ALWAYS CARRY A SILVER CROSS

I0891670

OTHER TITLES BY ANDREA ROBERTSON

Stand-Alone Novels

Captive

Invisibility

Loresmith Series

Forged in Fire and Stars

Cast in Secrets and Shadow

Bound by Sword and Spirit

Inventor's Secret Series

The Inventor's Secret

The Conjurer's Riddle

The Turncoat's Gambit

Nightshade Series

Nightshade

Wolfsbane

Bloodrose

Rift

Rise

Snakeroot

ALWAYS CARRY A SILVER CROSS

Andrea Robertson

Montlake

This is a work of fiction. Names, characters, organizations, places, events, and incidents are either products of the author's imagination or are used fictitiously. Otherwise, any resemblance to actual persons, living or dead, is purely coincidental.

Text copyright © 2025 by Seven Crows, Inc.
All rights reserved.

No part of this book may be reproduced, or stored in a retrieval system, or transmitted in any form or by any means, electronic, mechanical, photocopying, recording, or otherwise, without express written permission of the publisher.

Published by Montlake, Seattle
www.apub.com

Amazon, the Amazon logo, and Montlake are trademarks of Amazon.com, Inc., or its affiliates.

EU product safety contact:
Amazon Media EU S. à r.l.
38, avenue John F. Kennedy, L-1855 Luxembourg
amazonpublishing-gpsr@amazon.com

ISBN-13: 9781662533488 (paperback)
ISBN-13: 9781662533495 (digital)

Cover design and illustration by Liz Casal

Printed in the United States of America

For Eric, who understands the magic and never lets me get lost in the dark.

1

Guilt stalked Selene through aisles packed with king-size candy bars and preservative-filled snacks, still nipping at her heels when she reached a refrigerated case and stared at the rows of cans and bottles. She didn't need caffeine to stay alert, despite the excuse she'd made to herself for this stop. That reason would have made sense two hours ago, but not at a convenience store just past the sign welcoming Selene, and anyone else who happened to take that particular county highway, to Avondale, California.

This small town, nestled in an idyllic valley six hours north of Los Angeles, wasn't a logical rest stop to break up her long drive. She'd reached her destination . . . almost. Another few miles and she'd pull into the driveway of Emma and Allison Bancroft's house.

Selene's throat tightened as she watched her eyes become too shiny in the muddled reflection cast by the glass case. She'd promised herself she was done crying. That Emma wouldn't want her to keep suffering the loss. But Selene had broken that promise too many times to count.

Only Allie's house now, she reminded herself. *Allie's. And mine.*

Stomping out the flare of grief, Selene pulled open the door and shivered at the blast of cold air that hit her. Gooseflesh rose on her arms, a welcome distraction from the ravaging sorrow that threatened whenever she thought of Emma. Selene's best friend had died six months ago, but her loss remained a fresh, raw wound.

That was the reason Selene had stopped. To delay the inevitable. Despite all their discussions of what would be best for Allie's future, and realizing that meant returning to the place that felt like home to the grieving girl, the finality of moving to Avondale was what cemented the truth that Emma was gone. Forever. And Selene was faced with the impossible task of stepping into Emma's place in Allie's life. It wouldn't be easy for either of them.

But there was no putting it off any longer. She was here, and Allie was sitting in the car, waiting for Selene to drive those last few miles to the house.

To their home.

Selene grabbed an iced cappuccino and started toward the counter, but stopped, reconsidering. She'd been on edge the entire drive from Los Angeles, growing more tense the closer she came to Avondale. Hammering her already frayed nerves with espresso and sugar wasn't a good call.

Irritated with herself, Selene spun around and opened the case again. She shoved the cappuccino into its place, but in her haste the bottle didn't make it all the way into the slot. Instead, it slipped through her fingers and smashed onto the floor.

"Goddammit!"

A puddle of beige liquid punctuated by glints of glass shards spread around her feet.

You wanted a delay, Selene, she grumbled inwardly as she crouched and made a futile attempt to dam the flow of coffee. *Congratulations. You got it.*

"You don't need to do that, ma'am."

Selene yelped, lost her balance, and landed on her ass. Her jeans were instantly infused with frigid cappuccino. Wonderful.

When she'd entered the store, she'd spared a glance and a polite nod in the direction of the counter, catching sight of a teenage boy whose dark, longish hair flopped over his eyes. In her frustration with her clumsiness, she hadn't heard him approach. But there he was, mop in hand, frowning down at her.

"I'm so sorry." Selene grimaced. "I should have been more careful."

The young clerk offered her a tight-lipped smile. "It's no trouble."

With a reluctant nod, Selene pushed herself off the floor. And of course she planted her hand right on top of one of the glass shards.

"What the . . . ow!"

She wrapped her fingers around the cut on her left hand. It wasn't deep, but wow, capillaries really liked to bleed.

The clerk had gone very still . . . and yikes . . . very pale.

Oh god. He looks like he's going to pass out. Please, please don't pass out, kid.

He didn't pass out.

While he stared at the blood seeping from beneath her fingers, he said, "I'll . . . just . . . get you a BAND-AID."

He turned and in odd, stilted steps went through the employees-only door at the back of the store while Selene drowned in embarrassment and cursed herself for making this stop. Her procrastination punished with a damp ass that reeked of coffee and a sliced palm that smarted like a son of a bitch.

Less than a minute later, the clerk was back and brandishing a butterfly BAND-AID and some sterile gauze.

"Thank you." Selene pulled her fingers away from the cut and was rewarded with a fresh gush of bright-red blood.

The clerk inhaled sharply and pressed the gauze to the wound. Selene couldn't stop herself from hissing at the pain.

"Sorry," the clerk said. "Just thought I should stop the bleeding."

"It's okay," Selene replied. "Really. Thank you."

Despite his trembling hands, he applied the BAND-AID with care, offering her a timid smile when it was secured.

"All good?" he asked.

"Yes." Selene pulled her hand from his, then frowned. "Ugh. Now you've got blood all over your hand."

"It's no problem," he replied quickly, not bothering to look at his hand to confirm her words. "I'll just wash 'em after I clean this up."

Selene glanced at the mess on the floor. "I hate that I made extra work for you."

He laughed, but it was a tense sound. "Keeps things interesting. You can go ahead and take another bottle, then be on your way."

"Oh." Selene shook her head. "No. I'm okay, but let me pay you for the broken one."

"No, ma'am." There was that closed-lip smile again. "No charge."

"I don't want you to get in trouble."

"I won't," he told her. "My, uh . . . dad . . . owns the store. Don't worry about it."

Selene offered him a sympathetic smile. "Is that why you get the shift that sucks?"

She'd meant it as a jest but found herself frowning. He looked young enough to be in high school. It was after eleven. Awfully late for a kid to work on a school night.

"Yeah." He bobbed his head. "I guess."

Glancing at the front door, he added, "You probably have somewhere to be. I don't want to keep you."

"Are you sure I can't help?"

"I'm sure," he said quickly. "I hope you have a good night."

"Um, thanks?" Selene decided the best thing to do at this point was get out of his way. "I appreciate the first aid."

"Yep."

With a brief wave, Selene showed herself out of the store. She was halfway to her car when she realized her ass was still soaked with coffee and she should grab some paper towels from the bathroom to do what she could to keep the driver's seat dry.

Huffing out a breath, Selene marched back to the store. She grabbed the door handle . . . and froze. The teenage clerk was in her line of sight, still standing in front of the refrigerated case. He was . . . no, he wasn't . . . yeah, he was . . . licking his hand.

Her stomach churned. That wasn't the hand she'd bled all over, was it?

As quickly as the idea jumped into her mind, she dismissed it. No way. That was just too gross. He probably got coffee on himself when he was cleaning up. Still super gross. But gross was pretty much normal for teen boys, right?

Determined to scrub the image of that kid's tongue swabbing up her blood from her mind, Selene pivoted back to the parking lot. She could deal with a wet, coffee-smelling seat more readily than store clerks with zero hygiene boundaries.

Ugh. Poor Allie. That's her dating pool right there.

The girl in question waited in the passenger seat, her face washed by the bluish light of the phone screen she was bent over. Her thumbs flew across the digital keyboard.

Selene had opinions about kids and too much screen time, opinions backed up by articles she'd read, but given all Allie had been through, it hardly seemed fair to limit her ability to message the friends she'd been missing the past several months.

When Selene opened the car door, Allie's head jerked up and she flipped the phone over to hide the screen.

"Everything good?" Allie asked.

"Good enough," Selene replied, starting the car.

As she pulled out of the parking lot, Allie's nose wrinkled. "Why do you smell like Frappuccino?"

2

Someone was sitting on the front porch. The car's headlights briefly illuminated the stranger's silhouette as Selene turned into the driveway. Her hands tensed on the wheel, and her heartbeat kicked up a few notches. She couldn't think of a reason, at least not any good reason, someone would be lurking around a house this late.

Selene put the car into park, wondering if she should call the police or just wait to see what happened, but the moment the car stopped, Allie's door flew open, and then she was sprinting toward the front door.

"Allie!" Selene shouted as she wrestled with her seat belt and practically fell out of the driver's seat in her effort to race after the girl. "Allie, wait!"

But she came to an abrupt halt, her alarm turning into shock as the figure on the porch rose, triggering the porch's motion light, and opened his arms . . . arms that Allie leaped into. Her laughter, a bright sound that had been so rare since her mother's death, spilled into the night air as the stranger spun her around in circles.

The spell that stupefied Selene broke as she grasped for a rational interpretation of what she was seeing. A young man set Allie gently down, still holding her close.

"I missed you so, so much," Allie told him. "It feels like I've been away forever."

"I missed you too," he replied. "Every day. Every minute. Every second."

He released her, but only so he could cup her face in his hands. "Are you okay, Allie?"

She nodded. "I'm happy to be home. It's hard, but me and Aunt Sel—"

Allie drew a sharp breath and pivoted toward Selene. "Oh."

Yep, that's right, Selene thought, her mind still buzzing with surprise. *I'm here. Feeling awkward and a little like I'm watching a movie scene. But I guess this is real life? Who is this guy? Why haven't I heard so much as a peep about him?*

The guy in question took a step toward Selene, though he kept one hand linked with Allie's. Now that he was closer, she could see that he was young, walking the line that separated boy from man. He was tall, had thick brown hair and blue eyes, and offered Selene a confident smile.

"I've been looking forward to meeting you, Ms. Jones," he said. "I'm Josh."

Allie offered Selene a tremulous smile, then turned toward Josh, beaming at him with the force of a thousand suns. "Josh is my boyfriend."

Selene made herself take a beat even though she wanted to fire off about a million questions. She felt an all-too-familiar pinch in her heart followed by the treacherous inner whisper that she had no idea what she was doing when it came to parenting a teenager—well, a child of any age would be daunting, but teens came with extra . . . everything. And she'd been tossed into the deep end on day one in her new home because now there was a boyfriend.

Allison wasn't Selene's niece by blood. Emma, the sixteen-year-old girl's mother, had been Selene's college roommate and best friend.

Nothing, absolutely nothing, could have prepared Selene for the phone call she'd gotten six months ago. The police asking her to come to San Francisco to identify a body. Emma was dead. She'd been attending a weekend conference for work, and she'd been the victim of a mugging while walking from the convention center back to her hotel. A robbery gone wrong, they said.

Gone wrong. As if what had happened was a fluke. A simple mistake. Not a gaping wound in the hearts of the people who'd loved her.

Selene had gotten the call from the police because Allie was a minor and Allie's father had been out of the picture for years. Selene was named Allie's guardian in Emma's will, but she never thought she'd *become* Allie's guardian. Because only a nightmare would trigger that change in their lives. And the nightmare had happened.

Selene had collected a shell-shocked and grieving Allison and taken her home to live with her in Los Angeles until they could sort out a long-term plan. They'd been feeling their way along ever since. Both burdened by loss. Sometimes able to share their sorrow and find comfort, other times stumbling over each other in awkward, painful ways. For the most part, it had been good. At least as good as it could be, considering the circumstances. But not a day went by without Selene worrying that she either wasn't doing enough or was trying *too* hard.

Selene knew her tone was clipped when she said, "You have a boyfriend? Since when?"

"Since . . . a while." Allie returned her attention to Selene, her smile dimming a bit, but she held it in place.

Selene forced herself to count to five before replying in hopes of maintaining her composure.

"And I'm just hearing about it now?" Selene asked. Even after waiting, her voice came out a little strangled. But who could blame her? She and Allie had been living together for months.

It was Allie who hesitated this time. She and Josh exchanged a glance, and he offered her the slightest of nods.

Okay, they obviously planned this conversation. Was that what all Allie's furious texting on the drive up from LA had been about? She and Selene had barely spoken, but Selene had assumed that was because Allie was returning to a home filled with memories of Emma. Yes, they'd decided Avondale was where Allie wanted to be, hoping to ease back into a normal life where she'd attend a familiar school and be surrounded by friends. Allie's high school had been incredibly accommodating, allowing her to continue her classes remotely while she was in Los Angeles, which meant she'd be able to ease back into her schedule without being months behind. That didn't mean the homecoming wouldn't be bittersweet.

But given what Selene was witnessing at that moment, maybe not as bittersweet as she'd imagined. Now Selene wondered if she'd been projecting her fears onto Allie, while Allie had been eagerly anticipating this reunion with Josh.

"You've been so busy getting ready for the move," Allie began. "And sorting everything out with your job. I didn't want to give you something else to worry about."

Obviously there was more to it, but Selene held her temptation toward sarcasm at bay. "Allie, I'm never too busy for you to tell me what's going on in your life," she replied. "I always want to know." She fixed her gaze on Josh. "And I definitely need to know about—"

Selene's intention was to be firm, stern even, but holding Josh's stare was unnerving. The blue of his eyes startling and intense. For a kid, he had incredible presence. Despite the awkward situation, he gave no sign of embarrassment or worry, unlike Allie, who kept glancing anxiously between Selene and Josh.

Clearing her throat, Selene continued. "Important people in your life."

"I know, I know!" Allie blurted. "And I should have told you sooner, but I wanted to wait until I knew . . ."

She trailed off and turned toward Josh, cheeks turning a deep shade of pink, keeping her gaze slightly downcast but peeking up at him through her eyelashes. Selene sensed impending disaster.

"Until you knew what?" she asked.

"That what we have is real," Allie answered dreamily, and Josh took her other hand.

"It is," he said softly.

Allie took a step closer to him. "I know."

When it became clear they'd completely forgotten Selene existed yet again and looked like they were about to kiss, she panicked.

"Hey! Whoa! Time out, kiddos."

Time out, kiddos? Wow. I am so bad at this. So much for being the cool aunt.

Lack of cool notwithstanding, her outburst at least startled the teen lovebirds out of their reverie, so points for that. Allie was staring at her like she'd grown a second head. Josh simply looked amused.

"Are you okay, Aunt Selene?" Allie asked. "You're being kind of weird."

Grimacing, Selene decided to try a do-over. "I'm fine, Allie. You caught me off guard. I didn't think we'd have company the second we arrived in town, especially given that it's almost midnight."

"I know." Allie averted her eyes. "I meant to tell you on the way here, but I didn't know how."

"Right." Selene knew she was supposed to be the adult here, but it was becoming increasingly difficult to stop herself from giggling. She was overtired from the drive and the stress of, well, everything about the last six months. How perfect was it that she'd arrived at her new home and stumbled right into this—could it be a more classic teen-and-parent moment?

Selene needed to establish ground rules with Allie. And she would. But she was also a little relieved that Allie was caught up in something so normal when she had every right to be cocooned in sorrow, raging at the injustice of having her mom snatched away so suddenly and violently. Allie deserved every bit of happiness she could find.

For tonight at least, Selene decided to go easy on her. And Josh. They'd have plenty of time to sort this out, preferably in the light of day.

"Since we're talking about how late it is," she said, "and the fact that it's a school night, I think Josh should go home."

Allie made a grudging but affirmative noise.

"And Josh, I hope we can get to know each other better soon," Selene told him.

"I'd like that, Ms. Jones," Josh replied, the soul of politeness. "Allison is very *important* to me."

Selene didn't miss that he echoed and emphasized her word of choice from a few minutes ago. She wasn't entirely sure if he meant it to be respectful or if he was poking fun at her. That puckish glint was in his eyes again.

"Is it okay if I talk to Josh alone for a minute, Aunt Selene?" Allie asked. "To say good night?"

"Okay," Selene said. "It was nice meeting you, Josh. I'm sure we'll have the chance to talk again soon."

Josh and Allie exchanged a weighted glance that made Selene's brow furrow.

"I'm sure we will," Josh replied.

Though she still felt a little uneasy with the surprise-boyfriend situation, Selene returned to the car to grab her purse, then went into the house. The moment she stepped inside, her heart swelled with love then broke again. This place was a barrage of everything that had been Emma: warm lighting, cozy and quirky decor, polished wood, and dried flowers.

Selene closed her eyes and took a deep breath.

"I'm here, Emma," she murmured. "I wish you were too. So much."

She took another moment to steady her emotions, then went into the living room and sat on the couch. As she waited for Allie to come inside, she tried to conjure the right thing to say about boyfriends and curfews and maybe not giving poor Aunt Selene a heart attack on her first night in Avondale. Damn. She should have had that coffee after all.

Selene pulled out her phone and scrolled to pass the time, but it was impossible not to notice how long it was taking Allie to "say good night" to Josh.

Five minutes.

Ten.

Had Josh driven to the house? There hadn't been a car in the driveway or parked on the street, and she hadn't noticed a bicycle. Did he live in walking distance? Was that a good thing or a bad thing?

She drummed her fingers on her knee.

Maybe they're just talking. Allie's been away for six months. They have a lot to catch up on.

Fifteen minutes.

They are not just talking.

She was contemplating getting a bucket of ice water to throw on them when she heard the front door open, and a moment later Allie appeared in the living room, rosy cheeked and beaming.

"Thanks for not freaking out, Aunt Sel," Allie said, flouncing over to the couch to plop down beside Selene. "You're not, right? Freaking out?"

Selene lifted her hand, pinching her thumb and pointer finger together but leaving a slight gap. "Little bit. Maybe."

Ducking her head, Allie let out an awkward laugh. "Yeah. Sorry. I know that was weird—Josh waiting on the porch for us."

Selene pinched her thumb and finger together again. "Little bit."

"But you like him, don't you?" Allie prompted, all expectation and earnestness.

"I don't really know him yet, Allie," Selene answered cautiously. She'd been seeing a therapist about losing Emma, and her new responsibilities to Allie. The therapist had emphasized how important it was not to react instantly to a surprising or uncomfortable situation but instead listen to Allie's perspectives, consider, then address the issue cooperatively whenever possible. Time to put that advice to work. If she could manage it.

"But if you like him," Selene continued, "I'm sure he's great. And I'll find that out when he visits . . . but those visits shouldn't be after ten p.m."

"He is great," Allie effused, ignoring the curfew Selene had not-so-subtly attempted to establish. "He's perfect."

Selene started to grimace at the word *perfect* but forced her pained expression into a smile. "I look forward to seeing him around then.

Allie, look, I'm not here to dictate how you live your life, but we do need to set up some rules."

"I get that." Allie nodded quickly. "But really, you don't need to worry. Josh isn't, like, a 'bad influence.'"

Selene laughed at Allie's air quotes. "Good to know."

Grinning, Allie continued, "I mean it! Josh and I are being responsible."

Selene went very still.

Allie frowned, then clapped her hands over her mouth, which sort of muffled the shriek she let out before she blurted, "Oh my god. Oh my god. Oh my god."

Selene managed to find her voice, or rather, the frog's voice she borrowed, because what came out was mostly a croak. "Allie—"

"No," Allie cut her off. "I didn't mean, we're not, I'm not, we've haven't, I swear. Oh my god."

Allie turned and buried her face in a throw pillow.

Relieved, Selene patted Allie on the shoulder. "It's okay. I get the picture. But thank you for . . . clarifying. And for taking pity on me. The boyfriend was enough of a surprise. Maybe hold off a little 'til you make me deal with that thing you're not doing."

"Irmmugrrdd." Allie groaned into the pillow, but then she lifted her head and fixed a solemn gaze on Selene. "I'm not lying. We really haven't."

With a dramatic flop against the back of the couch, Allie stared up at the ceiling. "I can't believe I'm messing this up so badly."

"I believe you, honey," Selene told her. "You're not messing anything up. And if the time comes that you need to talk to me about anything with Josh, or anyone else who becomes *important* in your life, I'm here. Always."

She was never going to be able to say the word *important* without cracking a smile after this.

"I know," Allie replied. "That's not what I meant when I said I was messing up."

She sat up suddenly, fixing a determined gaze on Selene. "I have something else to tell you about Josh, and it has nothing to do with . . . that stuff."

Selene should have been relieved the conversation had moved on from "that stuff." Nevertheless, her stomach dropped. "Oh?"

The word came out like another croak.

"It's not bad, Auntie Sel," Allie assured. "I promise."

"Okay." Why did Selene feel like Allie was the adult in this situation and she was the kid dreading punishment? "What do you want to tell me about Josh?"

Allie straightened, taking a breath. From her expression, Selene surmised Allie had been rehearsing this conversation.

"The first, and most important, thing you need to know," Allie began, "is that Josh and I are serious."

"So, it's serious," Selene repeated warily. Her therapist always reminded her that she should never dismiss or patronize Allie's feelings, despite her gut reaction that a sixteen-year-old's idea of serious was definitely skewed. The most important thing was to listen. To solve problems as a family rather than set herself up as Allie's adversary.

This was a problem. "What does 'serious' mean? How long have you been seeing Josh?"

Alarm bells sounded in Selene's brain. Had Emma known about Josh? Selene couldn't remember her ever mentioning Allie having a boyfriend, much less a serious one. She had a hard time imagining a reason Emma wouldn't share that information. In fact, it was exactly the sort of thing Emma would have called her best friend about immediately to hash out potential pitfalls of Allie starting to date.

"Well, it's kind of complicated." Allie frowned. "Technically it's been eight months, including the six months I've been living with you. So we've been doing the long-distance thing, which was hard, but we talked every day. Being apart made us realize how much we needed each other."

Oof. That was a gut punch. Of course Allie needed love and understanding while grieving her mother. And there was nothing wrong with getting support from her boyfriend, but Selene worried the strength of Allie's feelings for Josh were knotted up with the depth of her loss, leading to impulsive decisions and declarations: a ticking bomb of emotions that would detonate in disastrous heartbreak.

As Selene rummaged through her memories for something she might have missed, Allie dug into her pocket and pulled something out. There was a blur of movement, then Allie shoved her right hand in Selene's face.

Selene blinked, closed her eyes, counted to three, and then opened them again. She blinked once more at the glittering object on Allie's right ring finger.

"What is that?" Selene asked numbly.

"It's a ring," Allie answered breathlessly, as if Selene's question wasn't ridiculous. "Josh just gave it to me. He told me he loves me and he missed me more than anything and he wanted me to know how much I mean to him."

Love. LOVE. Noooooo. No. No. Nope. After seven hours in the car, facing the upheaval of her whole life and the reality of starting a new one in a new home, Selene didn't have the mental fortitude to handle this kind of revelation. She barely knew what she was doing. How was she supposed to react?

She had to swallow before she could speak again, and when she did, all she could manage to focus on was the ring itself. "Is that silver?"

Somehow she already knew the answer, but she couldn't push past her own disbelief. She was grasping for anything reasonable in this moment of unreality.

Allie giggled and beamed at the bloodred stone flanked by flawless, colorless baguette-cut gems—*please let them be Swarovski crystals*—that sparkled on her hand. The bubbling laughter made Selene grit her teeth. She didn't find anything funny about this conversation. Exhaustion and stress set off a painful pounding in her temples.

"God no, it is *not* silver." More giggling, then Allie sighed dreamily. "It's a ruby and diamonds in platinum."

Selene wasn't trying to be dramatic, but she found herself on her feet. "Allie—"

"It's an antique. Josh says it's Art Deco," Allie cut her off. "He loves art history; he's so smart."

Selene bit her lip. *Listen. Remember to listen. Don't just react. God, this is hard. Was it easier for Emma? How did she do this?*

"Isn't it beautiful?" Allie said. "I was so surprised."

"Surprised?" Selene couldn't catch her breath. "That's a good word."

"Don't you think it's sweet of him?"

"Allison," Selene said. "Josh is your age, right?"

Her niece nodded, but after a moment of hesitation.

"How did he afford a ring like that?" Selene asked. "Does he have a job?" *As an investment banker? Did his parents sell a hot tech start-up and retire here?*

"Well." Allie kicked the edge of the rug. "That's the thing, Aunt Selene."

Selene's frenzied thoughts jolted to a stop as she waited for Allie to bring the hammer down.

"He's not like other boys at all," Allie said. She wound her fingers through her long blond hair and sighed again.

"Obviously not." Selene's eyes narrowed as worst-case scenarios bombarded her thoughts. "Allie, if he's dealing drugs, you cannot continue this relationship."

She didn't actually believe Josh was peddling narcotics, but her mind was spinning through the bad highlights reel of teendom: drugs, sex, car accidents . . .

"He's not a dealer, Auntie Sel." Allie laughed, then her expression turned wistful. "He's special."

"I'm sure he's special, sweetheart, but that doesn't answer my question." Selene couldn't imagine how much that ring cost.

"And he didn't buy the ring," Allie continued. "It's an heirloom. From his family."

Okay, that's way better than drug dealing. But it didn't make her feel any better about this whole "serious" issue.

Selene's heart skipped a beat. "Honey, I know two months can seem like a long time, but don't you think that's a bit early for Josh to give you a ring that has sentimental value for his family?"

"*Eight months*, and his family loves me," Allie said quickly, then amended, "or Josh promises they will . . . when I get to know them better. That's part of what I need to talk to you about."

"You haven't met his family?" That made Selene feel an eensy bit better. At least Josh's parents wouldn't judge her for being uninvolved before now. She wondered how much *they* knew about this suddenly serious relationship. And if they didn't know . . .

"Allison," Selene spoke quietly. "Did your mom know about Josh?"

The way Allie instantly averted her gaze was all the answer Selene needed.

"Is there a reason you kept your relationship a secret?" Selene asked. Her pulse began to thump hard. *Something is very, very wrong here.*

Allie's voice tightened, and when she looked at Selene again, her eyes were filled with tears. "It wasn't supposed to be a secret. We were getting ready to tell Mom and then—"

She began to cry, and Selene sat down, but when she tried to pull Allie into a hug, Allie drew away, shaking her head.

"No, I'm okay." Allie swiped her tears away. "I need to get through this. It's just that I really wish Mom was here. I was so excited for her to meet Josh."

Selene nodded, swallowing her own tears. "I wish she was here too."

She wasn't any less worried about the Josh situation, but at least she wasn't lacking any background information Emma might have provided.

Emma, if there's any chance you're listening and you want to tag team this situation in spirit, I'd be grateful.

Selene didn't have strong beliefs about ghosts or an afterlife, but it couldn't hurt to throw a plea out there.

Allie sniffed, then offered Selene a smile. "I'm okay now."

"You sure?"

"Yeah." As if to prove it, Allie sat up a little straighter. "So it wasn't meant to be a secret from Mom. I just wanted to wait a little while to tell her about Josh because of the circumstances with him and his family."

"There are circumstances?" Selene frowned. "That your mom wouldn't have liked?"

"I honestly don't know how she would have reacted," Allie said. "Because it's complicated. But I do know she would have loved Josh. Because I love Josh."

Selene nodded slowly. "So what's the deal with his family?"

"I mean, I have met them. At least some of them. It's kind of hard to explain," Allie said. "Josh's family is *really* important to him. He wants to make sure they'll accept me before I meet all of them."

Selene's eyebrows shot up. "There's a question that they might not accept you?"

"That's what I'm trying to tell you," Allie said. "Josh isn't like other boys. The rules are different for his family."

"Hold on," Selene said. "Is it a religion issue?"

"No, Aunt Sel," Allie groaned. "They're just . . . not like us."

Fed up with the weird clues, Selene said sharply, "Allison, what are you talking about?"

Allie stood up and crossed her arms over her chest, as if steeling herself for what she was about to say. "Josh is a werewolf."

3

Selene tried to remember how much she'd had to drink before this conversation. Nothing. She hadn't had anything to drink. But she was tired. That long, long drive. That was why she was hearing bizarre things instead of whatever Allie was trying to tell her.

"Auntie Selene?"

Tired. Very, very tired.

Allie poked her in the arm. "Are you okay?"

"What did you just say?" Selene stared at her niece.

"My boyfriend is a werewolf," Allie replied.

Maybe it's not me. "Have you been drinking?"

"No."

"Do you have a fever?"

"No."

"Is this a joke?"

"NO!"

Allie threw up her hands and left the room. Selene heard the front door open, followed by Allie saying to someone, "You were right. You'd better come inside."

When Allie returned to the living room, Josh was at her side.

"Hi again, Ms. Jones," Josh said.

Selene's eyes widened, and she turned a hard stare on her niece. "Allison, what is going on? You were supposed to say good night to Josh. Has he been waiting outside all this time?"

"It was my idea, Ms. Jones," Josh answered. "Please don't blame Allie."

In their brief meeting outside, Selene had noticed Allie's new boyfriend was cute, but seeing him in the full light proved that assessment severely lacking. He had an adorable mop of light-brown hair, shot through with golden threads, and a smile that could melt ice. Teenage dream incoming. No wonder Allie was smitten.

"Josh." Selene resisted his sweet smile. "We have rules in this house, and if you want to date my niece, you'll need to respect them. It's fine for you to come over, but not without letting me know."

"I understand that, Ms. Jones, and I meant no disrespect." Josh smiled again.

"I think you should show her," Allie said and took Josh's hand.

"Are you sure?" He turned wide sky blue eyes on the girl. He had dangerously long eyelashes.

Selene watched Allie's heart bloom.

Damn.

"Yes, she needs to know. And she won't believe me without seeing it." Allie rose to her tiptoes and kissed him.

"Allison." Selene frowned. "Now is not the time for PDA."

"Ms. Jones." Josh looked at Selene. His stark tone silenced her. "Please know that I will never hurt your niece . . . or you."

"Excuse me?" Selene could swear her heart stopped. *Why would he say that? Why would anyone say that?*

"Go on," Allie said.

"I'll need this in a sec." He snatched a throw blanket from a basket beside the couch and handed it to Allie. She nodded and moved closer to Selene.

"Just remember to breathe, Auntie Sel," she said.

Selene was about to reply when something happened to Josh. At first it looked like his muscles twitched. Then they rippled. In the next moment, his entire body convulsed, his torso lengthened, his face elongated. His shirt ripped and his jeans tore. The shredded remnants of his clothing dropped to the floor. Fur sprouted from his skin, and claws replaced his fingernails.

It all happened in the space of two heartbeats that felt like an eternity.

Selene gaped at the wolf that politely dropped to its haunches on her living room floor. Josh's blue eyes blinked at her.

Then she fainted.

◆ ◆ ◆

When her eyes opened again, Allie hovered over her. "Aunt Sel?"

"Allie?" Selene looked up at Allie. "Did I fall down?"

"You passed out," Allie replied. "Don't feel bad. That's a normal reaction."

"What?" Selene frowned.

"Are you okay, Ms. Jones?"

Selene's eyes followed the sound of the voice that asked the question. Her gaze landed on a boy standing in the living room. For some reason, he was wearing a blanket instead of clothes. He looked familiar.

"Who are you?"

"Oh boy." Allie huffed out a breath. "Aunt Selene. This is Josh, remember? My boyfriend."

Memories took shape within the haze of Selene's mind. Avondale. Moving day. A boy waiting in front of Emma's house.

"Josh, right." Selene pushed herself onto her elbows. Her vision swam. "Sorry. I'm not sure what happened. I'm a little lightheaded. I guess the drive really wore me out."

"Should we take her to the hospital?" Josh asked Allie. "I think she hit her head on the coffee table."

Selene squinted at him. "Why are you wearing a blanket? Where are your clothes? You need clothes."

"Auntie Sel." Allie spoke very slowly. "Do you remember what happened right before you fainted? What Josh showed you?"

There was a tiny voice clambering for Selene's attention, trying to tell her something vital, but Selene instinctively knew she did not want to hear whatever that voice had to say.

"I remember meeting Josh," Selene replied. "And you telling me that you guys are in a serious relationship. But Josh was supposed to go home. It's late. Josh shouldn't be here. You're both kids. And he needs clothes. Clothes are important."

Josh cleared his throat. "Maybe we should try this again tomorrow. She's not taking it well."

"No," Allie said firmly. "She needs to understand that it's real."

"That what's real?" Selene's head ached. She really wanted to lie down and close her eyes.

"Are you sure?" Josh asked. "She might be concussed."

Allie knelt beside Selene and inspected her skull. "I don't see any bumps. Aunt Sel, do you know what year it is?"

"I'm not concussed." Selene had no idea if she was concussed, but she was pretty sure she did know what year it was. She also knew she wanted this conversation to end. It was obvious she needed to go to bed.

Putting her arm around Selene's shoulders, Allie helped her sit all the way up. "Show her again, Josh."

"Show me what?" Selene didn't understand the dread that suddenly pressed against her ribs. Why would she be afraid?

Josh's expression grew somber, but he nodded.

"Aunt Selene, I need you to watch Josh," Allie instructed. "Don't take your eyes off him. Don't even blink."

In the moment all Selene wanted to do was shut her eyes as tightly as she could.

Allie seemed to sense that and whispered, "Please, Auntie Sel."

"I won't blink," Selene agreed, even as her gut clenched.

"Do it now," Allie told Josh.

Selene didn't blink, and Josh turned into a wolf.

This isn't real. This isn't real. This isn't real.

"Do you remember now?" Allie's voice sounded very far away. "Josh is a werewolf. He's my boyfriend, and he's a werewolf."

Maybe I never made it to Avondale. Maybe I fell asleep at the wheel. Oh god. What if the car crashed in a ditch and this is all some near-death hallucination? What if Allie is dying too?

That tiny voice piped up again, and this time Selene couldn't shut it out. *Why would you hallucinate about Allie and werewolves? You know that's not what's happening.*

As much as the voice's logic was bizarre, it was also accurate. Werewolves weren't something Selene dreamed about, or even thought about. Ever.

Also, the Josh-wolf was still sitting in front of her.

"Auntie Sel?" Allie gave her a little shake. "You're scaring me. Please say something."

A laugh of disbelief flew out of Selene's throat. "*I'm* scaring you?"

The wolf turned back into a teenage boy, who quickly wrapped himself in the blanket again. "I think that's a good sign. The sarcasm, I mean."

"I think so too," Allie said. She put her other arm around Selene and hugged her tight. "I promise it's okay, Auntie Sel. I know it's a lot to take in."

Werewolves are real. Oh my god. I can't believe it. I don't want to believe it.

"Josh," Selene said in a pained voice. "I'm having a hard time. You'd better show me again."

"No problem," he replied, and a moment later she was staring at a wolf again.

Werewolves are real, and my niece is dating one.

"You're a werewolf," Selene said flatly.

He changed back. "Yes, but I'm not dangerous."

"Since you haven't attacked me, I'm going to believe you." She rubbed her aching temples.

"I still think we should take you to the hospital," Josh said. Werewolf or not, he sounded genuinely concerned. "You did hit your head."

"I'm okay," Selene said. Her headache wasn't because she bumped her skull on the coffee table. That she was sure of. "No hospital."

"How many fingers am I holding up?" He waggled three fingers at her.

It took Selene a moment to answer. All she could think about was how a minute ago that hand had been a paw. "Three."

"Who is the president?" Josh asked.

"Josh, come on," Allie said. "She'll be fine."

"I'll get you a glass of water, Ms. Jones." He left the room, blanket flowing behind him like a cape.

"And some ibuprofen, Josh," Selene called. "I think there's some in the medicine cabinet of the powder room."

I can't believe I just said "powder room" to a werewolf. Oh my god. There's a werewolf in my house.

Black crept into the edges of her vision again.

"Are you sure you're okay, Aunt Selene?" Allie took her hand.

Selene shook her head, forcing it to clear. "How long have you known about this? Since the beginning?"

Allie looked away. "Yes. Avondale isn't like other towns. Most of the people who live here . . . aren't exactly people. I knew Josh was a werewolf when we started dating."

Selene gripped her niece's hand. "What? How? Why?"

She couldn't form an actual question. Maybe this was a dream. Yes. A dream. Eventually she'd wake up.

"I know it's a shock, but I swear it's not a bad thing," Allie said. "It's a whole new reality, but once you adjust, it's awesome."

Selene pinched the bridge of her nose, her world tilted so far on its axis, she was certain it was about to flip.

It could still all be a dream. Couldn't it? I could wake up tomorrow and none of this will have happened.

". . . but Josh is amazing." Selene realized Allie had been talking the whole time she'd been lost in her thoughts.

"I had no idea I could feel this way about someone." Allie sighed out the words, her expression cartoonishly smitten. Selene wouldn't have been surprised if her niece's pupils suddenly became hearts.

Okay, Allie is head over heels. For a werewolf. I'm still hoping this is a dream, but I'll roll with it for now. What else do I need to know? My therapist said to listen. I can do that. Not panicking. Listening.

"And his family are also werewolves? That's what you meant when you said things are different for them."

"Yes," Allie said. "But I should tell you, they're not technically his family. They're his pack."

"His pack," Selene repeated, her head wanting to spin again. She forced it not to. If she passed out again, Josh would make sure she woke up in a hospital bed.

"Josh has brought me into a whole world that's like having your dreams come true," Allie breathed.

"You mean there's more than the werewolves?" Selene wished she could walk out of the house, count to ten, walk back in, and find a mundane world where none of this was happening.

"I knew about, you know, the other side," Allie said. "You can't live in Avondale without being aware of it, but humans aren't invited in. We kind of coexist, and that was cool, but being part of it is soooo much better."

"Did your mom know about all this when she moved to Avondale?" Selene asked.

Frowning, Allie said, "You know, I'm not sure. I was so little, and she made me aware of it gradually. I started to notice stuff, and she filled me in as I got older, but she didn't talk about how she found out. She always said that from the moment she set foot in Avondale, she knew it was home."

Emma had spoken those exact words to Selene many times, but never had she hinted that Avondale was anything other than an idyllic small town. Why hadn't she said anything? This revelation was nothing short of earth-shattering, and Emma had kept it a secret all these years.

Had she not trusted Selene enough? Or did she worry Selene would never have believed her? No matter the answer, it stung.

"Basically, every myth you've heard is real, Aunt Sel." Allie had been talking again while Selene wasn't listening. "Everything. It's fantastic! Can you believe it?"

"I'm not sure." Selene rubbed her temples again. *Fantastic* was not the word she'd choose.

"Here you go, Ms. Jones." Josh knelt beside her. He handed her a glass of water and two pills. He was fully dressed, and he laughed at the puzzled expression on her face.

"I always carry an extra set of clothes around. Just in case."

"I see." She popped the pills and chugged water.

When she started to rise, she swayed a bit. Josh picked her up with one hand and set her on the couch. Selene gaped at him.

"Sorry," he said quickly. "Just trying to help."

"How strong *are* you?" she asked.

"Strong," he replied quietly.

"But he's always gentle," Allie said. "He would never hurt anyone."

Gentle when he's doing what, exactly? Selene shuddered and took another sip of water. After gathering her thoughts as best she could, she cleared her throat.

"Josh, I think Allie and I need some time. Just aunt and niece."

"Aunt Selene." Allie's tone was plaintive.

"Allison, I'm serious."

Selene turned back to Josh, hoping he read the help-me-out-here message she telegraphed from her eyes.

He gave a slight nod and flashed his high-beam smile at Allie. "Your aunt is right. You two should have a chance to talk this through. Now that's she's seen who I really am."

"Okay." Allie looked down and blushed.

Selene's brow knit together. She appreciated Josh's agreement, but the way Allie instantly deferred to him didn't sit well with her.

"I do have one request, Ms. Jones," Josh said.

Selene stopped frowning at her niece and looked at Josh. "A request?"

"My pack leader has asked to meet you," he told her. "Allison and I are petitioning for our relationship to be recognized by the pack. It's our tradition that this acceptance be extended to her family, and while the whole pack is involved in discussing our request, the final decision belongs to our pack leader."

Selene swallowed. "Your pack leader?"

"You've been invited for dinner on Saturday, if you're not busy."

Allie's eyes rounded and fixed on Selene, pleading. "Aunt Selene, it's so important. I mean, it's, like, a huge honor to be invited."

Selene wondered how pasty she looked. Given Allie's expression, she guessed her face resembled a puddle of glue. *Pack leader? Dinner? Should I be worried that we might end up on the menu?*

"I don't think I have plans," she said. "Who am I meeting exactly?"

"My pack leader didn't want you to be overwhelmed," Josh said with an eager smile. "So it will just be him, me, Allie, and you. The pack is pretty big, about one hundred wolves."

"One hundred?" Selene repeated, stunned by the number.

Avondale had just over one thousand residents. *Ten percent of the people who live here are* werewolves*?*

"But there will only be four of us at the dinner," Josh said again. "Two wolves, two humans. So it's a fair balance." He grinned.

This kid is a little too clever.

"Okay." Selene wanted to navigate these straits very carefully. It was becoming clear there were far more dangers lurking beneath the surface than she'd imagined. "And who is your pack leader?"

"Fenris Hall."

Selene dropped her water glass. Josh caught it before it hit the floor.

Holy reflexes, Batman, she thought before her mind shot back to the reason she'd dropped the glass in the first place.

"Fenris Hall . . . is a werewolf?" Her question came out strangled.

She'd only seen his name on checks. Fenris Hall was the single highest contributor to every fundraising campaign she'd managed that related to environmental conservation. The number of zeros on his checks always made her do double takes. But he never came to events and didn't return phone calls thanking him for his generous donations. She had yet to lay eyes on him. He was something of a legend in nonprofit circles. There were debates about whether he really existed and lived as a recluse, or if the name was a front for some kind of super PAC. It turned out the answer was option three: he was a werewolf pack leader.

Josh nodded. "He's eager to meet you. He admires your work."

Selene didn't know whether to say thank you or worry about offending a major donor at her first dinner among werewolves.

Worlds collide. Could this get any more complicated? Does my work even matter anymore when monsters are real?

Josh stood. "Can I tell Fen to expect you at eight o'clock on Saturday?"

Selene didn't trust herself to speak, so she nodded.

"Thanks, Auntie!" Allie threw herself onto Selene and hugged her. "I'll walk Josh out, then we can talk."

Yeah, we are so not doing that again. "Say good night here, Allie. You're right, we need to talk this out."

Her tone was enough to keep Allie from arguing. Instead, she threw a wary glance at Selene before giving Josh a quick kiss.

"See you tomorrow."

"Can't wait." Josh nuzzled her cheek.

When he was gone, Selene went to the writing desk in the corner of the living room, where Emma kept stationery and envelopes.

"Okay, Allie. Tell me the whole story about you and Josh." She opened a drawer to retrieve a pen, pausing as she took in Emma's array of elegant writing utensils.

Letter writing is becoming a lost art, Emma had liked to say. Selene agreed wholeheartedly, but the sound of Emma's voice in her head made Selene's heart ache.

"You're going to take notes?" Allie stared at the pen in Selene's hand.

"No," Selene replied. "I'm going to start writing thank you notes for the fundraising campaign I just finished. I think more clearly when I'm working."

And I need something from the realm of normality to keep myself from losing it.

She pulled up the list of donors' names and addresses on her phone. The third name on the list was Fenris Hall.

Shit.

Allie curled up on the couch while Selene began to write.

"What do you want to know?" Allie asked.

"How did you and Josh get together?"

Allie sighed. Selene pressed the pen harder against the note card.

"He says he watched me for a long time before he asked me out."

Selene's hand jerked and smudged the ink. She tossed the card and started over with a new one. "Like a stalker?"

"No!" Allie protested. "Aunt Sel, are you gonna be totally judgmental?"

"I want you to be safe." Selene tried to keep her hand steady.

"I am safe. Josh loves me."

And there's the L word. I am so in over my head.

"And he protects me."

Can he protect you from himself? Selene stopped herself from voicing the thought. *Listen first. Then act.*

"He only watched me because there are rules about paranormals dating humans," Allie said. "He couldn't ask me out without being sure he was really serious about it."

"Paranormals?" Selene managed to finish the first note.

I'm going to act as though all of this is real. I'm having this conversation as I continue with life. Go through the motions, and maybe I'll hang on to my sanity.

"That's what they refer to themselves as, as a group."

"And who are *they* exactly?"

"Well, there are the wolves, like Josh. Then there are vampires, witches, and faeries."

Vampires, witches, and faeries. Oh my.

"Is that all?" As if that didn't constitute more than Selene had ever wanted to imagine.

"Um, I think there are a few others, but those are the major ones. And they're the ones who interact with humans the most. The rest keep to themselves."

"So werewolves, vampires, witches, and faeries are in class with you. Every day." Selene frowned and reached for an envelope.

"Not vampires because of the whole sunlight-can-kill-them issue," Allie answered.

"No vampires," Selene said. "But the rest?"

Allie nodded.

"Is that a good idea?"

"Where else are they going to go to school?"

"Maybe they should be homeschooled." Selene licked the envelope and pressed it closed. "Just to be safe."

"God, Aunt Sel." Allie scoffed. "Are you seriously advocating paranormal segregation of schools?"

Selene's eyes widened. "Is that what you'd call it?"

"I would."

"It doesn't seem the same to me." Selene grabbed another note card and envelope. "You're talking about classmates who'd like to eat you. Don't werewolves and vampires eat people?"

"No, not anymore. They *don't* want to eat me. Well, maybe they want to, but they won't. They follow rules about that," Allie argued. "Besides, most of the paranormals don't go to school. They're much too old."

"Too old?" Selene returned to her list. She decided to skip the note to Fenris Hall. Maybe she would hand deliver it at dinner on Saturday . . . Dinner with the werewolf pack leader.

This cannot be happening. Normal, Selene, we're pretending this is normal. We are not panicking.

"Well, you know, they're immortal. Most of them have done all the school they need. Probably more than they need. They just pop in every so often for updates, when something major happens."

Selene tried to keep her voice even. "Updates?"

"I don't know. Technology mostly, I guess. Computers were big. And political stuff. Revolutions, new countries. That sort of thing. They need to fit in with the rest of us. It's toughest for the vamps since they can't go to school. But I think some of them take night courses."

Allie got up and wandered over to Selene, who had just ruined another note.

"I don't know any vampires, though," she continued. "Wolves and vamps don't like each other. Josh said it's something about a blood feud that started in Europe a couple thousand years ago. I guess they're still hacking it out over there, but the American groups have called a truce. They mostly avoid each other here, just to be safe."

"I see." Selene felt dizzy. She wondered if it was the conversation or the glue from the envelopes.

"I have met some of the Fae," Allie said.

"The Fae?"

"Faeries. They're fun, but they like to make trouble," Allie said.

Selene set down the pen. "Have they caused you trouble?"

Allie shook her head. "No one bothers me because of Josh. You don't mess with werewolves."

Selene stared at Fenris Hall's name. It was circled and had a note reminding her to try and track down his address—a feat no one had managed. Now she was invited to his home.

Money. Power.

She closed her eyes.

Fur. Fangs.

"Auntie Sel?" Allie frowned at Selene's pale face.

"I'm sorry, Allie." Selene shook her head. "I think that's all my brain can handle for tonight."

"Mine too, honestly. Time to crash." Allie stood up, then hesitated, tensing up. "You're still, um, taking the guest room?"

"Yes," Selene said quickly.

When they'd agreed that Selene would move to Avondale and live with Allie, Allie had asked if Selene wanted to take Emma's old room. It was the largest and had an en suite bathroom. But Selene wasn't ready for that. She suspected Allie wasn't either. They probably wouldn't ever be. Maybe, in time, they could recreate it as a shared space. A den or art studio or whatever. For the moment it remained a shrine to Emma.

Selene and Allie gave each other a smile and wave as they headed to their respective bedrooms. Closing the door behind her felt safe, like she'd shut out all the frightening things she'd seen and heard since Josh appeared. Pushing all thoughts of the supernatural away, she walked around the room, wondering if it would feel different now that she wasn't a visitor. Now it was home. Would the linens stop smelling of lavender, or had Emma done something to ensure that soothing, herbaceous scent lingered?

The room was filled with antiques that Emma—who'd been a casual collector of Victorian pieces—had procured over the years. A wrought iron bedframe, a wardrobe, a dresser, and a vanity set of rosewood that gleamed with warm, inner light. There were even lace doilies, which Emma admitted she knew were fussy, but she got a kick out of the fact that they were invented to stop men's hair oil from staining furniture.

"Can you imagine how awful that must have been?" Emma shuddered. "Or having to touch hair styled with that much oil?"

As Selene's fingers traced the pattern of the doily on the vanity, she smiled at the memory. It carried an ache, but it also made her smile. Emma would always be here, and Selene was grateful for that.

She picked up a silver-framed photo of Selene and Emma with Allie wedged between them. All three women were laughing, their features dappled by sunlight. Allie's golden-blond hair came from her father, but she had Emma's warm deep-brown eyes. Emma's hair matched her eyes, and in this photo it was styled in the chic inverted choppy bob she'd favored in recent years. It reminded Selene she needed to fix her own hair situation. Things were getting dire. She reached up and pulled her thick auburn hair out of the topknot she'd been throwing it into on a near-daily basis. Calling it a bun was generous. Her hair was too long to fit into a reasonable knot, and with each passing day it looked more and more like some sort of avant-garde sculpture. She groaned, rubbing her scalp as the long tresses loosened and spilled over her shoulders.

Selene walked to the window that overlooked the backyard, then began to close the drapes, when something caught her eye.

There was a dog in the backyard. A big dog. A really, really big dog. It was one of those dogs that they used in dogsled races. Those were called . . . huskies? Selene hadn't realized they were huge. But if they were pulling sleds through the snow, that made sense.

She frowned. The dog wasn't roaming around, sniffing. It was very still and almost seemed to be staring at the house.

Should I call animal control?

The dog didn't frighten her, but she worried about it getting hit by a car.

You're in the country now, Selene. Chill. Maybe people here let their dogs run around.

She certainly didn't want to piss off any of her new neighbors by getting their dogs sent to the local pound. If it kept showing up, she could ask around and see who it belonged to.

As she watched the dog, its muzzle lifted and its gaze moved to the second floor of the house, locking on her.

A laugh slipped from her throat. *Yeah right, that dog is* not *looking at me. I am way too tired.*

Even as the thought formed, the dog darted off into the night. Hopefully it was heading home.

All at once, a new disturbing idea slammed into her. Not a big dog. A wolf. A werewolf.

A werewolf that was watching the house.

But why would Josh be staring up at this room?

And while Selene didn't entirely trust her memory, she thought the wolf outside looked different from Josh. It had the wrong color fur, and if anything, it was bigger than Josh.

Selene closed the drapes, shivering. It was naive to think she could shut a door and forget that her world had changed forever. Life in Avondale would be like nothing she'd ever experienced. She'd expected that when she moved here, because she was now responsible for a kid and because a small town would be nothing like Los Angeles.

But she never could have anticipated that living with Allie meant accepting a home full of otherworldly beings. She flopped onto the bed, dismissing the idea of retrieving her suitcase from her car. Pajamas could wait until tomorrow. Tomorrow held promise. Selene could still wake up to a normal world. But if she didn't, what then?

Was that something she could live with? More importantly, was it safe for her and Allie to stay in Avondale?

Selene was asleep before she could settle on an answer to that question.

4

Selene woke up when Allie gave her a gentle shake. Blinking in the morning light, Selene asked, "What time is it?"

"Seven forty-five. I'm headed to school."

It took Selene a moment to get her bearings. School. Right. They weren't in Los Angeles anymore. Yesterday was moving day, and today was day one of a new house, new town, and new life, which also meant new routines.

"Do you need a ride?" She sat up and rubbed her tired eyes. She felt like someone had poured sawdust into them, and her body ached like she'd been hit by a bus. But why? Her mind didn't seem to want to answer the question—it was currently filled with dust bunnies.

"Josh is picking me up," Allie told her.

Josh.

The previous night came rushing back. Selene peered at Allie, hoping it had all been a delusion. "Josh the werewolf?"

She hoped Allie would laugh and call her crazy.

"Auntie Sel," Allie sighed. "Are you going to be weird about who Josh is? I really need you to not be weird."

The world is still upside down and inside out. There's your answer about why you're so messed up this morning.

"Not weird," Selene lied through her teeth. "I just needed to make sure I didn't dream it."

But maybe if I go back to sleep and wake up a second time, it will be a dream.

"Nope." Allie smiled. "No dreams. It's all real."

Allie made that declaration like it was the best thing ever.

"Great." Selene tried to return the smile but failed. "And we're having dinner with his . . . pack leader Saturday night?"

"Yep." Allie nodded. "I'm so excited! I'll see you after school."

Allie hugged her and skipped out of the room. Selene had never seen someone so excited to go to school. No doubt it had little to do with returning to class and a lot to do with the wolf-boy giving her a ride.

As much as denying this strange new reality was tempting, Selene didn't slink back under the covers. The best remedy she could muster for too much weird was balancing it with a normal routine. And she liked getting a morning jog in whenever she had the time.

Today she had nothing but time and a shaky grip on her sanity. There was still the U-Haul trailer to unpack, but that could wait until after hard pavement and sweat cleared her head.

A cup of coffee and a change of clothes later, she was outside, charging along the three-mile route she'd mapped out on her phone. The fast clip she forced herself to keep up as she ran through the neighborhood helped some but failed to completely quell her anxiety. She couldn't stop herself from imagining that a werewolf might bolt from behind some bushes and chase her down the block. At least the bright sunlight guaranteed she was safe from vampires.

Vampires?

Slowing to a walk because the abrupt surge of her heartbeat came from a bolt of panic rather than her pace, Selene tried yet again to wrap her mind around Allie's confession and Josh's revelation. She wasn't sure how to accept any of it. The world she'd always known was a lie . . . Well . . . maybe not a lie, but a half-truth.

Now the curtain was drawn back, exposing what still seemed impossible. Magic. Monsters. Apparently they'd been here all along.

And Allie was dating one of them. Selene pulled in a deep breath and let it ease out of her lungs. Her gaze roamed over the colors and contours of the neighborhood. She got why Emma adored this town with its gingerbread Victorians and cozy bungalows, every street canopied by ancient oaks and towering pines, abundant in parks and hiking and biking trails. Almost too good to be true.

It is, she mused as she walked.

Avondale was ruled by forces Selene couldn't begin to understand. Its perfection wasn't an accident.

Did that mean it wasn't safe? How could it be when Allie was dating a werewolf? Should they move? Allie would hate her, and Emma had made this town their home, but would Emma have changed her tune about Avondale's perfection if she knew Allie was involved with "the other side," as she'd put it?

First love. Talk about a force of nature. Selene knew trying to forbid Allie from seeing Josh would only make things worse. Nor could she turn back time and prevent Allie and Josh getting together, but she could and would do everything in her power to keep Allie from harm. The tricky part would be doing that without driving a wedge between her and Allie. They were still sorting out the changes in their relationship. She couldn't only be "fun Auntie Sel" now that Emma was gone. As Allie's guardian, Selene needed to make rules and stick to them. She remembered what it was like to be a teenager. Emotions volatile and unpredictable as a cyclone. Being a parent meant that sometimes Allie would see her as the bad guy. Moving away might be the right solution, but she wouldn't make that decision until she understood why Emma wanted to raise her daughter in Avondale despite its supernatural baggage.

So for now: damage control. In this new world, Selene didn't have the knowledge required to make rules for Allie. Selene needed answers. But how was she supposed to find them? She rounded the corner and headed back toward home.

"Morning, Selene!" A friendly voice pulled her out of her thoughts. "Welcome to Avondale."

Her next-door neighbor, Marley, waved to her with a dirt-covered hand. He was working in his enormous garden.

Grateful for a break from her existential crisis, she waved back as she started up her front walk. "Hi, Marley."

"Omelets a la Tim with fresh herbs from our kitchen garden this morning," he called. "Had breakfast yet? We'd love to get to know you better."

Protein, strong coffee, and human beings sounded like the lifesavers she needed. And Marley was right—they should get to know each other. They'd met a few times while Selene was working through the logistics of her move, but she had yet to visit their home. Having friends, especially right next door, might save her sanity. Plus, she'd never had someone cook for her from their own kitchen garden.

"Are you sure I won't be imposing?" Selene asked.

"We'd love to have you join us." Marley beamed.

"Let me grab a quick shower, and I'll be over."

"Fantastic!" He snipped herbs in a few efficient, graceful movements and headed into the house.

◆ ◆ ◆

"We're in the kitchen!" Tim called when she rang the doorbell twenty minutes later.

She stepped into the house and saw plants everywhere. Hanging from the ceiling, spilling out of sconces, climbing wrought iron trellises. Along with the living flora were bundles of dried herbs—lavender, rosemary, others she couldn't identify—that gave a pungent edge to the mélange of fragrances.

Selene wandered through the greenery of the living room to the kitchen. It was obvious Marley and Tim's house was designed by the same architect as Emma's—the layout was identical—yet she could swear their home was bigger on the inside.

"How's our new favorite neighbor?" Tim smiled when Selene entered the kitchen, which also seemed larger than hers.

He was stationed at the stove, burly and bearded. The omelets he was preparing smelled divine.

Selene glanced around the fully stocked gourmet kitchen, admiring its gleaming Viking appliances. "I confess, I have kitchen envy. This is incredible."

"We both love to cook." Tim grinned and flipped an omelet. Tim worked in real estate—he'd sold Emma her house, and Emma told Selene that knowing he and Marley lived next door was one of the reasons she'd purchased it. According to Emma, they were the best kind of neighbors: friendly and helpful but never intrusive.

"Sit down, sit down." He shooed her toward the kitchen table. "I'll have these finished in a jiffy."

"Yes, come keep me company." Marley beckoned from where he was already seated.

He stood as she joined him, kissing her on both cheeks before pulling out her chair. The couple was a study in contrasts. Tim was all bulk, tall and built like a pro-wrestler, where Marley was lean, with the litheness of a dancer.

"Fresh-squeezed orange juice, my dear?" Marley asked.

Selene nodded, and he set a juice glass before her and poured the pulpy orange liquid from a pitcher full to near overflowing. "What do you have on tap today?" Marley asked.

Making sure my niece's boyfriend has gotten his rabies vaccination.

"Not much," she said. "Unpacking, mostly."

"Ugh. Unpacking is so tedious." Tim transferred the fluffy egg creations to three plates and carried them to the table.

Marley brought over a plate of bacon. "Do you eat meat?"

"I do," Selene said. "Allie's the vegetarian, but I suspect I'll eat less meat now if I'm cooking for the two of us. God, this smells great!"

She grabbed a piece of bacon and happily crunched it.

"Are you settling in okay?" Marley asked. "How's Allie?"

"Allie seems good," Selene answered. "At least I think so, but . . . well, there's this . . ."

Selene trailed off, not sure if she should bring up her new parenting concerns on her first visit. She might never get omelets and bacon again.

Tim laughed and sat down. "Worried about the new boyfriend?"

"You know about Josh?" She gaped at them. "But Allie told me they were dating in secret. Emma didn't know."

Marley and Tim exchanged a long look that made her skin prickle.

"We might have seen Josh sneaking out of Allie's room one night when Emma was at the work conference in San Francisco," Tim confessed.

"It was giving *Romeo and Juliet* vibes," Marley said with a wink. In a more serious voice, he continued. "We confronted Allie about it, and she promised she was going to tell Emma as soon as she got home, but . . ."

"She never came home," Selene said quietly, her chest tightening.

Marley reached over and placed his hand atop Selene's. "We're so sorry for your loss. For Allie's. And for ourselves. We loved Emma. There aren't words to say how much she'll be missed in Avondale."

Selene nodded, appreciating their kindness. She bit the inside of her cheek so she wouldn't cry.

Tim must have sensed she was about to fall apart, because he said brusquely, "Getting back to Josh, I can understand your concern because teenage hormones: ugh. But I promise you he's a good . . . kid."

Selene put her head in her hands. She was never going to figure out this whole parenting thing.

"Selene," Tim continued. "Full disclosure. We had an ulterior motive in the breakfast invite this morning."

Selene raised her head. "What?"

"We thought you might need a little help adjusting," Marley said. "Mixed partnerships can be tough to navigate."

"Mixed partnerships?"

"Paranormal and human couples."

Selene's eyes went wide. "Paranormal . . . You know?"

Of course they know. Avondale is their home. Everyone here is in on it but me.

Tim smiled gently. "Yes."

"And we're in a position to offer advice," Marley added. "If you'd like."

"You are?" The wheels in her mind were spinning but only burning rubber.

"We've been in a mixed partnership for almost twelve years."

"A mixed . . . are you a werewolf?" Selene stared at Tim. He certainly had the physique of a potential werewolf, and a lot of body hair if one could judge by the dense covering on his arms.

He laughed. "No, god no. Marley's a faerie."

"Wait. Is this some kind of joke?" Selene glanced from Tim to Marley, frowning. "Because I'm not getting it. My brain might not be ready to process jokes about this stuff."

Tim laughed harder. "No, Selene. He's a real faerie. One of the Fae."

Marley was smiling and nodding, but he appeared perfectly human.

"Faeries are just like people?" she asked.

"No," Tim said. "Mar, you'd better lose the glamour so she can understand how it works."

"What's a glamour?" Her eyes darted back and forth between the men.

"Put down your glass, Selene," Marley said. "I don't want to sweep up the pieces."

Selene complied but didn't take her gaze off him.

The air around Marley shimmered, and a moment later she was staring at Marley. Except he wasn't exactly Marley anymore.

The same face smiled at her, but without the glamour, his arms and chest were bare. His skin had the bright-green hue of spring grass, and veins snaked over the surface of his body like vines twining around a tree branch. His hair had disappeared, and his head was now covered with what looked like fern leaves on the verge of unfurling.

But the feature that stopped Selene's heart were his wings. Marley had wings. Slender iridescent wings that sprouted between his shoulder blades. Gigantic dragonfly wings.

I am not going to faint. I am not going to faint.

"Selene, you've gotta breathe or you're gonna faint." Tim squeezed her shoulder.

She sucked in a long breath and then another.

"I'm okay." *The room is not tilting. It is perfectly still. I am calm. I am fine.*

"Of course you are." Marley beamed. "Maybe have some coffee?"

He fluttered across the table and picked up the carafe.

Selene fainted.

◆ ◆ ◆

She woke up on Marley and Tim's couch.

"You should have waited to fly in front of her," Tim said.

"I thought she looked okay. Her color was pretty good," Marley argued. He was still green and vine covered.

"I'm okay." Selene sat up. "Just embarrassed."

That was a bit of a lie. Yes, she was embarrassed—nearly four decades on this planet without losing consciousness, yet she'd passed out twice in the space of twelve hours. But more than that, she was overwhelmed. The hits were coming so quickly and without warning, her brain had decided to say "nope" and shut down.

She couldn't let it happen again. If this was her new reality, so be it. No. More. Fainting.

"I'm so sorry I reacted like that," she said.

"No need to apologize," Marley said quickly. "It's a shock."

"The first time Marley took off the glamour in front of me, I screamed and ran out of the room," Tim said.

"What made you come back?" Selene asked, still somewhat bewildered.

"He needed his clothes." Marley grinned. "We were in bed at the time."

"Like he said." Tim laughed and reached over to squeeze Marley's hand. "It was a shock."

"No doubt," Selene said and pushed her hair out of her face. "I fainted last night when Josh turned into a werewolf too."

"He shifted in front of you?" Tim asked in a hushed voice.

Selene nodded. "I didn't believe Allie when she told me. I guess the two of them decided seeing is believing. It is."

Marley and Tim were both frowning.

"What's wrong?" she asked.

"Werewolves aren't permitted to change form in front of humans," Marley said. He sounded nervous.

"Doesn't it make a difference that Allie is dating one?" Selene wondered if she'd reach a point where this sort of conversation felt normal.

"Josh would have gotten permission to shift in front of her before he ever asked her out. The wolves have a lot of rules about that sort of thing," Tim said. "It keeps certain situations . . . safer."

So they are dangerous. Selene forced her expression to stay neutral but filed away that information for future use.

"I've been invited to dinner with Fenris Hall Saturday night." She couldn't stop herself from tensing at the weight of yet another impending paranormal encounter. "Something about Josh and Allie's relationship requiring acceptance from the pack."

For a moment she thought Marley's eyes would jump from their sockets.

"Are you serious, Selene?" he whispered.

Her heart began to zigzag beneath her ribs. "Is something wrong with that?"

Tim drew a sharp breath, and Marley shot him a warning glance.

"Nothing is *wrong,* Selene," Marley assured. "But it might be a good idea for you to understand the hierarchy of the paranormal world. And of this town in particular. Since it's all new to you."

"Please fill me in," Selene said, the tension in her body easing a little. *Finally, some answers.*

"The wolves are at the top," Tim explained curtly. "And Fenris rules the wolves. In essence, he rules Avondale."

"Tim." Marley's tone was reproachful. "Fenris Hall has been very good to us. To everyone in this town. He keeps the peace and makes sure there isn't interference with our lives."

"I'm not saying he's anything other than good," Tim said. "But Selene isn't ready for him. Who knows what he's thinking since Allie—"

"Tim!" Marley snapped.

"What are you two talking about?" Selene asked. "What's happening with Allie?"

"Nothing," Marley said. "Nothing at all. She's dating Josh, and they want to formalize that relationship. That can't happen without taking specific steps. Steps that Fenris will oversee."

Tim looked away but didn't say anything further.

"Tim, why don't you bring the coffee in here, and I'll get Selene up to speed about Avondale."

Tim nodded and left the room.

"Marley, what's going on?" Selene frowned. "Is Allie in trouble?"

"Of course not," Marley said with a smile that looked like a flower bursting into bloom. "We couldn't ask for a better leader than Fenris, and now he's obviously open to the potential of bringing Allie into our world . . . and it sounds like you as well."

"I'm not following." Frustration crept into her voice. Yes, she was getting answers, but every answer birthed a new question. It made her feel like she was running in circles, chasing a truth that remained out of reach.

"How much has Allie told you about paranormals?" Marley asked.

"Not a lot," Selene said. "I got a little stuck at 'they exist.' I know there are paranormals at her school."

"There are more paranormals than humans in Avondale," Marley said. "It's a special town."

"That's crystal clear." Selene hoped she didn't sound too bitter about it. "But why Avondale?"

"There's a sacred grove in Crescent Moon Valley," he said. "Full of Old Magic. Lends power to whoever controls the site."

"I was planning to hike there!"

"Of course you were, it's lovely. Amazing views." Marley grinned. "But it *also* has a sacred grove."

"Right, sacred grove," Selene muttered. "Of course."

"Fenris came here with his pack about two hundred years ago and established the town with the idea that it would be a refuge for our kind," he continued. "He's been watching over the site ever since, and he pretty much decides who can and cannot live here."

"Hang on." Selene held up her hand. "Two hundred years?"

"Give or take," Marley said. "How do you think Avondale stays so small? We're the only town anywhere near the Bay Area that hasn't been swallowed by sprawl. The closest town is still twenty miles out."

Selene chewed her lip. "And that's Fenris? He makes that happen?"

"Yes."

"And it's mostly paranormals who live here?"

Marley shrugged. "Plenty of humans live in Avondale. But they're mostly magi."

"Magi?"

"Witches, warlocks, druids . . . We even have a couple of necromancers in town."

"Marley's best clients." Tim reappeared with a tray bearing coffee, cups, and saucers.

"Clients?"

"I'm the herbalist for Avondale." Marley smiled. "Exclusively. I also do some online sales, but I prefer to sell locally."

"So if the humans who live in Avondale are pretty much tied to the paranormal world, how did Emma end up here?" Selene asked.

Tim and Marley exchanged a look.

"We don't know," Tim said and poured her a cup of coffee. "No one can move here or start a business without Fenris Hall's permission. And nonmagical humans don't come here by accident. I'm guessing Natalie Lyon was responsible for Emma's arrival. If Natalie vouched for Emma, that would have been good enough for Fenris. Have you met Natalie?"

"Not yet." Selene knew Natalie was Emma's closest friend in Avondale. Their businesses were housed in the same building.

"As for you living here . . ." Tim left the statement hanging.

"He gives a lot of money to my campaigns," Selene told them. "Could that be it?"

"Possibly," Marley said. "You're already something of a known quantity, and there's no doubt Allie is a factor. Fenris wouldn't have left her without a loved one after Emma died."

"To be completely honest"—Tim offered Selene a sympathetic smile—"there's a good chance you're still on probation. Your dinner Saturday night is likely as much about judging your suitability for Avondale as it is about Josh dating Allie."

Selene couldn't handle unpacking that and skipped right over it. "So to review: the town is full of paranormals and humans who've been given permission to stay?"

"Yep, all kinds. The werewolves are the biggest contingent. Then it's the Fae and vamps. The rest are kind of a jumble. Pretty much everything you've read about in myth exists here."

Selene swallowed. "Allie mentioned vampires. She said they can't go to school because of the sun."

"That's true." Marley nodded. "Vamps are nocturnal. That's why so many of the shops in Avondale are open twenty-four hours."

Tim laughed, but Selene was frowning. "Are they dangerous?"

"The vampires?" His expression became solemn.

She nodded.

"They can be, if they're rogue, but Fen keeps a tight rein on the vampires in town. They get their blood exclusively from banks or groupies."

"Groupies?" Selene asked.

"Humans who volunteer to feed vamps," Marley explained. "For some it's a kink, for others it's the free room and board they get in exchange."

"Wow." The creep factor in that scenario made her shudder.

"Steady now," Tim said. "I know it's a lot to take in."

Selene nodded, grateful for their kindness and patience with her.

"What about the wolves?" Her voice lowered. "Are they dangerous?"

Marley glanced at Tim and reached out to take Selene's hand. A slender vine curled around her wrist like a tiny, reassuring embrace.

"The wolves hunt wild game. They don't go after humans."

"Allie mentioned something about a rivalry. Between vampires and werewolves. What's that about?" She took a sip of coffee and tried to ignore the fact that her cup was shaking in her hand.

"A blood feud. Really old, but mostly back in Europe," Tim answered. "Vamps and wolves don't get along. But they have the largest numbers and are the most powerful in our society. They're the ones who call the shots, so we all end up on one side or the other."

"But the wolves are in charge of the vampires here?"

"That's only in Avondale," Marley said. "There are other cities and towns where vamps have control. It mostly depends on who got there first and who's got the numbers—either a wolf clan or a vamp or witch coven. Here, it's the wolves."

"And Fenris Hall is king?"

They both nodded.

"So tell me." She sipped her coffee, mustering her confidence, and leaned back against the sofa. "What do I wear to meet the king of Avondale?"

5

Selene considered herself an LA-lifer. She loved the city's hodgepodge of incongruent, endless neighborhoods piled atop one another to the horizon and beyond. It never bothered her that the sprawl made having a car nonnegotiable, and she probably should have been charmed by her walk to Avondale's quaint downtown. If not for the fact that her every step was haunted by Allie's shocking revelation. Even so, she couldn't deny the little town was lovely.

During her visits Selene teased Emma mercilessly about the fairy-tale perfection Avondale manifested on every block. Come to think of it, even the facade of the convenience store she'd stopped at on the way into town reflected a carefully curated small-town appeal in the same way every tourist-bait location did, like the McDonald's in Lake Tahoe that mimicked a ski chalet. Avondale's zoning laws endeavored to cultivate whimsy and were strictly enforced.

Emma simply smiled at Selene's barbs, which was fair because despite all the cute and cozy, Avondale was not a tourist trap. Gorgeous, yes, alluring, for sure, but as far as Selene could discern, it wasn't fake. Nary a gaudy or garish trinket vendor in sight.

But none of that explained why Emma had moved to Avondale. And why did she stay if she knew it was filled with monsters?

Until last night, Selene believed she and Emma didn't have secrets. Their relationship was built on unshakable trust, unwavering love. Their shared history had taken them on a path from friendship to family.

After graduating from college, Selene and Emma shared a tiny LA apartment they could barely afford while they pursued their dream careers—Emma's as a promoter in the indie music scene, and Selene's as a fundraising and outreach coordinator for a variety of nonprofits, particularly those related to environmental conservation. Over the next handful of years, they advanced in their respective careers, eventually moving out of the shoebox they lived in and into their own places.

Along the way, Emma fell hard for Daniel Brix, the lead guitarist of a buzzy alt-rock band. When Emma got pregnant, they had a quick courthouse wedding—Daniel was about to go on his first national tour. To say their marriage was rocky was an understatement. Emma soon discovered that her husband viewed monogamy as a suggestion, not a requirement of their wedding vows. She was heartbroken, and he apologized, promising never to do it again. Until he did it again. And again. Emma hated it, but she was desperately in love with him, and he with her . . . as long as they were in the same room.

Then, without warning, shortly before Allie's sixth birthday, Daniel vanished. He didn't simply ghost Emma. No one knew what happened to him. Not his manager, nor his bandmates, who were all pissed because he'd bugged out in the middle of a European tour.

There was a search. Authorities were involved. But he was gone. No evidence of foul play. No conspiracy. Just no Daniel.

Emma was devastated and Allie confused and sad that her larger-than-life daddy was never coming home. But one night, after too many drinks, Emma confessed to Selene that Daniel's disappearance was something of a relief. She couldn't take the cheating, the broken promises. She could grieve him and let go in a way she hadn't been able to but had needed to for so long. She cried while Selene hugged her and convinced her she wasn't a horrible person for feeling that way.

In Selene's opinion, Emma and Allie were better off without Daniel. She'd been debating for several months before his disappearance whether to tell Emma that Daniel had made a pass at her one night when the three of them were meeting for drinks, but Emma had to cancel at the last minute. Selene and Daniel were already at the bar, and he convinced her to stay for a drink and then tried to talk her into taking him back to her apartment. She threw her drink in his face and left, but she hadn't told Emma, who already knew her husband was a cheating bastard.

Selene couldn't decide if making Emma aware of Daniel's new low would change anything for the better. Nothing to that point had convinced Emma to break things off with him, and Selene was afraid Daniel would twist things around and try to make it seem like Selene had been the one who hit on him. She wanted to think Emma would never believe she could betray her best friend that way, but Daniel was a master manipulator. Selene didn't want to risk losing Emma's friendship if he managed to convince her that he hadn't done anything wrong but Selene had. When Daniel went away for good, that problem was solved.

From the first, Selene was Allie's de facto aunt. Selene did everything she could to help Emma over the hurdles of being a mostly single mom. Daniel was always on the road and unreliable even when he was around. He liked playing at being Allie's father because the cute little cherub was his biggest fangirl. Her adoring, innocent love fed his ravenous ego. Allie was too young to grasp that his doting was born of narcissism, and Emma thought it would be cruel to break a little girl's heart with the truth.

A few years after Daniel disappeared, Emma decided she was done with Los Angeles and the nonstop pressure of trying to discover the next breakout band. Instead, she pursued a new career in holistic wellness, earning certifications in nutrition, yoga instruction, and massage therapy.

"Life is too stressful for everyone," Emma told Selene. *"I'd rather help people deal with it than keep drowning in it myself."*

Selene fully supported Emma's career reboot, but she was less enthused about Emma's decision to leave LA and move to a hamlet in Northern California that Selene had never heard of.

Avondale.

She'd considered going with them. She really had. So much of her work was remote, and when it wasn't, it involved traveling to locations all over the state. Emma and Allie were her family. It didn't matter that much where home base was, but Selene loved cities. Especially cities with international airports.

Yet no matter how many times she tried to persuade Emma to move somewhere in the Bay Area instead of a tiny town tucked away in the Santa Cruz mountains, Emma wouldn't change her mind. For some reason she'd fallen in love with Avondale, and nowhere else would do. But despite Emma's devotion to her new home, she had steered Selene away from visits, insisting that it would be better for her and Allie to come to LA or for the three of them to travel somewhere together.

At the time, Selene hadn't thought it was that strange and assumed Emma was catering to Selene's preference for cities. They shared every holiday. Took vacations together. Neither of them had other relatives. Selene had been raised in the foster system, and Emma was an only child whose parents were gone. They really were a found family. Their perfect little trio.

Emma dated, Selene dated, but no one had stuck. Emma was gun-shy after Daniel. Who could blame her? And Selene was so focused on her career that relationships felt like a hassle. Neither of them was particularly worried about finding "the one," even as they glimpsed middle age on the horizon. They had good lives. They were happy.

All the memories they'd shared were priceless. They would always be priceless, even if painful as sharp knives.

Selene crossed from the residential street into the heart of Avondale: a town square featuring a green quad with city hall at one end and a public library at the other. On the side streets, Selene spied the businesses that Emma raved about whenever she went on a spiel about the wonders of small-town life. There was the Midnight Broil, a twenty-four-hour diner where she'd shared a few scrumptious brunches with Emma and Allie. Queen Mab's Madness was a cocktail bar Selene had yet to try. Ciel was a MICHELIN-starred fine-dining establishment where Emma said it was near impossible to get a table. There was the Scottish-themed pub, Tam O' Shanter's Ride, and next to it a sewing and knitting shop called Darn It that advertised all locally sourced wool and fabrics. An art-supply shop leaned hard into Shakespeare with the name More Things in Heaven and Earth.

The surfeit of independent stores with cute, clever names bordered on ridiculous but was admittedly adorable. Selene made a beeline for Page Turner, the bookstore. Books were comfort, escape. And Selene was having a tough time with reality. Though part of her reason for heading to the bookstore was research. Maybe this magical town had a special section on paranormals that would help Selene navigate her new life. If she got really lucky, they might even stock a self-help book with rules for dating werewolves.

Selene stepped into the shop, a bell ringing as she pushed the door open. Page Turner managed to be gargantuan and tidy at once, reminiscent of an archive housing esoteric knowledge yet still distinctly cozy. Pure wrangled chaos.

"Welcome, my dear!" A voice warm as a crackling hearth beckoned her. "Looking for anything special today?"

Selene made her way to the front counter, where she found a silver-haired woman wearing glasses that gave her owlish eyes and the smile of a grandma who would sneak you candy from her purse.

"Not particularly," Selene hedged. She didn't know if it was okay to just come out and ask about Avondale's magic, and it felt risky to make any assumptions. "Just exploring the town. I moved here recently. Recently, as in yesterday."

"Did you now?" The woman's eyes narrowed.

"Yes," Selene replied, taken aback by the sharp suspicion of the question. "I'm a . . . was a friend, a close friend, of Emma Bancroft."

"Oh, my heart." Those narrowed eyes went wide and filled with sympathy, and her hands flew to press the space on her chest over the vital organ she'd invoked. Whatever reservations the woman held about Selene seemed to vanish. "Emma was just a darling. And her daughter is the loveliest girl. We were all devastated when we heard the news."

Selene's throat tried to close, but she answered. "Yes. I'm . . . um . . . I'll be taking care of Allison now. I moved to Avondale so I could do that."

The woman rested her hand on top of Selene's, which Selene hadn't realized was clinging white-knuckled to the edge of the counter.

"That is true friendship," the woman told Selene. "Welcome to Avondale . . ."

"Selene." Selene filled in the obvious gap. "Selene Jones. Thank you. And you are?"

"Betty," the woman replied, smiling. "This is my bookstore."

"Pleased to meet you, Betty," Selene replied, her returning smile genuine. "I love your store already." She took a deep breath. "The scent alone."

"I know," Betty said, looking pleased. "Nothing better in the world than the smell of books."

"Definitely a contender." Selene grinned.

"Oh, I like you." Betty laughed. "Now that we know each other, is there anything I can point you toward?"

"Not really," Selene replied. "Is it okay if I wander?"

"Of course," Betty said.

"Thank you, Betty." Selene made a silent promise to buy at least a dozen books, appreciating Betty's kindness.

"My pleasure," Betty replied. "Enjoy."

"I know I will." Selene smiled again before she meandered into the stacks. "Be back soon."

"Soon" turned out to be a miscalculation. Not only was the store even larger than it appeared, its stacks were labyrinthine, full of cozy nooks and hidden corners. Despite all the shelves bursting with books, Selene couldn't find anything beyond standard mythology texts when it came to magic. Everything else that featured the paranormal was fiction.

Oh well, if I can't do research, at least I can read for pleasure.

After selecting a couple of mysteries, Selene hunted down the young adult section and picked a few books she thought Allie might like. Continuing her exploration, she perused the aisles, pausing at a table marked by the sign **Betty's Favorites.**

Selene smiled as she picked up a book that featured an old-school bodice ripper cover. A woman swooning in a diaphanous gown that slipped from her shoulders was bathed in moonlight while a massive wolf stalked her from the shadows.

With a little laugh, Selene added the book to her pile. She loved a good romance, though she tended to favor rom-coms over fantasy. But if Betty recommended the book, Selene was happy to give it a try.

She was about to move on when the skin at the back of her neck prickled. Though she hadn't heard any footsteps, she sensed someone behind her, closing in quickly. Turning to greet the other bookshop patron—or maybe it was Betty coming to check on her—Selene painted on a friendly smile. Her pleasant mien dissolved when the aisles at her back were empty.

I could have sworn . . . She frowned. Whatever she thought she'd sensed had been conjured by her imagination. Given recent events, it would be very easy for Selene to imagine all manner of disturbing things.

Selene tamped down an irrational urge to hurry back to the front of the store, not only because it was silly but also because she wanted to see just how big this bookshop was. She continued toward the back, picking up more books along the way. She'd need to cut herself off soon. The pile she carried was getting unwieldy, and she had to carry it all the way back to Emma's house.

My house, she reminded herself, wondering if she'd ever get used to that. *My house and Allie's house.*

The store lights were dimmer and the shadows deeper in the rear of the store, and open bookshelves were replaced by locked glass cases. Antique and presumably rare books in beautiful bindings sat in neat rows on the other side of the glass. Selene peered into the cases but was unable to discern what the contents of the books could be as they hailed from a time before titles were printed on the spines.

She straightened abruptly, going still as her heart gave an uneasy thud, because there it was again. That feeling that she wasn't alone. This time she didn't try to look for anyone but kept her gaze on the case while she listened for any sign that her instincts weren't leading her astray. There was someone, there had to be, because her skin was practically humming with awareness. Closing her eyes, Selene sank into her other senses and waited. What compelled her to do this rather than simply search the stacks for whoever might be there, she neither knew nor understood. Only that her gut insisted she let it happen.

And then she heard it. A low, steady rumbling.

Her eyes snapped open because that had definitely been *a growl.* Something was growling in the back of the store.

Surely Betty didn't have a guard dog patrolling the back of the store. And if she did, why didn't she offer any warning?

Maybe this is a restricted section. Selene hadn't noticed any signs warning that the locked cabinets were out of bounds, or barriers separating the rare books collection from the rest of the store.

And if I've trespassed into a forbidden part of a store in a magical town, maybe it isn't a dog that's growling. Maybe it's something much worse.

The heavy thud of her pulse became a frenetic scamper as she debated her next move. Yes, she'd heard the growl, but she had yet to see the dog, or whatever it was, which meant, in theory, it hadn't spotted her?

Selene recalled that the worst thing you could do when confronted by an aggressive animal was run. Something about triggering a prey instinct? That knowledge was hardly comforting because, at this point, she really, really wanted to bolt to the front of the store.

She wasn't certain where the growl had come from, but since she hadn't run into any creatures on her way into this section, it followed that retracing her steps cautiously was the wisest course. Backing away slowly and expecting a snarling beast to stalk out of the darkness at any moment, Selene decided that if something did lunge at her, she'd hurl the stack of novels at it. That should at least buy her a few seconds to make an escape.

The lights above her grew brighter as she moved cautiously away from the locked cabinets, throwing an occasional glance over her shoulder, both to check for signs of the dog and to make sure she didn't ram into a shelf. She couldn't hear the growling any longer, and the bookcases on either side of her were once again the mundane bookshop sort, which she hoped meant she'd reached minimum safe distance.

Deciding it was worth the risk, Selene spun around . . . and crashed into a wall.

She let out a yelp. The books in her arms went flying as she stumbled back, having bounced off . . . not a brick wall, but the hard muscles of a man's chest covered by a gray Henley.

Flustered, Selene didn't know whether to apologize for running into someone because she'd been walking backward or demand where that someone had come from, because really, couldn't they have gotten out of the way? Rather than doing either, she crouched and began to reorganize the books into a manageable stack.

"Let me help you carry those," a quiet but deep voice offered.

She glanced up at him. And froze.

Oh. My. God.

Selene had never encountered a person in real life who could have modeled for the cover of a romance novel. And she'd never literally run into one.

But this guy . . . from the broad, wall-like chest to the tousled ash-brown hair that fell around his gray eyes and framed his sharp jawline, he could have jumped right out of any number of stepbacks (which were secretly Selene's favorite part of romance covers). Well, he would probably need to lose his shirt first, or rip it in some way . . .

Not helpful, Selene.

As she attempted to steer her brain in a reasonable direction, he knelt beside her and picked up one of the scattered books.

The stranger chuckled as he read the title. "*Nocturne's Burden*, a tale of forbidden desire. Well, it looks fascinating, to say the least."

Selene groaned inwardly. Of all the books, *that* was the one he had to look closely at?

She opened her mouth to reply, but his smile stole her words and made her knees weak. The shadow of stubble on his chin and jaw along with his Henley, jeans, and scuffed boots gave him a relaxed, outdoorsy look. He appeared to be thirty . . . ish. Younger than her, but maybe not . . . too much younger? He was tall, with a lean frame, and if crashing into him was any indication, there was nothing but muscle underneath his clothes. And now she was thinking about how that strong body felt, even briefly, against hers.

Forcing her gaze back to his smile didn't help because it drew her attention to his full, sculpted lips.

She realized she was staring when he began to pick up the rest of the books on the floor, and she quickly looked away.

"It's one of Betty's recommendations," Selene belatedly replied to his comment about the romance novel.

He glanced at her, and his smile became a grin. "Then it's a good pick. Betty has excellent taste."

"You're a regular then?" she asked, gathering the few books he had yet to retrieve.

"You could say that."

They both stood.

"I'm not," Selene said, then bit the inside of her cheek. "I mean, I haven't been here before. I just moved to town."

"Is that so?" He sounded amused.

His gaze moved over her face before slipping down to skim over her body in an unhurried manner. He did nothing to hide the fact that he was slowly taking her in. It should have made her uncomfortable, offended even, but instead she found herself leaning toward him. As her body canted in his direction, she heard him draw a deep breath.

Did he just . . . smell me?

The stranger's eyes lifted to meet hers. His gray irises had darkened to thunderclouds. His chest rose as he took another breath and stepped closer, his gaze drifting to her lips. When she felt his warm breath graze her skin, her eyelids drifted shut.

The low rumbling sound came again.

Selene jumped back, eyes snapping wide. "The dog!"

"The dog?" His mouth twitched at the corners.

And then Selene was blinking, dumbfounded, because he was standing a foot away, watching her with a notch between his brows, as if they hadn't been close enough to share body heat. As if he hadn't been about to kiss her.

Wait . . . Had she seriously been about to let a complete stranger kiss her in the back of a bookstore? Had she lost her mind?

Flustered and confused, Selene gestured at the shadow-drenched stacks. "There's a dog somewhere. I heard it growling. That's why I ran into you. I was rushing out of there, and I don't know why Betty didn't—"

"There's no dog." The man's voice was clipped. His expression shuttered. He might as well have thrown a bucket of ice water in her face. "I'll carry these to the front for you."

Selene stared in disbelief as he walked away.

What just happened? Had she imagined . . . all of that? The heat, the magnetic attraction?

Damn that romance cover. And the dry spell in her sex life that no doubt was the reason her mind was serving up fantasies of meet-cutes at the back of the bookstore.

Selene squinted into the shadows she'd fled. The fact that she hadn't had a date in recent memory might explain misconceptions of her run-in with the hot guy, but not the growling. It irked her that the handsome stranger had dismissed her fears and walked away, but she wasn't about to wander through the shelves and get bitten just to prove she *had* heard something. And given the true nature of Avondale, she could get lost in the stacks and come face-to-face with something far worse than a dog. That thought made her shudder.

Glancing around the floor to make sure there weren't any stray books she and Mystery Man left behind, Selene cast one last look at the dark recesses of the store, then made her way back to the counter. She rehearsed and dismissed a number of things to say to the attractive stranger because in her head they all sounded like awkward attempts to either get his number or insist that something *was* growling at the back of the store.

None of it mattered because when Selene reached the counter, and a brightly smiling Betty, he was nowhere in sight. The books he'd carried were neatly stacked near the register.

"Did you find everything you were looking for?" Betty asked.

"Yes, thanks." Selene gestured to the stack of books waiting for her. "More than I could carry myself."

After a meaningful glance toward the store entrance, Selene turned her attention back to Betty. She offered the shopkeeper an inquisitive smile, hoping Betty might fill in the blanks about her erstwhile hot helper. But Betty simply hummed tunelessly as she rang up Selene's purchases.

Selene sneaked a glance at the door again. Maybe her handsome helper was still nearby. If she caught up with him, she could . . .

I could what? Selene chided herself. *Suggest we get coffee after agreeing that I must have imagined some snarling creature in the bookstore?*

She huffed out a breath, dismissing the impulse to find the stranger. There were too many changes in her life as it was. Her focus needed to be on getting settled in Avondale and being whatever Allie needed her to be. And she didn't know where to begin when it came to the werewolf boyfriend.

"I'm throwing in a couple of canvas totes on the house," Betty quipped. "You'll need them to get this haul home."

"Oh!" Selene blushed because Betty was watching her in a way that made Selene suspect she'd been staring at the store entrance for a while. "You don't need to do that. I'm happy to buy them."

Betty winked at her. "I insist. Consider it a bribe to lure you back for repeat business."

"I'd be back without the bribe." Selene laughed. "But thank you."

As Betty put the books in the tote bags, Selene chewed on her lip and silently debated one last time whether she should ask who the man was. Then an unpleasant thought occurred to her: The guy was a local who knew Betty. What if she wasn't offering up his name because he'd asked her not to? Maybe Selene had made that bad of a first impression, bashing into him and freaking out about invisible beasts. But damn it, she'd heard growling. There was no way those menacing sounds had only been in her head. If she could talk to him again, she could explain . . .

Ugh, she was being ridiculous. He was just a guy, and she needed to let it go. It's not like he was that hot . . . Okay, he absolutely was, but she didn't need to bring poor Betty into her sudden, embarrassing infatuation. Instead, Selene made a deal with herself as she walked out of the bookstore. Avondale was a small town, right? She had no experience with life in a hamlet, but its size did increase the odds that she'd cross paths with him again. If that happened, maybe she'd take it as a sign. That's what you did with magic, right? Look for signs and portents?

What she really needed was a sign telling her whether she needed to get the hell out of this town.

6

Selene's next stop was one block off the town square. She paused on the sidewalk to look at the pair of signs over the shared entrance to two businesses: **A Snip in Time Salon** and **Om My Goddess Yoga and Therapeutic Massage.** It felt odd that this was her first visit to Emma's studio, but somehow life had always conspired to keep her away . . . Actually, when Selene perused her memories, it occurred to her that life hadn't steered her away from Emma's work in Avondale. Emma had.

The single entrance to the building opened to a small lobby furnished with minimalist chairs in neutral tones offset by an abundance of thriving plants, lending the glow of emerald and jade hues to the bare walls. Verdant, subtly herbal scents permeated the air, so pleasant that Selene drew a deep breath. A sensation chased that breath, somehow peaceful while at the same time invigorating. She began to smile, but the expression froze on her face then dissolved when she noticed the sign on the door to her left.

Om My Goddess Yoga and Therapeutic Massage: Closed Until Further Notice

No doubt the sign had hung on the studio door since Emma's death. Questions full of melancholy took up residence in Selene's mind: Would someone new take on the business? Or would the studio become something else altogether? How would Emma have felt about that?

Then the more mundane but pressing thought: What were the terms of the lease? No one had contacted Selene about an ongoing financial obligation, nor had Allie said anything. But maybe whoever rented Emma the space had been waiting for Selene to move to town when Allie's situation was more settled before broaching the subject, in person or via an attorney.

Selene pivoted toward the other door. Here the sign read:

A Snip in Time Salon, Natalie Lyon: Proprietor. Cuts, Color, Readings.
Appointments Recommended. Blessed Be.

The readings and "blessed be" told Selene that this was more than a normal salon, but she knew enough about Avondale now that it didn't surprise her. She hoped that on the other side of the door, she'd find answers to her questions, both the mundane and the bizarre.

Not exactly clear on whether the shop was open, Selene tried the doorknob and found it unlocked. When she pushed the door open, a cascade of silvery chimes filled the air. Expecting a continuation of the spa-like atmosphere of the lobby, Selene literally stumbled at the shocking contrast of the salon's interior. The first thing that came to mind was a nineteenth-century bordello replete with antique gold fixtures, velvet settees, and silk brocade window draperies, but the lingering music of the chimes and the air tinged with incense made Selene decide it was more like a fortune teller's den.

"I thought it might be you."

The clear voice came from the far corner of the room where a woman sat, holding a porcelain teacup. She set the cup in its saucer on the table beside her chair and stood.

"The cards suggested I clear my afternoon," the woman continued as she approached. "And I wondered . . . to be truthful, I hoped it meant you were coming. Welcome, Selene."

It was, without a doubt, the strangest greeting Selene had ever received. "Natalie Lyon?"

The woman laughed, her glossy coal-black curls bouncing when her shoulders shook. "I apologize. I can be a bit much for a civilian, but you'll adjust as you get settled in Avondale."

"A civilian?" Selene was beginning to feel like she'd walked into some kind of prank.

"You're not a magi," the woman replied. "And, yes, I'm Natalie. Feel free to call me Nat if you like. Lots of my friends do."

Selene set down her book-filled bags and took Natalie's hand, but rather than shaking it, Natalie clasped Selene's fingers with both of her hands and gave a light squeeze before letting go.

"Selene Jones," Selene replied. "But you seem to know that. And somehow you also know that I've been made aware of what makes Avondale so *special*."

Natalie sighed. "I apologize again. I didn't mean to put you on the spot. I could see you're looking at the world with new eyes the minute you walked in the door. Your aura is shifting between orange and silver."

My aura? Something else new to add to the list.

"But how did you recognize me?" Selene pressed. For the moment she didn't need to get into the whole aura thing.

"I've seen your picture at the house," Natalie answered, her voice warm. "Pictures of the three of you."

"Of me, Emma, and Allie," Selene said, putting the pieces together.

Natalie nodded, her eyes gleaming with fondness and grief. Extraordinary eyes, Selene couldn't help but notice. A deep blue that was almost violet.

"She talked about you all the time," Natalie said gently. "I'm so sorry for your loss."

"Thank you," Selene replied, her throat tightening. "And the same to you. Emma bragged that she had the best business neighbor, who was also a fabulous friend. I know you were close, though she managed to forget to ever show me a picture of you."

With a dismissive wave, Natalie said, "Not her fault. I hate being photographed."

Selene couldn't imagine why. Natalie was nothing short of gorgeous, the satin black of her hair and her mesmerizing eyes a striking contrast to her smooth ivory skin. In conversations with Emma, it had sounded like Natalie was at least middle-aged, but Selene couldn't find even a hint of fine lines on the salon proprietor's face. She either had a fantastic skincare routine, or she was a lot younger than Emma implied.

"It's wonderful to finally meet you," Natalie continued. "I wish it had been under different circumstances."

"Me too," Selene replied.

Gesturing to her abandoned cup, Natalie said, "We could sit and have tea, if you have time. No doubt you have many questions."

"I have time. And questions."

Natalie paused, giving Selene another speculative look. "Is there any chance you want your hair done? I'm in the habit of getting to know people while I'm working. If you don't want a haircut, I could do a deep conditioning treatment or a gloss."

Selene's hand went reflexively to her lopsided bun. "I'm embarrassingly overdue for a haircut. Are you sure you don't mind?"

"I'd be delighted." Natalie beamed.

She led the way to the far wall of the salon where a chair faced a giant gilt-framed mirror with a shampoo station alongside it. Selene settled into the chair, and Natalie freed her hair from its topknot prison.

"I love this color." Natalie carefully combed her fingers through Selene's auburn locks. "Do you add highlights, or are they natural?"

"At the moment they're natural," Selene told her. "I've been pretty neglectful the past six months."

"Understandably," Natalie murmured. "I think it's perfect as is, but if you want to change things up, I'm game."

Selene considered that. "Let's leave the color for now, but I'm wide open as far as a cut goes. My only requirement is that I'm still able to pull it back."

"I hear that." Natalie grinned at her in the mirror. "Let's get you shampooed."

A few minutes later, Selene was back in the chair, and Natalie was snipping away.

"Before we deal with the whole magic-is-real stuff, I don't want to forget to ask about some normal, practical issues. Like Emma's lease on the studio." Selene focused on keeping her head still while Natalie cut. "I haven't heard anything from the landlord about rent due or moving stuff out of there."

"That's because I'm the landlord," Natalie replied. "I own the building and live on the second floor."

"Oh! I didn't realize."

Natalie tilted Selene's head slightly, then returned to cutting. "There's nothing to worry about with the lease."

"Are you sure?" Selene frowned. While she appreciated Natalie's generosity, she didn't want to leave Emma's friend in a bind.

"Absolutely sure." Natalie moved around the chair and tilted Selene's head the other way. "I don't depend on the rent, and honestly, I'm not ready for another business to move in there. It's too soon."

"Okay."

Several inches of Selene's hair had piled up on the floor, and Natalie was working incredibly quickly. Turning this way and that, scissors in constant motion. A pang of nerves grabbed Selene until she remembered how incredible Emma's hair always looked, which Emma claimed was only thanks to Natalie being a genius with hair.

"So." Natalie smiled. "You ready to dive into 'magic is real'?"

"Ready as I'll ever be," Selene answered grimly.

"First of all, are you okay?" Natalie asked in a gentle tone. "You've been thrown into the thick of it without any warning."

"I . . . don't know?" Selene replied.

"That's fair," Natalie said. "But you didn't shove Allie in your car and drive straight back to LA."

With a grimace, Selene admitted, "I'm still considering that option."

Natalie arched an eyebrow.

"Not really," Selene said. "I couldn't do that to Allie. At least not without learning more about what living in Avondale really means. This is her home, and she wants to be here."

As Natalie continued to work on her hair, Selene struggled with how to put together the right words.

"I don't know how she could hide this from me," she said at last. "I thought we knew everything about each other, and now it feels like . . ."

She couldn't finish the thought. Strings of reactive, impulsive thoughts were fighting their way through her brain, powered by confusion, jealousy, fear.

Natalie seemed to understand. "She couldn't tell you, Selene. A condition of Emma, or any human, residing in Avondale is a secrecy akin to the most airtight NDA you can imagine."

"I don't understand," Selene blurted. "Why would she agree to that? Everything I'm hearing about Avondale makes it seem like humans don't belong and maybe aren't even welcome. How did she end up here? She told me she took Allie camping in the area one weekend and fell in love with the place. That isn't true, is it?"

With a sympathetic smile, Natalie replied, "Humans who live in Avondale have one foot in the paranormal world. Either a partner or a relative or unforeseen circumstances brought them into contact with the supernatural. In Emma's case, it was the latter. A work friend of hers was a . . . client of mine. Emma drove that friend to Avondale one weekend. It was an emergency situation, and that's how she met me."

"An emergency haircut?" Selene couldn't help her incredulous tone.

Natalie shook her head. "I do other work that helps people who need to get out of abusive relationships. It's a whisper network of sorts, so it's not something I advertise openly."

"Oh wow," Selene said, chagrined. "So Emma's friend . . ."

"Was in a bad situation, and I helped her," Natalie said. "Emma felt drawn to my work and asked how she could be a part of it. For a long time, she volunteered as a contact in the greater LA area, but over time

Emma came to love Avondale and wanted to make her home here. I had to pull a few strings to get her permission, but I was able to convince the powers that be that Emma would be an asset to the paranormal community."

Selene stared at their reflections in the mirror, processing Natalie's words and rewriting the history of her best friend's life.

"I don't know if it helps," Natalie said gently. "But Emma told me many times that she hated keeping the truth from you. It weighed heavy on her heart."

"It helps," Selene replied, knowing the lingering hurt she felt was selfish and not worth hanging on to. "How is it that I got permission to move here?"

"Your circumstance is exceptional," Natalie admitted. "But with Emma's death and Allie wanting to continue living here, decisions had to be made quickly. It was agreed that you'd be allowed to move to Avondale on a conditional basis."

"Is anyone planning on telling me the conditions?" Selene groused.

"They're simple," Natalie replied. "Allie would talk to you, revealing the true nature of our community, then you'd decide to stay or go. If you stay, you'll have to follow the same rules as other humans. Keep Avondale's secret."

"And if I go?" Selene frowned. "What stops me from blabbing about magic and monsters being real?"

"We have the means to ensure your silence," Natalie said with a shrug.

Selene's eyes widened. "Are you saying I'd be hunted down and killed?"

"Goddess, no!" Natalie gasped. "Sorry. I should have worded that differently. There are spells that would make you forget but wouldn't otherwise harm you. Humane and effective."

With a shudder, Selene pushed aside the vision of wolves chasing her through Topanga Canyon. "It's a moot point anyway. We're staying, at least for the time being."

"I'm glad." Natalie smiled and patted Selene's hand. "I'd miss Allie like crazy if she moved away. Having her here is like still having a little bit of Emma. And getting to know you keeps Emma close too. She loved you so much."

Selene was touched, but her eyes were welling up, and she needed to change the subject.

"Out of curiosity, how did Allie break the news to you?" Natalie asked.

"She told me about Josh," Selene replied.

"Hold up a sec, there's a Josh?" Natalie asked. "Who's Josh?"

"Allie's boyfriend." Selene began to frown. "Wait, you don't know about Josh?"

As soon as she'd asked the question, she realized it made perfect sense that Natalie hadn't known about Josh. Emma wasn't aware Allie had a boyfriend. Tim and Marley only discovered the relationship by accident.

"First I've heard of him," Natalie told Selene.

"Josh is Allie's boyfriend," Selene explained. "And according to her, 'it's serious.'"

"Of course it is." Natalie grinned. "She's sixteen. First love and all that."

"I know, right?" Selene said wryly. "Probably why Allie thought it was a good idea to introduce me to the real Avondale by telling me her boyfriend is a werewolf. Telling me and then showing me because seeing really is believing, and—"

Selene stopped talking when she noticed Natalie had gone eerily still.

"Nat? Are you okay?"

"Allie is dating a wolf?" Natalie asked after a lengthy pause.

Selene nodded. "Emma didn't know. Allie was planning to tell her, but Emma died before that could happen. To be honest, it's strange Allie kept Josh a secret. She and Emma were very close."

"She kept it a secret because she knew Emma wouldn't be happy." Nat was shaking her head, brow furrowed. "Tell me more about this guy."

Emma wouldn't be happy. Natalie's words dropped like stones in Selene's stomach.

"I don't know much," Selene replied, "other than that Josh goes to school with Allie."

With an uneasy laugh, she added, "Suddenly I'm dealing with a real-life *Teen Wolf*."

"He's no teen," Natalie said quietly as she began to razor layers into Selene's hair.

"What?"

"None of the wolves in Fenris Hall's pack are that young," Natalie continued. "He's got strict rules about bringing new wolves in. He hasn't approved the turning of a human as long as I've been here."

"Turning?" Selene's heart skipped a beat.

"From human into a werewolf," Natalie said. "I'm surprised Fenris has allowed one of his pack to consort with a human. That's not like him. He keeps his wolves away from outsiders."

"I'm not sure how much he's allowing it." Selene met Natalie's gaze in the mirror. "Josh said he and Allie are petitioning the pack to accept their relationship. I don't know exactly what that means."

"It means Fenris hasn't forbidden Josh from dating Allie, but he hasn't decided if he'll allow it to continue." Natalie didn't meet Selene's eyes, making Selene more uneasy with every heartbeat. "Nothing happens with the wolves unless he okays it. He's got the last word on everything, and not only for his pack. For all of Avondale."

"Tim and Marley said the same thing," Selene said. "And that I'm probably still under review as far as Fenris Hall is concerned. I've been invited to have dinner with him on Saturday. I'm guessing it's some kind of test."

"Fenris doesn't play games." Natalie pumped styling crème from a glass bottle on the rolling caddy filled with her supplies. "If he wants to know something about you, he'll ask. You're charged with caring for Allie. And Josh is Fenris's responsibility. The two of you are in a similar position. Maybe you'll find common ground and it will make you feel better about this whole situation."

"Common ground?" Selene scoffed. "Me and the wolf tyrant?"

"I wouldn't call him a tyrant." Natalie rubbed the styling crème on her palms and ran her fingers through Selene's hair. "You'll like him. Fenris Hall could charm the skin off a snake."

"But do *you* like him?" Selene asked. Charm wasn't always a good thing. Emma's ex-husband, Daniel, proved that over and over.

"Actually, I do," Natalie said without hesitation. "Quite a lot. He's a good pack leader, and he keeps Avondale in great shape. I've heard horror stories about towns controlled by vamp covens. I can't imagine living anywhere else, and my life wouldn't be as good without Fenris's oversight of this place."

"Then what's the problem?"

Natalie thought for a moment, then sighed. "There really isn't a problem, Selene. And I'm sorry to make you worry. I love Allie, and I'm hoping you'll be happy in Avondale. Dating a wolf will be complicated. I don't want your lives to get complicated when you're already dealing with so much change."

"Too late." Selene smiled thinly. "I'm guessing dinner with Fenris Hall won't make things any less complicated."

Natalie's expression became sly.

"What?" Selene frowned as Natalie smirked at her.

"I'll be very curious to hear what you think of our dear Fenris. He's . . . well, I won't give any spoilers," Natalie said with a laugh. "Especially since this is all brand new to you."

"If I don't faint, I'll consider it a win," Selene groused.

"Faint?"

Rolling her eyes, Selene explained. "I fainted when Josh turned into a werewolf. Then I fainted again when Marley took off his . . . I don't remember the word, but he showed me he has wings and green skin."

"He removed his glamour," Natalie said.

Selene nodded. "I wasn't ready for it. He looked so normal and then WINGS."

"Hold that thought." Natalie got out a blow-dryer.

Selene watched Natalie in the mirror, mulling over their conversation. She couldn't imagine ever being so at ease with a world full of magic as Natalie was. Had she ever been as stupefied as Selene felt? Then a terrible suspicion dawned as Natalie put away the blow-dryer.

"Natalie, are you human?" Selene blurted, then gasped. "Oh god. Is it horribly rude to ask that?"

Shaking her head, Natalie laughed again. "It's not rude, but I wouldn't recommend going door-to-door asking everyone in Avondale what they are. It's best to let paranormals reveal themselves as they choose."

When Selene continued to watch her expectantly, Natalie grinned and spun the chair around so they were facing each other.

"I'm human, for the most part."

"What does that mean?" Selene hadn't thought "human for the most part" was a possible answer.

"I'm a witch," Natalie answered. "And I come from a long line of witches. Very powerful witches. Forgoing any disasters, I'll live a lot longer than your average human would, and I'll look like I do now until I choose to enter my crone phase."

"Crone phase?" Selene repeated.

"That's witch speak for old lady," Natalie replied. She regarded Selene for several beats, pursing her lips.

"You're making me nervous." Selene twisted her fingers together. "Why are you looking at me like that?"

"I'm trying to decide how much you can handle."

"Is there a lot more to handle than magic and monsters being real?" Selene groaned. "Because that's plenty."

Natalie reached out to fuss with Selene's dried hair. "It might be more than you want to know, but I believe it's important that you understand you belong here, Selene."

"I'm not following."

"And I can't give you much," Natalie confessed with a sigh. "Only that you, like me, are human . . . for the most part."

Selene scoffed. "I'm not anything but human, Nat. I'm pretty sure I would have noticed if I had magical powers."

"All I can tell you at the moment is that beings with supernatural power resonate at a different frequency than mundane humans," Natalie said firmly. "Those of us attuned to the paranormal always sense one another. You resonate like one of us."

"Is that something you see in my aura?" she teased, but Natalie nodded in all seriousness.

Selene tried to cover the spike of fear in her gut with a smile. "I hate to tell you this, but your paranormal radar is malfunctioning. There's nothing magic about me."

Natalie looked like she wanted to argue, but she pursed her lips, then said, "When you're ready, we'll talk."

Selene made a noncommittal noise, ignoring the electrical storm coursing through her veins.

A weighty silence fell as Natalie continued to style Selene's hair.

"There you go," Natalie said after a few minutes and turned the chair to face the mirror again. "What do you think?"

Selene couldn't answer because her jaw was hanging open. Was that even her gaping back at herself in the mirror?

"I could pretend to be afraid you're speechless because you hate it, but that's not my style." Natalie pulled the cape off Selene and shook it out. "I am damn good at what I do."

"I didn't think my hair could do this," Selene exclaimed when she found her voice again. "Do you know how much money you could make in LA?"

Natalie winked. "Not interested. Avondale is where I belong."

When Selene opened her purse, Natalie clucked her tongue. "No charge."

"But—"

"It's my welcome-home gift to you," Natalie said. "I'm really happy you're here, Selene."

A business card appeared in her hand, seemingly from nowhere. She dropped it into Selene's open purse. "I feel it's only fair to tell you that if you don't call me immediately after your dinner tomorrow night, I'll be devastated. That's the kind of gossip that could be the foundation of our friendship."

"Guess I'd better call," Selene attempted to deadpan, but she couldn't stop a smile from overtaking her face.

7

Selene set the table and rehearsed her speech again. She had no idea if the rehearsals were doing any good. They certainly weren't making her any less nervous.

Talking with Natalie had helped, but then Selene came home and made the mistake of diving into another internet rabbit hole, searching for the most vital facts about werewolves, and streamed movies, but she had no idea if what she gleaned from them was fact or fiction. How could she? Before yesterday it had *all* been fiction.

For the rest of the afternoon, her mind had been stuck in a loop of disturbing questions: How dangerous were the paranormals in Avondale? Did they welcome human residents in their town or simply tolerate them? Did Allie fully grasp the potential threat of dating a being who, at least at an instinctual level, was a predator? Could those instincts ever truly be controlled?

The last two questions were the most troubling and pushed Selene to the conclusion that Allie should take a time-out to think all these things through. They'd talk about the pros and cons, maybe make lists, or graphs, or spreadsheets that would prove to Allie how the risks of being with Josh outweighed the rewards. Okay, so the graphs and spreadsheets were probably overkill, but talking and lists would hopefully do the trick.

Not knowing what to do with herself, Selene decided the best thing to do was bake cookies for Allie to ease the pain of hearing that Selene thought dating a werewolf was a terrible idea and Allie needed to break up with Josh immediately. And bonus: they could skip the dinner with Fenris Hall, which Selene was getting more and more anxious about.

Unfortunately Selene didn't bake, and now she was staring at a shriveled pile of charred cookies that she'd pulled out of a smoking oven.

"Hey, Aunt Sel!" Allie bounced into the kitchen and dropped her backpack on the floor. "Oh wow. Your hair looks amazing. Did you go see Natalie?"

"Yes, I did. And thank you for the compliment," Selene said with strained brightness. "Did you have a good day?"

"Yeah," Allie said. "Not too much homework, and Josh was really happy you didn't freak out about us. He says hi."

Me fainting wasn't freaking out? Selene somehow managed to hold on to her smile.

Allie's nose wrinkled. "Is something burning?"

"I made cookies." Selene pushed the plate of cookies in front of Allie. She should have thrown them out because they were a crime against nature.

"Oh." Allie eyed the cookies, put on an impressively brave face, and selected one that was marginally less burned than the others.

Selene snatched the cookie out of Allie's hand before she could take a bite. "If you eat that cookie, you'll regret it. I don't bake. I don't know what possessed me to try."

She knew exactly what had possessed her, but she wasn't going to tell Allie.

"I'm sure they're not that bad," Allie said as she set the cookie down, then pushed the plate to the far side of the table.

"Can we talk, Allie?"

"That's not a question, Aunt Sel," she replied. "That's you saying you want to tell me something and I should listen."

"Yes, but the way I said it was much more polite." She sat down.

"I'm just trying to keep our communication honest." Allie grinned.

"Fine." Selene sighed. "I have some concerns. Just sit down."

Allie settled in a chair at the kitchen table and pulled her knees up to her chest. She'd grown out of the gangly phase and moved with confident grace now. Selene tried not to think about the first time Josh noticed that.

"Sweetheart." Selene hoped her tone was casual. "How old is Josh?"

The strategy she'd chosen for this conversation was introducing the problem of the age gap and then weaving it into the werewolf issue. A reasonable two-pronged approach.

"What do you mean?" Allie frowned. "He's sixteen. Like me."

She got up and grabbed an orange from the fruit bowl.

"I did some reading today—" Selene started.

"Your hair really does look awesome, by the way," Allie interrupted. "Isn't Natalie great?"

Selene couldn't hide her smile, running her hands over her hair. "She is, but don't change the subject, Allie."

"Josh is sixteen," Allie said stubbornly. She stopped peeling the orange and stared at her aunt.

Selene doubled down. *Here goes nothing. Firm, but compassionate. That's how this gets done.* "No. I know that he looks sixteen. And he may have been frozen in time at sixteen. But how old is he, really?"

"Aunt Sel, come on." Juice dripped onto Allie's fingers from where she was squeezing the half-peeled orange too hard. "He's sixteen."

"Are you sure?" She was pushing Allie, hoping that with encouragement Allie would choose honesty. If they could be honest with each other in the face of tough issues, it might stave off unnecessary heartache.

"What is this?" Allie's voice grew shrill. Josh was definitely not sixteen. And this conversation was not going the way Selene wanted.

"Honey," Selene began, trying for a soothing tone. "This stuff you're going through is actually pretty common, you know. Well . . . in the fiction aisle, anyway. And movies."

"What does that have to do with anything?" Allie's eyes were darting around the kitchen, looking everywhere but at Selene.

"It's really my only way of, um . . . researching issues you might encounter in your relationship," Selene said. "It's not exactly easy to know what's true and what isn't. I'm hoping you can help me with that."

"You're trying to dissect my relationship by reading novels and watching movies . . . about werewolves?"

Yep, that's outrage in Allie's voice. Not a good sign.

"Not just werewolves," Selene countered. "Vampires, faeries, all of it. Everything you've mentioned seeing since you learned who Josh and his family really are. No stone left unturned."

"Oh my god." Allie dropped the orange. It rolled along the counter and fell to the floor.

Selene ignored the orange and Allie's dramatics. "And what I've found is that in *all* the stories, the same issue arises. The poor smitten girl can't help but fall head over heels because the boy is witty, sophisticated, and charming. And do you know why he's all those things? Because he's *several hundred years old*!"

Allie groaned. "Auntie Selene, you're being ridiculous."

"This is a serious issue, Allie," Selene insisted. "Josh is not only a werewolf, he's also not a kid like you. He's been around for several generations. You need to think about the implications that has on your relationship."

"Why does it matter?"

"Because, sweetheart, while you are a capable and intelligent woman, you are still sixteen. And if your boyfriend witnessed the Civil War, I think you're going to find it problematic. If not now, eventually."

"He didn't witness the Civil War," Allie said in a mulish voice.

"Maybe not," Selene replied. "But Natalie told me that no wolves in Fenris Hall's pack are as young as you're telling me Josh is."

Allie flinched. "You were talking to Natalie about me?"

"Natalie cares about you," Selene said. "She was close to your mom, and she's someone I trust to give me good advice. She's helping me to understand Avondale."

"So you trust her more than you trust me?" Allie's voice wobbled.

"That's not it at all," Selene explained. "But Natalie can offer a different perspective on this situation. That's important when strong emotions are involved. I'm not dismissing your feelings. It's the opposite."

Allie's posture became less defensive, and Selene continued.

"Honey, romantic partnerships have to offer balance. Shared responsibility, equal power. I can't see how that's possible when you are sixteen and Josh is two hundred. You aren't a magical creature, and he's an immortal werewolf."

"He is not two hundred! And I don't care that he's a werewolf!" Allie shrieked. But Selene could see in her niece's wild eyes that panic was taking over. Allie didn't want to lie to her, but she was terrified of what telling the truth would mean.

"Allie, please. Just hear me out." Selene winced, all too aware she was losing control of the conversation.

"Stop it! Just stop it!" Allie jumped out of her chair with such force that it tipped over backward and crashed to the floor.

Selene stood up, forcing herself to speak calmly. "I'm not trying to be hurtful, Allie. I just want to keep you safe. How can you guarantee his wolf instincts won't take over one day and make him attack you?"

"You don't know anything about werewolves!" Allie hadn't lowered her voice at all. "I don't care what you read on the stupid internet. Josh is amazing. No one has ever made me feel the way he does. He loves me, and he would never hurt me!"

Cursing herself inwardly at the way the conversation was spiraling, Selene made another attempt.

"You have to care, Allie. You have strong feelings for Josh, but you haven't been dating him long at all. For most of the time, you weren't even in the same place. I'm asking you to consider what kind of connection you can truly have when you come from completely different worlds."

"Oh, we connect," Allie blurted. "More than you'd like to know. More than you could ever handle! And I am more than my own person with Josh than I've ever been before. Would you like to read my diary? Or maybe you've already done that!"

Selene flushed and then paled. "You are way out of line, Allison. Calm down and think about what I'm saying. I'm only bringing this up because I'm worried. I love you, sweetheart. I want you to have healthy relationships. That are full of trust and companionship."

"You can't tell me what to do," Allie hissed. "You're not my mom. If she was here, she'd understand. She'd listen to me."

Selene looked away from Allie as grief ripped through her.

But Allie wasn't finished. "And what do you know about being in love anyway? When was the last time you even had a boyfriend?"

The accusing questions stung, not only because Allie fired them off mercilessly, but also because they were accurate. Selene hadn't dated anyone in longer than she liked to admit. As for love, she honestly didn't know if she'd ever been as far gone for someone as Allie was for Josh.

"May I go to my room?" Allie asked stiffly.

Selene nodded but kept her eyes averted. The tears stung before they rolled down her cheeks. Everything she worried might go wrong with that conversation had. She didn't know how to do this. What she needed, more than anything, was to do right by Emma. And she was failing. She waited until her own shame and fury had passed before she climbed the stairs and knocked on Allie's door.

"Yeah?" She could hear regret in her niece's voice.

"May I come in?"

"Yes." And guilt.

Allie was sitting on her bed. Her face was tear stained.

"I'm sorry for what I said," she murmured. "About you not being my mom."

Selene smiled weakly.

"Thank you for apologizing." Selene sat next to her niece. "Allie, I didn't want to upset you. I know your feelings are real, and Josh seems like a good guy to me, but I know almost nothing about him or about the world he comes from. This new relationship is a little scary for me. I want to protect you."

"I know," Allie said quietly. "But I really do love him. And I trust him."

"Can you tell me how old Josh is?" Selene asked carefully. "I just want to know. I promise not to judge."

If I can show Allie she can trust me with this, we're making progress. We can tackle the wolf stuff another day.

"Promise?" Allie's eyes got big.

Selene nodded.

Allie picked up a pillow and squeezed it against her chest. "He became a werewolf in 1932."

Selene kept a straight face but dug her nails into the coverlet. *Well, at least he was born in the last century.*

"It was during the Depression. His family had a farm in the Dust Bowl. They lost everything. Josh came west to try to find work," Allie said. "He was starving when Fenris found him on a road outside Avondale. Then life got much better for him."

"Fenris Hall turned Josh into a werewolf?" Selene asked.

"Yeah," Allie said. "Josh says Fen has been like a father to him ever since then."

We're calling him Fen now?

Her eyes gleamed. "Fen would be such a cool dad."

That would be a yes. So Fen it is.

Selene's stomach twisted. Allie's own father had disappeared. Of course she'd idealize a strong leader and guardian, which, according to everyone, seemed to be precisely who Fenris Hall was.

"Auntie Selene." Allie grabbed her hand. "You'll feel so much better about all this after dinner tomorrow. Fen is really cool and smart. And the wolves are like a big family. They all take care of each other."

Selene nodded. "About the family thing—I was surprised Josh said it would just be the four of us at dinner. Isn't Fenris married?"

Her jaw tightened a bit as she waited for Allie's answer. That was . . . odd.

"No," Allie said. "I guess his mate died a long time ago."

"His what?" The stomach clench Selene felt at the word made no sense whatsoever.

Allie blushed. "Josh says that werewolves don't get married. They find their mate. He says it's actually a much stronger bond."

"I see." Selene studied Allie's face. *Does she think she's Josh's mate? What does that even mean?*

Selene ground her teeth. There was so much in play here that she didn't understand. How could she ever catch up and steer Allie toward the right path? Maybe Natalie was right, and she'd discover that she and Fenris Hall were on the same team—the this-relationship-is-going-way-too-fast-for-my-sixteen-year-old-niece team. No matter what his opinion on Allie and Josh was, Fenris would have answers. And Selene was desperate for more information.

"I don't know how Fen's mate died," Allie continued. "The wolves don't like to talk about it. But I get the sense it was really tragic. Fen has ruled their clan alone since she died."

Again with the gut clench.

Selene nodded, then braced her heart before looking at her niece. "Allie, about what you said downstairs about me not understanding love—"

"I'm really sorry, Aunt Sel," Allie said quickly. "I didn't mean it. I know it must be hard, finding someone at your age."

At my age? Thanks a lot, Allie.

With a grimace, Selene replied, "I know, honey. It's not about me. I'm just concerned . . ."

The last talk might have ended up being nothing like she'd anticipated, but it was obvious that she and Allie needed to have the *other* talk. *Deep breath, dive in.* "Are you and Josh having sex?"

"Aunt Selene." Allie turned her face quickly and stared out the window. "Come on. I told you we weren't."

"We're having the talk," Selene said, as much to herself as to Allie. "And we're having it now."

"It's really not necessary." Allie refused to meet her gaze. "Mom had the talk with me."

"And we need to have it again," Selene insisted. "Hypothetical sex is not the same as being sexually active. I'll decide what's necessary. Please answer the question."

Allie squeezed the pillow again. "Not yet . . . but we're talking about it."

"Are you taking precautions?" Selene kept her voice firm but calm.

Allie nodded.

"I need specifics. What are you doing to be responsible and protect yourself?"

"Werewolves can't get humans pregnant," she said, a little too quickly.

Selene took a moment to digest this.

"Allie, pregnancy isn't the only risk. STIs can have lifelong consequences."

"I know, but we're just talking about stuff. I'm not ready, and Josh isn't pressuring me. I promise."

Selene tensed up, and she waited a beat before speaking. "I'm really glad to hear that."

"He would never pressure me. That's not who he is," Allie said. Her voice cracked when she added, "I love him, Auntie Sel."

"Oh, honey." Selene felt her throat tighten. First love. No matter what she said, it couldn't compete with the intensity of Allie's feelings. All she could do was be there for her niece through the ups and downs, ready to pick up the pieces when things fell apart. And despite what Allie insisted, Selene knew trouble lay ahead.

"Please don't say I can't be with him. Please." Allie hiccuped then started to cry. "I think he's the one."

"Okay. I hear you." Selene pulled Allie into her arms. All the while her heart banged around her chest like a pinball. Being a teenager was so, so hard. Allie's unexpected love life was stressful for Selene, sure, but enduring the maelstrom of hormones and oh-so-intense emotions was much worse. Selene remembered those years, and she'd never want to go through them again. "I'm not going to say you can't date him. Just keep taking one day at a time."

Selene smiled through tears, and Allie hugged her tightly.

"And the wolf thing is new to you, too, not just me," Selene said. "We both have lots to learn about them. I need you to promise me something."

Allie stiffened. "What?"

"If you decide to have sex with Josh, it needs to be because you believe it's what you truly want and what's best for you. Not because it's what Josh wants. If he loves you, he'll wait until it's the right time for *both* of you. Can you make me that promise?"

Allie nodded. "I promise."

"Okay."

"I love you, Aunt Sel," Allie replied with a sniffle.

"I love you too. Wanna try and bake cookies together? If you're supervising, I might not burn them."

Shaking her head, Allie smiled. "Let's order pizza instead."

8

"Aunt Sel, we're gonna be late!"

After five days holed up in her new house, unpacking and getting settled, Selene still thought Saturday night arrived far too quickly.

Selene finished putting in her earrings as she hurried down the stairs. "Sorry."

Allie whistled. "Look at you."

"You think this will be okay?" She glanced down at the blue silk sheath she regularly wore to big-ticket campaign functions.

"More than okay," Allie said. "You're gorgeous."

"Well, you said their dinners are usually formal."

"They can be kind of old-fashioned that way." Allie gestured to her own outfit. "Why else do you think I put on a skirt? I hate skirts."

Selene laughed and slipped into her coat. "Let's go."

They drove to the edge of town and then a mile and a half down a drive marked **PRIVATE** that brought them to an imposing set of wrought iron gates.

"They know we're expected," Allie said. "The gates should open in a sec."

Even as she spoke, the tall barrier slowly swung back. The road behind the gates wound through a dense forest for another mile. They passed formal gardens and manicured lawns, and when, at last, Fenris Hall's home appeared, Selene's jaw dropped.

"Allie, this is not a big house. This is a small—no, make that medium—castle."

The building looked like a cross between an English manor and a fortress. Selene stared and waited for someone to cue the rumble of thunder and flash of lightning followed by a river of bats surging out from beneath the parapets.

"Come on, Aunt Sel," Allie replied. "Don't make a big deal. Fenris is old. Like Crusades old. He's had time to make money. And a lot of the wolves live here, so it's not like they don't need the space."

"Crusades old?" Selene's eyes widened as she parked the car. She envisioned a battle-scarred, grizzled man with bent limbs and one eye. She hoped she wouldn't stare too much when they were introduced.

Allie shrugged, unbuckled her seatbelt, and exited the car. She scurried up the steps to the massive oak doors of the building. Selene walked slowly up the stairs, glancing nervously around.

"Why are you so slow tonight?" Allie said impatiently and waved for her aunt to join her at the front door.

"How did you get used to this?" Selene murmured. "I'm trying to take it all in. I feel like I need a map and a tour guide."

"It's really cool." Allie took her hand. "You're gonna love it."

"Should we knock?" Selene stared at the door.

But before Allie could answer, the doors swung open.

"Oh my god," Selene whispered.

Her oh-so-hot and mysterious helper from the bookstore smiled. "Hello, Ms. Jones."

"You—" she blurted. "What are you doing here?"

He'd traded the Henley and jeans for a crisp white dress shirt, collar unbuttoned, sleeves rolled to his elbows, and dark twill pants, but it was definitely him.

"Aunt Sel," Allie frowned. "You already met Fenris?"

Fenris? Selene stared at the young face, the tousled ash-brown hair, and the playful smile. *This guy is Crusades old?*

"Good evening, Allison." He kissed the girl's cheek. "Your aunt and I bumped into each other downtown the other day. Literally."

Selene blushed but quickly went from flabbergasted to annoyed. "I didn't know who you were, but you knew perfectly well who I was, which is hardly fair. Why didn't you say something?"

"Forgive me." His gray eyes were warm, if mischievous. "I didn't want to introduce myself until the appropriate occasion arrived. I'm Fenris Hall, but call me Fen. I'm honored you accepted the invitation to dine with us this evening. Learning about our world can be something of a shock."

Allie laughed. "She fainted when she found out. Did Josh tell you?"

"Allie!" Selene grimaced. So much for good first impressions. Though technically this was a second impression. Which meant she was zero for two.

Fen extended his hand. "Please be assured, you have nothing to fear from us, Ms. Jones. And if you faint again, I'm sure we have smelling salts somewhere."

Smelling salts? I guess he is from another century.

"Thank you, and it's Selene." She smiled, appreciating his effort to make her feel better, and took his hand in a light clasp. "It's a pleasure to meet you, Fen."

She'd become slightly distracted by the way the touch of his fingers made her skin tingle when he jerked his hand back with what sounded like a snarl. Selene's eyes rounded. He took in her startled expression and frowned.

"I apologize," he said quietly. "Your ring. Would you please remove it?"

"My ring?" Selene stared at him and then at the simple Celtic knot that adorned her right ring finger. Emma had given it to her as a birthday gift when they were in college. She wore it almost every day.

He turned over his palm to reveal a glaring red welt. "Silver burns us."

"Aunt Selene!" Allie's shrill exclamation hammered Selene's eardrums, and she knew she'd committed some heinous werewolf faux pas. *"You wore silver?"*

"It's fine, Allison." Fenris smiled gently. "Our sensitivity to silver is an odd concept for humans."

"Oh, oh god," Selene stammered. "I am so sorry." She pulled the ring from her finger and the earrings from her ear lobes and shoved them into her purse. "I don't know the rules yet."

"It's nothing. I heal very quickly." He showed her his palm again. The redness was already fading.

He stepped back so they could enter. "Please, come in. Josh is waiting for us upstairs."

Allie glared at her as she moved through the doorway. Selene bit her lip and glanced apologetically at Fen. He turned the knee-buckling smile on her, and she tripped over the doorstep. Fen caught her elbow and righted her. His firm grasp sent tendrils of heat over her skin, and she nearly stumbled again. She looked up at him, and their eyes locked. Her heart tripped the same way her feet had.

Oh no.

Selene couldn't remember the last time she'd had such a visceral reaction to a man. In fact, she didn't think she'd ever felt this sudden lightning strike of desire. An irresistible urge to get closer to him. To feel his touch.

"Careful," he murmured as he released her.

Selene had the distinct feeling he wasn't talking about her lack of balance. She fought for composure, irked at herself for being so easily distracted. This dinner was about Allie and Josh.

So she was attracted to Fen. What of it? He was charming, handsome, and powerful. Anyone would be drawn to him. Besides, the allure she felt had to be one sided. Fen probably had women falling at his feet constantly.

That last thought stung.

"Anu will take your coats." He gestured to a slender girl who appeared from the shadows.

When the girl stepped into the light and extended her arms, her skin looked mottled and rough, like bark.

Selene slid her coat from her shoulders and handed it to Anu, who took Allie's coat as well, nodded to Fen, and then slipped back into a dark hallway.

Selene's eyes followed the girl. "She's . . ."

"A wood sprite," Fen said. "My household requires a substantial staff to maintain. I have a large number of Fae in my employ."

He took her arm and guided her from the front door into a spacious foyer with a wide staircase at the far end. Their footsteps echoed on the polished marble floor, and Selene kept her jaw cemented shut so she wouldn't gape at the sculptures that ringed the space or the immense tapestries that lined the walls. Allie trotted happily at her side, unbothered by the opulent surroundings.

They climbed the stairs and started down a hallway that, for all appearances, was endless.

"Our formal dining room is a bit large for four people. I've arranged for us to dine in the conservatory," Fen said. "I thought it would be more intimate."

She wasn't sure if she'd imagined that his fingers caressed the inside of her forearm when he said "intimate," but goosebumps appeared on her skin as if he had.

"Oh!" Allie exclaimed. "The conservatory is my favorite room in the mansion."

"Josh may have mentioned that." Fen smiled at her.

They stopped in front of a large oak door, which Fen opened. He stood aside.

"After you."

Allie darted into the room. "Josh!"

Josh crossed the space between them with impossible speed, picking Allie up and twirling her around. "Hi, beautiful."

Allie kissed him soundly on the lips, which made Selene's stomach clench, and then said, "I missed you today."

Selene forced herself not to roll her eyes and glanced at Fen. He watched the young couple with a slight frown. When he caught Selene looking at him, a sardonic smile flickered on his lips.

"The rapture of young love."

She returned his smile. "Something like that."

"We should talk," he said quietly. "Soon."

"I agree."

His gaze moved over her slowly, a crease forming on his brow.

"What's wrong?" she asked.

Fen's scrutiny had her fighting the impulse to touch her hair and ensure it wasn't in disarray.

"At the bookstore, I wondered—" He cut himself off, seeming to think better of what he'd been about to say. "It's nothing."

But he was still looking at Selene as if she was a puzzle he needed to solve.

As Fen studied her, she was seized by the impulse to move closer to him, to lift her chin in challenge to the power he radiated.

Aside from Josh's obvious physical strength, he was by all appearances a teenager. A very cute, but still ordinary, sixteen-year-old boy.

There was nothing mundane about Fenris Hall. He radiated quiet confidence and unquestionable authority. It was so obvious now, Selene wondered how she could have missed it when she ran into him at Page Turner.

Maybe he had the ability to rein in that aura of strength when he wanted to. What color would that aura be?

She didn't know anything about auras, but Natalie could teach her how to see them. Or she could just ask Nat what color Fen's aura was.

God. Why am I suddenly obsessed with his aura?

Unable to bear the increasing tension between them, Selene quickly turned away and glanced around the room. The conservatory could hardly be called small. Its ample space held a grand piano in one corner as well as a cello, a violin, and a few guitars on stands nearby. Soft light that filled the room came mostly from candles on the table and in sconces flanking the windows. She felt like she'd walked into a Jane Austen novel.

Fen guided her to a small circular table that had four chairs and four wine goblets but only two plates. He pulled out the chair in front of one of the plates, then pushed it back to the table once Selene had settled in it. Josh did the same for Allie. Fen took the seat to Selene's right. Allie sat on her left with Josh between Allie and Fenris.

The door opened and Anu appeared with a bottle of wine. She showed the label to Fen.

"Sir?"

He glanced at Selene. "Do you have a preference? This is an interesting Malbec with an emphasis on spice. It will pair well with tonight's menu."

"That sounds lovely."

He smiled at her and then nodded at Anu. The wood sprite uncorked the bottle, poured Selene's glass, and began to move around the table. When Anu arrived at Allie's side, Fen held up his hand.

"Selene?"

She looked at Allie. The girl's eyes were large and hopeful.

"It's fine, if she would like to have a glass."

Allie beamed and squeezed her aunt's hand under the table.

"*One* glass," Selene clarified.

When all their glasses were filled, Fen raised his. "Welcome to our home. May this be the first of many evenings we share."

His eyes didn't release Selene's as he sipped his wine. A pleasant warmth crept along her neck and wrapped around her shoulders, lingering when she broke their gaze a moment later.

Get ahold of yourself, Selene. This isn't a date.

Selene tasted the wine, which was exquisite, then noticed the empty place settings in front of the two wolves. "You're not eating?"

Josh looked uncomfortable, but Fen didn't flinch.

"Humans sometimes find it difficult to watch us eat."

Selene wasn't sure she wanted to know but couldn't stop herself from asking. "Why is that?"

"We only eat raw meat."

Selene glanced at Allie with a slight frown. "But you're a vegetarian."

Fenris raised an eyebrow and tilted his head at Josh. "She's a vegetarian?"

Josh looked somewhat abashed.

"I eat fish." Allie fidgeted in her seat and looked at Fen as though seeking his approval. "Sometimes."

"Do you have a problem with vegetarians?" Selene asked.

"It's somewhat unnatural to us, but nothing we object to." He turned to Allie. "You should have mentioned your preference earlier. I'm afraid we're serving pheasant this evening. My sincere apologies."

"That's fine," Allie said quickly. "I didn't want to cause a fuss. I'll just eat the sides."

"Didn't want to cause a fuss?" Selene countered with an incredulous laugh. "Allie, you always make arrangements for a vegetarian option when we go out."

"You should try some pheasant, Allie," Josh urged. "I'm sure you'll like it."

"Okay," Allie murmured and stared at her plate.

Nope. Selene set her glass down firmly and fixed a hard gaze on Josh. *Not on my watch.* It unnerved her to watch Allie agree with Josh without any discussion. She'd never seen Allie behave in such a meek manner.

"Josh, Allie is a vegetarian. She's been a vegetarian for a long time," Selene said. "Please respect her choice to not eat meat. It's perfectly reasonable."

"Aunt Sel!" Allie's eyes widened. "It's okay. I don't mind. I should try new things."

Josh smiled at her.

"You've got to be kidding me." Selene crossed her arms over her chest. She knew she was committing a cardinal sin by calling Allie out in front of other people, but this was too important to let slide. "You haven't eaten meat since you were ten. You make gagging sounds if I try to grill a steak, and you refuse to eat in the same room with me."

"Josh," Fen's voice was low, almost a growl. "If Allison prefers to eat only the side dishes that have been prepared, so be it. We do not impose our preferences on our guests."

"Yes, Fenris." Josh suddenly cowered in his seat. "I'm sorry, Allie."

Allie looked horrified. "No, no. Please don't apologize. It's fine."

Her eyes threw daggers at Selene.

The door to the conservatory opened again, and two more wood sprites appeared, bearing trays loaded with grilled asparagus, glazed carrots, roasted red potatoes, and the aforementioned pheasant. A young man with fingers like twigs carved the bird and placed slices of steaming meat on Selene's plate.

"None for the young lady, Gil," Fen said.

"I'll have a small piece, please," Allie interjected and wouldn't look at her aunt.

Selene's lips pressed together in disapproval, but she remained silent. Josh winked at Allie, which Selene didn't appreciate *at all.* If she thought Allie was making the choice for any other reason than to please Josh, she wouldn't have made a fuss. Then again, maybe Allie was insisting on having the pheasant because Selene had embarrassed her.

Ugh. How am I supposed to know when to put my foot down and when to mind my own business?

Fen watched without comment. Part of Selene wished he would reprimand Josh again, but that would mean ignoring Allie's decision. As much as she didn't like Allie changing her behavior for Josh, it *was* her choice, and Fen seemed to be respecting that, which Selene couldn't fault him for.

Selene and Allie began to eat in uneasy silence, stainless steel utensils clinking against china, until Fen spoke up.

"Selene, your professional accomplishments are impressive. How did you come into your line of work?"

She'd been savoring the pheasant, which had her taste buds jumping for joy, and was startled by the question. She chewed quickly and swallowed.

"In college I did a lot of volunteer work for the causes I was interested in and completed a couple of internships," she told him. "I started doing consulting and public relations for nonprofits on a part-time basis when Allie's mom and I lived together in Los Angeles. I realized that work was my passion, and I'm lucky that I was able to build a successful career out of it as an independent contractor."

"I don't think luck had anything to do with it," Fen replied, tipping his glass toward her.

She smiled at him. "Thank you for your generous contributions. They are deeply appreciated."

"Don't thank me," he said. "The causes are worthy."

"I'm glad you think so." She picked up her wine glass. The liquid gleamed like garnet in the candlelight. "Running your own business can be a lot of work. I couldn't move to Avondale until a few days ago because I was in the middle of a campaign."

She smiled apologetically at her niece.

"Come on, Aunt Sel," Allie said. "You know I'm proud of what you do. It's great."

"And do you mind making your home in Avondale?" he asked. "Many in your position would prefer living in the city."

Selene tensed and stared at her dark-red wine. Her next thought seemed strange and disconcerting.

Blood in the water.

"There was no question of moving here," she answered. "Allie's happiness is what matters."

When Selene noticed Allie biting her lip, she quickly added, "And Avondale couldn't be more lovely."

Selene suspected Fenris knew she was holding back, but this dinner wasn't the place to voice her doubts about staying in Avondale.

"What did Emma tell you about our town?" Fen prompted.

Selene shifted in her chair. His questions felt oddly leading, as if he already knew the answers but was digging for something beneath them. It didn't quite make her uncomfortable, but it did leave her wary.

"Very little." She focused on cutting her meat into smaller bites than necessary so she could speak without looking at Fen. All the while she fought to regain some sense of control over the conversation. "Emma moved here a few years after—"

She looked at Allie. They didn't avoid talking about Emma, but it was never easy. And they rarely talked about Daniel leaving. She wasn't about to plunge into this emotional quagmire without Allie's agreement.

Allie was pushing her piece of pheasant around her plate and didn't seem to have eaten a single morsel of the meat.

"It's okay." Allie reached under the table to clasp Selene's hand. "I've talked to Josh about Mom and my dad . . . and what happened."

Selene nodded, waiting for a moment to give Allie a chance to change her mind. When Allie stayed quiet, Selene steeled herself and lifted her eyes to meet Fen's steady gaze.

"You know that Allie's mother, Emma, was killed," she said quietly. "It was devastating for both of us. It still is. But I'm thankful every day that Allie is in my life and that we're able to be together."

"Me too," Allie said, giving Selene a sad smile.

Fen steepled his fingers, then asked, "Allie's father didn't object to you assuming guardianship?"

The question startled Selene and riled her temper. Was this really any of his business?

"Allie's father isn't in the picture," Selene said curtly. "He's been gone for a long time."

"You have no idea what happened to Allie's father?" Fen's tone was dark. "Or where he is now?"

Selene gritted her teeth. She was on the verge of demanding why he thought he had the right to ask, but Allie interjected.

"His name was Daniel Brix. He left when I was little. Or went missing. Or something. I only kind of remember him. When I asked Mom about him, it made her sad, so I stopped asking and basically started thinking of him as a sperm donor."

Allie spoke so matter-of-factly that Selene simply stared at her. The way Allie described Daniel didn't track with what Selene knew about their relationship. Allie had had a starry-eyed view of her dad because Emma didn't want to break her heart with the truth. Even so, if Allie wanted to frame Daniel as never having been an important part of her life, that was fine by Selene.

Allie managed to keep a straight face for a few more seconds and then she burst into giggles.

"I can't believe I just said *sperm* at the dinner table." She cast a sheepish glance at Fenris. "Sorry, Fen."

Fen grinned and shook his head. "No need to apologize for honesty. I appreciate your candor."

The entire exchange knocked Selene off balance again. Nothing had been predictable since they arrived at this fortress of a home.

What do you expect, Selene? You live in a world full of monsters and magic now. And your super-hot dinner host is Crusades old.

She guzzled more wine than advisable.

Fen refilled her glass without comment, then gestured to her plate. "All my questions are keeping you from your meal. Please eat."

Selene smiled gratefully and returned to the feast before her. She needed a break from the interrogation, and she'd had too much to drink without enough food in her stomach to buffer the alcohol's effect. She was starting to feel a little dizzy.

Fen turned his attention to Josh and Allie. Selene finished her meal while the young couple answered his questions about their week at school. The main course was cleared, and the wood sprites replaced her plate with a ramekin of crème brûlée.

"This is decadent," she said as Fen signaled Anu to open another bottle of wine.

"Does it please you?" The question made her toes curl.

An innocent question. Not a double entendre. Calm down.

Selene nodded even as she crossed her ankles to keep herself from squirming. "Everything was delicious."

"I'm fortunate to have a talented witch in our kitchen. Never a disappointing meal."

"But you only eat raw meat." She raised an eyebrow.

"I have many guests who are not werewolves," he replied.

Selene suddenly felt childish. Until that moment she'd assumed she was somehow special for having received the dinner invitation. But of course that wasn't the case. Fen was arguably the most powerful man in Avondale, and her own work bore witness to the fact that he had influence well beyond the borders of this small town. He likely had a revolving door of high-profile visitors.

She became quiet as she finished dessert. Allie chatted happily about the latest antics of some faeries in her gym class that involved their substitute teacher, a pommel horse, and petroleum jelly.

When all the dishes had been cleared away and Selene realized that she was on her fourth glass of wine, *oh boy*, Fen turned to Josh.

"Would you play for a bit?"

Josh nodded and went to the piano. Allie rose and followed him across the room. She settled beside him on the bench.

Music after dinner? I am in a Jane Austen novel.

When Josh began to play, Fen moved his chair closer to Selene and spoke in a low voice. "I am concerned about Allie's involvement with Josh, and I'd like to hear your thoughts on the matter."

"I also have concerns." Selene watched as Allie leaned her head on Josh's shoulder. "First and foremost is that Allie is very young, and I don't know that rushing into a serious relationship is wise."

She looked at Fenris. "That would be the case with anyone. Josh's . . . unique qualities add another dimension to my worries."

"As they should," he replied. "Considering how recently you learned about our world, you're remarkably levelheaded about the situation."

"Even though I fainted?" Selene laughed, cheeks pinking.

Fen shook his head, expression solemn. "You didn't try to hurt Josh after you saw him change."

"I didn't . . ." She stared at him with dawning horror. "Of course I didn't. I would never—"

"Many would," he said, and she saw the weight of too much pain in his eyes, but it was chased by a razor-sharp smile. "Despite the futility of such an attempt."

Twin urges filled her. The first, to shudder, she resisted. Despite the menace in Fen's latter words, Selene understood the reason for it. The second she gave in to, resting her hand on top of his.

"I'm sorry that fear so often provokes violence," she told him. "It's the source of too much pain and destruction in the world."

"It is." He was staring at her hand, and she started to draw it away, but he turned his palm up and wrapped his fingers around hers. "You also didn't run."

She smiled at him despite the sudden galloping of her pulse. "Violence or running? Those are my options?"

"Those are the options too often chosen by humans upon first encountering our existence." He brushed his thumb over the back of her hand, and she had to swallow a gasp at the flurry of sensation it provoked. "But there are other, much more pleasant options."

"Like dinner?" Selene slowly pulled her hand from his. Fen's touch was setting flares off all over her body, stoking desire she wasn't prepared for.

He didn't stop her retreat, instead nodding. "For example."

"You have options too," she said. "It's obvious you have considerable influence over Avondale, and I imagine even more over your . . . pack?"

"I do."

"But Josh was free to pursue Allie?" Selene asked. "Despite her being human and him being what he is?"

She cringed at her phrasing. "I'm sorry . . . who he is. I'm still figuring this out."

"No offense taken, Selene," Fen assured her with a teasing smile. "You're doing very well. And it's a good question. The answer is both yes and no."

"Forgive me if I don't understand how it's not one or the other," she teased back, leaning toward him.

He leaned in as well, which sent Selene's pulse skipping.

Damn it. Galloping. Skipping. My heartbeat will probably do a jig next. This can't be good for my blood pressure.

"Though our world is mostly hidden, we live side by side with humans," Fen told her. "Crossover, interaction, and mingling are unavoidable and not necessarily bad. Though they often have tragic outcomes."

The shadow of pain slid over his eyes once more and had Selene fighting the urge to reach for his hand again.

"Even if I forbade relationships with humans," he continued, "it would only be a matter of time before someone broke the rule, and I don't want to be forced to punish my pack for crossing that line without good reason."

A chill crawled up her neck. "What would constitute a good reason?"

"If the relationship would do more harm than good."

"But how do you determine what's harmful and what's good?" Selene asked.

"I don't," Fen replied. "Time does."

When Selene frowned, he explained. "Rules have been established—formalities, if you will—to ensure that any relationship between a human and one of the pack is born of true love and can withstand hardship."

"I understand rules," she replied. "How does time factor in?"

"When immortality is involved, time plays an essential role," he said. "Our relationships can span infinite lifetimes; thus, they may only be entered into by proving true devotion."

Selene sat up, stunned. *Infinite lifetimes.*

Her voice came out in a whisper. "Allie is only sixteen."

"Yes." Fen's reply was gentle. "Josh genuinely cares for her. He is a good person, and I do not doubt his affection for Allison. But affection alone isn't enough."

"So what happens now?" Her eyes found Josh and Allie, snuggled together at the piano, a picture of sweet, youthful adoration. She didn't want to cause them heartbreak, but everything Fen was saying made perfect sense.

"Josh has requested formal recognition of his relationship with Allie," he told her. "I asked you to dinner this evening because I will not allow that to happen without your consent. Allison is your ward, and as you've already pointed out, she is very young. Even younger in my eyes."

Selene swallowed a hard lump in her throat.

Allie is going to hate me forever. But how can I say yes to an eternal relationship?

Fen read the imminent despair in her expression and placed his hand on her shoulder, his steady gaze calming her. "Let me explain what will happen if you agree and then you can tell me what you think is best."

She nodded, and he briefly pressed his fingertips into her skin. Another array of sparks went off in the wake of his touch. It was a cruel twist of fate that the man she was this attracted to happened to be the linchpin of her first major parental crisis. She couldn't afford to let her attention become divided.

"After receiving recognition, Josh and Allie would begin formal courtship," Fen continued. "If, after ten years, they remain committed to one another, the pack would approve a mating."

It took some time for Selene to process that. "Did you say ten years?"

He smiled slowly, and her stomach flipped over.

Stop it, she silently scolded her body. *Just stop.*

"At any time during their courtship, either party may end the relationship," Fen told her. "And other members of the pack may submit concerns they have about the viability of the relationship."

Selene considered that. "So, in other words, it takes a village?"

"I prefer *pack*," he returned. "But yes."

"Ten years," she mused aloud. "That will make Allie twenty-six."

After she's eighteen, she's an adult. I can give her my advice, but what she chooses at that point is out of my control. And a lot can change in ten years. Maybe she'll be past her supernatural crush phase, if that's what this is. In the meantime, I'm no longer the bad guy. That will go a long way to helping Allie and me adjust to making a life together in Avondale. Wow. And just like that, I'm a big fan of werewolf traditions.

"Okay." Selene released a long breath. "I think I can handle the ten-year courtship. Or at least I'm willing to give it a chance. What you've described is hardly unreasonable."

Fen nodded. "I'm glad you're open to our custom."

"You're not making it that hard." Selene scoffed. "If you told me Allie had to become a werewolf tomorrow, we'd be having an entirely different conversation."

"I would hope so," he said and rolled his broad shoulders back.

Her eyes wanted to track the movement of that thick muscle, so she quickly shifted her gaze to Allie and Josh at the piano.

She couldn't stop herself from asking quietly, "Do you think they'll make it?"

Fen watched the young pair for several heartbeats before answering. "It's impossible to know."

The sudden lump in her throat caught Selene off guard. "Isn't it always?"

"Yes." She felt a gentle touch at her elbow, and she turned to find herself pinned by that odd searching gaze Fen had captured her with earlier.

This time she didn't look away, holding his eyes for long moments.

I shouldn't let this happen. I need to lock up whatever these feelings are and lose the key.

Fen stood and offered her his hand. "Shall we enjoy the music?"

It was too easy to slide her fingers into his grasp. She rose and walked with him to stand closer to the piano. Like most of the immortal boys in the movies she'd streamed, Josh was a piano virtuoso. He drew a lilting, mournful tune from the ivory keys.

After listening for a few measures, Selene stifled a laugh.

"You don't care for Beethoven?" Fen asked, bemused by her reaction.

"Absolutely, I do. And Josh plays beautifully. But the 'Moonlight Sonata'? This . . . castle? And werewolves?" she whispered, not wanting to be rude but unable to resist the moment. "I feel like I'm on the set of a Gothic film."

"You would prefer something else?" he asked. His voice was neutral, but she thought she spied a challenge in his gaze. As if her observation had raised the stakes of their exchange.

She started to shake her head, but Fen lifted his voice.

"Josh, would you indulge me?"

Josh gave the briefest nod, and his fingers flowed smoothly from the Beethoven sonata into a new melody. After a minute of listening, Selene smiled.

"You know the piece?" Fen watched her closely.

"I love Fauré," she murmured.

"Fauré, environmental protection campaigns, and romance novels. A woman of eclectic tastes. I like it."

"I also speak Klingon," Selene said without looking at him.

"I . . ." A long pause. "Did you say Klingon?"

She stole a glance at him and kept her expression blank for about five seconds.

"Your face. Oh my god." She gasped between laughs. "You believed me."

Fen was stunned, which made Selene laugh even harder. Tears leaked from the corners of her eyes. The piano went silent.

"Aunt Selene?" Allie had turned on the bench and was peering at Selene with a frown. "Are you okay?"

"I, I'm . . ." She couldn't catch her breath, hiccuping instead, and she dissolved into giggles again.

"She's fine, Allie," Fen said. "I promise. Please continue, Josh."

Notes lilted through the air again, and Selene finally quelled her mirth. She smiled at Fen, feeling a new lightness. She'd needed a release desperately, and it felt so good, she wasn't even a smidge embarrassed by her outburst. She felt even better when she saw Fen smiling at her.

"I take it you don't speak Klingon?"

"Sorry if that disappoints you," she said. "Though I do love *Star Trek*."

"I'm more of a *Star Wars* man," he replied. "But I won't let that mar my opinion of you."

"And I've never believed in picking sides," Selene told him. "The more sci-fi adventures I can get, the better."

"You're an intergalactic peacemaker then," Fen teased. "How admirable."

Refusing to let herself preen, Selene pointed at the piano. "I'm not even going to ask if you play because I know the answer is yes. And if not, what have you been doing with your time? I hear you're Crusades old."

She bit her lip, wondering if she'd pushed too much, but Fen only chuckled.

"I do play," he replied. "But I prefer the cello."

Okay. I want to swoon a little. Just a little. "I have a weakness for the cello."

"It's a wonderful instrument." He looked at her. That seeking gaze. "Do you dance, Selene?"

Puzzled by the question, she gave a tentative nod. "On occasion."

"Would you give me the pleasure?"

"Are you serious?" Her knees threatened to become jelly.

Do people actually dance in conservatories after dinner? Wait, okay. Reset. I'm not dealing with people. It's a whole new ball game.

"Absolutely." He turned to face her. "Don't worry, I'm not decrepit. I may be Crusades old, but I'm not pyramids old."

Laughter, light as fizzing champagne, escaped her. "Well then, how can I refuse?"

His hand slid along her waist, and before she knew what was happening, she found herself turning in languid circles through the conservatory, Fen leading her steps effortlessly.

Dancing. We're really dancing. What is happening here?

She flushed and glanced at Allie, but the girl's head was nestled on Josh's shoulder as his fingers moved over the keys.

"Do you always dance after dinner?" she murmured.

"No." The crease between his brows returned. "I can't remember the last time I did."

She fell silent, and he smoothly guided them through slow, graceful movements. Each turn brought them closer. Closer. The heat of his body seeped through the fabric of her dress, warming her skin. She could feel the contours of his chest. Hard lines against her soft curves. It was impossible to not melt against his body. The feel of him irresistible.

Oh. My. God.

"You haven't given me an update," he said softly. His hand slid from her waist to follow the curve of her hip and along her lower back, where his firm touch rested, fingers splayed. A shiver chased up her spine.

"An update?"

He bent his head. Before he spoke, she heard him draw a long, deep breath.

Is he . . . smelling me? She couldn't decide if that was flattering or just weird. A flash of memory from the bookstore—he'd done the same thing. What did it mean? Was it a werewolf thing? Werewolf thing or not, she couldn't stop herself from taking her own deep breath, and . . . oh . . . he smelled like the deep forest after rain.

"*Nocturne's Burden*, the tale of forbidden desire." His warm breath skimmed over the shell of her ear. "Has it usurped the other books on your nightstand yet?"

He straightened, and she blinked at him. *Does he really want to discuss romance novels with me?*

"And has the wolf had his way with the heroine?" His eyes were full of mirth, but beneath that, something else lay in wait. "Ripped the bodice from her heaving bosom?"

She staved off lurking temptation by zeroing in on the conversation. *Okay, romance novels it is.*

"There has been some bodice ripping," she said dryly. "And some heaving bosoms. It's just that sort of book."

"I'm glad it hasn't been a disappointment." His smile was like a caress over every inch of her skin.

So much for keeping lust at bay.

Spirals of warmth curled in her belly and began to work their way down, becoming a hot pulse between her thighs. Her breasts grew heavy, beginning to ache. When her overly sensitive nipples brushed against him, she had to bite her lip to keep from gasping.

He just had to bring up the bosoms, didn't he?

Fen leaned closer and pulled in another slow breath. Selene felt a vibration in his chest accompanied by a low sound. A growl. Her own nervous sip of air stopped halfway into her lungs. His gaze became hungry. Feral.

Oh god. He's a wolf. He can smell *that he's turning me on.*

She tried to calm herself, but her heart wouldn't stop pounding, and her skin grew hotter by the minute. She was startled and embarrassed by the sudden wetness drenching her panties, and there was nothing she could do about it.

Fen's arm tightened around her waist, molding her body to his own. Her eyes widened. His erection was like a lead pipe against her stomach. She bit her lip to stop herself from moaning at the sudden throb in her core. Every inch of her being screamed to sink into him, to surrender.

But.

Reality.

Responsibility.

I am not here for this.

"My niece is ten feet away," she hissed through clenched teeth.

"She is distracted." His response barely hid the laughter behind his words.

It was annoying that he seemed to be so much more in control of himself than she was.

"I just met you." She tried to pull away, but his powerful arms kept their bodies locked together.

"In flesh, perhaps," he murmured. "In soul, perhaps not."

Wait, what? That shouldn't sound so right.

She felt dizzy. "I don't think that way. I can't."

He bent his face close, and when he spoke, his lips nearly brushed against hers.

"Open your mind, Selene."

She shook her head in attempt to clear the sweltering fog that swirled and obscured any clear thoughts. "What do you want?"

"I would think that's obvious."

"Stop. I need a minute." Her blood was on fire, but she dug her nails into her palms until pain cut through the haze of desire.

"You fascinate me. I never thought to feel this . . ." he said. His lips grazed her cheek. "I want to know you. Intimately."

She swallowed and looked at Allie and Josh. *I have to take care of her. I can't do . . . whatever this is.*

Turning a hard gaze on Fen, she managed to twist out of his embrace.

"Why are you doing this?"

"I beg your pardon?"

"You want to know me? Intimately? Is that some kind of line?" She was angry and more than a little afraid. But she couldn't be sure of the fear's source—the fact that he perceived so much about her, or the insistence of her own body's craving for him. She fought to calm her breath and wished she could pull her eyes from his. Damn those storm-dark irises, so unfairly compelling. How addictive it was to be the focus of that intense gaze, as if he wanted to look at nothing but her ever again.

"I don't make a habit of inviting humans into my life, and I didn't expect to tonight. At least not on my own behalf." He stepped toward her. "But you are too intriguing to ignore."

"I'm not." She moved back and avoided his attempt to recapture her in his arms.

"This is about Allie and Josh." She kept her voice low. "It has nothing to do with me."

"Is that so?" His gaze followed her, a wolf tracking its prey.

"I think it's time for us to leave." Her hands were shaking. She couldn't sort through her clashing emotions. "Thank you for dinner."

"Selene—"

Shaking her head, Selene wouldn't risk looking at him. She didn't trust her resolve.

"We've had a lot of wine," he said carefully. When he touched her arm, she closed her eyes.

I want him so much. Why do I have to want this man?

"You could stay—" Fen whispered. He was close again. She felt his warmth, inhaled his addictive scent. It would be so easy to give in. To forget the rest of the world.

She cut him off before it was too late and made herself face him, forcing her gaze to battle with his as she buried her desire deep, deep, deep. "Were you planning on getting me drunk and into bed in a single night? Is that how you werewolves operate?"

Her tone was harsh, and he stepped back so quickly it stung, but outrage was the only armor she had, and she was desperate to shield herself from this unexpected siege.

"Never," he said, a quiet rumble. "But I won't allow you to drive. Your safety matters to me."

I will not cave because he said something nice. I will not feel like a jerk for drawing a line. "Then I have no doubt you have someone who could take us home."

She saw a flicker of amusement play across his face.

"Josh can bring my car over tomorrow," she continued, clinging to the scraps of resolve she'd mustered. "I'm sure he and Allie have plans to see each other."

He watched her for a moment. She couldn't believe how much she wanted to touch him again. The ache of it was painful. She started to tremble and was about to concede, to agree to stay, to beg him to hold her again, when he smiled. Flat and polite. A distant smile meant for strangers. She hated it.

"I'll have a car waiting for you at the front door in a few minutes." Without another word, he left the room.

Selene didn't know if she felt worse about the cold sensation that gripped her skin at his sudden absence or the thought that her campaigns might never see another check from Fenris Hall. Both made her want to run after him and apologize. That made her angry all over again. She'd done nothing wrong.

The music stopped.

"Why did Fen leave?" Josh looked at Selene. Something in his expression made her think Josh knew more about Fen's amorous behavior than he wanted her to suspect.

"It's late," Selene said crisply. "This has been a lovely evening, but it's time for us to go home."

"But, Aunt Sel," Allie protested. "Josh invited us to stay over. There are soooooo many rooms. It wouldn't be a problem."

"No buts, Allie," Selene said. "We came for dinner, not a slumber party. Fen has someone who will drive us home. I drank a little more than I should have."

A lot more.

She looked at Josh. "Would you mind driving my car over tomorrow?"

He offered a wary smile and took the key fob she held out to him. "Sure."

Allie's sulking vanished. "Can he come for breakfast?"

"If you're making it," Selene said, suddenly bone tired. Her chest hurt, like she was about to cry. "I'm sleeping in."

Josh watched Selene, his expression guarded. "Thank you again for coming to dinner, Ms. Jones. I'll see you in the morning, Allie."

He rose, and they followed him out of the conservatory and back through the spacious foyer. Anu was waiting at the front door with their coats.

"Fenris offers his apologies that he won't be able to bid you good night himself. He had urgent business to attend to."

Selene's stomach sank into her shoes, but she nodded politely.

I definitely pissed him off.

A glossy black SUV was parked in front of the mansion, engine idling. The driver opened the back door, and Allie climbed in. Selene glanced around the grounds one last time. She wanted to kick herself for wishing that Fen would turn up at the last second to see them off.

Get over it, Selene. You know nothing about this guy. Just because he's the first man to get you hot in forever, it doesn't mean anything.

She repeated the thought for the duration of the drive home and hoped she'd eventually believe it.

◆ ◆ ◆

Fenris Hall wasn't accustomed to being unsettled, but he was deeply so tonight. He dropped to his haunches, having shifted to his wolf form the moment he stole from the manor and watched the car pull away. He'd been too restless after spending time with Selene Jones to remain in his human skin. The door to the mansion swung open, and a slightly smaller wolf slinked from inside and trotted beneath the cover of trees.

Did she agree to the courtship? Josh paused beside his pack leader.

Yes. Fen's eyes remained locked on the road down which the car had disappeared. He pawed at the soft earth, frustration rising. He'd revealed too much, but his reaction to the woman had been so primal. He hadn't been prepared for that. It was not a mistake he would make again.

Josh paced restlessly in front of Fenris. *She left very suddenly.*

That is my fault. Fen turned his eyes on the younger wolf. *I . . . am drawn to her. And I frightened her.*

Josh paused, and his ears flicked back and forth. *Will that change things for me?*

No. Fen sniffed.

Ms. Jones wants you. Josh's tongue lolled out. *I could smell her heat from across the room.*

When Fenris snarled, Josh dropped to his belly.

I meant no offense, he whined. *Only that your mate is well chosen.*

I do not know if she is a true mate, Fen growled. *I should not have to remind you that such things cannot be rushed. That is as true for me as it is for you. The rules of the pack will not be broken. Not even for its leader.*

Josh inched toward Fen. *Apologies, pack leader. I am grateful that you will allow my courtship of the human Allie. Very grateful. And I wish you happiness if you pursue Ms. Jones.*

Fen bared his teeth in acknowledgment.

With a low whine, Josh dared to ask, *And the other? You have spoken to him?*

A message has been sent, Fen replied with a growl. *We will see if he is wise enough to heed that warning.*

Fen's bristling ceased. *Enough of this talk.*

He stood, shook his ruff, and looked at Josh. *Are you hungry?*

Josh hopped up. *Starving. I was almost ready to eat that burned bird on the table.*

Then we hunt.

9

Selene and Allison were barely in the front door when Allie bounded up the stairs.

"Josh is coming over early. I'm going to bed!"

"Don't stay up all night messaging him," Selene called.

A part of her wanted to follow Allie upstairs and talk about how worried she was that her niece seemed to be changing to please the boy.

Can I still call Josh a boy given how old he actually is?

He might look sixteen, but he had decades of life under his belt. Nevertheless, at the moment Selene was too tired and shaken to deal with the inevitable argument that would follow that conversation. And she had her own problem to deal with and a promise to keep.

She pulled out her phone.

Natalie picked up after the first ring. "You're up late."

"So are you," Selene said. "I'm sorry for calling at this hour."

"Are you kidding?" Natalie said. "I never go to bed before two a.m. Why do you think I won't make appointments before noon?"

Selene laughed, but the sound echoed her unrelenting nerves.

Natalie picked up the tension. "What's going on, Selene?"

"Any chance you could come over?" Selene said. "I just got back from dinner at Fenris Hall's mansion. I don't think a phone conversation will clear up my head."

There was a long pause.

"Nat?" Maybe it was too early in their friendship for late-night invites.

"Sorry, Selene," Natalie said. "Of course I'll come over. Just give me about twenty minutes."

"Thanks," Selene said.

"No problem." Natalie hung up.

Selene set a pot of coffee to brew in the kitchen. Caffeine probably wasn't a great idea, but she didn't see sleep anywhere in her near future, so what the hell. The coffee maker started its gurgling, and Selene pulled out the trash from under the kitchen sink. She tied off the bag and went out the back door. She was halfway to the garage when someone stepped from the shadows.

Selene gasped and dropped the trash bag.

"Who's there?" Selene thought briefly about running back to the house and locking all the doors. Then recognition slapped her in the face. But . . . how could it be? She'd had a lot to drink, but not enough to hallucinate.

"Daniel Brix?" She stayed where she was, poised to bolt if necessary. "Is that really you?"

"Hey, Selene." Daniel cocked his head at her. "Aren't you happy to see me? It's been a minute."

Goddamn. It was Daniel. Emma's ex. Allie's father. His face was the same as it had been the last time she'd seen him. His hair and clothes were different. Daniel was sporting a leather coat and jeans that molded to his muscular thighs. His hair was styled in the manner that seemed popular among teen boys of late, as if he was still trying to court a younger audience, which he probably was. A thatch of thick blond strands each seemed to be competing to travel in a different direction across his head. Unfortunately, the look suited him. He could probably put on an orange clown wig and still look hot. Asshole.

Selene spoke through clenched teeth. "What the hell are you doing here? You scared me to death."

He smiled his signature lopsided grin. Emma said it was that smile that did her in. Selene could see why. All these years later, it still had impact. There was no arguing that Daniel was attractive. Even if he hadn't become a rock star, he would always have looked like one.

"Come on, Selene," he said. "Don't be like that."

"Don't be like that?" she hissed. "You disappeared ten years ago. Where have you been? We thought you were dead."

For some reason that made Daniel laugh. Hard.

"It's not funny." Selene's head was spinning.

First the world is magic, now Daniel comes back from the dead. What is it with this week? Aliens are probably going to abduct me tomorrow. Dear god, please don't let aliens abduct me tomorrow.

"Oh, it's funny," Daniel told her. "Hi-fucking-larious. You're just not in on the joke."

And that was enough of that.

"Get out of here, Daniel," Selene snapped. "Whatever you want, I'm not interested."

Maybe it wasn't fair to dismiss him out of hand, but her instincts wouldn't let her do anything else. Daniel had broken Emma's heart time and time again. She didn't believe he had anything to offer Allie but pain and disappointment. Allie shouldn't have to deal with her deadbeat dad. Not with everything that was going on. Scratch that. Not ever. He didn't deserve her. Selene needed him gone.

He kept smiling and grabbed the discarded trash bag, the movement so quick Selene couldn't follow it.

"Let me take care of this for you, and then we'll talk."

She stared after him as he deposited the trash bag in its bin. When he returned, she was trembling and a little nauseated.

He gave a low whistle. "Gotta say, Selene, the years have been good to you."

"Fuck off."

He nodded, and for a moment the self-assured smile disappeared. "So that's how it's going to be? You know, I always thought we had a connection."

Of course you did. You assume every woman worships the ground you walk on.

"Think again." Selene gritted her teeth.

Should I let Allie have a say in this? She's sixteen. Am I being too protective? Damn it. Why are parental boundaries so hard?

Daniel was Allie's father, but what good could he bring into her life? He hadn't even asked about his daughter. The first thing he'd done was hit on Selene just like the Lothario she remembered and despised. Suddenly a cold, sickening wave rolled over her.

"Do you know about Emma?" Her voice shook.

He looked at her for a long time before he answered. At first Selene thought he didn't understand what she was talking about, but then he sighed.

"Yeah . . . I know." He dragged his hand through his hair. "That's kind of why I'm here."

"Oh." That was all Selene could muster. She was already so wrecked from dinner and . . . well, everything. Now it looked like she was going to have to deal with Daniel, and it felt like losing Emma all over again.

"How did you find out?" Selene asked weakly.

"It's a long story," he said and glanced at the house. "Can I come in and talk? You look like you're about to keel over."

She shook her head. "Not tonight, Daniel. It's not a good idea. I *am* tired. And you can't just show up after all this time."

"Come on, Sel." The smile was back. "I can explain. I'm dying to see Alley-Cat."

Hearing that nickname was a sucker punch. Selene had forgotten about it. The way it made little Allie giggle. And he just basked in Allie's and Emma's love and adoration without giving anything back. She could have forgiven him for being dead. But not that.

How could she even begin to help Allie with this if Daniel insisted on seeing her? As much as her knee-jerk response was to reject anything Emma's ex wanted, he had legal rights as Allie's father. He could take Selene to court.

Selene wanted to slap him. "Allison is in no way prepared to see you. Do you have any idea what your little disappearing act did to her? From age six to sixteen, she had no father. Six months ago, someone killed her mother, and she had to move in with me. What makes you think she'd want to see you at all? She doesn't even know you."

His expression darkened. "I have the right to see her."

That was what Selene was afraid of. What could she say to convince him otherwise?

"You gave up that right when you left," Selene said, remembering what Allie said at dinner. "I think it would be better if you stayed away, Daniel. As far as Allie's concerned, she doesn't have a father. She's happy, and I don't know what having you back would . . . Things don't need to be more complicated for her. Leave it alone. We're making a good life here."

"I can see that." Daniel glanced at the house again. "And I've been reading about your work. Congrats, Selene. You've always been an impressive woman. I know I messed up the marriage thing with Emma—relationships were never my strong suit. But I've changed. I can prove it."

He took her hand, and she jerked it back.

"Don't touch me," she snapped, shaking out her fingers. "How long have you been out here? Your hands are freezing."

He simply smiled, a languid curve of his lips. "I'd love a hot cup of coffee. Please invite me in."

She wavered, feeling suddenly dizzy, but she shook her head. No way in hell was he going to pull that charming act on her.

Selene looked away from his playful mien. "No, Daniel. I don't know what you expected, but a warm welcome isn't what you're getting."

When she turned back, she glared at him. "Things weren't fine even before you took off. Emma should have kicked you to the curb the first time you cheated on her."

"Yeah, yeah, I'm the asshole." He grimaced. "Sure, we can go with that. Just let me tell you what happened to me. Things got complicated."

"I don't care."

He scowled at her for a moment, then smiled again. "Look, I've been in town for a little while now."

When she frowned, he hurried on. "I've been waiting for the right time to let you know I'm here. I didn't want to show up while you were in the middle of relocating."

His words caught her off guard. Daniel would never have been that considerate in the past. To anyone. He never remembered Emma's birthday, much less their anniversary, or even Valentine's Day, when you couldn't walk five feet without advertisements full of hearts and roses smacking you in the face.

He smiled thinly at her shocked expression. "Yeah, I know. I am different, Selene. Believe it."

"Daniel—" She couldn't imagine that anything he'd say would convince her he deserved another chance. He'd already had too many and wasted them all.

"I'm worried about you and Allie," he continued. "I've been hearing some things."

Her heart skipped a beat. "What things?"

"Can we please talk about this in the house?" He took a step toward her, staring intently.

She blinked, dizziness hitting her again.

A car door slammed, and her mind cleared.

"Oh god." Selene turned toward the house. "That's Natalie."

"Natalie?" Daniel glared in the direction the sound had come from.

"A friend," Selene said. "She's stopping by for a little while."

"You have friends over at this hour?"

She scoffed. "When I have people over is none of your business."

He shrugged, and she glared at him. "Leave now."

"You need to hear what I have to say, Selene," he countered.

"I don't need anything from you," she snapped. "Neither does Allie."

She gasped when he grabbed her, his fingers digging into her upper arms painfully.

"Don't say that."

"What the hell are you doing?" She struggled in his hold. "Let me go!"

"Promise you'll hear me out," he murmured.

"Daniel . . ." Her head swam.

I hate this man. I hate this man. She shut her eyes as confusion roiled in her mind. Why did she want to listen to him? Why did he sound so sincere?

"Promise." His voice seemed to echo all around her.

"Another time." Selene caved. Her body was trembling. She felt like she was fighting to stay awake. Her limbs were so, so heavy. Maybe it wasn't so bad that Daniel was holding her. "We can talk another time."

He smiled and loosened his grip on her arms, stroking up and down her shaking limbs before releasing her. "Until then, sweetheart. Give Alley-Cat a kiss for me."

She stood there, swaying on her feet, and watched Daniel melt into the shadows. The moment he was out of sight, she stumbled backward as if a tether holding her in place had snapped. She bent over, rubbing her face with her palms to clear away the lingering confusion.

What the hell had just happened? Had Daniel Brix really been in her backyard?

Yes. As much as she'd prefer to have imagined the entire episode, Selene knew it was real. For whatever reason, Daniel was back. And he wanted to see Allie. She had no idea how she was going to handle it.

Still dazed, she went back into the house.

The doorbell rang.

Selene stumbled through the house and flung the front door open. Natalie was standing there holding two large tote bags.

"Get inside, Nat," she said, grabbing her friend's elbow and dragging her over the threshold.

"Oh gods, Selene," Natalie's eyes were wide as Selene hurried to lock the front door. "What's going on? Why are you crying?"

Selene touched her cheek and was startled to feel hot moisture on her skin. She didn't know when she'd started crying, but she hoped it had been after Daniel left the backyard.

Natalie's face was ashen. "Fenris didn't hurt you, did he?"

Selene almost collapsed. Her original reason for calling Natalie had been erased by Daniel's appearance. The whole evening came rushing back, and she had to steady herself against the door.

"No." Selene heard the tears in her voice. "Fen was just . . . Oh my god, Nat. What is happening to my life?"

She began to sob.

Natalie dropped the bags to put an arm around her and led her into the kitchen. She settled Selene in a chair and poured two cups of coffee. She set the coffee on the table and then brought over a box of tissues and set it in front of Selene.

"Thanks," Selene said and tugged out a handful.

"Start at the beginning." Natalie took a seat, watching her friend with narrowed eyes.

Selene blew her nose. "I think I have to start at the end."

She glanced at the back door. For all appearances, her surprise visitor was gone.

"Daniel showed up tonight."

"What!" Some of Natalie's coffee sloshed onto the table. She jumped up and went for a kitchen towel. "Daniel, as in Daniel Brix? Emma's ex-husband? Allie's dad?"

Selene nodded and sipped her coffee. Her hand was shaking so badly, she also spilled quite a bit.

Natalie mopped up Selene's coffee, too, then returned to her seat. "Hasn't it been, like, ten years since he disappeared?"

"Yes," Selene murmured. "Yes, it has."

"And before this you've heard nothing?" Natalie frowned. "No letters, emails, phone messages?"

"Not anything," Selene said. "As far as I'm aware, no one has. He vanished. I thought he was gone forever. He was presumed dead, Nat."

Natalie sat back in her chair. "That's crazy."

"I know." Selene pinched the bridge of her nose. "I can't believe it. I can't believe any of this. A week ago, my life was so normal."

Smiling sympathetically, Natalie said, "It's more than anyone should have to handle. Allie and Josh, the truth about Avondale . . . That would be too much on its own. And now Daniel. But you'll be okay, Sel. I promise. And I will be with you every step of the way."

"Thank you for saying that." Selene pushed her coffee away. She knew it had been a mistake. Her mind was already buzzing, and now her hands had joined in the fun, fingers dancing on the table.

"So why did he show up?" Natalie asked. "And where has he been all this time?"

With a shrug, Selene replied, "Where he's been? I have no idea. He didn't say, only that it was a long story. He wanted to come in, but I said no."

"Good." Natalie stood up and went to the kitchen cupboards.

"What are you doing?" Selene asked.

"Making you tea." She filled the kettle and set it on a burner. "I can handle coffee at two a.m., but you're about to pull your hair out. And I can't have that. Everyone will think I gave you a terrible haircut."

Selene laughed, and Natalie winked at her. Affection and gratitude took the edge off Selene's frazzled state.

"The fact that Daniel just showed up without warning tells me he's assuming a welcome he doesn't deserve." Natalie leaned against the counter.

"Exactly." Selene started to reach for her coffee cup as a reflex but stopped herself. "He's claiming he's a changed man, but who the hell knows what that means. And god knows I have no reason to believe anything he says. He's never hesitated to lie to get what he wants. It made Emma miserable."

Her head dropped back against the chair, and she stared at the ceiling. "I can't stand him, and yet I told him I'd talk to him again. Why did I say that?"

"I get why you'd want him to stay away," Natalie said. "But as much as you very reasonably would prefer otherwise, he is Allie's father. That gives him legal rights to see her. If he digs his heels in, you'll need a court order to make him leave. Probably best to see what he wants."

"I know." Selene made herself sit up again, giving herself a firm mental reminder that she was tired, not defeated. "He said something strange. That he's been in Avondale for a while, waiting for a good time to approach me, but that he's been hearing things that made him worry about me and Allie."

Natalie paused in her rummaging through the pantry. "Like what?"

"He didn't say," Selene answered. "He just kept asking to come in the house so we could talk."

Natalie emerged with a glass jar of loose tea. "This is one of Marley's herbal blends, right?"

"I have no idea," Selene replied. "The tea was there before I moved in."

"Pretty sure it's Marley's, and it will help you unwind." Natalie put the jar on the counter before retrieving a teapot from a cupboard.

"Daniel's been in Avondale awhile?" Natalie spooned tea into the pot. "That's strange."

"I know," Selene said. "It feels kind of stalkery. I don't even know how he found out I moved here."

"It does," Natalie agreed. "But that's not what I meant. Remember how I said humans can't just move to Avondale?"

Selene went still. "I didn't, but Daniel didn't say he was living here. Maybe he's been keeping tabs on me and Allie but staying somewhere else. Because if he is living here, that would mean—"

The words died before she could finish.

"It would mean Fenris knows Daniel is in Avondale," Natalie said quietly.

The teakettle shrieked, and Selene jumped out of her chair. Natalie moved the kettle off the hot burner and came to Selene, taking both her hands.

"Easy," Natalie murmured. "Breathe, Selene."

"He didn't say anything." Selene shook her head slowly. "Not one word all night."

Natalie tightened her grip on Selene's fingers. "Don't jump to conclusions, Sel. Especially when it comes to Fenris Hall. If he does know that Daniel has been in Avondale and didn't tell you, he has his reasons for staying quiet."

"Like what?" Fen's silence cut her like a betrayal, but that was silly. He didn't owe her anything. They'd only officially met a few hours ago. Were they even friends?

"Like he's decided it isn't his business," Natalie suggested. "Or he's waiting to see what happens before he decides to run Daniel off. That sounds more like Fen. He's a law-and-order kind of wolf, but it's live and let live until someone crosses a line. He doesn't punish preemptively."

Selene groaned at the logic. "That's . . . fair."

"Fenris is very evenhanded when it comes to ruling Avondale." Natalie returned to the stove and filled the teapot with steaming water. "It's one of the reasons I like living here. And to be honest, it makes me feel better about the whole Daniel situation because it's likely that Fen does know he's here, and that means he'll keep an eye on the situation."

"And he'll step in if necessary?" That idea both thrilled and terrified Selene. What would it mean for a werewolf pack leader to confront Daniel Brix? She was dying for a front-row seat to that show while another part of her hoped it would never happen.

Natalie carried the teapot to the table along with a new cup for Selene. "Yes."

She sat down. "But if you don't want to wait for that, I can always hex Daniel for you."

Selene stared at her.

"Seriously, Selene," Natalie said with a sly smile as Selene considered the possibilities. A hex was . . . interesting, and more than a little tempting. Daniel had definitely earned one, or several.

"I think I'll just wait and see," Selene said at last. "I'd rather have you in the capacity of friend than witch for hire."

Natalie shrugged. "Just keep in mind that your witchy friend can multitask if needed."

"I appreciate that," Selene said, wondering what a hex would entail. Boils maybe? Or parts falling off?

"Since Fen has already entered the conversation, let's keep backtracking through the night," Natalie said. "You called me before Daniel showed up, right?"

Selene nodded as Natalie poured her a cup of tea.

"So what happened at dinner with the wolves that had you so worked up?"

"Two things." Selene pulled the teacup close and inhaled the herb-scented steam. Her shoulders instantly relaxed.

"Okay." Natalie leaned back in her chair. "What's the first?"

"It's Allie," Selene said and met Natalie's probing gaze. "She treats this Josh kid like he's the second coming. I'm worried she's changing who she is to try to please him. As if the whole werewolf thing wasn't enough."

Natalie smiled gently. "Sorry, Selene, I think that might just be part of first love. You're in free fall until you crash, and then you climb back up. If the love is real, it's still there when you stop trying to be the person you think your partner wants you to be. Allie's sixteen. She's got some time to figure that out."

"You're right," Selene sighed. "I'd just like to save her the trouble."

"You can't," Natalie said. "She's the one who has to learn. You could tell her everything you know, every mistake you've made, every regret you have, and she'd still have to do it all herself. That's what growing up is. Plus, the more you try to control her relationship with Josh, the tighter she'll cling to him."

Selene nodded and thought about the pheasant. "No question there."

"But you should keep an eye on it a little," Natalie continued. "Werewolves can be very dominant."

A hot flush crept along Selene's neck. "I noticed."

Natalie's eyes widened. "Are we at the second issue?"

Selene swallowed, blushing. Natalie watched her closely and straightened, putting on a serious face.

"Oh, dear goddess. Fenris? Is he . . . Selene, what happened?"

"He, uh." Selene bit her bottom lip. "He made it very clear he's interested."

"How clear?" Natalie's eyebrows drew together.

"Trust me, there were no mixed signals." Selene took a deep breath. Even the memory of Fen's words, and his hands on her back and waist, made her skin come alive and her pulse jump.

"Be specific."

Selene looked at Natalie, expecting to see a teasing smile on her friend's lips, but there was only a stern, worried expression.

"What do you mean?" Selene was startled by the serious cast of Natalie's face.

"What did he ask of you?" Natalie pressed.

"He didn't ask anything," Selene wrapped her hands around her cup. "We were talking about Josh and Allie. I was feeling a little better about the whole thing because he isn't sure their relationship is a good idea either, and he told me about the rules werewolves have about courtship."

"Yep," Natalie said. "They are big fans of rules and ritual. I'm too impatient for that kind of thing, but I agree that when it comes to Allie's situation, it's a good thing."

"Definitely." Selene paused to sip her tea, gearing up for what she was about to say. "So that was fine. But the more we talked, the more it felt like flirting. I don't know, Nat, he's so . . . It's like he has this pull. I've never felt anything like it. At first I thought it was just me. I mean, he's really hot, and he has this *presence*."

"He does." Natalie lifted an eyebrow at the sharp look Selene gave her. "Everyone feels his power, Sel. I'm not into him, but the way you just reacted tells me a lot."

"I didn't—"

Natalie held up her hand. "Don't make excuses. Just tell me what happened."

Chagrined, Selene continued. "He asked me to dance after dinner."

"Very old school." Natalie smiled.

"It should have felt silly." Selene returned the smile. "But it didn't. I loved it, even though I was overwhelmed by my . . . response to him."

"And his response to you?"

"God, Natalie, I didn't know a man could get that hard."

Natalie tipped over her coffee cup. A trail of dark liquid spilled over the edge of the table and dripped on the floor. "I thought you said you were just dancing! Is that some new euphemism you're using for sex?"

"We *were* just dancing." Selene laughed and put her hands to her flaming cheeks. "But it almost felt like sex. Really, really good sex . . . I can't believe I just said that. I haven't been out there for a while."

Natalie patted her hand before reaching for the kitchen towel again. "I don't blame you, Selene. Fenris Hall is a beautiful creature. But he's not just a man, he's a wolf. Not just any wolf either, he's *the* wolf."

"Yeah." Selene frowned. "I don't know what to make of that."

Natalie crouched near the floor to sop up the spilled coffee. "If you get involved with him, it won't be dating. It will be something else."

"I know," Selene said. "Rules and rituals."

Natalie went to the sink and tossed in the soaked towel. She kept her back to Selene and stared out the darkened kitchen windows.

"Selene, if what I think is happening here is really happening . . ." She paused and gripped the edge of the sink.

"Are you okay?" Selene was about to rise when Natalie abruptly turned around and strode back to the kitchen table.

"I can't tell you what to do about Fen," she said. "And please don't misunderstand my reaction. He's a good man. I have immense respect for him. He wouldn't have been so forward with you if his intentions were dishonorable. If you're interested, I wouldn't want to interfere. But I also need you to know that I don't think Fenris would ever have a fling. If you get involved with him, it won't be casual."

"How am I supposed to know if I want things to be serious this early?" Selene exclaimed. "We had dinner for the first time just a few hours ago. It wasn't even supposed to be a date. I still don't think it was a date. And he seemed to be surprised by his feelings as much as I was. He said he doesn't usually invite humans into his life."

"That's true," Natalie said. "And that's another reason there's no such thing as casual when it comes to Fenris. Hang on, I'll be right back."

Natalie left the kitchen, and Selene sipped her tea, considering what her friend was telling her. It wasn't exactly a warning, but it was obvious Nat wasn't comfortable with Selene dating Fen, and not because Fen was a bad person.

Given how strong Fen had come on at the end of the evening, Selene knew Nat was right to caution her. Selene was still shaken by how heated things got between them in such a short space of time. She'd never been one to jump into relationships. It scared her to admit that Fen tempted her enough to consider throwing caution to the wind. She wanted him that much.

Natalie returned carrying the tote bags she'd arrived with. She set them down, reaching into one.

"I was going to give you these things regardless, but it's even more imperative that you have them, given that it's obvious you won't be on the periphery of the magical world. You're already in the thick of it."

Selene didn't try to deny it. She was in the woods all right, deep in that dark forest fairy tales warned about.

"What things?"

"The means to protect yourself." Natalie drew a slender black case from the bag and opened it.

For a moment Selene stopped breathing. The dagger was sleek and gleaming. Its blade was eight inches long and appeared to be paper thin. The hilt was inlaid with luminescent milky stones.

"If you have trouble with a wolf, this will protect you. It's silver set with moonstones."

When Selene found her breath again, she tried to laugh. It came out as a husky puff of air. "This is a joke, right?"

Natalie's lips thinned. "Look, Selene. I doubt you'll ever need to use it. Like I said, Fen is a good ruler, and he keeps the creatures in Avondale in line, especially his wolves. But your life has changed. Forever. Once you know about paranormals, they are no longer constrained by laws about keeping themselves hidden from you. You're part of their world now. You need the equipment to stay safe if something goes wrong. You believe in self-defense, right?"

Selene nodded and continued to stare at the dagger. She'd never owned a weapon of any kind.

"I brought a couple of other things." Natalie rummaged in the bag. "The vamps in town are afraid of Fen enough to behave, but every once in a while, one of them goes rogue. Wolves almost never attack humans. I wish I could say the same for vamps. You should carry this with you when you're out at night."

She handed Selene a slender chain with a cross suspended from it.

"The cross will keep a vampire at bay. Plus it's silver, and so is the chain. That's another line of defense against the werewolves, and it's small enough to hide in your purse."

"I was wearing a silver ring tonight," Selene told Nat. "It burned Fen when I shook his hand."

"Oh my goddess." Nat snorted out a laugh.

"Don't laugh," Selene complained. "I was mortified. And Allie was furious."

"I'm sorry." Natalie tried to stop laughing and almost succeeded. "Fen must really like you if he didn't send you home the moment that happened."

"I didn't know!"

Still grinning, Natalie shook her head. "Allie should have given you some ground rules. No silver is pretty basic."

"Yeah, I get that," Selene said dryly. "But now you're telling me to wear a silver cross at night. Is that true if I'm with Fen?"

"So you are going to keep seeing him?" Natalie asked, her smile fading.

Selene frowned. "I don't know."

Giving Selene a sympathetic look, Nat said, "You don't have to know right now. It's a lot. Be patient with yourself. And to answer your question: you should not wear silver if you're with Fen, but like I said, carry it in your purse. I also have an aerosolized spray bottle filled with holy water. Doesn't do anything to wolves but hurts vampires like hell and gives you the chance to run. That's what you need to do if you're attacked by a vamp. Run and get somewhere safe. You won't win a fight with one."

"Okay." Selene's heart was pounding, both from the thought that she might try to date Fenris Hall and because she was talking about fighting off creatures of the night with silver crosses and holy water. "What else have you got in there? A shotgun for zombies?"

Natalie laughed, but it was a brittle sound. "Shotguns aren't for zombies. We don't have zombies around Avondale, as far as I'm aware. Shotguns are for werewolves. You just need silver ammo. But let's hope I never hand you a gun. Because we wouldn't be talking about self-defense at that point."

"What would we be talking about?" Selene asked.

"War," Natalie said, and her tone made Selene's blood turn to ice. Her mind began to spin, barely able to process everything that had taken place over the course of the past several hours. It all melted together into a confusing puddle of strange and frightening scenarios. None of which seemed quite possible, despite what Selene had witnessed with her own eyes.

Natalie returned to her bags and pulled out a box set of DVDs. "Old school, I know, but I wasn't sure what streaming channels you subscribe to. You do have a DVD player, don't you?"

Selene nodded and picked up the first box. "*Buffy the Vampire Slayer*?"

"All seven seasons," Natalie said. "Consider it your crash course in paranormal self-defense. I also included a Brazilian jujitsu DVD. You should practice."

"Should I get Allie to watch these?" Selene asked.

"Yes," Natalie replied. "But the weapons and jewelry are just for you."

Selene looked at her with surprise. "Why?"

Natalie sighed. "I want you to have this stuff because I think it's important that you feel safe. And I need to know I'm doing everything I can to protect you if things go sideways. But not everyone would share my opinion."

"Like who?"

"Fenris," Natalie said. "The werewolves have laws about items they consider threatening to their kind. He'd see this as an affront to his clan. Particularly the dagger. There are very few things that can kill the wolves, but the dagger is one of them. It's powerful and deadly."

"Maybe you should hang on to it." The conversation had taken a turn that made Selene uneasy. "I'm not exactly an expert when it comes to weapons."

"I wish I didn't think it was necessary to give it to you, but you're in a new world with new rules," Natalie countered. "Don't let anyone see it. It's only for use as a last resort."

"Okay," Selene said. "Thanks, Nat."

"No worries." Natalie smiled. "I know it's late, but do you want to watch some *Buffy*? Seriously, it's a great show."

10

Allie's scream jolted Selene from sleep. She'd been dreaming about whittling stakes with her new silver dagger, and it took her a minute to realize she was no longer preparing to fight vampires.

But something had frightened Allie enough that she'd cried out so loudly it carried all the way to Selene's room. That sound sent sheer terror spiraling through her limbs. She scrambled out of bed and grabbed the dagger she'd left on the nightstand when she'd finally stopped watching *Buffy* at 4:00 a.m. Selene was no vampire slayer, but she'd fight like hell in the waking world if Allie needed protecting.

"Allie!" Selene rushed down the hall and flung open her niece's bedroom door.

She thought her heart stopped when she saw Allie pinned to her bed. A huge brown wolf hovered over her squirming niece, its fangs bared.

Selene stared in shock at the real-life manifestation of every nightmarish thought she'd had since she'd learned magic and monsters were real. Her fear that a werewolf boyfriend was a danger to Allie was confirmed beyond doubt.

"Get off her!" Selene shrieked, raising the dagger.

The wolf caught the flash of silver. It blinked, leaped away from Allie, and cowered against the wall.

"Aunt Selene, no!" Allie sat up, her face white as the sheets on the bed. "Stop!"

"Ms. Jones." The wolf was gone and Josh lay on the floor, human again, pale with fear and stark naked. "What are you doing?"

Selene froze as her certainty that Josh had been attacking Allie faltered. She gripped the dagger tightly but didn't take another step. Though the immediate threat appeared to be gone, or at least stalled, her pulse continued to hammer.

She pointed at Josh with her free hand. "You attacked Allie. I heard her scream."

Allie groaned and threw Josh a pillow, which he used to shield his lower body.

He glared at Selene. "I did not attack her!"

"I had the hiccups!" Allie cried, still glaring at Selene. "I couldn't get rid of them."

That made absolutely no sense.

Selene frowned at her niece. "Why are you talking about hiccups?"

"I was trying to scare her so they would go away," Josh said, his eyes still wild.

The adrenaline kick from choosing fight over flight the moment she woke up still held Selene's body captive. As her panic receded and her tense limbs went wobbly with relief, she didn't know whether to laugh or cry.

"Oh god." She folded her arms over her chest. "I thought . . ."

I thought you were about to be shredded by fangs and claws. I knew I would do anything to save you, and you're staring at me like I'm *the enemy. And you think I'm completely nuts.*

"Why did you run in here?" Allie was still furious. "You don't even have pants on."

Selene looked down. She was only wearing a nightshirt. *At least it hits at mid-thigh. Good to know I could have been even* more *humiliated.*

"I just—" Selene started and then gave Allie a hard look. "Allie, you screamed bloody murder. It woke me up. What did you expect me to do? Ignore it?"

Allie's belligerent expression didn't waver. "Josh would never hurt me."

"I really wouldn't," Josh said as he inched toward a duffel bag across the room.

"I'm sorry," Selene said.

Josh's eyes fixed on the dagger. "Where did you get that?"

Selene set the gleaming weapon on Allie's bookshelf and held up her hands. "I am sorry, Josh. I misunderstood what was happening. I only wanted to keep Allie safe."

"That is a bounty hunter's weapon. Their sale is forbidden here." Now that his fear had dissipated, he snarled. "Where did you get it?"

Selene's eyes widened. *Oh no.*

Only for emergencies. That's what Natalie said.

Way to get an F on my first assignment.

"I ordered it online," she lied, her instincts screaming at her to keep Natalie out of it. "I had it before I knew about you." *Please let him believe me.* "When I heard Allie scream, I grabbed it off my dresser."

"You keep a dagger on your dresser?" Josh was not buying it.

Shit. Shit. Shit.

"That dagger is illegal in Avondale," he continued. "I need to know where it's from."

"Why is it illegal?" Selene tried to maneuver out of her predicament. Hoping with all her heart that Josh would believe her if she kept playing dumb. "What do you mean it's a bounty hunter's weapon?"

Radiating defiance, Josh straightened to his full height and tossed aside the pillow. Selene averted her eyes while he rummaged in the duffel bag, presumably for his clothes.

"Some people make their living by hunting us," Josh growled.

When Selene heard the sound of a zipper, she turned back to face him. Josh had a pair of jeans on and was pulling a T-shirt over his head.

"Why would anyone hunt werewolves?" Selene frowned.

"Sometimes it's assassination," Josh said, his eyes dark with suspicion, as if she was a threat he hadn't seen coming. "We have politics of our own, and they can get dangerous. For others it's profit—werewolf pelts and fangs have mystical properties. They command a high price on the black market. And there are some who just do it for sport. We aren't easy to kill. They see it as a challenge."

This is getting worse and worse. No wonder Natalie told me to keep the dagger hidden.

Selene glanced at it. "And that's a bounty hunter's weapon?"

"Any weapon crafted of pure silver was meant for a bounty hunter," Josh snapped. "They have no other purpose. Where did you get it?"

Selene didn't answer. Natalie had said something about laws and the dagger being a problem, but Selene had been a mess, her mind jumbled by back-to-back encounters with Fenris and Daniel.

Josh growled and stepped toward her.

"Answer me."

Allie jumped off the bed and stood between them.

"Hang on, Josh," Allie said. "I get why you're upset, but you're overreacting. Just like Aunt Selene overreacted when she heard me scream."

Josh looked at Allie, his expression softening slightly. "Allie, there are laws—"

"Laws she doesn't know anything about," Allie insisted. "She doesn't hang out with bounty hunters, and she didn't even know that werewolves were hurt by silver. For god's sake, when she shook Fen's hand last night, she had a silver ring on."

Josh stared at Allie, who nodded. Then he looked at Selene like she was a complete idiot.

"Seriously?"

Okay, not fun to be insulted, but less scary.

"It's true," Selene muttered. "I apologized to Fen for the mistake."

Josh shook his head. "That is . . . really something."

"I'm sure the dagger is some kind of antique she found. She picks up weird stuff on eBay all the time. Right, Auntie Sel?" Allie gave her a piercing look before taking Josh's hand and tugging him close.

Selene smiled weakly and nodded. "The dagger caught my eye because it's beautiful. The scrollwork on the hilt is very ornate. That's why I keep it on my dresser."

Did that sound like I know what I'm talking about?

A new tack jumped helpfully into her mind. "It's next to my antique brush, comb, and mirror, which are also silver plated. I'm sorry. Silver has never been an issue before. The dagger matched, and I thought it made the whole ensemble a little edgy. Like the cover of a mystery novel. I realize that sounds ridiculous."

Josh seemed to relax. "Look, Ms. Jones, I'm sorry I got angry, but you need to understand how serious this is. Fen's mate was killed by a bounty hunter. That's why the laws in Avondale are so severe—all silver weapons are forbidden. Trafficking them is a capital crime."

"Someone *killed* Fen's mate?" Selene gasped and looked at Allie for confirmation, but her niece appeared astounded by Josh's revelation.

Josh nodded, his face becoming drawn with grief. "Five wolves were hunting in the foothills when bounty hunters, poachers, ambushed them. We lost all five of our pack mates. Fen's mate was one of them."

Selene couldn't speak. It was Allie who asked the next shaky question. "Poachers? Are you saying that Fen's mate was killed . . . *and skinned*? By humans?"

"Skinned and beheaded. It was like that for all five wolves," Josh said quietly. "Fen was mad with grief. There was a time when we thought he wouldn't come back from it."

Selene's stomach roiled with such violence, she had to grab Allie's dresser to steady herself. Skinned and beheaded. She'd been obsessing about werewolves being a danger, but the true monsters in this story were people. She couldn't grasp how twisted someone would have to be to commit such an atrocity.

She only spoke when she was certain she wouldn't vomit, which meant that several seconds of uncomfortable silence passed before she could ask, "When did this happen?"

"About ten years ago," Josh answered.

Ten years. From the raw sorrow on Josh's face, Selene had expected him to say it had happened more recently. But she thought of Emma and knew that years from now, the pain would be just as sharp. Loss was loss.

And how had Fen spoken of werewolves and their mates? *"Our relationships can span infinite lifetimes."*

The promise of an eternity of love had been stolen from him in the most horrific way. Her heart ached for him. How many years had they been together before she was killed? Decades? Centuries?

Daring to ask that question was unthinkable, so instead Selene whispered, "Did he ever find out who the hunters were?"

"No," Josh said, cold fury edging his words. "Unfortunately, bounty hunters are very good at what they do. They know how dangerous it is to prey on werewolves. They also know a pack will try to come after them, so they cover their tracks. Finding a bounty hunter after a kill is almost impossible."

"Josh, I am so sorry," Selene murmured. "I'll get rid of the dagger."

"That would be a good idea," Josh said. "And I . . . I won't mention it to Fen. He really likes you, and he would be . . . I won't say anything."

He would be what? Selene wanted to scream. *Hurt? Disappointed? Angry?*

Probably all of the above.

Selene couldn't fault Natalie's intentions, and she wished she'd been paying closer attention to her friend's warning.

"If you'll excuse me," Selene said. "I should get dressed."

Selene fled to the bathroom. She turned on the shower and leaned against the basin as steam filled the room. Her throat burned, and her chest felt like it had been pummeled by a battering ram. Visions of flayed wolves without heads flashed in her mind's eye. She'd never been confronted with such gruesome violence. Its horror would haunt her, but the revulsion she felt would never compare to the pain and suffering of Fen and his pack. No wonder he'd passed laws banning weapons like the dagger.

Selene stripped off her nightshirt and was about to step into the shower when there was a soft knock at the bathroom door.

"Aunt Selene, it's Allie."

Selene grabbed her bathrobe from a hook on the wall, wrapped it around her, and opened the door. Allie slipped inside the room and closed the door.

"What is it, hon?" Selene asked.

"I sent Josh home because I need to ask you something." Allie shifted her weight from one foot to the other. "What are you going to do about the dagger?"

"I said I would get rid of it. I will." She couldn't imagine having anything in her house associated with such an abhorrent practice.

"I meant about the fact that you got it from Natalie," Allie said.

Selene stared at her. "How . . ."

"I woke up and heard voices downstairs," Allie continued. "I recognized Natalie's, so I came down to say hi, but when I realized what you were talking about . . . I kind of eavesdropped. Sorry."

"What did you hear?" Selene tensed.

Does she know that Daniel is back?

"Well I already knew that Natalie was a witch," Allie said. "So that wasn't a surprise." She smiled impishly. "I didn't know you were into Fen."

Okay, after Daniel. Good. Wait . . . Fen? Oh no. Not good.

Selene blushed at the same moment her heart lurched. "I don't know what to think about Fen."

And after learning what happened to his mate, I'm even more lost. Why would he be the least bit interested in me given all that history?

"Give me a break, Aunt Sel." Allie grinned. "That's not what you said last night."

"I am mortified that you heard any of that, Allison," Selene said. "Please erase it from your memory."

"Not likely," Allie said. "I think you should go for it. I love Fen."

"What else did you hear?" Selene ignored Allie's delighted expression.

Her niece's smile faded. "Well, that was when Nat started talking about self-defense. At first I was kind of annoyed, but then I thought she was probably being realistic. I mean, Josh and Fen are great, but I'm sure there are bad paranormals out there. Just like there are good and bad people."

Selene nodded. "That's smart, Allie."

"I think Nat is just trying to be helpful," Allie concluded.

"She is," Selene said. "Are you going to say anything to Josh?"

"No, Nat is awesome. She's like my super-cool aunt."

"Your super-cool aunt?" Selene scoffed. "What does that make me?"

"Obviously you're my *favorite* aunt." Allie stuck out her tongue, then beamed at Selene. "Anyway, I don't want Natalie to get in trouble. And I love Josh, but some of the werewolf rules are a little over the top. Did you know they want us to date for ten years before I can be Josh's mate? That's *forever*."

"Fen told me about that rule, and I don't hate it," Selene said, making Allie scowl. "I know ten years sounds like a long time, but you still get to be with Josh during that time. It means you'll really know each other before you make a commitment that is literally forever."

"Whatever. It's way too long," Allie mumbled. "But I get the law against weapons, knowing what happened to Fen's mate."

Selene couldn't stop herself from shuddering as she nodded her agreement.

"Josh didn't mention it before this morning?" Selene asked.

Allie shook her head. "I knew she had died. It was a huge tragedy for the pack, and Fen took it really hard. But that story, what the poachers did . . . it's too horrible."

"It is." Selene wrapped her arms around herself.

"Aunt Selene." Allie's voice became so quiet, Selene instantly went on alert. A haunted look crept over her niece's face. "When

Mom died . . . you had to identify her at the morgue before she was cremated . . . You saw how she looked after it happened."

"What's wrong, Allie? What do you need to know?" Selene asked gently. They'd talked about this before. She'd decided against hiding the truth about Emma's murder. Allie deserved honest answers no matter how difficult the questions.

"The person who killed her." Allie stopped, swallowed a couple of times. "They didn't do bad things to her body. Like the hunters did to Fen's mate. Did they?"

"Your mom was stabbed in the throat," Selene said, keeping her voice even. But memories of the morgue, of the sheet being drawn back to reveal Emma's lifeless body, clawed at her heart. "It was an ugly, awful thing, but no, it was nothing like what happened to Fen's mate and the other wolves who were killed by the hunters."

Allie's shoulders slumped in relief. "Okay. Good. Thank you for telling me." She sniffled, wiping tears from her cheeks, but she dodged when Selene tried to hug her.

Selene wanted to tell Allie she didn't have to put on a brave front, that crying was always okay, but she also understood that Allie was at a moment in her life where she wanted to prove she was independent. Strong. If that was what Allie needed, Selene would support her.

"Is there anything else you want to ask about that?" Selene laced her fingers together because she wanted to brush the hair that hid Allie's eyes away from her face. But Allie would hate that.

"No."

They stood quietly.

"I feel so sorry for Fen." Allie gave her aunt a speculative look. "Maybe that's a good reason you should date him. You could, like, teach him to love again after all that tragedy. It would be super romantic."

Selene would have been thrown by the sudden shift in tone, but there was a hint of pleading behind Allie's words, telling her that Allie needed a new focus. Happier thoughts. Brighter possibilities.

"I don't think it works that way," Selene said.

"Why not?" Allie frowned.

The tumult of her own feelings came roaring up. Was she attracted to Fen? Absolutely. Could she handle all the complications tied to that attraction? She honestly didn't know.

"Can we not talk about this right now?"

Something in her expression brought Allie up short. "Sorry."

"You don't need to apologize, sweetheart." Selene didn't want to shut Allie down when they hit on uncomfortable topics. If that happened, it was far too easy for small problems to turn into major crises.

Speaking of crises.

Selene paused and thought about telling Allie about Daniel's sudden appearance. But she quickly dismissed that idea. She wanted to know more about his intentions before Allie was involved at all. A part of her hoped that Daniel would decide never to show up again. It would fit his usual pattern to flake out.

"I don't know that it's a good idea for me to get involved with anyone right now," Selene told Allie. "It's not that long before my next contract starts up. You know how busy I get with work. And your love life has enough complications for both of us, don't you think?"

"No way, Auntie Sel," Allie snarked. "You don't get to use work for an excuse. Or me. Go out with Fen. I'd be really happy for you."

"Well since I have your approval, that erases all my doubts," Selene quipped before bopping Allie on the nose. "Should I send a dozen red roses to Fenris at his castle?"

Allie laughed. "I just think you'd be happier if you had someone like Fen in your life."

"I'm not unhappy, Allie," Selene murmured.

"Not regular happy, Auntie Sel," Allie drawled. "Love happy. It's different, and you know it."

All Selene could do was sigh.

"Oh," Allie continued. "One more thing. Can Josh come to dinner tonight?"

"Breakfast and dinner?" Selene clucked her tongue. "Allie, that's an awful lot. Josh can't be your whole life."

"Please, Aunt Sel," Allie said. "He was really shaken up by the dagger thing. I think it would mean a lot if he thought you wanted him around. You did wave a deadly weapon at him this morning."

Guilt socked Selene in the gut. "Yes, I suppose I could make amends for that. Okay, he can come for dinner."

Allie's eyes lit up.

"But don't push it, Allie," Selene said. "I know the werewolf world works differently, but I will never, never approve sleepovers."

Allie's cheeks went pink. "And I would never, never ask."

◆ ◆ ◆

Selene remained distracted and a little agitated when she drove into town. She was still puzzling over what she was supposed to serve a werewolf for dinner when she walked into Natalie's shop.

Natalie turned from the chair and grinned at her. "Let me guess, you just watched the last episode of Season Two. Rips your heart out, doesn't it? Have a seat, and we'll talk about it. Don't worry, Angel comes back. Sorry. I should have said spoiler alert."

"Sorry, I'm still mired in the first season. Buffy and Angel just kissed for the first time." Selene had winced when the cross around Buffy's neck burned Angel's skin like a brand. That hit too close to home. "I'm here to ask about something else."

"Heya, Selene." Tim waved at her from the salon chair. "Good weekend?"

"It's been interesting."

"Natalie said you had a close encounter of the Fenris kind." He waggled his bushy eyebrows at her. "I have to admit, I'm a little jealous."

"Nat!" Selene glared at Natalie as she brushed stray hairs from Tim's shoulders.

"Oh, come on," Natalie said. "You're going to end up asking Tim and Mar for advice anyway. I figured I'd give them a head start."

"Thanks," Selene replied in a flat voice.

"You're all set, Timothy." Natalie pulled the cape off his shoulders.

"Excellent." Tim rose. He went to one of the velvet sofas where a wooden crate sat. It was full of small jars of dried herbs. He picked it up, did a quick scan, and then carried it over to Natalie.

"I think this makes us even."

"Say hi and thank you to Marley." Natalie took the crate from his arms.

"Of course." He kissed her on the cheek.

"Selene, you stop by any time you want to talk about your new romance."

"There is no new romance," Selene insisted.

"We'll see." Tim smiled. "We don't have to talk about navigating a paranormal romance. If you just want to tell me what Fen looks like naked, I'm all ears."

"Oh my god." Selene buried her face in her hands.

"That's my girl." He gave her a pat on the back and left the salon.

When Selene lifted her head, Natalie was still holding the crate, watching her.

"Are you okay?"

Selene shook her head, guilt wrapping around her. She'd never forgive herself if her mistake caused trouble for Natalie. "Something happened. We need to talk."

"What is it?"

"Josh saw the dagger you gave me." Selene ripped the BAND-AID right off. "He was pretty freaked."

Natalie's grip on the crate tightened. "How did he see the dagger? I asked you to keep it hidden except for emergencies."

"I thought it *was* an emergency," Selene protested. "When I woke up this morning, Allie was screaming, and Josh was a giant wolf standing over her. It looked like he was attacking her, but they were just kidding around. I'm sorry, Nat. I know I made a huge mistake."

Natalie bit her lip, then nodded. "That would be an easy scenario to see the wrong way. Did you tell Josh where you got the dagger?"

"No," Selene hurried to answer. "Allie told him I got it on eBay as an antique, not knowing what it was for. He accepted that explanation."

"Allie said that?" Natalie's eyes widened.

"Yes," Selene said. "The little scamp eavesdropped on part of our conversation last night. She wanted to cover for you."

"I'll have to thank her." Natalie smiled weakly. "She didn't hear about Daniel, did she?"

"No, thank god," Selene said. "I'm still trying to figure out what I'm going to do about that."

"It's a pickle," Natalie agreed.

"Nat, I need to know more about this weapon thing," Selene said. "Josh said having it is forbidden and that selling the weapons in town is a crime."

"Yes," Natalie said. "It is."

Selene waited for the punch line, but Natalie remained stern faced. At the least, Selene had expected a denial or confusion.

"Why did you give me this dagger?" Selene pulled the weapon from her bag.

"Put that away. Quickly," Natalie ordered and waited for Selene to comply. "Now go turn the dead bolt to the front door and then follow me. I need to show you something."

Selene went to the door. "Show me what?"

"How much I trust you."

Selene trailed Natalie through the salon and into a supply room filled with hair color, shampoos, conditioners, styling products, and various tools. They passed through another door into a dark room that flickered with candlelight. A pentacle was carved into the hardwood floor, and what looked like a shrine stood against one wall.

Natalie set the crate of herbs down near the shrine and then walked to the opposite corner of the room.

"Is this your witch room?" Selene looked around the shadowy space.

Natalie laughed wryly. "It *is* where I cast spells, throw bones, and draw cards."

She kicked the edge of a circular rug until it rolled back to reveal a trap door. She pulled open the door and beckoned Selene to follow her.

"Promise you're not taking me into a dungeon." Selene tried to smile to cover her flare of nerves.

"Scout's honor," Natalie replied.

The trap door opened onto a small flight of stairs, which took them into a basement that looked as spotless and sterile as a hospital. Fluorescent lights filled the space with a washed-out brightness. Selene gasped. The walls were lined with weapons. Swords, long knives, wickedly curved daggers, axes. Each one pure silver. There were also several racks lined with rifles and shotguns. Shelves held stacks of ammo boxes that Selene could only presume were silver bullets.

As she walked through the room toward a desk and computer, Natalie reached out and pulled open a slim drawer—one of many in cabinets that were scattered through the basement. Selene followed Natalie toward the desk. When she glanced in the open drawer, she saw that it was lined with velvet. An array of crucifixes gleamed against the black fabric.

"Natalie, what is this?" Selene breathed.

"I told you I do other work," Natalie replied. "This is it."

"You traffic illegal weapons?" Selene gazed around the room. The glint of silver answered her question.

"The weapons are a part of it," Natalie replied.

Selene's hands were shaking. "But, Nat, how could you? What Josh said about bounty hunters . . . they sound like monsters. No money could be worth that."

Natalie's jaw clenched. "I don't sell to bounty hunters, and if they contact me trying to buy, I make sure I get their names to Fen . . .

anonymously. I would never truck with those scum. Josh is right, they are monsters. As far as I'm concerned, hell is too good for them."

Well then.

"But why all this?" Selene gestured to the walls. "Who are they for?"

"Selene, bounty hunters are bad news. No question," Natalie said. "But bounty hunters aren't the only ones who need weapons. Not all paranormals are honorable like Fenris's pack. There are some who are dangerous, others who are downright evil. And not all places are storybook towns like Avondale. We're blessed. It can get bad out there. Really bad."

Selene nodded slowly.

"I only sell weapons for self-defense," Natalie continued. "For the same reasons I gave you the dagger last night. Domestic abuse isn't limited to the human world. It's rampant in the paranormal world too."

She pointed at the computer. "I run an underground network for people who are being abused by paranormals. I help them find safe houses, and I get them the tools they need to protect themselves. In most cases the survivor was dating someone too good to be true and then finds out they're a vamp or a wolf. My client wants out. The abuser says no and decides to turn their victim by force. If the survivor is lucky, they figure it out and head for the hills before it's too late."

"Turn them into what?" Selene stared at Natalie. A cold sickness wormed in her belly.

"Whatever the abuser is," Natalie said. "It's not hard. Wolves only need one bite to create the change. It's a very particular bite, an intentional bite, that secretes magical venom, but any wolf can manage it."

"Josh could just bite Allie?" Selene's nails dug into her palms. "And that would be it? She's a werewolf forever?"

Natalie took Selene's hands and unfolded her tight fists. "Josh won't. You have nothing to fear there."

"How can you be sure?" Selene asked. She wanted to run home that instant and make sure Allie was okay.

"Because Fen would kill him," Natalie said. "Without hesitation. That's how serious it is. If Josh turned Allie without her consent and the consent of the pack, the only way Josh would survive would be to take Allie and run. He'd be an exile, hiding for eternity. Wolves can't tolerate a solitary existence. They need their packs."

That was marginally reassuring, but Selene didn't resist when Natalie dragged a chair over and made her sit. Nor did she decline the glass of wine Nat poured and put into her hand.

"You still with me?" Natalie asked.

Selene nodded and drank some wine.

Natalie's smile was razor thin. "Vampire transformation is a little more involved, but considering how much stronger vamps are than humans, forcing someone to drink their blood isn't too much of a challenge."

Selene paled. "You have to drink a vampire's blood to become one?"

"Yes."

"There are no abuse shelters or support groups for people who've been caught up in the darker side of the magical world," Natalie continued grimly. "They can't go to the police, they can't get help from friends or family. I wish I could say my services aren't in high demand. They are."

"That's incredible," Selene murmured. "But Nat, the laws. Why on earth are you doing this in Avondale?"

"Because Avondale has become a refuge for a number of survivors who are hiding out from abusive partners," Natalie said. "Outsiders are reluctant to broach Fenris's territory. He's very old and incredibly powerful, and he won't brook abuse of humans. He never permits an involuntary change from human to paranormal. This town is something of a safe harbor. But these survivors still need a second line of defense if their abuser decides to risk coming after them into Avondale despite Fenris. I provide that defense."

"But what if you're caught?" Selene asked. "Aren't you worried?"

"I've been doing this for years and have kept it hidden," Natalie explained. "Fenris only cracked down on weapons dealers after his mate was killed, but I was underground from the beginning. There are plenty of others who've wanted to stop my operation for much longer than our local wolf king. I'm extremely careful. Though I clearly should have taken the time to tell you more about this before I gave you that dagger."

"I'm so sorry," Selene said again. "Really, Nat. It's making me sick that I put you in danger. Even more so knowing the risk you take to help people who need it the most."

"It's not your fault." Natalie sighed. "I've been tiptoeing around this stuff because I don't want to scare you. But you deserved more honesty from me. Now you have it."

"Do you mind if I pass this information on to Allie?" Selene asked.

"Not at all," Natalie said. "It sounds like Allie was the one who saved my ass this morning. Plus, if she's serious about Josh, she should know about the underbelly of the paranormal world. You can enjoy the good, but you can't ignore the bad."

"I'm starting to get that," Selene replied.

11

"That is a mountain of food," Allie said when she walked into the kitchen.

"I figured Josh might be one for eating a lot," Selene replied and continued slicing cucumbers.

"He is," Allie said. "But even for Josh, this is overkill. I guess it's a good thing that Fen's coming too."

The knife slipped, and Selene almost amputated her pinky.

"What did you just say?" She stared at Allie, willing her niece to have misspoken.

"Fen called this afternoon and asked if he could drop something off at the house for you." Allie put on an oh-so-innocent smile. "Josh thought it would be nice if he came to dinner too. You weren't around to ask, but I decided it was a great idea."

Selene continued to gape at her niece. Allie kept smiling, eating up the moment with obvious delight, and pointed at the food.

"And I was right. Now you won't have heaps of leftovers."

"Allison." Selene's tone was dangerous. "Do not try to play matchmaker for your favorite aunt."

Allie batted her eyelashes at Selene. "I have no idea what you mean."

She turned and skipped out of the kitchen, calling, "But Fen sounded *very* happy. He'll be here at six thirty!"

Selene glanced at the clock and panicked. It was almost six. She'd planned on dining with the kids in her T-shirt and yoga pants. Now that Fen was joining them, she actually cared about the way she looked. She set aside her kitchen prep, dashed up the stairs, and discarded her loungewear in favor of her most flattering pair of jeans and a draped linen-blend shirt.

Glancing in the mirror, she decided there wasn't time to do anything with her hair, so she pulled it up into a casual twist that she fixed in place with a vintage hair comb—bronze, not silver. That she kept some antiques in her bedroom hadn't been a complete lie. She hurried back to the kitchen and rearranged the food from a buffet on the counter to a more formal setting on the kitchen table. She scanned the room one last time to make sure it was clear of any silver utensils or implements. The doorbell rang as she was pouring glasses of water.

Selene took a deep breath, smoothed her shirt, and went to the door.

"Good evening, Selene." Fen smiled and handed her an armful of crimson tulips and an envelope. He was also dressed casually in jeans and a dark-blue merino wool sweater that set off the gray of his eyes.

He absolutely took her breath away.

"Thank you." Selene admired the abundance of red blooms in her arms. "These are lovely."

"From our gardens," he said. "On a clear day you should come to see them. They're quite expansive. It would be a lovely walk."

"That sounds very nice," Selene said, unsure if it had been an offhand remark or an invitation. "Please come in."

She looked at the envelope, and her heart sped up. "Would you like me to open this card now?"

"It can wait." He stepped through the door.

When she closed it and turned, he was right there. Inches away. One step and she'd be in his arms. He was watching her, perhaps considering . . .

She panicked.

Selene pivoted toward the staircase. "Allie! Josh! Fen's here. Please come down for dinner."

"You have a beautiful home," Fen said, taking a step back and glancing around the entryway.

"Thank you," she said, breathing a bit easier now that there was space between them but wondering what would have happened if she hadn't called for Allie and Josh. "It might be a little cramped compared to what you're used to."

"But less drafty," Fen remarked, and Selene laughed.

Josh and Allie came down the stairs like a herd of elephants despite there being only two of them.

"Hi, Fen!" Allie beamed and threw her arms around him in an enthusiastic hug.

Selene's eyes widened at her niece's show of affection. Fen smiled and returned Allie's embrace, lifting her off her feet with a chuckle.

"Hello, Allison," he said. "That's quite the welcome."

"I'm just so happy you're having dinner with us," Allie said brightly. "Aren't you, Aunt Sel?"

"Of course." Selene swallowed a groan. How hard was her niece going to push the matchmaking thing? "Allie, would you find a vase for these?"

She handed the tulips to her niece.

Allie leaned in, her whisper conspiratorial . . . and obvious. "He brought you flowers?"

"Yes, it was very thoughtful," Selene said quickly. "Vase. Now."

Allie trotted away, giggling.

"Josh, why don't you show Fen into the kitchen." Selene needed a moment. Or an hour. "I'll be right there."

"This way." Josh waved, and Fen fell in step alongside the younger wolf.

Selene went to the living room and dropped onto the couch. Taking a deep breath, she stared at the card Fen had given her. It was heavy cardstock, and the flap had been sealed with bloodred wax. She fought the temptation to open it and discover its contents, instead forcing herself to set it on the writing desk. Right now she had guests, and as Fen said, the card could wait.

She found them already seated at the table, and when she walked in the room, Josh and Fen exchanged a glance. They were both grinning like kids on Christmas morning.

"What?" Selene asked, self-conscious under their beatific gazes.

"You made sushi," Josh said.

"It's raw meat." Selene approached the table. "I thought you'd be able to eat it."

"We can." Fen said. "And we're delighted. It was incredibly kind of you to prepare something we can all enjoy together."

Selene smiled, more than a little pleased by his words, and took her seat between Fen and Allie. "I'm glad it works for you. I wasn't sure what to make."

"It's perfect." Fen smiled, and Selene's heart did a backflip.

More cardiac acrobatics. Wonderful.

Dinner proceeded with none of the tension that had marked their meal the previous evening. Fen and Josh both appeared to enjoy their sushi immensely, though Selene noticed they ate only the sashimi and touched none of the rice or rolls on the table.

I guess the raw-meat-only thing is a hard line.

Conversation flowed comfortably, and while, for the first part of the meal, Selene watched for signs that Josh had changed his mind and told Fen about the dagger, everything seemed to be fine. She let herself relax.

When they'd finished eating, Josh and Fen cleared the table. Selene leaned back in her chair, feeling deeply content and fizzingly happy with the evening. She'd successfully hosted a dinner for, as Nat described, a "very old, incredibly powerful" werewolf pack leader. How many people could say the same?

"Aunt Selene, may Josh and I be excused?" Allie asked. "I have to watch a PBS documentary for my American history class."

"Sure, Allie," Selene said. "Fen, you're welcome to join them if you'd like. I'll take care of the dishes."

"They can go ahead," he replied. "I'll help you clean up."

Allie and Josh headed for the living room, leaving Selene and Fen alone in the kitchen. The room suddenly felt much smaller and charged with electric tension. Selene's dreamy contentment devolved into sparks of nerve.

She went to the sink and filled it with hot water and dish soap.

"If you give me a towel, I'll dry." Fen came to stand beside her.

She pulled a dish towel from a drawer and handed it to him.

"When was the last time you did dishes?" she asked, a smile tugging at the corners of her mouth. A wolf king in the kitchen faced with a stack of dirty dishes after being served dinner. How often did that happen?

He paused and then laughed when she passed him a wet plate. "I honestly can't remember."

"I thought that might be the case," she said with a quiet laugh.

For a minute or two, they focused on the dishes without speaking.

It was Fen who broke the silence. "Selene, I want to apologize for my behavior last night."

"You don't have to." She scrubbed a plate more vigorously than necessary and kept her gaze firmly on the sudsy water. "I'm sorry I left so abruptly. I was very rude."

"No, you weren't," he said. "The fault is solely mine. I haven't . . ."

He fell silent. She stopped washing and looked over to find him wearing a sheepish grin.

"You haven't what?" she asked, puzzled by his expression.

"I haven't wanted to pursue a relationship for many years. And I've never attempted to court a human."

Court? Selene bit back a laugh. There were those werewolf formalities again. In truth she found the whole notion of courtship rather sweet.

"Last night I responded to my attraction as I would had you been another wolf, and I worry that I intimidated you." His eyes were gentle, and she had to look back at the bubbles in the sink. "That troubles me."

"You did a little," Selene admitted. "But I know you didn't mean to."

"Will you accept my apology?"

"Of course." She kept her focus on the dishes.

"And an invitation to dinner at Ciel on a night of your choice?"

"You'd take me out to dinner to watch me eat?" She shook her head at the idea but couldn't deny the thrill of his offer. Ciel was the only fine-dining restaurant in Avondale.

"I would enjoy the conversation and your company," he said. "And Ciel serves an exceptional beef carpaccio and lamb tartare. You wouldn't be eating alone."

She turned to face him. "Fen, I'm deeply flattered by your interest. And I don't want you to take this the wrong way. I'm not sure if it's a good idea."

"Dinner at Ciel?" He played innocent.

"You know that's not what I mean."

He watched her closely. "And why is what you mean a bad idea?"

She began to dry her hands. "Josh told me about your mate. I'm so sorry. I don't think I've ever heard a more horrific story."

His expression hardened, and he looked away. "Losing Miriam and our other packmates is the worst thing that's ever happened to me. And I've seen many terrible things in my time in this world."

Her name was Miriam. Selene wanted to know so much more about Fen's mate. *What did she look like? Where was she from? Why did he fall in love with her?*

His gaze returned to Selene, and his irises flickered with warmth. "But loss isn't the end of life. Simply part of it."

Setting her towel aside, she placed her hand on his wrist. Even that light touch sent a current up her arm and through her body. She looked at the place her fingers rested on his skin, willing herself to understand why she felt such a connection to him.

"Are you afraid of me?" Fen asked. "Or of what might happen between us?"

She could feel her pulse thudding as she lifted her eyes to meet his. "I'm afraid you'll break my heart."

Her confession seemed to put him at ease, which surprised her.

"Because of Miriam?" His eyes searched hers.

Rather than answering the question directly, she asked, "How long were you together?"

"A little over a century," he answered, not breaking her gaze.

"A century—" Her throat closed, but it wasn't fear or jealousy that stopped her words. It was the fist that tightened around her heart. "Oh, Fen."

Without thinking, she reached up with her other hand and cupped his cheek in her palm.

"I won't deny that I loved Miriam," Fen told her, leaning into her touch. "But it's important to me that you grasp the nature of our relationship. When you are with someone for that long, they become a part of you. Our connection was a gift, and I don't regret it, despite the pain of losing her. However, we became mates not because we fell in love, but because we met at a time when we were each leading a pack of our own. Joining the two packs made us stronger in a time when separately we were vulnerable to our enemies. That initial partnership was built on friendship and respect, and over the years love did grow between us. But it was love sustained by trust and affection, not passion. Do you understand?"

Selene withdrew her hand and nodded.

"If I promised to never cause you heartache, it would be a lie," he continued. "Because opening yourself to another is the greatest kind of risk, and I cannot predict the future. Nor can you. But I want to take that risk by sharing this truth with you: I want you as I have never wanted another. I am drawn to you in ways I can barely describe."

She didn't speak . . . because what was there to say to something like that? No one had ever uttered words that reached inside her and unlocked the door to her soul. It left her shaken, needy. Overwhelmed but captivated.

His confession frightened her but also reassured her. Fenris didn't see her as a replacement for someone he lost. And his attraction to her unnerved him in a way that mirrored her inexplicably primal response to him. That someone as powerful as Fen was willing to reveal his vulnerability made him even more alluring.

"Let me into your life, Selene." He turned his hand over and clasped her forearm. His fingers stroked her skin. Selene's breath became quick, shallow.

She desperately wanted him to kiss her. But Fen remained stone still, and after a minute she found herself stepping toward him. When his lips curved in a slow smile, ribbons of heat snaked over her hips, between her thighs. That heat became a throbbing ache as his other hand slid around her waist.

He bent his face toward her. Her free hand came up and touched his jaw, and her thumb traced the shape of his lips.

"Do you want me to kiss you?" He caught the tip of her thumb between his teeth, making her gasp.

"I would think that was obvious," she said, and he laughed at the echo of his own words from the previous night. A low rumble of mirth that she felt all the way to her toes.

"Ask me."

"What?" Selene frowned at him.

"Ask me to kiss you," he said.

"Why?" Frustration made her wriggle against him.

He held her fast, his gaze intent. "Because I won't take anything from you that you aren't ready to give."

Oh.

Her muscles turned to liquid, and he had to steady her to keep her from falling. "Fen, I need you to kiss me. Please kiss me."

Instead of bending his face to hers, Fen lifted her up, setting her on the kitchen counter. He stepped between her legs and tugged her forward until her hips were flush against his, and when she encountered the undeniable evidence that he wanted her, she whimpered.

"Yes, Selene." Fen brought his mouth to hers in a light caress. "Feel how hard you make me. Know how much I crave you."

His hand slid into her hair, pulling the comb free so waves of auburn tumbled over her shoulders. He wrapped a thick handful of strands around his fist and tugged, tipping her face up. Then he nipped her lower lip, chased the bite of pain with a soothing brush of his tongue, then took her mouth. There was no gentleness in this kiss. Only hunger and heat. His claim.

Selene clung to him. Her nails dug into his shoulders when his tongue stroked hers. He tasted rich and wild. Every breath she drew carried his scent of rain-soaked woods. Wrapped up in him, she felt like she'd stepped into another plane of existence. One made entirely of sensation.

Instinctively, her legs wound around his waist. She was already pressed tight to him, but she needed to be closer. To feel more of him. When her ankles locked at the small of his back, Fen growled and rolled his hips. The thick, rigid length of his cock rubbed against her sensitive core, an illicit connection that made her shiver.

Nothing in her life had ever felt so good. The exquisite ache left her wanting, needing. He rocked into her again. Her body quaked. An unmistakable tension coiled within her, molten and insistent. She almost couldn't believe it was happening—that he could manifest such an erotic torment when she was fully clothed. But there was no denying how quickly and easily he had her riding a knife's edge of pleasure. And he knew it. Every purposeful shift of his powerful body, each seductive caress of his hands made that clear.

Fen broke their kiss to look into Selene's eyes. "I could make you come right now. But I think you'd rather I didn't, given the place and time."

There was no doubt Fen could bring her to climax on the next breath. She was that close. And god, she wanted it. She was desperate for it. She was ready to forget herself, forget the world. She was ready to beg. But he was right. Not the time, definitely not the place. The idea of what he could do, would do to her when not bound by propriety, tantalized and overwhelmed her.

Though her body screamed its frustration at her, Selene unhooked her ankles from his waist and pulled away. Her skin was still so hot, she wouldn't have been surprised to see steam coming off it. What Fen did to her . . . She'd never experienced anything so intense.

"I need to get you alone," Fen murmured, stroking her hair. "I'm dying to taste you."

His gaze was hooded, his irises fogged with lust. It made her less self-conscious about her wanton response to their very first kiss to see that he was similarly affected.

Smiling, she touched her swollen lips. "Isn't that what you've been doing?"

Selene thought she was teasing him, but Fen's returning smile stole her breath.

His palm curved around her thigh, gliding slowly up, pausing just before he reached the juncture between her legs. A place she still ached.

"I had something else in mind."

Her eyelids drifted shut as his thumb traced the crease of her hip and thigh. "Fenris."

The image he'd just planted in her mind had her on the edge all over again. She dragged in a trembling breath, holding on by a rapidly fraying thread. If he moved his hand to her core, she knew the slightest touch would make her come apart.

She felt his breath on her neck.

"Tell me when, Selene. Tell me when I can give you what we both need."

His teeth grazed her earlobe.

Whether it was the low rumble of his words, the promise they held, or that last, teasing nip of her sensitive skin, Selene didn't know, only that she had to turn her face into Fen's neck to muffle her cry as unspeakable pleasure stormed through her, lightning strikes of ecstasy streaking from her core, racing to the crown of her head and the tips of her toes.

Sensing what had happened, Fen pulled her tight against his body, holding her as the echoes of her orgasm shuddered through her limbs. He kissed her temple, the shell of her ear. His fingers traced the length of her spine in soothing strokes until, at last, her body stilled.

When she drew back to look at him, still reeling from the most intense physical experience of her life, he couldn't quite mask the mischief tugging his features into a self-satisfied smirk.

"I didn't intend for that to happen," Fen said.

Selene could tell he was sincere, and yet . . .

"You didn't? Because you look a little smug."

"Can you blame me?"

She laughed and shook her head. With her blood finally cooling, the reality of what just happened sank in.

"Fen." She looked at him. God, he was beautiful. And what he could make her body do with the slightest provocation was . . . well, there certainly was no precedent. "I don't know what to say."

"You don't have to say anything." He helped her down from the counter, then took her hand, bringing the tips of her fingers to his lips. "But I want to know when I can see you again. For a proper date . . . among other things."

And he can still make me blush.

"I might need you to stop talking." Selene snatched her hand away even as she smiled shyly.

When he grinned at her, he'd never looked more wolfish.

And she liked it.

The doorbell rang.

"Are you expecting someone?" Fen asked. His nostrils flared, and his eyes narrowed.

"No, I'm not," she replied, frowning. "Please excuse me."

The doorbell rang again.

"Aunt Selene! Someone's at the door." Allie shouted from the living room.

"I've got it, Allie," Selene called back.

She opened the front door, gasped, and slammed it shut again. Insistent knocking began immediately.

Selene sucked in a steadying breath and opened the door a foot, positioning herself so she blocked the sight line into the house.

Daniel was laughing. "What the hell was that about?"

"What are you doing here?" Selene hissed.

"I'm here to talk." He leaned against the doorframe and grinned. "You said another time. It's another time."

"It's not a *good* time," Selene said. "If you want to talk, you need to schedule something with me. Please leave."

She glared at him, but he continued to smile. In the backyard his features had been obscured by shadow. Under the porch light his skin looked strange, washed-out and chalky. It suddenly occurred to her that Daniel might be sick, and it might be serious. Was that why he turned up after all this time? He was facing his own mortality and wanted to make amends?

"That excuse won't keep working, babe," he said.

The pinch of sympathy she'd felt a moment earlier vanished.

"Do not call me 'babe,'" Selene snapped. "And I'm serious about it being a bad time. We have dinner guests."

"Really? You have quite the lively social calendar these days." He straightened and smoothed the front of his shirt. "May I come in? I'd love to meet your friends."

"Don't be ridiculous."

"I'm not," he replied. "I'm serious about being back in Allie's life, and that means your life, too, Selene. Invite me in."

Her pulse gave a hard thud that felt like a warning. "No."

"Why not?" Daniel asked with a teasing smile. "Don't you think your friends will like me?"

The door suddenly swung open, and a pair of strong hands settled on Selene's shoulders. Though the pressure wasn't anywhere near painful, she had the sudden impression of being bolted to the floor.

"Probably not," Fen said quietly.

Daniel snarled. Selene's eyes widened because he had just *snarled.*

"You must be Daniel," Fen continued in a voice softer than death. "Do you know who I am?"

Cold fury blazed in Daniel's eyes. He nodded reluctantly.

"Then you'll understand my disappointment at seeing you here," Fen said.

"I don't think I like you touching Selene." Daniel glared at him, then shot a pleading look at her. "Listen, beautiful, you need to invite me in. Now."

"Do not *ever* invite him into your home, Selene." Fen's grip on her shoulders tightened. "Once extended, the invitation can't be revoked. He's too dangerous. And I won't always be here to protect you."

"What are you talking about?" Selene was a little relieved when she turned to look at Fen and he didn't attempt to hold her in place. "Fen, how does he know you?"

Fenris kept his eyes on Daniel.

"You no longer have a claim on this family or this household," Fen said. "You forfeited that right when you joined the forsaken."

"You may be some kind of dictator in Avondale," Daniel shot back. "But you have no right to keep a man from his child."

Fen's smile was brutal. "You are no longer a man."

"I'm more of a man than you are, dog," Daniel said, his lips curled back. Something glinted in the porch light. Long, sharp canines.

Selene gasped.

Daniel. Had. Fangs.

Oh my god. He's . . . he can't be . . . not that.

"Auntie Sel, what's going on?" Allie appeared from the living room with Josh right behind her. "Who's here?"

"Allie, wait!" But Selene was too late.

Allie's eyes fixed on the figure in the door. She frowned and then her eyes went wide.

"Daddy?" Her lower lip quivered. "Is that . . . is it really you?"

She spun to face Selene. "Auntie Sel. That's Daniel, isn't it? That's my dad."

Selene's heart tore slowly in half. "Allie, honey."

What do I do? I don't know what to do!

She heard a growl rumble in Fen's chest as Allie turned to look at Daniel again, her lip trembling. "Dad? You came back?"

Daniel grinned. "Hey, Alley-Cat. Look how you've grown up. I've missed you so much."

As his gaze focused on Allie, his eyes seemed to glow. "Come give me a hug."

His voice was oddly resonant, lingering in the air. And it was familiar. He'd spoken in a similar tone when Selene found him lurking in the backyard. Something about it was off.

Tears began to drip along Allie's cheeks, but she looked bewildered, almost dazed, and took a step toward the door.

"You go too far." Fen took two strides forward, and, with what looked like a casual sweep of his hand, he lifted Daniel off his feet. Daniel sailed in an arc from the porch, landing with a solid thud in the middle of the front yard.

Allie screamed.

"Josh, get her out of here!" Fen ordered.

Josh had Allie in his arms and up the stairs so swiftly, Selene barely saw it happen.

Fen was already out the front door. She rushed after him but stopped when she saw Daniel on his feet, brushing grass from his jeans.

How is he even conscious?

He glared at Fen. "I'll tear your throat out."

"Do you think you can threaten me, leech?" Fen laughed. "The only reason you're alive is that I don't kill members of Marie's coven without discussing the matter with her first. Consider yourself fortunate."

Selene cautiously approached them. Pale skin, glowing eyes, fangs, a coven. Truths crashed into one another, like domino after domino leading to a horrible conclusion: Daniel was a vampire. Allie's father hadn't died ten years ago. He'd joined the ranks of the undead. But how? And why?

Daniel's eyes found her. His teasing demeanor had vanished, and his stare was nothing but malicious. "You stupid bitch. You know what he is, and you're having dinner with him?"

Selene stumbled back as if she'd been slapped. Though she shouldn't have been so surprised by his abrupt change in demeanor. Here was the Daniel she remembered and loathed.

Fen's fist laid Daniel out on the lawn once more. "Do not ever speak to her that way."

Daniel licked blood from his lips and scrambled to his feet. He smiled, though his eyes were full of rage. The fangs were even sharper than when she'd first seen them. He hissed but backed away from Fen.

"Daniel, what happened to you?" she murmured.

"The greatest adventure you could imagine." He laughed and ran his tongue over his sharp teeth. "I'd love to tell you about it when you're not being held hostage by Cujo here."

"If you come near Selene or Allison again, you'll find yourself chained to a tree waiting for dawn," Fen said in a flat voice. "Marie will tell you the same thing."

"And what if Selene comes near me?" Daniel snapped. He turned to her. "Are you going to let him tell you how to live? Please, Selene, I'm sorry I got angry. This asshole is pissing me off. You need to hear me out. For Allie's sake. For Emma's."

When he spoke Emma's name, Selene flinched. Her hand pressed to her sternum, which suddenly burned with grief.

Fen looked at Selene, and for a moment his eyes flickered with uncertainty. He remained silent. She searched his face and then looked at Daniel's hate-filled glare. Stepping closer to Fenris, she folded her arms across her chest.

"I owe you nothing, Daniel," she said with more confidence than she felt. "Stay away from us."

Daniel offered her a half-cocked smile. "You don't mean that. You and I . . . there's always been something there."

He continued to address Selene, but it was Fen he smirked at. "Don't try to deny it."

Selene dropped her gaze to the lawn because the ground suddenly felt like it was tilting beneath her feet. When she lifted her eyes again, Daniel had vanished.

12

"Selene! Selene! Are you all right?" Tim bolted across his front lawn toward her. Marley was just behind him, wings fluttering while he hefted a pail with water sloshing over the edges.

The panicked pair stopped just short of them.

Marley hovered a few feet off the ground, holding the bucket aloft, as his eyes flashed around the lawn. "Where did the bloodsucker go? Where is he?"

"He's gone," Fen said. "I doubt he'll be back tonight."

The moment he spoke, Tim and Marley both froze. They exchanged a glance and simultaneously inclined their heads to Fen.

"Fenris," Marley murmured as he landed and slowly lowered the bucket. "We heard the commotion and wanted to help."

"We didn't mean to imply that you couldn't handle the situation," Tim added and edged closer to Marley.

"It's fine. I'm glad to know that Selene has such vigilant friends nearby." Fen smiled, and they both relaxed visibly.

"Why do you have that bucket?" Selene pointed at the tin pail.

"Holy water," Tim said wryly. "We keep a big plastic tub of it on hand. But it was in the backyard shed; that's why it took us so long."

Fen's laugh was so much like a roar that Selene jumped away from him.

"I'm sorry you didn't get here sooner." He grinned. "I would have liked to have seen that fool doused."

"We'll keep it close to the front door from now on." Marley smiled sheepishly.

"Let's hope you never have call to use it." Fen's amusement faded. "There will be hell to pay if he fails to heed my warning."

Tim's gaze had fixed on Selene, who had begun to sway on her feet. "Uh oh. Selene, are you breathing, honey?"

"Are you going to faint again?" Marley peered at her.

She managed to shake her head, but the lawn still felt like it was rocking beneath her.

Daniel Brix is a vampire. They were going to throw holy water on him. Because he is a vampire.

"I should get her inside," Fen said and put a supporting arm around her waist. "She's had a bit of a shock."

"Who was the vamp?" Marley frowned. "Why would any of them come after Selene?"

"Allie's father," Selene said. "He's . . . a vampire." Even as she said it, she stumbled, and Fen pulled her against him.

"You'll be all right, Selene," he said quietly. "We'll talk inside."

"Daniel?" Marley gasped. "Allie's father came to Avondale?"

Selene nodded. The ground lurched again, and she vomited on Fen's shoes.

"Oh dear," Tim said. "I see you had sushi for dinner."

"Do you want this water, Fen?" Marley offered the pail.

Fen shook his head. "I'll leave my shoes on the porch and clean them off later."

He lifted Selene into his arms. "I do appreciate you watching out for her. Good night."

Marley's and Tim's eyes were owlish as they watched Fenris carry Selene back to the house.

Fen brought her inside, and she squirmed in his hold. "Put me down. I'm fine now."

"I don't—"

"Put me down, Fenris."

He didn't argue again, setting her gently on her feet.

"I need to brush my teeth," she said, not looking at him. The sour taste was overwhelming, and not just because of the sushi.

"I'll be waiting in the kitchen."

She nodded and went to the powder room, locking the door behind her. It wasn't that she expected Fen to try to follow her, but she needed to feel secure. Even the tiniest bit helped.

Selene turned on the basin tap and rinsed her mouth out several times, then splashed cold water on her face. Too many feelings slammed around inside her: shock, confusion, embarrassment, fear.

Her first encounter with a vampire—and it had been Daniel Brix.

I was alone with him last night. Bile tried to rise in her throat again.

Natalie's words slid into her mind. *"Forcing someone to drink their blood isn't too much of a challenge."*

If he'd attacked her . . . But he hadn't. That wasn't what Daniel wanted, was it? To turn her into a vampire? To turn Allie?

He hadn't explained why he was here. A long story. That was his excuse yesterday. Is that why he came to the door tonight? To tell Allie and Selene his story? Or was it all a lie? A way to get in.

"Do not ever invite him into your home, Selene."

Fen. Fen knew who Daniel was. What else did he know? And why the hell didn't he say anything? Daniel was dangerous. He'd become hostile the moment he realized Selene wasn't going to give him what he wanted. Fen not only witnessed Daniel's aggression, he'd anticipated it and had answered in kind. Yes, Fenris had protected her and Allie, but on his terms. She resented that he'd kept so much vital information to himself when he'd had opportunities to tell her the truth about Daniel. Hell, he could have even hinted at it.

Selene dried off her face and went to the kitchen.

"What can I make for you?" Fen asked, pulling out a chair for her. "Tea? Unless you'd prefer something stronger."

"No, thank you," she said in a flat tone as she sat. "But there's ginger ale in the fridge."

Fen frowned but found the ginger ale and brought it to her.

"I should talk to Allie," Selene said to herself as she opened the can.

"Yes," he said. "But you and I should have a conversation first."

Selene took a sip of ginger ale as she ran over what had happened since the doorbell rang, coming to the same conclusion she'd arrived at when clearing her head in the bathroom. Fenris had kept silent when he should have done the opposite. She needed to understand his reasoning and determine whether she could live with it. She sat up straighter and looked at Fen with narrowed eyes.

"You're right." Her voice was sharp. "We should."

Her tone made his eyebrows shoot up.

"You knew Allie's father was a vampire." Her rising anger made the dizziness subside a little.

"I did," he replied calmly.

"And you knew he was living in Avondale."

"He only recently arrived in Avondale," Fen said. "No more than two weeks ago."

"Two weeks?" Her eyes widened. "When were you going to tell me about this?"

How could he have kept that from her? What if Daniel had gone to Allie first?

"I'd hoped I would never have to tell you," he answered in the same matter-of-fact tone.

She stared at him, incredulous.

"Selene." He sat in the chair next to hers. "Daniel has caused Allie pain in the past and would only cause you both more pain in the future. I thought it would be better if you never encountered him again."

"That wasn't your decision to make," she said quietly but firmly. Inside her mind, things were far less peaceful. She knew she'd come to pretty much the same conclusion when she'd decided not to tell Allie that Daniel had returned. But while Allie might be on the cusp of adulthood, she was still a child. If Fenris saw Selene in the same way, it was condescending and insulting.

Is it because I'm human? Does he think I'm unable to make wise choices when it comes to the paranormal? If that's true, he doesn't respect me or my responsibility to Allison. Not in the way I need him to, especially if we're . . .

She cut off that painful line of thought. It was hard to believe that a short time ago, in this very kitchen, she'd shattered with pleasure in Fen's arms. Now she was kicking herself for her naivety. She was foolish to trust him, much less let him get so close. He was hot. Okay, exceptionally hot. It didn't matter. She knew better than to act on impulse. Look where it left her. How she'd endangered Allie.

I've been so irresponsible. Her eyes burned. *I will not cry. I refuse to cry.*

As Fen watched emotions roll over Selene's face, his gaze hardened.

"It wasn't my intention to manipulate you, Selene," he said. "The regulation of paranormals moving in and out of Avondale remains in my control. Daniel became subject to me the moment he entered this town. His interest in you and Allie complicated matters somewhat, but not extraordinarily."

Not extraordinarily. Selene wrapped her hands around the can of ginger ale and tried to gather her thoughts.

"Marie came to me and expressed concern about Daniel's intentions toward you and Allie," he continued.

"Who is Marie?" she interrupted.

"Marie is the leader of Avondale's vampire coven," he said. "Any vampire who chooses to make their home here answers to Marie. And Marie answers to me."

She frowned. "What did she say about Daniel's intentions?"

Fen looked uncomfortable. Selene leaned forward.

"What?"

"Whether he's been entirely truthful to Marie is uncertain, but he claims he returned to Los Angeles looking for Emma and Allie," he said. "He'd been traveling abroad prior to a few months ago. When he discovered Emma was dead and Allie was living in Avondale, he followed."

"Why?"

"Immortality seems very glamorous at first," he replied after a small hesitation. "But an eternity of solitude is more punishment than reward. It seems likely Daniel seeks to reclaim that which he discarded all those years ago."

She stared at him and then drew a sharp breath.

"Are you saying he came to Avondale to make Allie a vampire?"

"I believe so." His voice was low. "But I can't be certain."

"Will he do that?" she whispered, suddenly cold and as shaky as she'd been in the front yard.

"Not without permission, from both Marie and me," he replied. "And I would never permit such a thing to pass."

She cleared her throat. "All right—but as a hypothetical. What if it were something Allie wanted?"

He looked at her sharply, and she held up her hand. "Hypothetical, Fen. Daniel is her father."

His jaw tightened. "You believe Allie would consider a life where she never felt the sun again?"

"No. Of course not." She shuddered. "But I need you to answer the question."

He offered her a razor-thin smile. "The turning of a mortal to either vampire or werewolf can happen . . . if it truly is voluntary and for the right reasons."

"What are the right reasons?"

"Love would qualify." He answered quietly as he watched her. "Fear of death would not."

She shifted uneasily under his scrutiny. "I really should talk with Allie now."

"There's one more thing, Selene," Fen said.

"What?"

"Josh told me you're in possession of a weapon. An antique silver dagger that you purchased online." His tone was rougher than gravel.

Damn it, Josh. He'd broken his promise after all.

Selene swallowed, her voice becoming very small. "Yes."

"May I see it?"

Her mouth went dry, and her pulse tripped. "You want to see it?"

He nodded. Selene rose and went to find her purse. She'd tried to give it back to Natalie, but her new friend insisted that it was better to risk having it than be without defense. After learning about Natalie's secret work, Selene decided to keep the dagger. The fact that Daniel was a vampire gave her even more reason to hang on to it. She drew the gleaming blade out and carried it back into the kitchen.

Fen rose as he watched her approach. She extended the dagger toward him. His eyes moved slowly over the weapon, but his face registered no reaction.

"You can take it," she said shakily. "I'll wrap it up in something so it won't burn you."

"There's no need," he said. "It belongs to you."

His gaze returned to her face. "You understand why such a weapon is offensive to my pack, to me?"

"Of course," she said. "I'm so sorry. I didn't mean—"

He smiled gently. "I'm glad to know you wouldn't hesitate to defend yourself and your family when endangered. Josh told me why you brought out the dagger in the first place. His decision to frighten Allie with his own transformation was foolish. You must have been terrified."

"I was."

He glanced at the dagger once more. "I'll leave you to your conversation with your niece. Send Josh down. I'll take him back to the mansion."

"Okay." She set the dagger on the kitchen table.

Fen followed her to the bottom of the stairs. She took two steps.

"Selene, wait."

She turned to face him.

"What Daniel said on the lawn." Fen's jaw clenched. "Was it true?"

His expression was guarded, and Selene didn't understand why. "Was what true? I don't know what you're asking."

"He said you've always had a connection." He ground his teeth as he spoke. "Were you involved with him at some point?"

"Never." If not for the strain etched on Fen's face, Selene would have laughed. "He made a pass at me once, but if a stop sign had breasts, Daniel would try to get it into bed."

She'd obviously shocked Fen. He stared at her, lips parting as if to offer a retort. Then he shook his head. "I'm sorry I asked. It was petty of me."

Selene looked at him for several heartbeats. The pull was still there. She wanted to go to him. To ask him to hold her. If only it were that easy.

"It's nice that you care, Fenris," she said finally.

He looked up, frowning. "Of course I care. Selene, I—"

When he moved toward the staircase, she backed up a step. He froze.

"It's too much, Fen." She had to force the words out. "Whatever this is . . . What I feel for you. I'm not ready. There's so much about your world I don't understand."

Since the night she arrived in Avondale, Selene had been caught up in a whirlwind of life-changing revelations and heart-stopping emotions. Her mind was under siege, battling for rational responses to unbelievable scenarios. She'd already made so many mistakes. Revealing the dagger. Blundering through her encounters with Daniel, which in hindsight had offered glaring signs of what he'd become. And she'd missed it. What else was she missing because she was distracted by her own desires? There was no way her selfishness wasn't putting Allie at risk. She couldn't go on like this.

Fen turned his face away. When he looked at her again, his expression was unreadable. "If that's what you want."

All she could do was nod because her heart and body were shrieking at her to throw herself into his arms. To beg for him to touch her again. To confess to him that every time he was close, she felt more alive, more powerful.

A part of her wished he would argue or kiss her until she wanted him too much to push him away. But he watched her silently until she turned around and continued to climb the stairs.

Selene knocked on Allie's door. It opened a crack, and Josh's face peered out.

"Josh, Fen is waiting downstairs to take you home," she said.

"Aunt Selene?" Allie called from within the room. "Auntie Sel, is that you?"

Josh stepped aside and let the door open. Allie flew off the bed and into Selene's arms.

"Oh my god," Allie sobbed and clung to her. "What happened? Are you okay?"

"I'm fine, sweetheart." Selene hugged her niece and stroked her hair.

Allie lifted her face and glared at Josh. "He wouldn't let me out of the room."

"I had to keep you safe," Josh argued.

"Go away," Allie snapped and turned her back on him.

Josh threw a pleading glance at Selene.

"Allison, Josh meant well," Selene said, deciding he deserved a break. "Fen ordered him to take you upstairs. He didn't have a choice. And I wanted you to be safe too. It was the right thing for Josh to do at the time."

"Thanks, Ms. Jones." He smiled weakly and looked at Allie. "Please don't be mad."

Allie peeked out at him from where she'd buried her face against Selene's neck.

"Please." He fluttered his very long eyelashes, and Allie sighed.

"I was just worried about Aunt Sel."

His smile broadened. "I know. It's okay."

"I'll see you in school tomorrow," Allie told him.

"Sure," he said. "Thanks for dinner, Ms. Jones. The fish was really good."

"Good night, Josh," Selene said. He bobbed his head, eyes lingering on Allie before he left the room, and a moment later she heard his footfalls on the stairs and the front door close.

"Do you want to come downstairs to talk?" Selene looked at her niece's tear-streaked face.

"Let's just talk here," Allie said. She went back to her bed and pulled a pillow into her arms. Selene sat beside her.

"What happened after Josh brought me up here?" Allie asked.

"Fen told Daniel to stay away from us," Selene said. "They argued, but Daniel eventually left."

"Did you know he was in Avondale?" Allie asked in a quiet voice.

"He was here last night," Selene said. "It was late. After we got back from dinner. That was the first time I'd seen him since he disappeared. I didn't even know he was alive, Allie. Seeing him was a complete shock."

Allie was silent.

"I'm sorry I didn't tell you, Allison," Selene continued. "I wanted to know more about why he was here before I talked to you about it. It was horrible that you had to find out when he showed up at the house tonight. That's my fault."

"Did you know he was a vampire?" Allie asked.

"No." Selene shivered.

"I get why you didn't tell me right away." Allie traced shapes on the quilt with her fingertip. "I thought I'd hate him. And I always imagined that if he showed up, I might not even recognize him. But when I saw him, it was like he'd never left. He was just my dad."

She sounded ashamed.

"It's okay, Allie." Selene put her arm about the girl. "You loved your dad, and he loved you."

Daniel's version of love was showering Allie with gifts and affection whenever he was around, and Allie had only been six when he disappeared. Far too young to understand the heartache he caused her mother. When Allie talked about Daniel, Selene detected a yearning in the girl's voice. She wanted Daniel to be a good person. A father she could admire.

Goddamn him.

"Josh said we can't trust him," Allie said. "He said vampires are really manipulative and dangerous."

Great. Daniel was manipulative before *he was a vampire.*

"I don't know any vampires," Selene said. "So I don't know what to say about that. Except that Fen also thinks Daniel is dangerous to us."

"I don't know whether to believe Josh," Allie continued. "He might just be racist."

"Racist?"

"Werewolves hate vampires," Allie said. "Maybe racist isn't the right word. Speciesist? But he has a bias for sure. Fen would have it too."

Selene frowned. "Allie, do you want to see Daniel? Even though he's a vampire?"

She despised that idea, but now that Allie knew Daniel was in Avondale, she felt she had to ask. And if Allie wanted to talk to Daniel, Selene would be with her niece every step of the way. With lots of crosses and holy water. Just in case. She made a mental note to stop by Tim and Marley's house to fill a water bottle or two from their supply.

Maybe picking up a few of those Super Soaker water guns would be a good idea.

Allie looked away. "I don't know. Do I have to know right now?"

"Of course not," Selene said. "But no matter what you feel, please be careful."

"What do you mean?"

"Even if Fen and Josh are biased against vampires, I think we should take their warning to heart," Selene said. "Please don't go out alone after dark until we know more about this."

"Okay," Allie said, then after a moment she tilted her head. "Did anything happen with Fen tonight? Are you guys dating?"

Selene ignored the knife in her heart. “I’m going to shelve that idea for a little while. I like Fen, but life just got a lot more complicated. Distractions seem like a bad idea. And dating is a huge distraction.”

Allie nodded. “Tell me about it.”

Laughing, Selene wrapped her niece in a hug.

◆ ◆ ◆

Fenris turned the car up the narrow lane at the edge of town, pausing to allow the iron gates of his estate to slide open.

“Do you expect the vampire to heed your warning?” Josh asked.

Fen kept his eyes on the road. “No. He is arrogant . . . and reckless. He won’t back down.”

“Then you’ll kill him?”

“Yes,” Fen replied. “But Marie deserves the chance to bring him in line. She’s led the Avondale coven for nearly a century. It’s important that these events occur in the proper order, lest it be seen as personal. And who knows, she may be able to sway him.”

“If you say so.” Josh shrugged.

Fen laughed gruffly. “I could kill him outright, but it would be an unpleasant disruption among the paranormal factions when we’re accustomed to peace. Politics matter. Tyranny never breeds contentment.”

“What about the other issue?”

“That presents a problem.” Fen grimaced. “A very ugly problem.”

“It’s not an antique,” Josh said and watched Fen’s jaw clench.

“No,” Fen said. “It’s a new weapon. And the enchantment on the moonstones had been cast recently. I could sense the remnants of the spell even a few feet away.”

“So it came from someone in Avondale?”

“Yes.”

“What are you going to do?” Josh asked.

“What we always do when our laws are broken.”

13

"Bye, Aunt Sel," Allie called as she opened the front door. "I'll see you tonight."

"Have a good day at school!"

Selene carried her coffee cup from the kitchen into the living room and sat at the writing desk. She still had thank-you notes to finish up from the campaign, and while her next job didn't start for another three weeks, she hoped to have some organizational leg work finished before the contract began.

But she mostly wanted a distraction, and work had always been the best way to keep her mind occupied when she was upset.

And Selene was upset.

The worst part was that she didn't know what she was the most upset about. There were far too many problems competing for the number one slot on her anxiety list:

Her niece was still dating a werewolf.

For her own part, Selene was far more interested than she wanted to admit in dating yet *another* werewolf.

Her new, yet closest, friend was trafficking illegal paranormal weapons in and out of Avondale.

Allie's presumed-dead father had reappeared and was now a vampire.

Since she had no immediate solution for any of her problems, Selene decided to focus on things she excelled at instead. Unfortunately her new life with paranormals seemed to intrude no matter what she was doing.

This morning that intrusion was the card she'd left on the desk when Fen had arrived for dinner the previous evening. In the chaos of Daniel's appearance and the fight on the lawn, Selene had forgotten that Fenris even handed her the envelope.

She picked up the card and turned it over in her hand. Her name appeared in fine calligraphy, dark ink against the creamy linen fibers. She broke the wax seal and pulled out the card. As she quickly read its contents, her brow knit.

She'd been expecting some kind of personal note from Fen and was embarrassed by how quickly her heart had been beating as she anticipated what it might say, after she'd effectively ended their involvement last night. She suspected if Fen had written anything remotely romantic, she'd fall for him all over again.

But it wasn't a letter from Fen. It was a formally engraved invitation to an event she'd never heard of.

Selene frowned and read the card again.

Mr. Fenris Hall Requests the Honor of Your Presence
at the Annual Beltane Rite
Saturday, the Thirtieth of April
at Sunset
The Sacred Grove
Crescent Moon Valley Park
No RSVP Required

Selene picked her phone up from the desk.

"I know I woke you up, sorry. I'm your super-annoying new friend," she said. "I have a question . . . Yeah, it's about paranormal stuff. How would you feel about breakfast at Midnight Broil?"

She waited a moment. "What if I told you Daniel showed up again last night? It turns out he's a vampire."

Selene had to hold the phone away from her ear at the sudden screech.

When she deemed it safe, she continued, "So I'll see you in twenty minutes?"

◆ ◆ ◆

"Sorry again for waking you up this morning," Selene said.

They were tucked into one of the booths at Midnight Broil because, once again, Selene was desperate for Natalie to help make sense of her very messy, magic-infested life. She knew infestation wasn't a fair description, but right now it felt apt.

Natalie had shadows under her eyes. "Don't worry about it. You should have called last night."

"I think I was in too much shock last night to talk about it."

"What can I get for you ladies?" Their waitress appeared with two cups of coffee and set them on the table.

"Egg-white veggie omelet," Selene said and handed her the menu.

"I'll have blueberry pancakes," Natalie said.

The waitress nodded and left.

Selene glanced around the restaurant, a little worried about having their conversation overheard, but only a few tables were occupied. It was late enough to have missed the breakfast rush but too early for the lunch crowd. Some solitary diners using the café as a workspace clacked away at their laptops. A young couple huddled in a shadowed corner of the restaurant. They looked hungover, slumped in their chairs, sipping Bloody Marys. The man's face was covered by a hooded sweatshirt, and they seemed much more interested in each other than the food that sat untouched on their plates. A group of senior citizens were the closest to Natalie and Selene, and they were still two tables away.

Natalie was shaking her head. "I can't believe Allie's father is a vamp."

"Neither can I," Selene said.

She nodded, then pressed the heels of her hands into her eyes. She was simultaneously exhausted from lack of sleep yet still wound up so tight that getting a nap in was out of the question.

"So what happened?" Natalie asked.

"Fen wasn't happy that Daniel was there," Selene said. "He knew Daniel was in town and a vampire. Daniel wasn't supposed to bother us."

Natalie shrugged. "That's not a surprise. If Fen's interested in you, there is no way he'd let any vamp near you. Particularly one that has a personal history in your life. He's probably worried Daniel might try to turn you."

"Yes," Selene replied quietly. "That's what Fen said."

"Who knows if that's the case." Natalie sipped her coffee, then continued. "Daniel would have to jump through a lot of hoops to get permission to change two humans. It doesn't matter who they were in his past. In Avondale, changing humans to paranormals is taken very seriously. The transformation must be voluntary and be approved by the bigwigs. Daniel has to know that. Everyone here knows that."

Selene frowned. "So is it just bias then?"

"What?"

"Fen said Daniel is a danger to us. Josh told Allie the same thing. But is that true? Or is it a werewolf-versus-vampire, jealousy thing? They just don't want Daniel around us?"

"It might be partly jealousy," Natalie said. "But I wouldn't say Daniel is safe under any circumstances. He's still a vampire."

"Why does that make him more dangerous than Fen or Josh?" Selene asked.

Watching Fen toss Daniel, who was not a small man, halfway across her yard served as a sharp reminder that werewolves were unbelievably strong.

"Vampires are less predictable than the werewolves," Natalie replied. "They aren't as social. Wolves live in packs. They always answer to a pack leader, and the leader is usually old, wise, well liked, and interested in keeping peace with the human world."

"But don't vampires live in covens?"

"Vampires live in covens by choice if they decide they want to try to fit into society," Natalie said. "But many prefer to lead a solitary existence. They don't like the restrictions that are imposed by covens."

"Like what?"

"Not preying on humans."

Selene didn't respond, and Natalie sighed.

"I'm sorry, Selene," she said. "Werewolves may eat raw meat, but they don't need human flesh. They're just as happy feasting on wild game. Or cows, for that matter. They can curb their predatory instincts. Vampires *need* human blood. They always crave it, and that makes them a danger to any humans they're near."

Selene nodded and glanced at the water bottle she'd filled at Tim and Marley's before coming into town. She probably didn't need to carry it with her during the day, but its presence was reassuring after a very rough night.

"Vampires aren't all bad. The local coven leader, Marie, is an interesting woman. I've always liked her." Natalie looked apologetic. "And maybe Daniel will turn out to be one of the more trustworthy vamps out there."

"He doesn't have a great track record when it comes to trustworthiness," Selene muttered.

"Yeah, I thought that might be the case." Natalie reached across the table to pat Selene's hand. "I'm sorry."

Selene let out a long sigh. "I guess I'll take Fen's warning to heart then."

"That's probably wise," Natalie agreed. "I have to say, Daniel is either brave as hell or crazy. No one challenges Fen."

"I'm starting to notice that. One other thing." Selene lowered her voice. "Can you get another silver cross? I'd like Allie to have one."

She didn't think Allie would try to seek Daniel out on her own, but if some impulse to meet up with her father took root, Selene wanted to be sure Allie had something to defend herself on hand. Though it might take some convincing to get Allie to carry around anything silver that would burn Josh.

"Of course," Natalie said. "Just send her by the salon this week."

Their waitress reappeared with plates of food. "Egg-white omelet and blueberry pancakes."

"Thanks, Amy." Natalie smiled and reached for a fork.

"Anything else I can get you?"

"I think we're fine," Selene replied as she shook pepper onto her eggs.

Amy left, and Selene glanced at Natalie. "You know the waitress?"

"She's a client," Natalie said simply.

Selene watched the waitress disappear into the kitchen. A client for which business? Was that young woman hiding out from some monster? Or did she simply have a cute haircut courtesy of Nat?

"Something else is bothering you." Natalie speared her pancake with a fork. "Besides Daniel."

"I told Fenris I can't get involved with him," Selene told her.

"How did he take that?" Natalie asked.

"He took it fine," Selene replied, grimacing. "I think."

Natalie took another bite of pancake, regarding Selene with interest.

"Why are you looking at me like that?" Selene asked.

"You didn't like it," Natalie said.

Selene tore her omelet apart with her fork, pushing the pieces around her plate. It was hard to have an appetite when she was so tense. "Didn't like what?"

"That he took it fine."

Shoveling in a heaping forkful of egg so she didn't have to reply immediately, Selene considered lying, but she suspected Natalie would see right through her attempt to dodge.

"I should be happy he was respectful," Selene began, but her stoic facade crumbled. "But, Nat, we have this connection. I've never felt anything like it. It was really hard for me to break things off with him . . . and they hadn't even officially started. I thought he felt the same way, but then he just accepted what I said. Not a single protest."

Natalie smirked. "Did you want him to throw you over his shoulder and take you back to his castle to have his way with you?"

"Of course not!" Selene dropped her fork. When Natalie continued to watch her silently, Selene confessed. "Okay, maybe a little."

"Just a little?" Natalie teased.

"Even if I do want that, it's not smart. Not with Daniel around, and I need to keep my eye on what's happening in Allie and Josh's situation," Selene said, stabbing more egg.

"But?"

"There's no 'but,'" Selene insisted.

Natalie took a long slug of coffee, then said, "Yes there is."

Selene chose to eat rather than reply, but she only got through a few more bites. She set down her fork and pushed her plate away.

Leaning forward and lowering her voice, she said, "He made me come on the kitchen counter."

Natalie spit out the sip of coffee she'd just taken. She swore and grabbed napkins to sop up the mess.

"Sorry." Natalie laughed. "But you should have waited until I swallowed."

Selene took her own napkin and wiped coffee from her face.

"I thought this was a family dinner," Natalie remarked.

"It was."

"Where were Josh and Allie when Fen was . . . taking care of you?" Natalie tried to stifle a giggle and failed.

"Watching TV in the living room," Selene said with chagrin.

Natalie gaped at her. "You got naked in the kitchen when Allie was in the next room?"

"I was not naked!" Selene blurted, then her cheeks flooded with heat. She glanced around the room, worried she'd raised her voice, but none of the other customers were looking in her direction.

"Then how . . ." Natalie's brow furrowed.

"That's the thing." The heat in Selene's cheeks seeped into other parts of her body at the memory of Fen's hands on her. His mouth. His voice. "We kissed. More than once. But he didn't touch me. No, I mean, he was touching me, but not the way I would usually need—"

That was as far as she could get without bursting into flames.

Fortunately, Natalie nodded. "I get the picture. And wow."

"It was very wow." Selene squirmed in her chair. "I didn't know there could be that much wow. But I can't keep seeing him. It's too risky."

Natalie signaled Amy for more coffee. When she arrived with the pot and a washcloth to finish cleaning up the table, Selene went quiet and Natalie did the same.

"You don't sound very convinced, Selene." Natalie spooned sugar into her new cup of coffee. "You still want him."

"It doesn't matter," Selene said quietly.

Natalie clucked her tongue. "Of course it matters. Yes, you're taking care of Allie. And yes, it sucks—no pun intended—that her jerk of a dad showed up and happens to be a vampire. But you still have a life, Selene. From what Emma said about you, I know you work way too hard. If you want Fenris, don't ignore that."

"What if he doesn't want me anymore?" The question flew out before Selene could stop it.

"I'm not following," Natalie said.

"He didn't argue with me." Selene let all her worries race after the first. "He didn't tell me that I was making a mistake. He walked away. It was easy for him to do."

Natalie shook her head. "You don't know that."

Selene stared into her coffee cup, having a pity party for one.

"You told him what you need," Natalie continued. "He *listened.* That's all that happened. If you change your mind, tell him. He'll listen again."

"But—"

"No buts this time," Natalie cut her off. "Fen doesn't roam around Avondale offering women orgasms as some kind of community outreach."

This time Selene almost spit out her coffee but managed to simply choke on it instead.

"The point is," Natalie continued, grinning, "he wants you. Only you. And I guarantee he's willing to wait. The man has been alive for centuries. He knows how to be patient. The question is, How long are you going to make him wait?"

Selene had to finish coughing before she could speak. "I don't know what to do about Fen, but he did give me this last night."

She pulled the invitation from her purse and pushed it across the table. Natalie's eyes narrowed for a moment and then an impish smile danced across her lips.

"My, my." She stirred her coffee. "That's an interesting move. I guess I don't have Fenris Hall figured out yet."

"What?" Selene frowned. "What's Beltane? I've never heard of it."

"It's a pagan holiday," Natalie replied. "Also called May Eve."

"A holiday that celebrates what?" Selene asked, taking another bite of her omelet. Only a little coffee had splashed her plate.

"A few different things. The arrival of summer—the bright side of the year, we call it. Honoring the goddess. There's a ritual, and . . ."

Natalie's voice trailed off, and she frowned.

"What's wrong?" Selene put her fork down.

"Are you planning to attend?"

"Maybe," Selene replied. "Will you be there?"

"Yes," Natalie said. "I have to help with the ritual."

"What does that involve?" The hairs on the back of her neck prickled at the word *ritual.*

"That's what I can't figure out about this invitation." Natalie's gaze grew distant.

Selene had to swallow the lump that formed in her throat. She didn't like the expression on her friend's face.

"What do you mean?"

Natalie took a long time to respond. She appeared to be weighing her answer, and that made Selene even more nervous.

"Fen will be involved in the ritual this year," Natalie finally said. "I wouldn't think he'd want you to see—"

She broke off and frowned.

"Oh my god." Selene swallowed a knot of dread. "It's not a sacrifice, is it? Is he going to kill something? Like a goat?"

Natalie looked stunned, then exploded into laughter. "No, no! Nothing like that. There's actually very little sacrificing that occurs in the magical world. At least not that I'm involved in—or Fenris, for that matter."

"Then why—"

"Never mind," Natalie said quickly. "You should come. It's a great party. Ask Tim and Marley about it. They'll be going for sure."

"Okay," Selene said, still wondering what had given Natalie such pause a moment ago. "Should I bring Allie?"

Natalie shook her head. "I don't think you'd want Allie there. It's not really an aunt-niece kind of event. Some stuff might be over her head."

"Thanks for the warning label." Selene smiled.

"No problem," Natalie said.

◆ ◆ ◆

Daniel Brix couldn't stand that he'd been reduced to spying, but he snuck another glance at Selene from across the restaurant.

"Ow!" He jerked his leg back when the tip of a steel-toed boot met his shin.

"Stop looking at them," Rowena snapped. "You know you can't go over there. Marie would rip your intestines out."

"I'm not going over there." Daniel rubbed his shin. "And I can look. She's not going to see my face." But he pulled the hood of the sweatshirt down further just in case.

"What are you going to do today anyway?" Rowena asked. "Sulk again?"

"Shut up."

"You're getting pretty good at it," she sniped.

"I'll just watch her." Pathetic. All this skulking around. It was beneath him.

"Watch her from where?" Rowena's ruby-lipped smile wasn't kind. "It's pure luck she showed up here. There aren't that many businesses that have underground doors and tinted windows for vamps who want to be out in the day."

"It's not pure luck," Daniel snapped. "I know the kinds of places Selene likes. I figured she would come here. She and Emma would always go out for breakfast when they were upset. Something about food helping them problem solve."

"Weird," Rowena muttered.

"Do you know the woman she's with?" Daniel's eyes traveled across the room again.

"Only by reputation," Rowena said. "That's Natalie Lyon. She's a witch."

"A witch?"

"And she owns a salon," Rowena continued. She lifted her fingers to toy with her long hair. "I've thought about getting an appointment, but she has a waiting list a mile long. Then there's the whole witch thing. I don't like witches."

Daniel agreed. Witches were bad news. Couldn't be trusted, and some of their spells were downright nasty. The only good thing about them was that they weren't hard to kill—as long as you caught them by surprise.

The waitress paused at their table. She looked like she wanted to laugh. "Is something wrong with your food?"

"No, everything is fine," Daniel said quickly.

The waitress shrugged and continued on.

"This is stupid." Rowena wrinkled her nose. "I can't believe I'm sitting here. The food is making me queasy."

"Just drink your blood," Daniel said.

"Why did we even order food?" Rowena asked. "It's not like the waitress doesn't know we're vamps. The owner is Fae. They serve blood. We're covered."

"We need to blend in," Daniel grumbled. "We have food so we look just like the other customers."

He pushed the eggs on his plate around with his knife. Rowena was right. They reeked.

"I don't know why I let you talk me into this." Rowena covered her plate with a napkin, then sucked on the straw in her glass.

Daniel snagged her hand. "I thought you were on my side."

Rowena jerked free, folding her arms across her chest. "I said I thought Marie should have stood up for you when Fenris came to the coven. The werewolves have a stranglehold on this town. Marie needs to grow a pair. She's a vampire. We don't bow down to other paranormals, and I think she's forgotten that. But I didn't say you should stalk your daughter and her guardian."

"What would you do if you were in my situation?" Daniel countered.

She laughed harshly. "I would forget the woman. When a werewolf pack leader chooses a mate, you don't get in the way. Not if you want to keep all your limbs."

"I'm not going to just stand by and let that dog paw someone I want."

"You're thinking with your dick instead of your brain," Rowena chided. "If Fen wasn't interested in Selene, would you even give her a second look?"

Daniel scoffed and snuck another glance at Selene. Rowena wasn't wrong. Not completely. His dick was definitely leading the charge toward Selene, but that wasn't a new thing. She was an itch he'd always wanted to scratch, but he'd never managed to talk her into a hookup. It bugged the hell out of him. Women didn't turn him down.

"Is it because you fucked up with your wife and you think Selene's a good replacement?" Rowena pressed. "I guess that makes sense. God knows you'll need someone to take care of the kid when you turn her. Teenage vampires are a nightmare. And that's saying something."

Daniel snarled at Rowena. "Never talk about Emma. I've told you that before, and I mean it."

He didn't need to be reminded that he fucked up with her.

"Whatever." Rowena rolled her eyes. "I'm right, though. You should find someone to play Mom. No way in hell it's gonna be me."

"I wasn't asking." He took a pull from his glass, forgoing the straw. The blood was lukewarm. Tolerable, but it left him longing for the hot flood of copper pumping against his tongue when he sank his fangs into someone. There was nothing better. Sex was a close second. Very close. At the moment he was still getting pussy on the regular, even if he was a little bored with his playmate. But it had been way too long since he'd sucked a person dry. The fucking rules of this town. And all because of some wolf blowhard.

Daniel couldn't wait to turn the tables on Fenris. The sweetest thing would be to make the werewolf watch while he drained and fucked Selene at the same time. That would be tricky to pull off, but man it would be incredible. A tranquilizer dart and silver chains. He could take down the wolf, restrain him with chains that would burn the motherfucker the whole time. Daniel would have to wear gloves when he was wrapping Fenris up, but that was a small inconvenience with a big payout. He got hard thinking about it and had to adjust the sudden bulge in his jeans.

"When I turned you, I told you what it would mean," Rowena said in a plaintive tone. "You seemed happy enough with the concept at the time."

"I don't regret the change." Daniel reverted his attention to her instantly. He needed Rowena to make this work. She watched his back and fed him information via Marie, who she was friends with from way back. "You know how much it means to me, Row. But Allie is my kid."

"We just came to town to see what was up," Rowena countered. "You only got possessive when you found out about the wolves."

"Would you want your daughter hooking up with a wolf?" Daniel snarled. "No way I'm letting that go on. And Fenris doesn't get happily ever after with Selene. Fuck that guy."

He couldn't stand that Allie was crushing on some furball. She was Daddy's little girl, always staring at him with those big eyes like he was a superhero every time he came home. He didn't remember a lot about that time in his life, but he remembered that, and it had rocked. Sure, she was more grown up now, but she could sure as hell show a little loyalty to her father.

Rowena shrugged. "I'm not saying I wouldn't be happy to mess with Fenris Hall. He's a pompous ass. And it's not like you're the first vamp to want the partner and rug rats for all eternity. Though the appeal is beyond me. Kids. Ugh."

She gave a little shudder.

"You wouldn't abandon me now, would you?" Daniel reached under the table to give her thigh a squeeze. "Not after all the good times we've had."

He had to be sure he was managing Rowena. She got whiny if she felt ignored.

"I brought you to Avondale, didn't I?" Rowena leaned toward him. She took his hand and dragged it farther up her leg. "And I stayed with you and joined this coven. I'm still not sure if I like it. I've always been a drifter. And why I'm hanging around when you want to throw me over for a couple of humans is beyond me."

"I'm not throwing you over, Row." He flashed a tantalizing smile at her as he lied. The truth was, he needed a change. Rowena had turned him, and he was grateful to her for showing him the ropes of being immortal and all that shit. But it bugged him that being so much older than him, she was stronger. He kept imagining the fear in Selene's eyes while he held her down. She'd fight him, he was sure of that. But in the end, she'd give it up and beg for more.

Yeah. Selene would be perfect for him. And Rowena was starting to get clingy. He'd given her a decade. What more did she expect?

Daniel scooted his chair closer so he could cup her pussy under the table. "You're my first and last, babe. And I promise we'll have fun with Selene. Sharing is caring, right?"

She laughed and blew him a kiss, squirming against his teasing fingers. "As long as we're clear, I'm not made for Stepford. I want the road life."

Daniel sat back, and she made a pouty lip that he ignored. "We can get out of here, get back on the road, as soon as I work out what's going to happen with Selene and Allie. It won't be much longer. I promise."

Rowena's eyes flashed. "If you manage to seduce that woman out of the wolf's arms, you'd better be ready to get out of town. You'd better be ready to run like hell."

14

"Please, Auntie Sel?" Allie made her puppy eyes even bigger. It was clear she'd been practicing the look.

"No."

"But—"

Selene shook her head. "There's no way. I'm barely convinced I should be there. If I didn't think it would be rude, I'd stay home with you."

"Yeah, right." Allie flopped back on the bed. "It's so unfair. Josh is going."

"Josh isn't my responsibility. You are." Selene knew she'd have little luck convincing Allie that she meant what she'd said: she had more than a few reservations about attending the Beltane celebration. Avondale's supernatural side was too unpredictable. Every time she thought she was beginning to understand the rules of her new world, another wild card turned up.

"But I'm his girlfriend, and this is a really important holiday," Allie whined. "One of the biggest pagan days of the year. He needs me there."

"Then why didn't you get an invitation?" Selene asked pointedly.

Allie slumped into a pile of pillows and looked out the window.

"Fenris told Josh I could only come if you said it was okay," she grumbled.

Selene smiled. "No wonder I like him."

Allie's begging gaze was back. "Please, please, please!"

"Allison." Selene sighed. "Natalie said this ritual isn't appropriate for you. Marley and Tim agreed. They all know you well. If they say it's not a good idea—and they know way more about this event than I do—then I'm not going against their advice."

If she were in Allie's position, she'd want to go to the pagan party, too, but until Selene understood what precisely it entailed, she wasn't comfortable bringing Allie.

"What am I supposed to do tomorrow night?" Allie asked. "All my friends will be at the Beltane rite."

"Don't you have any nonparanormal friends?" Selene asked.

"I stopped hanging out with the kids who aren't part of the paranormal scene when I started dating Josh." Allie pushed out her lower lip.

"That's a winning look." Selene scoffed. "I'm terribly convinced you're mature enough to attend this pagan holiday."

Allie startled, blushing. "You're not being fair."

"Neither are you for punishing me because I'm acting like your guardian instead of your buddy," Selene replied. "Now do you want to go shopping with me tonight or not?"

"I want to go to the movies with Josh tonight," Allie said, still sulking. "Since I *won't get to see him tomorrow.*"

"Okay," Selene quipped, refusing to be drawn in again. "I'll be home later. Have a good time with Josh."

"Bye." Allie flipped over on her bed so her back was to Selene.

◆ ◆ ◆

When Selene had embarked on her shopping expedition in downtown Avondale, she hadn't realized that finding an appropriate outfit for her first pagan ritual would be so involved. Selene turned over the tag on the blouse she'd picked out and scanned the list of materials. She sighed and put the blouse back on the rack. After seeking advice from her paranormal friends, she'd come away with specific parameters regarding what she should wear.

Natalie had pursed her lips and said, "I'd wear a skirt, something you can move easily in. There will be lots of dancing."

"Really?" Selene hadn't known what to expect, but dancing in the forest hadn't been on her list of possibilities. With everyone talking about how important the holiday was, she assumed it would be something more staid.

Natalie nodded. "And make sure you wear only natural fibers."

"Natural fibers?"

"Yeah. Cotton, wool, silk. Nothing synthetic."

Selene frowned. "What are you wearing?"

"I have to wear ritual clothing because I'm assisting in the ceremony," Natalie said, then added, "And leave your phone at home. No technology."

Tim and Marley hadn't been much more helpful.

"Don't wear too much," Tim said. "If you're overdressed, you'll regret it. It always gets hot."

"Hot? You're kidding." It was still April, and the air rolling in from the coast at nights brought the temperature way down.

Tim just smiled. "Trust me."

"You could go skyclad," Marley said slyly.

"Knock it off, Mar." Tim laughed. "She's asking for our help."

"What's skyclad?" Selene asked and sipped her coffee.

"Naked." Tim rolled his eyes.

Selene managed to stop herself from spitting coffee all over their kitchen table. But just barely. She was not a fan of this pattern. Though it was an improvement over the fainting.

"Will there be many naked people at this event?"

"At least a few." Marley laughed. "But you might not recognize them as people."

Selene's eyes widened.

"Let's just say that among the Fae, Marley is one of the most human-looking," Tim said.

"Don't worry, Selene. You'll handle it just fine," Marley said, then his face grew serious. "But make sure you wear only natural fibers."

And that sent Selene on a hunt through the few clothing stores in Avondale on Friday night, sorting through racks of clothes in search of an all-natural-fiber, not-too-heavy outfit. It wasn't easy. She was rather astounded by the number of synthetic materials that made up at least a part of most clothing.

The first two stores yielded nothing, so it was with delight that she discovered that the third, Arachne's Web, appeared to carry only natural-fiber items. Selene kicked herself for putting the store at the bottom of her list. The name had creeped her out. She was not a fan of spiders. If she'd gone there first, it would have saved her a couple of hours, and now it was close to closing time.

With an armful of skirts, tops, and dresses, Selene approached the store clerk sheepishly. "I'm so sorry. I know you're about to close, but would it be possible for me to try these on?"

The store was set to shut in ten minutes. There was no way she'd get through her mountain of options in that time.

The woman eyed the pile and smiled knowingly. "Shopping for the Beltane rite?"

Selene almost blurted, *How did you know?* then thought better of it.

When she nodded, the woman laughed. "I can never decide what to wear. Here, let me look at what you have."

They walked over to the counter, where Selene spread out her choices.

Tapping her index finger against her lips, the woman made a humming sound and began to pluck items from the counter and deposit them in Selene's arms.

"This. This. Not this. Maybe . . . no. Definitely not this. Oh, this would be lovely. But this could work too. Ah, the slit in this skirt isn't high enough. You don't want your movement to be restricted. We'll put that aside. But you should try this one instead."

She surveyed the slightly smaller pile Selene held. "You should find something in there that suits you."

"Are you sure you don't mind?" Even having reduced the number of choices, it would still take her a while to try them all on.

"Not at all." The woman eyed Selene again. "Is this your first Beltane?"

Selene nodded.

"You're in for a treat." She offered Selene her hand. "Perhaps I'll see you there? I'm Arachne."

"This is your shop?" Selene shook Arachne's hand. "It's a pleasure to meet you. I'm sorry to make you stay late."

Arachne waved away her apology. "My studio is in the back of the shop. I always weave for a few hours after I close. If you don't mind, I'll lock the front door and go to work. Come find me when you're finished."

"You weave?" Selene asked.

Nodding, Arachne replied, "I create most of the fabrics for the clothes I sell. Avondale is home to a number of independent and incredibly gifted seamstresses and tailors who I hire to take my fabrics and turn them into everything you see in here."

Gifted, Selene thought, *means magic.*

Arachne watched her with an obvious if-you-know-you-know expression.

"That's wonderful," Selene replied. "I regret that I haven't been in here until today. It's silly, but . . ."

"Go on," Arachne urged.

With a nervous laugh, Selene confessed, "I don't understand the name of your shop."

"You don't like spiders." Arachne smiled gently.

Selene couldn't stop herself from rubbing her arms. Even thinking about spiders gave her the creepy crawlies.

"Do you know the story of my namesake?" Arachne asked. "The first Arachne?"

Selene shook her head.

"Then let me tell you," Arachne continued. "You might change your mind about spiders. At least a bit."

"Okay." Selene doubted anything could change her opinion of spiders.

"In ancient Greece Arachne was an incredibly gifted weaver," Arachne explained. "She gained so much renown for her talent that she got a little too full of herself and decided to challenge Athena to a weaving contest."

"Athena, as in the goddess of wisdom?" Selene asked.

"The very same," Arachne replied. "Athena is also the goddess of crafts, and let me tell you this, if there is one rule to be followed in life, it is this: Never brag about yourself to a deity. Hubris is always punished. When Arachne realized how deeply she'd enraged Athena, she hung herself. Athena took pity on Arachne and saved her life but did so by changing her into a spider so that she could weave for all eternity."

"An immortal spider then," Selene remarked.

"Yes."

"Is that supposed to be a happy ending?" Selene frowned. The story would make her see spiders differently, but she wasn't necessarily more inclined to like them.

Arachne shook her head. "Myths rarely offer happy endings. The blessing is mixed. The lesson is what matters."

"No bragging when the gods can hear you," Selene said. "Got it."

"And the gods can always hear you," Arachne added. "I named my shop not only after myself but also as a reminder that my love of weaving is a gift that I shouldn't take for granted. Now let me show you to a dressing room."

Arachne led Selene to a generous space in one corner of the shop that could be curtained off for privacy. After the shop owner excused herself, Selene pulled the curtain shut, stripped off her clothes, and began shuffling in and out of her options.

With Arachne working in her studio, the shop was eerily quiet, the silence around Selene only broken by the rustle of fabric as she changed.

Having discarded several possibilities for the Beltane celebration—but also setting a few aside to purchase anyway because they were simply gorgeous—Selene gazed in the mirror and stroked her hands over a sleeveless pale-blue silk blouse with a low-cut shirred neckline. The sea-fog color set a pleasant contrast to the calf-length, butter-soft suede skirt she'd paired it with. The skirt had a generous slit up the left side that wouldn't hamper any dancing. Selene remained unconvinced that she'd be warm enough on a spring night in this outfit, but she had a cashmere shawl at home that she could wear if needed. She put her hands in her hair and twisted it up above her head.

Updo or loose?

A snicker came from just behind her. "Nice, babe. That blue makes your hair look like flames. I'm into it."

Selene gasped and whirled around. Daniel stood inside the dressing room, his back to the curtain. He was grinning as he openly ogled her.

"You've sure taken a long time to pick something," he said. "What's it for? Big date?"

His grin didn't fade, but his eyes flickered with annoyance.

She stared at him, then she slowly turned and stared at the mirror. Her own reflection looked back at her. There was no one else in the room. She pivoted back to Daniel.

"How long have you been here?"

His smile grew sly. "Long enough to know that outfit's my favorite."

She tried to keep her breath steady. He stepped toward her and put his hand where her waist curved into her hip.

"Long enough to know you've still got a body every man wants." His voice was low as the light touch of his fingers became a firm grip.

"Let go." She grabbed his hand and tried to pull it away. He didn't budge.

"Come on, Selene," he purred. "We haven't had the chance for a proper reunion. You're a hard woman to catch alone."

"You've been warned to stay away from me," she insisted, trying to voice the anger sizzling in her veins, but the gleam of his eyes kept distracting her. The strange, luminous quality of his irises drew her in, making it difficult to look away.

"I know you want to talk to me." His voice was calm, lulling. Melodious in a way she didn't recall. Daniel was a guitarist, not a singer. "I know you have questions that I can answer."

"Questions?" A part of her was screaming to run. To get away that instant. But she couldn't look away from his face. The glimmer of his irises became a mesmerizing sparkle that pulsed rhythmically and riveted her in place.

"About where I've been," he murmured. "Why I had to leave. Why I need you now. I need you so bad, babe."

What the hell? Daniel didn't need her. The idea was ludicrous, as was his assumption that she'd welcome his attention.

He pulled her against him. His hand slid from her hip to her lower back, fingers slipping beneath the blouse to stroke her skin. She gasped. The touch was cold as ice, yet it set off an unwelcome flare of heat deep within her.

Her stomach lurched. That wasn't possible. No matter how handsome a package Daniel came in, Selene knew the contents were toxic. She wanted none of it. And yet her body was tilting toward him.

No. This isn't right. Something is happening to me.

"What are you doing?" Even her voice sounded wrong. Sluggish and hoarse. Her heart pounded. She tried to step back, but his arm held her like a vise.

"Showing you who I am," he said. His other hand stroked her cheek, over her lips, and trailed down her chin and throat, down, down. Her breath caught in her throat when he cupped her breast. Why did that feel good? She hated that it made her want to arch her back.

I can't stand this man. Why am I reacting like this?

She fought the rising tide of desire that wanted to sweep her under. Her mind had gone hazy, the way it felt when she was caught between a dream and waking and she had only marginal control over her thoughts and actions. Her mind tried to resist, but her body was giving in.

He traced circles around her hardening nipple with his fingertips and smiled. “That’s a good girl.”

She opened her mouth to protest, and his lips were on hers. His kiss was cold, but the caress was like frozen silk. Despite the chill of his touch, it set her skin on fire. When he began to use his tongue, her resistance crumbled. She kissed him back. Her hands stopped pushing against his chest and slid around his neck. She twined her fingers in his thatch of golden hair.

Deep within her, panic surged, fighting through the trance of desire.

Somehow Selene turned her face away to choke out words. “I don’t want . . . I can’t—”

“Shhh.” Daniel walked her back until she bumped against the mirror. “You don’t have to fight it, Selene. Not that I mind you being feisty. But you won’t win. You’re mine now.”

Determined to prove him wrong, Selene dragged her hands back, fisting them at her sides. The effort exhausted her. She had to dig her nails into her palms to stop herself from reaching for him again.

“So stubborn.” Daniel grabbed her chin. “Look at me.”

His gaze pierced her. She could feel it chaining her to him. She wanted to close her eyes, to break the contact that compelled her, but she couldn’t.

When she whimpered, he laughed. “That’s right, babe. I’m in charge.”

He took a step back and raked her body with his eyes. “Now turn around. Put your hands against the glass, above your head.”

She spun to face the mirror before the conscious thought to obey him surfaced. Her palms pressed flat on the cool, reflective surface. He spoke. She acted.

A war waged inside her. Her mind, her soul, clawed at the cocoon Daniel had trapped her in. Her body ignored her commands, only hearing his. Selene barely recognized her reflection. Her eyes were glassy, her lids drooping. Again, she was the only one in the mirror, which made the sound of Daniel's voice, the coolness of his breath on her neck, all the more disturbing.

"This mirror thing is a fucking drag," he complained. "I'd really like to watch what's about to happen."

Daniel's hands gripped her shoulders, then slid over her shoulder blades to each side of her rib cage then down to her hips.

"This ass," he murmured. "I'm not lying when I say I've dreamed about it."

He stepped close, fitting her body against his so she felt his hard-on. She closed her eyes as her stomach twisted with disgust. Then she realized, something had changed.

He broke eye contact.

His touch disgusted me.

My body didn't like it.

He's been controlling me somehow. He invaded my mind and stole my willpower.

Selene swallowed hard and tried to focus her thoughts. It was difficult but she was able to push against the trance now that he wasn't holding her with that gaze. His eyes. Now that her back was to him and he had no reflection, she would be able to avoid eye contact. And she could fight him.

He made a mistake.

Daniel was licking her neck, laughing softly.

He doesn't know.

Carefully, Selene opened her eyes, keeping her lids heavy. She only had one chance to make her move. If Daniel realized her mind had broken free, he'd capture her again before she could fight back. What would stop that from happening?

Remaining as still as she could, Selene glanced around for anything in reach. The pile of clothes wouldn't help, but there was her purse. Right at her feet. But could she get to it?

That was when she felt the pain. It was barely noticeable—just a slight prick. Then the pressure grew. A sharpness paired with the satin strokes of his lips. The sharpness of teeth. Daniel's face was buried against her neck. Her eyes widened, and her shock tore away the last threads of desire that had enveloped her mind and body.

He's biting me.

"No!" Selene panicked and dove for her purse, digging into the front pocket. Her hand found what she was searching for, and she spun on her knees as Daniel descended like a vulture. Her hand flew up, hitting his throat. He shrieked and rolled to the side.

Her fingers went to her neck and found no wetness. No blood. He hadn't punctured her skin. She gulped down a relieved breath and scrambled to her feet. She kept the silver cross Natalie had given her extended toward him. Daniel hissed at the cross and pressed his hand against the smoking skin of his throat.

Wow. It really works.

"What the hell are you doing?" he snapped.

"What the hell were *you* doing?" Selene countered. "You attacked me."

He snorted. "Attacked? I was having a good time. So were you."

"No," Selene said angrily. "I didn't want that. I will *never* want that. How did you control me? A spell?"

He glared at her, but he kept his distance. "Hardly. All I can do is amplify what you're already feeling. I got rid of your inhibitions the way a nice cocktail would."

"You're lying." She clenched her teeth. "I don't want you."

"Sure you do." He grinned. "You just don't want to admit it. I was helping you get there."

Furious, Selene took a step forward and was gratified when he shrank back. "I never liked you, Daniel, but I didn't think you were this stupid. Listen to me: I don't want you. I have never wanted you. Go. Fuck. Yourself."

He snarled, baring his fangs. "You're mine. Even if you don't want to believe it."

"I don't belong to anyone," Selene said.

"That's not how the wolf tells it," he hissed. The hatred in his eyes made her stomach knot.

"This isn't about Fenris," she said and tightened her grip on the cross. "Listen to me, Daniel. The only thing you proved tonight is that you have no place in Allie's life. You're vile. Irredeemable. You are no longer her father. It's over."

His smile was pure evil. "We'll see about that."

And then he was gone.

15

Selene clutched her purse tightly as she moved through the shadowed forest. It contained not one, but three crosses. After the incident at the shop, she wasn't taking any chances. Natalie had been happy enough to bring them over, and she'd been sympathetic about Selene's request for wooden crosses rather than silver. After all, the invitation to the pagan festival had come from Fenris. She didn't want to offend him by showing up with a purse full of silver. Natalie's insistence that no vampires would be at the rite of Beltane hadn't altered Selene's resolve to keep crosses with her for the entire evening.

"I'm serious, Selene," Natalie had assured her. "Vamps don't get into the pagan-holiday cycle. They see themselves as above the old rites. They hate being reminded there are things in the universe more powerful than they are. Plus, it's Fen's event. They'd keep their distance no matter what."

Selene smiled weakly and turned the cross over in her hands. Its solid weight was comforting.

"Are you going to tell Fen what Daniel did?" Natalie asked.

Selene shook her head. "I want Daniel to stay away. I don't know that I want him dead. Yet."

"Then you can't tell Fen." Natalie had offered her a thin smile. "But if Daniel tries something again, I think you'll have to."

A gust of wind rustled the tiny spring leaves on the trees. She shivered and pulled the shawl more tightly over her shoulders.

Thanks, Tim. I'm freezing my ass off out here.

The spring day had been pleasant enough, but with the sun setting, the temperature was already plummeting.

She wore a moss-green silk wrap dress that swirled around her in the cool breeze. Gooseflesh rose on her calves. At least her feet were warm in the soft leather ankle boots she'd deemed sturdy enough for an outdoor event.

After Daniel had vanished from Arachne's Web, Selene sank to the dressing room floor. Her heart raced and her mind spun as she tried to regain her bearings. A vampire had attacked her. She felt sick and stunned, but she won. That was what mattered. She had the means to protect herself, and she didn't hesitate to use them. More than that, she no longer had any ambivalence about Daniel. He was a predator. Dangerous. Manipulative. It wouldn't be an easy conversation to have with Allie, but she would be honest, and Allie would be safer and, in the long run, happier because of it.

It still took a good fifteen minutes for her to gather her composure, change clothes, and find Arachne. As much as she'd loved the shirt-and-skirt combo she was wearing when Daniel surprised her, his comment about it and what followed made it unwearable.

Now she was tromping through the woods in green silk, trying to find a pagan festival. She'd considered staying home, but she didn't want to dwell on what had happened with Daniel. She was resolved to put that, and him, behind her. She also didn't want Fen to misinterpret her choice if she stayed away. As much as she was wary of a romantic entanglement with the pack leader, she couldn't deny the strength of her feelings for him. It was time to . . . explore that. The festival seemed like a good place to start.

Selene stopped on the path and glanced at the crinkled page upon which Natalie had jotted down directions to the grove.

East at the standing stone, then follow the path.

And there it was: a hulking gray column just off the trail, slightly obscured by the stately trees that flanked it. She wandered to the eastern side of the rock and peered into the woods, which grew darker by the minute. As she moved deeper into the trees, she forced herself to believe she was following a path, because she certainly couldn't see it. It was no more than a narrow space between the tall oaks and a noticeable lack of underbrush. Selene walked east through the lengthening shadows and hoped she was headed in the right direction.

The forest began to change. Tree trunks thickened, becoming wider than her Prius was long. The branches snaked over her head and twined around each other, so her path—and it was a path now, clearly—was canopied by a latticework of bark and spring leaves.

She didn't know how far she'd walked when darkness began to cover everything, obscuring her vision. She stumbled over tree roots that snaked across the thin trail. Her heart beat erratically, and she fought for calm breaths. Black shadows took shape through the tree trunks, alive and moving, watching her. She couldn't see the path at all and didn't know if she was even still walking on it.

I'm lost.

Selene reflexively dug in her purse for her phone, then remembered it was in her car because of the no technology rule. Bringing a flashlight hadn't so much as crossed her mind. Did a flashlight count as technology? Was she supposed to carry a torch?

Feeling ridiculous and a little frightened, Selene was about to turn back and hope she'd somehow find the jogging lane, when a sparkle caught her eye. The winking light flashed and was gone. She stared into the ink-dark woods, wondering if she'd imagined it.

Another flash. Then another.

Selene moved warily toward the tiny lights. A silver haze spilled over the ground. Her eyes turned skyward, and she gasped.

The rising moon took up most of the sky. Its fullness dominated the heavens in a way she'd never seen. The growing light pushed back creeping shadows, and Selene saw that she was indeed still on the path. Moonlight kissed her skin, and a frisson of awareness traveled through her. It felt like a greeting. A welcome.

She moved forward with faster, more confident steps.

The lights danced and flickered, and she saw they were a multitude of colors, ranging from pale rose to electric blue. The path widened and opened into a broad space the size of a football field but in the shape of a perfect circle. The trees that ringed the grove were larger than she'd believed any deciduous tree could grow, taller and broader than the sequoias she'd marveled at when visiting Kings Canyon National Park.

At the center of the grove was an immense bonfire, and the clearing was filled with people. Laughter and music filled her ears. The air was full of the scent of spring flowers: lilac, honeysuckle, tulip, lily of the valley. She saw many dancers, though the styles of dancing varied widely. Some couples waltzed in the grass, and others were jigging. She even caught sight of a cluster of breakdancers next to a group that was line dancing.

Come as you are, do as you will, Selene thought, and smiled. She pulled her shawl from her shoulders and wrapped it around one of her purse straps. The temperature had risen at least twenty degrees the moment she'd stepped into the sacred grove.

She walked forward and tried to convince herself that she could fit in at this gathering.

Not too bad. Not scary at all. Selene glanced around the clearing. *Bonfires. Costumes. It's like a college party. Or Burning Man.*

She ignored the little voice that tried to remind her she'd been at least a decade younger for each of those. Even so, nothing about this pagan festival seemed that extraordinary.

She looked at the string of colorful lights that hung like a web over the grove. Then she frowned. The lights weren't hanging at all. They were moving, zigzagging across the sky.

Fireflies, she thought with delight. She'd never seen so many at once.

A lime-green ball of light swooped down and hovered before her eyes. Selene froze.

The twinkling light had wings. And a body. A tiny naked man wiggled his antennae at her, buzzed closer, and kissed her nose. Then he giggled like the tinkling of bells and flew away. Selene stared at the mass of tiny beings that flew above her.

Not fireflies. Mini Marleys.

She walked farther into the grove in a stupor, unable to take her eyes off the sparkling winged creatures.

That was when the gnome headbutted her knees.

"Hey, lady, watch it," the gnome groused.

"I'm sorry," she said.

There was no mistaking him for anything other than a gnome. He even had a pointed red hat and a pipe caught between his teeth. The smoke that curled up toward her smelled of cloves, cinnamon, and peat moss.

The gnome glared at her and tottered off. Selene stared after him.

"Avoid the gnomes if you can!"

Selene turned to see Tim waving at her. He was shirtless and had a wreath of flowers on his head. "The little buggers are cranky as hell."

When she reached him, she lowered her voice. "They look just like the garden figurines."

"Yeah, they've got the patent on that image," Tim replied. "Keeps them from having to work."

She didn't know if he was joking.

"Selene, you made it." Glamour-free Marley, green and leafy as ever and wearing only a kilt with silk pleats that looked like flower petals, fluttered over on his dragonfly wings and pecked her on the cheek.

"Wouldn't miss it," she murmured, even as she wondered if it would have been wiser for her to stay at home with Allie. She felt like she'd walked into Oz on steroids.

Tim grinned at her. "You're going to love it. Beltane is my favorite Sabbat in the wheel of the year."

"The year is a wheel?" Selene replied, puzzled. Her year was a grid calendar, phone alerts, and spreadsheets.

"Absolutely," Marley said. "We have eight holidays, and they are all so much more fabulous than your commercialized human variety.

Though they did manage to get their hands on Samhain and muck it up beyond recognition."

"Samhain?" Selene wasn't any less confused.

"Halloween," Tim answered.

"Ugh." Marley shuddered.

"Blessed Beltane, Selene." Natalie walked up, wearing a broad smile, and embraced her.

A long silk dress, a white nearly as luminous as the moon above, skimmed over Natalie's body. The fabric was caught at her waist by a wide girdle, woven with intricate Celtic knotwork patterns in gold and green.

"Hi, Nat." Selene was relieved to see her friend. "Nice party."

Natalie laughed. "Always is. Wanna dance?"

"Sure," Selene said, but she quickly scanned the crowd.

Tim smiled knowingly. "Sorry, sweetie. Fen's got official duties for this gig. You probably won't see him tonight."

Selene sputtered with embarrassment, and Natalie frowned slightly.

"We'll keep you occupied. But Tim's right," Natalie told her. "You won't see Fen before the ritual."

"That's fine," Selene said, wishing they'd find a new topic. "Let's go dance."

◆ ◆ ◆

There was dancing. There was drinking. There was an abundance of luscious fruit and edible flowers that tasted better than Selene expected. Marley and Tim were vigilant, steering her clear of anything they deemed problematic or unpredictable when it came to side effects on mere mortals.

The night wore on, and the chaos of swirling bodies around them thickened. Took strange shapes. There were people around her, but there were other things too. Things with wings, with horns, with the heads or legs of beasts. Things with body parts she couldn't name. Things that looked friendly. Things that didn't.

Any time Selene's eyes rounded or her heart tried to crawl out of her throat, Natalie would squeeze her hand and Tim would wink at her. And everything would be okay again.

She couldn't find the source of the music. It seemed to be coming from the earth itself, spouting up into her feet and carrying her body with its own rhythms. They'd been dancing for hours, and she had yet to lose her breath or feel tired. She was twirling in ecstatic circles when out of the corner of her eye, she caught Natalie halt in the midst of her belly dancing gyrations. Tim and Marley broke out of their two-step and stiffened. All three of her friends stared at something just behind Selene. Their bodies tense, eyes wide. She was about to ask what was wrong when a familiar voice answered the question for her.

"Good evening, Selene."

She spun around. Fenris stood a foot away from her. He was flanked by four solemn-faced men, and all Selene could think was *brawn.*

Like Marley, Fen wore only a kilt. But where the faerie's garb was brightly colored silk, Fen's kilt was leather and resembled armor more than festive clothing. The imposing quartet that stood just behind him also wore leather. They all appeared ready for battle—Bronze Age battle.

Her mouth went dry as she took in Fenris. Every inch of his bare torso looked like it had been chiseled from gleaming stone. His skin was covered by a pattern of tattoos in vivid blue paint that mirrored the knotwork on Natalie's girdle. A crown rested upon his head composed of twisted material that curled and stretched out in sharp points. A crown of antlers. He was frightening and beautiful, almost inhumanly so, as though he'd stepped out of some heathen pantheon.

"You look like a god," she murmured, then mentally kicked herself for speaking aloud.

At her back, Natalie sucked in a sharp breath.

Fen's mouth twitched into the ghost of a smile.

"I wanted to apologize that my obligations will keep me from your side tonight, as much as I'd like to be there," he said and took her hand. "I'm pleased and honored you accepted my invitation."

His touch made her shiver. Warmth traveled from her fingers up through her arm and spilled into her body. Selene didn't trust her voice, so she nodded.

He brought her fingertips to his lips. They brushed over her skin, featherlight. Her knees tried to buckle, and she had to close her eyes and draw a steadying breath.

"Enjoy the night, Selene," he said softly, releasing her.

When she opened her eyes again, Fen had turned away. The four men alongside him simultaneously inclined their heads to Selene, then followed their leader's exit.

"Wow," Tim said quietly and began to fan himself. "Just wow."

Marley fluttered to Selene's side. "You must work fast, Selene. I've never seen anything like that. Nice job."

Selene didn't reply. She couldn't take her eyes off the rippling muscles of Fen's shoulders, remembering how they'd felt when her fingers gripped them. The way he looked without a shirt . . . She didn't have words.

"I'm pleased and honored you accepted my invitation."

Her heart was doing somersaults, and she felt a bit lightheaded. It was wonderful.

"Shit." Selene heard Natalie mutter as she watched Fen and his entourage melt into the shadows.

"What?" Selene turned to face her.

There was a tightness around Natalie's eyes as she took in Selene's expression.

"I have to tell you something, Selene."

Selene frowned. "Tell me what?"

"About the ritual." She sighed. "There are things that might happen . . . things you won't like. You need to understand it."

"Why do you think I won't like it?"

"Because of the way you look at Fenris," she said. "I didn't realize . . . If I'd known, I would have told you not to come."

Selene's somersaulting heart rolled into a ditch with an unpleasant thud. "If you'd known what?"

"That you're falling for him. Falling hard."

"I never said that." Selene looked away, her chest suddenly tight. "You can't know that. I don't even know that. I barely know *him*."

Natalie looked at her sharply. "It doesn't always work that way. You may have known him before. You recognize your soul's true mate."

"What are you talking about?"

"In another time, another life," Natalie said quietly. "On another plane of existence."

"Oh, please." Selene stifled a laugh, but Natalie's face was somber.

"I'm sorry, Selene," she said. "But you need to accept that the rules have changed now. You've stepped into our world, and it seems to have claimed you."

Natalie frowned and scrutinized Selene. "I can't figure it out. That doesn't always happen."

Selene took a step back, uncomfortable with Natalie's probing gaze. "What doesn't always happen?"

"You're part of our circle. Not an outsider," Natalie said. "I think you might have ties to us in your past that you don't know about."

"That's ridiculous," Selene said, but she was finding it difficult to breathe. What Natalie was suggesting couldn't be true. Past lives. Soulmates. That was fiction. Fantasy. She wasn't part of this. Nothing about Selene was magical. She might be an unwitting spectator, but she was not a willing participant.

Natalie sighed, shaking her head. "Well, there isn't time to look into it now. But you should come to my shop soon. I'll do a reading. Tea leaves. Maybe cards. Now about the ritual—"

Her words were cut off by a deafening roar of the bonfire. Flames leaped toward the sky, a pillar of searing heat that reached impossible heights. The column grew and changed, the tower of flame morphing into a gargantuan tree, its blazing branches stretching toward the full moon.

"Damn." Natalie gazed at the fiery display. "I have to go, Selene."

"What's happening?" Selene stared at the gargantuan tree of flames.

"The ritual," Natalie said. "It's time. I have to assist."

She gripped Selene's hands. "Remember, Selene. No matter what you think you're seeing, it is sacred. The ceremony honors the goddess—whomever is chosen. It's not about you and Fenris. Don't take it the wrong way. I can explain more after it's finished."

Selene stared at her friend, hundreds of questions crowding into her mind. Natalie gave her a quick hug before she turned and wove through the crowd toward the bonfire. Even as she moved, the massive crowd of paranormal beings began to part. A path opened that Natalie walked along, but the eyes of the throng didn't follow Natalie. They were fixed on a cloaked figure who stood before the fire, arms raised. The figure, shrouded in dark, heavy robes, was bent and spindly. Natalie stood to one side of the cloaked person. A young girl Selene didn't recognize stood to the other side.

An arm slid around Selene's waist.

"Come on," Marley whispered. "You don't want to miss this."

He pulled her forward into the crowd.

The figure raised its arms again, and the hood fell back. It was a woman. Her face was ancient, riddled with lines that made patterns on her face like intricate cobwebs. Her hair cascaded down her bent back almost to her ankles—its waves shifted and undulated as though it were composed of both the leaping flames of the bonfire and the pour of moonlight from the sky above.

When she spoke, her voice wasn't that of an old woman. Instead, it was clear and resonant. A chorus.

"From whence comes the Great Hunt?"

Natalie and the girl spoke in unison. "The hunters appear."

Selene gasped as Fen and his warriors stepped out of the great flaming tree, seemingly untouched by the fire. They ringed the three women so that Fen stood directly in front of the oldest woman.

"Hunt well, and the goddess will honor the consort," she said and seemed to be speaking only to Fen. He dropped to one knee and removed the crown of antlers from his head, placing it in the old woman's hands. She lifted the crown above her head. It shimmered, becoming one with the moonlight, then vanished.

"Prove your worth that you may be crowned once more," the woman said.

"Let the goddess choose her vessel that I may serve her in the Hunt," Fenris replied.

"The goddess chooses her priestess on this May Eve." The old woman reached into her cloak and began chanting.

The flames of the tree began to pulse, and the moonlight intensified. A silver spiral, a double helix of light, stretched from the heavens to encase the three women and the circle of hunters. The old woman's chant reached a feverish pitch, and the spiral spun around her, so bright that Selene had to avert her eyes. There was a flash, a crack of lightning. The chanting stopped abruptly, and the light became a soothing glow.

Selene returned her gaze to the ring of men and the three women. The old woman had dropped to her knees. She was staring at several small objects on the ground.

"What's happening?" Selene leaned into Marley to whisper.

"She's reading the bones," he replied.

The old woman stood and turned from Fen to face the crowd. Her face was filled with a shimmering radiance, and she wore a mysterious smile.

"The goddess has spoken," the old woman called. "Let the chosen step forward to receive her blessing."

She stretched forth a long, bony finger. The crowd parted and turned. There was a moment of absolute silence, followed by gasps and murmurs.

Selene stared at the old woman and the age-gnarled finger pointing directly at her.

"The Triple Goddess names Selene Rhiannon Jones. Come, daughter of the Lady, chosen vessel of this holy night. Come forward and claim your place in the rite of Beltane."

◆ ◆ ◆

Allie curled up on the couch with a bowl of popcorn, aimlessly scrolling through movies and TV shows. She sighed for the millionth time, so bored and wishing she was with her boyfriend at the Beltane festival instead of stuck at home. It was so annoying that Aunt Selene made her stay home. She wasn't a kid anymore, and somehow Aunt Selene and Fenris didn't get that. Josh did. He never treated her like a kid. She'd hoped he would skip the festival to hang with her at home, but apparently whatever was going on in the sacred grove tonight was more important than her. How old did she have to be before adults took her feelings and opinions seriously?

The doorbell rang. She set the popcorn down and rushed to the door, feeling a thrill of hope that Josh had changed his mind. It would be so romantic if he'd come to surprise her, to sweep her off her feet and into the night to a wild pagan party. And he could literally carry her all the way to the sacred grove. Allie wasn't embarrassed to admit that Josh's strength was super hot.

She opened the door, grinning with anticipation, and her spine curled in on itself. Her smile vanished.

"Heya, Alley-Cat." As Daniel grinned, his eyes began to glow. "Got a minute for your dad?"

16

The old woman beckoned to Selene once more with a crook of her gnarled finger.

Leaning over to Tim, Selene whispered, "Is this some kind of joke? Make the newbie get up on stage so she can play the fool?"

"No." Tim's voice was shaky as he tugged Selene's purse from her grasp and tucked it under his arm. "No joke."

He glanced at Marley. "Goddess have mercy. What do we do?"

"She goes to the crone," Marley said in a hard voice. His grip around her waist tightened. "Come on, chosen one."

She hadn't realized how strong Marley was until he lifted her off her feet and flew her to the front of the throng. Selene felt blood drain from her face as she approached the tree of flames and the trio of women. The ring of warriors drew back into a line and dropped to their knees when Marley set Selene on the ground.

"Behold the Great Lady," the men intoned in unison.

"What the hell is happening? How did she know my middle name?" Selene couldn't keep the fear out of her voice.

Her eyes flickered to Fenris. His expression was one of surprise but also satisfaction.

Natalie stepped forward. "Selene, it's okay. You've been named to participate in the ritual."

Her voice was calm, but her eyes were wild.

Everything is not okay.

"Participate how?" Selene protested. "I know nothing about this ritual. I'm just visiting. Pagan tourist."

She tried to laugh, but the sound died in her throat.

A gentle touch drew her gaze down as small fingers slipped through her own. The young girl smiled up at her.

"The goddess will guide you."

The girl's wide, innocent eyes, sky blue and full of puffy white clouds and sunlight, sent a wave of calm through Selene. But a panicked voice shocked her back into the present . . . and a new storm of fear.

"Fen! Fenris!" Josh pushed his way free of the crowd. He stared at Selene, his face filled with distress. "How did this happen?"

The old woman cackled. "The goddess works in mystery, boy." She smiled toothlessly at Josh, but he remained visibly upset.

Fen rose from his kneeling position and stepped forward. His eyes found Selene's. She had to bite her tongue so she wouldn't gasp. His back was to the flaming tree, but somehow the fiery trunk and branches were dancing in his dark irises.

"Selene has been chosen." Fenris looked at Josh and spoke in a voice pitched low and unyielding. "She is the vessel and will take part in the rite of Beltane."

Color leached from Josh's face. "Please, Fenris, she's my girlfriend's aunt! *This is her first Beltane.*"

Selene's heart skipped a beat when she saw the boy's hands quivering.

"It's gotta be a mistake," he pled.

"The crone has spoken," Fen said quietly and fixed his eyes on Selene. "There is no mistake."

Josh's shoulders slumped, and he stepped back.

The old woman raised her hands once more, and the crowd fell silent.

"The night of Beltane is upon us. Let the Hunt begin."

The warriors rose to their feet. Selene was too shocked to scream when Fen and his followers turned around and walked directly into the flaming tree. And then they were gone.

Selene swayed a little on her feet. Fainting yet again when faced with paranormal surprises would be embarrassing, but she decided she'd be okay with passing out and waking up in her own bed. This night was getting to be too much.

"Come on." Natalie took her hand. "We have to get you ready."

"Ready for what?"

"For your part in the ritual." Natalie fell in step behind the old woman, who moved with surprising speed. The young girl skipped alongside her, holding Selene's other hand.

Selene swallowed hard and hoped she wasn't going to have to walk into anything that was on fire.

"Natalie, why am I here? I have no idea what I'm supposed to do."

"You will when the time comes," Natalie said. "The goddess will guide you."

"What the hell does that mean?"

"It means what it means." Natalie followed the old woman into a pavilion that Selene didn't remember seeing anywhere in the grove earlier that evening. The enclosed space was decorated with vines and flowers, and the sounds of a flute and harp filled the air. It was crowded with people and creatures whose chatter rose into an excited buzz when Selene entered. Fragments of conversation assailed her ears.

"The Lady! It's the Lady of Beltane!"

"Wait, is she human?"

"I don't know her. Do you know her?"

"She has a strong aura."

"Why would the goddess choose a stranger for Fenris?"

Natalie stopped just inside the entrance and turned Selene to face her. She must have done something witchy because the voices all around them were suddenly muffled, freeing Selene from that distraction.

"Listen to me, Selene." Natalie's eyes were bright. "The goddess chose you as her vessel tonight. I don't know why. But it means you're not who you think you are—at least not completely. You're tied to the paranormal world. You wouldn't have been selected otherwise. Damn it, I knew I needed to trace your genealogy."

"I don't know what you're talking about," Selene argued.

"I know you don't," Natalie said. "I wish I could explain better."

She sighed and suddenly embraced Selene.

"It is a great honor to be chosen. Remember that."

"Okay." Selene tensed at the fierceness of Natalie's tone.

"We're going to give you ritual clothing. It's a dress like mine," Natalie said.

Selene nodded.

"You'll be brought to the site of the ritual. And then you have a choice."

"What kind of choice?" Selene asked.

"You'll be asked a question," Natalie explained. "The answer will come to you. When it does, be honest. And after that . . . well, follow your instincts."

"Have you been chosen before?"

Natalie blushed. "I have."

"Is it hard?" Selene frowned. "What if I mess up?"

Natalie blinked at her and then she began to laugh. She laughed so hard that tears trickled down her cheeks.

Selene's brows knit together. "This isn't funny, Nat."

"Oh," Natalie said, wiping moisture from her cheeks, "it is. It's very funny."

"You're the one who's been telling me how much I'm not going to like this ritual," Selene said. "Now I'm in the middle of it."

Natalie's face became serious again. "Yes, but now that you *are* in the middle of it, I don't know how you'll feel about what happens. It changes things. It changes everything, actually. That could be better or worse."

"Can't you just tell me what's going to happen?"

"No. But please know that to be chosen is a *great* honor."

"You already said that. Why won't you tell me anything else?"

"If I did, it would influence your actions. What you do tonight must come from your soul," Natalie said solemnly. "Outside interference is forbidden."

Selene pouted, and Natalie's smile became playful. "Sweetie, even if I could tell you what was about to happen, you'd never believe me."

"Try me and we'll see."

"No."

Selene was about to object again, but she was surrounded and pulled away from Natalie by people dressed in ritual garb. Whatever was happening to her involved a lot more than a wardrobe change. Her clothes were stripped off, and she was cleansed from head to toe with warm water and massaged with oil that smelled of apple blossoms and honeysuckle. And to be honest, that was pretty great. After all she'd been through lately, she was in dire need of a massage.

Flowers were woven into her hair while a choir of angelic little girls sang to her in a language she didn't recognize. A luminescent silk dress was slipped over her head, though, unlike Natalie's, her dress was left to flow freely along her figure, and she was given no girdle to bind her waist. Someone placed a chalice in her hands.

"Drink, blessed one." The young girl from the trio of women at the fire smiled up at her.

"What is it?" Selene asked warily.

"Mead," the girl answered. "Fermented from honey of the sacred hives, blended with herbs sacred to the goddess."

Sacred groves. Sacred hives. Sacred bees. Sacred herbs. Seriously? Maybe I should ask for some sacred coffee to get myself through the rest of the night.

Selene thought about making the joke but decided it wouldn't go over well. All the sacreds might be weird to her, but everyone else was taking the ritual and her role in it very seriously. She didn't want to insult anyone, and she couldn't ignore the fact that her grasp at humor was simply a defense against how nervous she felt.

She raised the cup to her lips. The amber liquid was sweet and smoky but unlike anything she had tasted before. She swallowed more of it, and warmth spread from her throat into her chest and stomach. She hadn't expected mead to be so strong. Or maybe that was the herbs. No one had warned her that they might have strange effects. Though admittedly those effects were not unpleasant.

Her skin came alive, crackling with pure energy. Her blood began to pulse with a rhythm drawn from deep within the earth. Something primal stirred deep inside her, waking up parts of her consciousness she hadn't known were asleep. A connection to the very essence of creation.

Somewhere in the distance, she heard the sound of a horn.

The old woman shouted from the other side of the pavilion. "The Hunt returns!"

Shrieks of delight sounded in the small space. Then Natalie was standing before Selene.

"It's time."

She guided Selene from the pavilion toward the giant flaming tree in the center of the grove. A cadre danced before them, waving branches and tossing petals in the air. A steady drumbeat sounded all around them, deep bass thrums that rose from the earth and lingered in the shadows. The crowd of celebrants was there, but they were still and silent.

The fire of the tree abruptly flared and then vanished. Curls of smoke rose into the night sky. The full moon shone directly above the extinguished fire. Silver light streamed into the grove and revealed an immense stone slab that stood solitary in the place of the flaming tree. In the center of the gray surface rested the crown of antlers Fen had worn earlier that evening.

Natalie guided Selene to the edge of the bonfire's remnants and dropped her arm from Selene's waist. Without knowing why, Selene kept walking. She moved forward until she stood beside the great, flat stone, which reached her waist in height.

Her bare feet rested on cool naked soil. There was no sign a fire had burned here, no soot nor ash, only fresh spring earth. The rich scent of it, of all that potential to bring new life into the world after the stillness of winter, surrounded her, suffused her. Moonlight pooled around her, spiraling as it had around the crone. She felt something move along her skin, then beneath it. A rustling of wind or a breath of air that filled her being and pulsed in her veins. The power of possibility. The promise of renewal.

Five shadowy figures emerged from the forest that surrounded the grove. Four of them stopped at the edge of the woods. The last stepped from the darkness into the sphere of silver light. Fen's skin gleamed in the moonlight. The blue tattoos on his torso had come alive. They swirled, shifted, and recreated themselves in new patterns as he strode toward Selene. He no longer wore a leather kilt. The living ink was the only covering on his body.

Selene spoke in a voice that was hers and not hers at the same time. "The Lady awaits her consort. Who comes forth to prove he is worthy?"

The power that spoke through her seemed to reach deep into the earth and to the heights of the heavens, the moon, and the stars. It was full of starlight. She was past, present, and future.

Fenris approached her and dropped to one knee.

He kept his head bowed but raised his hands toward her, palms facing up. They were covered in blood. But she felt no alarm; her body was awash with serenity, grace, and a subtle thrill of triumph. She was herself and yet more, but not altered in a way that frightened her. Rather, she was filled with a sense of familiarity, of purpose, as if from the moment of her birth, she'd been searching for this place, this moment.

"The Great Hunt is complete. I return to serve the Lady," Fenris said, and she recognized his voice but heard a deeper voice beyond Fen's as he spoke. It was a strong and vibrant sound, full of sun, trees, rivers, lakes, and the swell of the ocean waves. "Do you accept my offering?"

Along with her own pulse, she was aware of thousands of heartbeats, the thrum of life itself, all around her. And with it, a word that was murmured in her ears and reverberated in her soul.

Choose.

In that moment she understood the power that belonged to her. She could accept the offering and end the ceremony without doing anything further. Or she could follow a new path and become more, be forever bound to the mystical force that sung within her and danced on the air in this sacred grove. She saw what that would mean, who she could be, to whom she would belong.

Selene chose.

She lifted the crown of antlers from the stone and placed it upon Fen's head. She took his crimson-stained hands in her own and pulled him to his feet.

"The High King is returned," she said. "The goddess welcomes the god. Let the earth be renewed and life begin again."

She released Fenris's hands and brought her fingers to the thin straps of her silk dress, sliding them down her shoulders, and the dress fell in a white pool around her ankles, leaving her naked.

Power unfurled deep within her, bursting forth from a seed hidden deep in her soul. It grew, spiraling through her veins, whispering of the arcane. Of knowledge she had within her grasp—knowledge that belonged to her. All she had to do was reach for it. Claim it.

"Honor the goddess," Selene said, opening her arms to him. "Worship her vessel."

Fen lifted Selene and laid her on the stone slab. The smooth surface was warm against her back. The length of his body stretched over hers. He cupped her face with one hand. His other hand slid beneath her, canting her hips to fit against his body. Moonlight twisted in a tighter spiral around them. The silver aura shimmered and brightened until she could see nothing but the light and Fenris.

Selene pulled Fen's face to hers. Her lips parted to welcome his kiss as her legs twined around him. She was no longer grounded to the stone but floating above it. Her skin, her blood, and her breath wove together with his as they became one with the shining moonlight.

They rose into the stars and left the world behind.

17

Fen's kiss felt like heaven and eternity. When their lips parted, the veil of moonlight surrounding them drew back to reveal a clearing—a perfect circle ringed by giant trees with leaves that gleamed silver. The grass beneath Selene's bare skin was soft as silk, and the air around her warm and windless yet seeming to shiver with anticipation.

The night forest was silent. And they were alone.

"Where are we?" Selene's question was a reverent whisper.

Fen gazed down at her, brushing his fingertips along her cheek. "The true sacred grove. The site of union between the hunter and the chosen vessel, open only to those whom the goddess gives her blessing."

They were both naked, pressed skin to skin, but Selene felt no shame or self-consciousness, only harmony and the sense that she existed in perfect balance with the universe. The power that had filled her during the ritual still hummed in her veins.

"This is the union?" Selene asked Fenris. "Us, in this place?"

"It can be." He smiled, then bent and nuzzled her jaw. "Or it can be more. Nothing is required of us beyond what we desire. What we choose to offer."

"What we desire." Selene pressed her hips up, letting Fen know she was very aware of his hard length trapped against her stomach.

"Yes." He groaned but kept his body still. "Tell me what you want, Selene. I will give you anything you ask for."

She knew what her deepest desire was, what every fiber of her being cried out for, but one question remained. "We are the hunter and the chosen vessel, but are we still us?"

He laughed softly. "Does it feel like we're still us? Do you know who you are? Who I am?"

"Yes." She smiled up at him. "I know who we are, Fenris."

"You have your answer, Selene," he said.

"Then I want everything." She lifted her hand to caress his face.

His lips brushed her temple. "The goddess has truly smiled upon me this Beltane."

Fen cupped the nape of her neck, his fingers diving into her hair as he captured her mouth in a lush kiss. His tongue stroked over hers, and he tasted like smoke and honey. She drew his lower lip between her teeth and bit down gently, reveling in his instant response. His kiss became more frenzied, then he broke away only to lick and nibble along her jawline, to suck at her throat.

His palm molded to her breast, teasing its weight before his fingers toyed with her nipple. Rolling, tugging. Heat arrowed from his touch, surging through her body to stoke a fire in her core.

Selene writhed beneath him as his lips and tongue mapped a path from her collarbone to her breast, where he paused to draw her nipple into his mouth. Wet heat surrounded her sensitive flesh, and he drove her mad with slow licks and deep pulls that hollowed his cheeks before he released her breast to rain kisses upon her abdomen, along her hip.

She lifted her head, eyes locked on him, mesmerized as he nuzzled the tight curls between her legs, breathing deeply. His hands gripped her thighs, pushing them wide. A low steady growl rumbled from him, and he gazed at her exposed sex as if he wanted to devour her.

And then he did.

A moan escaped her throat as Fen's tongue speared into her, his face buried in her sex. She writhed with each slow thrust into her core. He withdrew, and she ached to be filled again, but by more than his tongue. He licked and laved her sensitive flesh, taking his time, savoring her until she was panting and mewling.

When he lifted his head, his eyes sought hers. Whatever he found in her gaze made him smile slowly. He leaned down and tongued her clit. Selene's hips bucked, and she cried out his name. Fen tightened his grip on her now trembling thighs, keeping her spread for him and pinning her to the earth as he continued his exquisite torment, lashing her with his tongue, then suckling. Sensation layered upon sensation, bringing her up, up.

Oh god.

She crested on a ragged sob, pulsing with release. Fen stayed with her, easing her down with gentle licks and languid caresses. She was still shaking with the intensity of her climax when he kissed his way up her body and stretched out beside her.

"You taste even better than I imagined, Selene."

A breath shuddered out of her along with his name. "Fenris."

She knew he wasn't finished. Neither was she.

Fen levered himself over her. She felt his cock, long, thick, and so hard, pressing into her hip.

Selene turned slightly, creating enough space so she could reach down and grip him. She reveled in the contrast of his satin skin and the iron rigidness of his erection. Fen groaned as she stroked him. His breath hissed out when she ran her thumb around the head of his cock, teasing the slit. He thrust into her grip as his hand found her breast. She made a small noise of pleasure, and he kissed her hungrily.

She became a creature made only of wanting, of need. Her blood poured hot through her veins, settling low in her body, another pleasure peak rising. Fen's fingers and mouth teased and demanded, driving her body into a frenzy of need. She released his cock and ran her hands down his back. Her fingers dug into his hips and ground the hard line of him against her pelvis. She'd never felt desire like this, so sharp it was almost painful.

"Please." The word came out trembling.

He drew back. His eyes were dark, alive with desire as he watched her.

"Tell me what you need." He spoke quietly, his voice rough, as his fingers traced the shape of her lower lip.

"I need you," she breathed, arching up, trying to draw him inside her only to have him grasp her hips and hold her still.

He smiled and moved his other hand between her thighs. She cried out when his fingers stroked the silken heat he found there.

"How do you need me?"

His fingers moved again and drew an answer she'd buried in her very soul. A truth she feared but couldn't deny. The reason she'd given herself fully to the ritual.

"Fill me," she gasped amid the relentless strokes of his hand. "Make me yours."

A growl, deep and possessive, vibrated against her. "Yes."

His hand slid under her hip. He tilted her pelvis up and reached between them to notch the wide crest of his cock at her entrance. She moaned and rocked against him, whimpering as the tip breached her slick heat. He growled again and thrust deep, burying himself to the hilt and holding himself there.

"You are mine, Selene," he murmured against her lips. "Feel me claim you."

Their bodies moved with a steady rhythm that started slow, so careful it was almost excruciating. He drew the length of himself from her and pushed in again, deeper, harder. Her body shook, coming alive with fire and starlight that chased each other along her skin. The pace of his thrusts became faster. Seizing her hips, Fen dragged her lower body up as he rose onto his knees, still deep inside her. When he drove into her, the new angle stroked his cock over a secret, perfect place. Her inner muscles clenched, her body bowed, and she was crying out with her release. Fen's body stiffened, the pistoning of his hips grew wild, and she heard him shout as he reached his own climax. He collapsed, rolling them onto their sides, limbs still entwined and skin glistening with sweat.

They lay quietly, moonlight pouring over them.

Then Fen kissed her softly. Then not so softly, and she felt him harden inside her.

"Again?" he whispered.

Selene tightened her arms around him, rolling onto her back, urging him to follow. When he was looking down at her, eyes full of tenderness yet dark with lust, she smiled.

"Again."

18

Selene opened her eyes. She lay on her back, sheets twisted around her bare limbs. The familiar scent of her laundry detergent drifted into her nose. Her own sheets. Her cheek rested against her own pillow. Her body nestled comfortably in her own bed.

The room was bathed in the dusky orange and rose hues that marked dawn. Selene felt a little dazed but not hungover. While whatever she'd drunk last night had done something to her, it hadn't caused nasty, lingering side effects. She could almost believe that she had dreamed up the entire episode. But the fact remained that she was naked.

And then there was that other fact of the man in bed with her. Who was also naked.

She knew he was naked because she could feel his skin molded against her own, every inch of his bare body and his hard muscles, and the scratch of his chest hair. He had one leg draped over hers like a long, thick coil of rope that bound their bodies together. She swallowed and glanced at him.

Fenris still slept. His lips were slightly parted, and Selene could feel his warm breath feather over her bare shoulder.

Okay, Selene. Your first pagan holiday where you might have traveled to another plane of existence where you had mind-bendingly good sex with the werewolf pack leader who is now in bed with you. So much for keeping your distance. Next move?

Her gaze wandered to the bedside clock. Seven. She began to plot her escape, stealing another glance at her unexpected guest. She wasn't going to abandon Fen. She just needed a few minutes alone to get her head on straight.

But her heart missed its next beat.

Fen's eyes were open and locked on her. His gray irises were dark as gathering storm clouds.

Simultaneously and inexplicably, Selene wondered what she should say and what she looked like. On the latter count the best she could hope for was mussed, the worst depraved; on the former she wavered between "good morning" and "how the hell did we end up in my bed?"

Before she could speak, he moved swiftly, positioning his body to hover over hers. His eyes perused her naked form before returning to meet her gaze. The look he gave her was heated yet playful. His head dipped, and his mouth moved across her neck, his tongue exploring the hollow of her throat.

Fen's hands were on an expedition of their own, skimming down her torso, tracing the swells at the sides of her breasts. His lips stroked over her collarbone, and he kissed lightly over her heart before his hands moved to cover her breasts. She gasped when his thumbs grazed her nipples, then his fingers teased them with gentle tugs. The gasp became a moan when he took the tip of one breast into his mouth.

Her mind still struggled with what had taken place the night before, but her body remembered very well, and it was clear Fen's body remembered too. Selene heard her own sigh and felt her pelvis arch into him, begging for his attention.

I need to stop this and talk to him. We need to talk.

"Fen, wait."

He instantly became still. "Is something wrong?"

"No," she assured him. "I'm just trying to get my bearings after last night."

"I understand. Take whatever time you need, Selene." He smiled at her, his gaze moving slowly over her features. "You are so beautiful."

She was suddenly, inexplicably shy, considering the intimate night they'd shared. "So are you."

She looked up into his gray eyes and marveled at the depth of emotion she found there. His expression made her shiver, sparked heat low in her body, even though she was trying very hard to stay calm. Need curled in her abdomen, made her thighs quiver. She closed her eyes, remembering the moonlight, the grove. She had never screamed like that. And the way she was responding so quickly to him told her she could reach that peak easily if he took her again. Then she remembered where she was.

Her eyes flew open, wide and alarmed. "Oh my god, Allie!"

She sat up and started to scramble across the mattress.

Fen laughed and caught her wrists, towing her back.

"She's not here."

"Where is she?"

"I asked Josh to take her out for the day," he said.

He dropped her wrists and slid his arms around her waist. He pulled her against him, and she could feel how hard he was.

Wow. Crusades old or not, the man has stamina.

"I didn't want us to be disturbed."

She struggled to concentrate even as her body betrayed her. It helped if she didn't meet his eyes.

"Did she know you were here?"

"No," he said. "We didn't arrive until the early morning hours. Allie was asleep. I asked Josh to wake her for breakfast and to explain that you'd likely sleep for some time due to the late night. She doesn't know I stayed with you. I thought you'd want to speak with her yourself."

"Thank you for that," Selene replied, wondering how she could even begin to explain this to Allie.

Fen leaned in to kiss her.

"Wait." She put a hand on his chest and tried to create space between them. It wasn't easy. She desperately wanted him to touch her, to have his hands and mouth on every inch of her skin. Pulling away from him went against every nerve of her being. Something inside her needed their bodies to be locked together again, hunting that shared ecstasy.

But they really did have to talk.

"What is it?" he asked, letting her inch away.

She forced herself to meet his eyes and found his expression slightly injured and full of concern. That wasn't what she wanted.

"I need . . ." She took a deep breath. "Fen, what happened to me last night? How did we get here?"

Her memories from the ceremony and the grove were clear. After that, things got hazy.

"You were in the thrall of the goddess, her vessel," he said. "And I walked in the shadow of the god as the hunter."

"The thrall?" she frowned. "But how? Was I drugged?"

She remembered the sweet golden liquid she'd drunk just before the ceremony began. The girl who'd given it to her had said it was mead with herbs. But Selene didn't know what those herbs were or how they might have altered her state of mind.

His eyes hardened. "Of course not. Is that what you think of us? Of me?"

"No," she said quickly. "That's not what I meant. There was never a time I didn't know what was happening, or what I was doing. It's just . . ."

She struggled for words. Fen looked deeply offended.

"I seemed to be in my body, but I don't know how I did what I did, even though I chose it. And I did choose. I remember that. But I don't understand where the words I said came from." She pulled her lower lip between her teeth. "I've never felt anything like that. And I was given a drink. Did that do something to me?"

The tension in Fen's expression eased. "The mead you drank was infused with herbs that enhance the divine aspect of existence already within you. It simply made you more aware of that which is usually unseen—the secrets beyond the veil. When you accepted your role, the goddess spoke through you and acted through your body. Just as the god moved in me."

She couldn't stop her smile, despite her worry. "So you *were* a god last night?"

"Yes," he replied. "Such is the rite of Beltane."

Her smile faded. "Wait. That happened and—oh my god, did we have sex *in front of all those people*?"

She bolted upright, dragging a sheet over her naked body as if that could erase the fact that a throng of paranormals had witnessed her taking her dress off.

Fen shook his head. "They saw you invite me to the altar and invoke the goddess, but in the grove we were alone. Everything that transpired there belongs only to us."

She felt the color draining from her cheeks. "Thank god. I am not an exhibitionist."

"Neither am I." He chuckled.

"I don't know how to accept that I took part in it at all." She shuddered at the idea that she'd gotten naked with Fen on a stone slab in the middle of the woods with most of the town looking on.

"You must see the divine that moves around you and through you, those forces that guide us all." He reached for her, but she shrank from him.

"Selene." His voice was soft but chiding.

"I should at least have been asked," she insisted, then frowned.

But she had been asked.

Choose.

The word had been so clear. That, she did remember. But why had she continued with the rite after placing the crown on Fen's head? She could have stopped it there. She'd understood that was an option, but she hadn't. Why had taking the next step felt so right? So necessary? In the light of day, her reasoning seemed much less clear.

Stubbornly, she continued. "I could have been told what would happen before it all went forward."

"It doesn't work that way," he said. "There are many ways the ritual can proceed. The choice belonged to you, and you chose the path of the sacred union."

He suddenly smiled. "We were brought together in the rite. It was a great blessing."

"You're talking about things I don't believe in." Selene slowly shook her head. "None of that is part of my life."

He moved too swiftly for her to dodge and caught her in his arms. She surrendered to the warmth of his body for a moment, resting against him. He felt so good. Why couldn't he have been a park ranger? Or a teacher? Anything but a werewolf pack leader. She knew she was too tangled up in him to walk away, but that didn't mean she wouldn't go down fighting.

"You have the mark of the goddess." He nuzzled the small tattoo on her shoulder. "You have already honored her and acknowledged her place in your life."

The tattoo was old, faded. The woman in the indie ink parlor a few blocks from UC Berkeley had told eighteen-year-old Selene that it was the moon in three phases. And something else . . . maiden, mother, crone. *Oh shit.*

"Uh, no. No, no," she said with another shake of her head, electing to dismiss that evidence. "I got that in college. Budding feminist, rebellion against parents, insert other lame cliché here. But tattoos used to be much more shocking than they are now. It's a woman-power thing."

"Yes." He nodded. "You are powerful. Chosen by the Lady. It is an honor to caress you, to be welcomed into your body."

Selene couldn't stop her blush, but she still frowned. "Lady? What Lady?"

"The goddess." His tone was patient, but she could tell he was amused by her resistance. "But you already know this, Selene. Trust your instincts."

"I'm an atheist."

He laughed, a deep rumble of thunder. "Can you honestly say that after your experience last night?"

"I'm still not sure what happened last night," she said. "I don't know if I'll ever understand it."

"It may take you time to accept your role in our world," he murmured. "It's very reasonable to have questions, and I will provide what answers I can, as will your other friends."

His lips brushed over hers and stole her breath.

"But we are no longer the god and goddess. Only Fenris Hall and Selene Jones. This is all I've craved since I first saw you. To be with you. To be yours. And you mine."

That took her by surprise. "Even at the bookstore? You pretended you didn't know who I was."

"I engineered that encounter," he admitted, and Selene was charmed to see that he was embarrassed by his confession. Once again Avondale's fearsome leader had made himself vulnerable for her sake. "You'd just arrived in town, and I needed to take your measure, to gauge whether you were suited to life in Avondale, but I wasn't prepared for the reaction I had when I came face-to-face with you. I chose to dismiss that response as simple lust. It . . . has been a long time since I've taken a lover."

Fen's hesitation signaled to Selene that, for the time being, that statement was better left alone. She stayed quiet despite her curiosity.

He ran his finger down her neck, along her shoulder. "I already knew you were intelligent. Driven. Protective of your niece. I had no idea you would be so beautiful."

Leaning closer, he pulled in a slow, deep breath. "Or that your scent would be irresistible. It created a quandary for me. I had to decide how to act in a matter of seconds, and I chose not to reveal myself to you that day. I apologize for the deception."

"You were feeling all that?" Selene remembered his easy smiles and casual, friendly manner in the bookstore. "You must have an incredible poker face."

"I do." He grinned, then his smile became wolfish. "Now let me show you how much I wanted you from the first. How I will always want you."

Fen gave the sheet Selene had covered herself with a hard tug, stealing it from her. The expression that came over his face when her body was bared to him again was the death knell for what remained of Selene's resistance. His growl made her thighs clench. She waited for him to lunge at her, the anticipation making her breathless.

Instead he leaned down to place a kiss just above her knee. He kissed her again, moving a hairbreadth up her thigh. His tongue flicked out, caressing her sensitive skin. She was already coiled so tight, aching, fully aware of Fen's endgame. But he was surely going to kill her by taking his time getting there.

He licked her again, then kissed his way back toward her knee.

Oh no. That was unacceptable. Fen might have built up centuries of patience, but her stores were dwindling rapidly.

Selene's fingers twitched as she considered grabbing a handful of his thick hair and dragging him to the juncture between her thighs. The situation was getting that desperate.

There was another rumble, but this one came from her stomach.

Fen lifted his head, laughing. "You're hungry."

"Apparently." Her stomach had the world's worst timing.

Would it be rude if I pushed his head back down? Though it was tempting, she couldn't imagine actually doing that.

"It's no wonder." He rose to his knees and reached out to stroke her cheek. "You haven't eaten all day. It's nearly dusk. Let me take you out for a very late breakfast, or early dinner if you prefer."

"Dusk?" Selene straightened and looked at the clock. Seven thirty. She'd assumed that was a.m. She glanced out the window. The hazy, pastel light was still there, but the shadows were deepening. "We slept all day?"

"We were up all night," Fen answered.

She was tempted to ignore her growing hunger and suggest they return to what it had so rudely interrupted, but her stomach growled again. This time it bore an alarming resemblance to a roar.

God, why am I so hungry all of a sudden?

She cast Fen an apologetic glance, but he pressed his fingers against her lips before she could speak.

"Don't worry, Selene." He smiled. "Once you're fed, I plan to have you beneath me again, or on top of me. Whatever you prefer. Consider this a brief intermission. But first a shower. And while we eat, I'll answer the questions I can see you're still desperate to ask."

He slipped his arms beneath her and rolled them both off the bed, landing effortlessly on his feet.

"By the way, are you ticklish?"

She was shrieking with laughter when he carried her into the bathroom.

19

Allie was surrounded by beauty. Flowers filled the air with their sweet spring scents, and early evening shadows made the ivy look like it was climbing and twisting over the stone before her eyes. It should have been a magical evening, but she couldn't enjoy it. Her mind was too full of thoughts tumbling over one another. Thoughts about her dad, about family, about love and loyalty. When she sighed, Josh squeezed her hand.

"What's wrong, Allie?"

"Nothing." She avoided meeting his eyes, afraid he'd see she was keeping things from him. "I just think I should get home. Check in with Aunt Selene."

Allie wanted to hear what her auntie had to say about the Beltane ritual. Josh had been frustratingly reticent about the whole thing. And she was desperate to tell Auntie Sel about her dad coming to the house. It didn't feel right to tell anyone else before her aunt knew. Ugh. If she was completely honest with herself, she was nervous about Josh finding out. She knew that he, that all werewolves, despised vampires.

"Aren't you enjoying yourself?" He used his grip on her hand to reel her in for a kiss.

Butterflies swarmed in her belly, and she smiled against his lips. Even when she was distracted by worry, he made her body fizz with delight.

"I am," she told him. "You know I love the garden. Especially at sunset."

"That's why we're here." He grinned and kissed her again.

"You're being awfully nice." She narrowed her eyes at him. "We've done all my favorite things today. Donuts for breakfast, a bike ride, ice cream, pizza, now the garden."

"I wanted to make up for last night," he said. "I missed you."

She snuggled into the curve of his arm. "Thanks. I missed you too. I'm bummed I couldn't be at the party."

It probably wasn't fair to be suspicious. Josh liked to spoil her, and it was no surprise he felt guilty he'd left her alone last night. He'd left her alone . . . and look what had happened. None of it was his fault, but her mood had soured because of it.

"Is that all it is?" He rested his chin on the crown of her head. "You've been kinda out of it all day."

"I'm just worried about my aunt." That was a half-truth. Her insides had been jumping around with nerves since the moment her dad showed at her front door and the one person she needed was unavailable.

"I told you she had a great time last night," Josh said. "She's fine."

"Can you please take me home?" She pulled away so she could look at him. "I'd really like to talk to her."

Josh shuffled his feet, avoiding her gaze. "I think she's busy."

"What do you mean she's busy?" she asked. "You said she'd be asleep all day."

Allie didn't get why he was being so weird. Josh was usually warm and cheerful with her, but he'd been guarded all day. Maybe she'd been so distracted by her own problems that she'd done something wrong. Great. Now she was paranoid that Josh was mad at her.

"If I let you know what's going on, you can't tell your aunt," he said with more than a little reluctance.

Her worry that she'd upset him mingled with a new fear that Aunt Selene was in trouble. Had she messed up the Beltane ritual? Oh god, was she in paranormal jail? "Tell her what?"

"That I told you who she's with right now."

"She's with someone?" Allie's eyes widened. "I thought she was at home in bed."

"She is," he answered, voice sly.

"Josh!" Allie gasped. "You'd better tell me what's going on, right now!"

He laughed. "She's with Fen."

Allie stared at him. "Aunt Selene and Fenris . . ."

She felt like shock had turned her limbs into stone as his words sank in. All she could do was stand there and stare at him. The words coming out of his mouth couldn't have been further from what she'd imagined.

He kept laughing.

When she convinced her body to move again, she slugged him in the arm. "Stop!"

"Your face was priceless," he said and touched her cheek. "Why are you frowning? I thought you'd be happy."

"I'm just surprised," Allie said and shifted her focus to a nearby rosebush. In bed with Fenris was better than paranormal jail but still troubling. A few days ago it wouldn't have been, but today . . .

"Why surprised?" Josh asked. "We've talked about this. Fen and Selene make a good match. It was just a matter of time."

"I know . . . but that was before—" She cut herself off.

His brow crinkled. "Before what?"

"Never mind," she said quickly. "But I do really want to talk to her. Can I go home now?"

She couldn't tell Josh. Not yet. Not when everything she'd believed about her life and what it should look like had been turned on its head. Frustration bubbled, churning in her belly.

"I just told you that she's not alone," he countered. "It might be awkward—"

"I know, but I need to go home," she said and kicked the gravel path with the toe of her shoe.

Josh shook his head. "That would be a bad idea."

"It's almost dark, Josh," Allie said. "Do you really think they're still . . ."

Heat poured into her face, and she couldn't finish the sentence. Wishing her aunt would get a happy ever after was one thing. Thinking about her doing things with Fenris was something else entirely.

"Knowing Fen, I'd bet on it." He smirked. "He won't be able to get enough of her. And there is no way I'm going to risk pissing him off."

Nope. She didn't like this at all. And it felt really disrespectful for Josh to be so casual about something Allie thought was serious. She crossed her arms over her chest. "That's my aunt you're talking about! Knock it off."

"I didn't mean any offense," he said quickly. "He won't do anything to hurt Selene. I told you that. I don't want to interrupt their time together. It's not only about sex. He has important things to discuss with her."

"Like what?"

"I'm not allowed to talk about it before he's given me permission," he said, expression shuttering.

"That's not fair," Allie said. "There are so many things you can't tell me. I don't like it."

Maybe my dad was right. Maybe Josh isn't being honest with me. Maybe I can't trust him as much as I thought.

Josh shrugged. "I don't cross the pack leader."

He gave her a serious look and slipped his arms around her waist. "Neither should you."

"Josh!" A gruff voice reached them from the direction of the manor.

Allie had been about to push Josh away, still angry that he was dodging her questions, when she turned to see two tall, broad-shouldered men walking swiftly toward them.

"Hey, Bannock. Hey, Ewan." Allie shifted nervously on her feet as they drew near.

Most of the werewolves seemed like regular people to her, but Fen's personal guard always made her blood run cold. They were as old as Fenris, his closest advisers and fiercest warriors. Josh had told her too many stories about their exploits in defense of the wolves' territory. All tales brimming with violence and death.

"Allison." Bannock's long chocolate-hued hair was caught behind his head, the length tied with a strip of braided leather. He flashed teeth at her. She knew it was a wolfish smile, but she still had to fight back a shudder. Sometimes werewolves were just plain scary.

"Evening, lass." Ewan was never anything but formal and overly polite, and echoes of an ancient Scots brogue gave everything he said a pleasant lilt. His sweep of ebony bangs fell in front of his eyes when he inclined his head in her direction.

"We need to speak to Josh for a moment," he continued. "Will you excuse us?"

"Sure." Allie was happy enough to give the guards space, but Josh kept one arm tight around her waist. She was simultaneously annoyed and comforted. How much sense did that make? Too many things were happening too quickly. The sudden pivots of her own emotions were exhausting, and she had no idea what to do about it. On the one hand she wanted to turn and bury her face in Josh's chest; on the other she was tempted to flip him off and run away.

"What is it?" he asked.

"We finished the trace this afternoon," Bannock said. His eyes flickered to Allie.

Even that brief glance made her lean into Josh, which made it sting deeply that he was the one to step away from her.

"You'd better give us a few minutes, Allie," Josh said.

"I'll just wait for you by the fountain," she said, not liking how quickly she could go from feeling like she was at the center of Josh's universe to being set aside for more important matters. Was that what it meant to be a werewolf? The pack always came first?

She glanced back once to see the three men huddled in a tight circle. Josh's body tensed, and as the other men spoke, he looked more and more unhappy. An icy trickle of foreboding slid along the back of Allie's neck. She shook off the strange, unpleasant feeling and continued down the path until she reached a large marble fountain at the center of the garden. Taking a seat on the edge of the rippling pool, she trailed her fingers through the clear water. A few days ago she would have tossed a coin in the pool and wished for something to happen between Aunt Selene and Fen. Now she was close to wishing the opposite. Her dad had confused everything.

Why did he have to be so nice?

She'd spent years being angry at him for leaving, and she'd forgotten all the good things about him, especially how funny he was. He'd hung out with her for several hours last night. They'd watched TV together. He'd listened to her stories about school. He'd even been okay about Josh—and she knew he couldn't be crazy about the fact that her boyfriend was a werewolf. Vampires and werewolves rarely got along. He did offer some warnings about the drawbacks that could come along with wolves and their strict pack rules, but nothing he said was unreasonable.

And then he'd hinted that he wanted to be a family again. Not just with her, but with Aunt Selene as well. According to Daniel, once upon a time her mom, her dad, and Selene had been inseparable. Neither Allie's mom nor Auntie Sel had ever said anything about the good times Daniel insisted they had, but both women pointedly avoided talking about Daniel at all after he disappeared. Maybe it had been too sad for them to share happy memories about her dad when they didn't know what happened to him and thought he was probably dead. Her mom always seemed very sad on the rare occasions Daniel did come up in conversation, which made Allie reluctant to ask about him. It had been easier to pretend he'd never been important. Why make up a perfect dad if she was never going to really know him? She did have fond memories of surprise visits, parties, and presents. And she had to admit, it was pretty cool he'd been in a band that toured around the world.

Would it be so bad if he and Aunt Selene became friends again? And eventually, maybe, something more?

At first that idea struck Allie as super weird, but her dad kept saying that close friendships could grow into love, and he had so many compliments about Auntie Sel. How happy he was that she was taking care of Allie, how loyal a friend she'd been to Allie's mom. The more he talked about him and Aunt Sel, the better his suggestions sounded. And now she couldn't stop thinking about how nice it would be to make a family that linked the past and the future. Was it wrong to want to have a dad who wanted to be in her life as much as Daniel seemed to?

Yeah, the vampire thing was . . . not great. But he'd also explained a lot about the prejudice werewolves have toward vampires. That the wolves told lies about vamps to turn other paranormals against them. It was all about power, Daniel said. From what Allie learned in her history classes, that rang true. Daniel wanted to take her and Aunt Selene to Europe, where they could visit towns ruled by vampire covens. Places he swore were more beautiful and luxurious than she could imagine. Where, as his daughter, she'd be treated like a princess.

It sounded so silly she wanted to laugh out loud, but a part of her craved that kind of attention. To feel special and magical. Especially since the werewolf rules meant she had to wait ten years before she could join the pack and become Josh's mate. Daniel agreed with her that it was an old-fashioned, stupid requirement. If she were in love, what could be more important? He treated Allie like her opinions mattered as much as, if not more than, his own.

Their conversation had knotted her up inside. She was thrilled by his attention and the promises he made, but guilt poked at her because she knew Josh would be unhappy that she'd seen him. Keeping her dad's visit a secret felt like she was betraying her boyfriend, but she knew if she told Josh, he'd find a way to keep Daniel from seeing her. She didn't want that to happen.

Knowing her aunt hooked up with Fenris at the Beltane celebration messed everything up. She didn't understand why Aunt Selene had changed her mind about Fen so suddenly. Hadn't she told Allie she wanted to wait? That it was too soon for her to get involved with someone she didn't really know? But then she turned around and spent the whole night with him!

They hadn't even had a real date, had they? She worried her aunt had been lying to her all along because she didn't want Allie to have sex with Josh. That was so unfair, and she was a little angry about it, but mostly she was confused. She just wanted to talk to Aunt Sel and find out what was really going on.

"Allie." Josh appeared on the path. Bannock and Ewan were nowhere to be seen.

"Everything okay?" she asked. From the look on his face, it wasn't.

"We need to talk." He sat next to her. "How close are your aunt and Natalie Lyon?"

Allie was certain her heart stopped beating for a moment. "Why?"

"Something very unpleasant is about to happen."

◆ ◆ ◆

Selene and Fen settled into a booth at Midnight Broil. She decided that breakfast sounded about right after all, and this diner was the only place in town that served it twenty-four hours a day. She looked at the menu and pushed her hair back from her forehead. It was still damp from the shower, but she'd been too hungry and distracted to bother drying it.

She was still distracted. It was difficult to think about what she might like from the menu. Her mind kept wandering to the things Fen had done to her in the shower. Good things. Wickedly good. Impossibly good.

Sneaking glances at him across the table as she perused the menu, she already wanted more. She couldn't get enough of him.

Not for the first time, a part of her wondered if she'd been in a car accident on the drive up from LA, and now she lay in a coma dreaming up this wondrous world, this incredible man. Accepting that this new, magical reality was real never seemed to get easier. Real or not, her mind was humming with ecstasy, and her body crackled with desire and joy.

"I like to see you looking so happy." Fen reached across the table to touch her hand. "Is it truly because of me?"

She nodded, blushing, and curled her fingers around his. He gave her that slow smile she couldn't resist, and her heart sped up. She caught herself speculating about whether it would be out of the question for him to strip her clothes off and ravish her in the booth. Then she realized that given he was Fenris Hall, wolf king of Avondale, the restaurant would probably politely clear out and leave them to it. That shouldn't have been such a tempting idea.

She lightly squeezed his hand and then pulled her fingers away from his, determined to behave like a sane person.

I never should have read that stupid book. Too many bodice-ripping scenes are stuck in my head. Sure, keep telling yourself that, Selene. You know the book has nothing to do with it.

"Coffee?" A pale-faced teenage waiter hovered alongside the booth and cast nervous glances at Fen.

"Yes, Tom," Fen said. "Thank you."

"For me too," Selene added, peering at their server. Something about him was familiar . . .

"Great." Tom bobbed his head and scurried away.

Selene laughed at his abrupt departure. "Do you always make wait staff act like that?"

"No," Fen replied with a wry smile. "He's a vampire. They're a little more skittish around me than others."

Selene stared after the waiter. "Vampires work here?"

"Only the night shift."

"Of course." Selene laughed ruefully. "I'm still getting used to all this."

"Be patient with yourself."

"It's happening a little too fast for patience," she said.

"I suppose that's true."

Tom reappeared with two mugs of coffee.

"Are you ready to order?"

"Selene?" Fen gestured to her.

"Sure." She scanned the menu. "I'll have the steak and eggs. And a side of bacon."

She frowned. She never ordered steak and eggs.

"How would you like your steak?"

"Rare," she replied automatically and frowned again. She always ordered her steak medium.

"And the eggs?"

"Um . . . scrambled. No wait, over easy."

Tom jotted down her order. "Hashbrowns or home fries?"

"I don't need any sides," Selene told him. What was up with her today? She loved hashbrowns. Especially the crispy edges. But at the moment they sounded gross.

"Mr. Hall?" Tom looked at the werewolf.

"Another order of bacon and an order of sausages."

Tom raised an eyebrow. "Would you like anything else? Off the other menu?"

"No, just what I already mentioned." Fen inclined his head. "Thank you, Tom."

"Of course, Mr. Hall." He took their menus, jerked forward in something that almost resembled a bow, and then walked away.

"What's the other menu?" Selene asked.

"They have special items that paranormals can eat," Fen said.

"Like raw meat?"

"Yes."

Not weird, Selene insisted to herself. *I already knew that's what werewolves eat. Don't freak out because the diner has a secret menu with raw meat on it and probably other stuff I shouldn't think about.*

"You can order," she said. The idea of a slab of bloody meat on Fen's plate was far less repulsive than she would have thought. "I wouldn't mind."

"I'm not hungry."

"You're not?" Her stomach wouldn't stop rumbling, convinced that if it quieted, Selene might ignore it. If she was this hungry, how could

Fen not be? Wouldn't he need to eat more than she did? Maybe she was wrong in presuming werewolves had enormous appetites.

"We hunted last night as part of the rite," he told her. "I'll be full for a while."

"You hunted," Selene said, considering the implication of his statement. "And you ate what you hunted?"

He nodded.

"What did you hunt?"

"Deer."

That's pretty normal, I guess. Don't think about Bambi's mom, Selene. Don't go there.

"Why did you order more bacon and sausage?" she asked.

"I suspect you're hungrier than you realize."

She laughed. "I already ordered more than I'll ever eat. I'm hardly a vegetarian, but I never eat this much meat. I don't know what I was thinking."

He didn't say anything, and he wasn't smiling, but his eyes were.

She took a sip of her coffee and ran her tongue over her lips. "Speaking of the rite, I have another question for you."

"Ask away." Fen leaned back, slinging one arm along the top of the booth.

Selene suddenly wanted nothing more than to crawl beneath the table and snuggle under that arm.

But I will not. I will not. *Because that is not normal. Pagan rite or no, I am still a nonmagical, normal person. That whole goddess-thrall thing was definitely a one-time deal.*

"Who were the men with you last night?" she asked, needing to distract herself.

"My guard."

Selene tilted her head at that answer. "You have a guard?"

"Bannock, Ewan, Gabriel, and Kipp," he said. "The oldest wolves in the pack and my closest friends. We left Europe together to form a new pack in America. We spent decades exploring the country, gathering more wolves into our pack along the way, until we found the sacred grove here. Along with me, they are the founders of Avondale."

Selene's eyebrows shot up.

"They advise me on political matters." His tone brimmed with fondness and respect. "They watch over the town, and they are leaders in a fight when violence is called for."

"Does that happen often?" Selene whispered the question.

The closest to a werewolf fight she'd experienced was when Fenris tossed Daniel across her yard. He'd remained in human form then, and it had been scary enough.

"More often than I'd like," Fen said. "But it's been some time since we've had a major incident."

"You said the guard are your closest friends?"

"I did."

"What about Josh?" she asked. She only knew what Allie had told her, which wasn't very much and was filtered through both Josh's and Allie's perceptions of the relationship.

Fen's smile was warm. "Josh is like a son to me. Our bond has been strong since the day I found him lying on the side of the road, near death, and made him part of my pack. He is a warrior and very intelligent, if not yet wise. He'll get there, but he's young for a wolf. One day he'll have a place among my advisers, but not until he's seen another century."

Selene blinked at his casual reference to the passing of hundreds of years. *Will I ever get used to that? Probably not.*

"Do you have other questions?" he asked.

"Yes." She shifted uneasily in the booth, dreading what she was about to ask, but she needed to know. "If you really don't mind."

"Please." He watched her expectantly.

"Last night I was chosen," she began and couldn't keep the nervous edge out of her voice.

She felt like she was drawing back a curtain and wouldn't be able to unsee what was revealed if she didn't like it.

"You were," Fen replied, perfectly at ease.

"But if someone else had been chosen, then you would have . . ." She let the phrase hang in the air between them and looked away when he frowned.

"*You* were chosen," Fen said firmly.

"But I might not have been." She couldn't let it go. The idea of Fen with someone else in that rite . . . It made her sick with jealousy, furious and heartbroken all at once.

"No one else could have been chosen last night," he insisted, but his expression gentled at the worry in her voice. "But if another had been called by the goddess, I suspect—no, I am certain—the ritual would have played out in a different manner. It can take many forms. What happened last night, our union, was only possible because of who we are to one another."

"But you couldn't have known it would be me," she countered. "I saw your face after the old woman called my name and pointed to me. You were surprised."

He paused. "I didn't know," he admitted. "No one did. Only the goddess can reveal who the chosen will be. But I know now that it could not have been different. Our paths were set well before last night."

"Natalie said she's been chosen in the past," Selene argued.

"She has."

"So when it was you and Natalie, you didn't . . . ?" Yet another question she wasn't sure she wanted the answer to.

Fen looked genuinely startled. "I wasn't involved. A different consort is chosen every year, as is a different Lady, and as I said, the ritual doesn't always involve the sacred union. Though it did when Natalie was chosen—"

"Natalie got naked in front of everyone too? Who was the guy, or girl, or person?" Selene blurted before she could catch herself, having destroyed her effort to be cool with the more salacious aspects of pagan festivals. But it made sense now—the way Natalie had tried to warn

Selene that she might not like the Beltane ritual. Natalie had known the rite could get sexy, as apparently it had when she'd been chosen.

Fenris shook his head, obviously a bit frustrated with her unevolved take on possession by pagan deities. "Selene, you're worryingly fixated on the naked part. Nudity isn't shocking for pagans. I know that challenges the paradigms you're accustomed to—"

"I'm sorry, you're right," Selene interrupted. "And I get it. Or I'm trying to. Fenris, I'm not denying that what happened during the ritual felt like more. So much more."

When he nodded, pleased, she couldn't stop herself from saying, "But could you tell me who it was with Natalie? 'Cause I'm dying to know."

He shook his head, chuckling, then his voice grew thoughtful. "It was Gabriel. One of my guard."

"How interesting . . ." Selene couldn't wait to corner Natalie and grill her about the night she'd been chosen by the goddess. Consider it payback for not cluing Selene in on what was going to happen.

Shoving that idea aside for the time being, Selene refocused. "So you aren't always the consort? Even though you're the king of Avondale?"

"I was selected this year because of special circumstances," he replied. "The hunter is named before the rite because of what is required of them, which is the reason I knew what my role would be before you discovered yours."

A wave of relief poured over her. As much as Fenris insisted that what took place at the rite was different every year, and that the intimacy the hunter and Lady shared wasn't always what took place, Selene was too far removed from the paranormal world to completely accept that. It would have been . . . awkward, to say the least, knowing he'd participated in the rite year after year, including once with her closest friend. His explanation also pushed her a little closer to believing what he and Natalie kept saying about fate bringing her and Fen together. But just a little.

"What were the circumstances?" she asked.

"Beltane coincided with the full moon and a specific planetary alignment," he said. "The power raised in the circle was much stronger last night than in other years. The crone said that only a true king could fill the consort's role for this particular rite."

"And you're the true king?"

"Yes." There was no arrogance in his voice.

"What does that make me?" Selene asked.

"The one who belongs at my side." He spoke softly. "I already believed that, and last night our deities proclaimed the truth of that belief."

And there it was again. Fate. Gods and goddesses. "How can you talk about this stuff so easily?"

"I am immortal, and I rule among immortals," he said. "The divine is always close in our world."

He leaned forward and caught her in a gaze that stopped her breath.

"Now I have a question for you, Selene."

She nodded, not trusting her ability to speak.

"What are your feelings for me?"

"What?" Fen tended to be direct, but asking her how she felt about him outright, in public, caught her off guard.

He grinned, enjoying her bewilderment. "Was the question unclear?"

Not unclear, but very uncomfortable.

Instead of looking at him, she focused on the steaming coffee in her mug. She knew the answer to his question, despite the excuses she could make about what she'd told him amid their lovemaking, but it felt much too raw . . . too exposed to let the words hang in the air between them.

"Selene." His tone drew her eyes upward.

She met his dark-gray irises and shivered. The emotion roiling in his gaze demanded a response. An honest one.

"What do you want me to say, Fenris?" she murmured. "That I'm falling for you? That it scares me? That I don't understand why I feel so strongly when we've spent only a short time together?"

"I only want to know what's in your heart, Selene."

"Pretty much everything I just said," she told him. "But I don't know what to do with it. To be honest, Fen, I'm overwhelmed."

"I hear you."

"We met a little more than a week ago." She frowned at him, hoping her words weren't hurtful. "That isn't enough time to know you. Not really."

His smile was mysterious and carried an impish edge. "You're limiting the possibilities of knowledge too narrowly."

She shook her head, snickering. "You paranormals and your ideas about past lives. Natalie said something like that too. I can only say that I met you in the here and now. I don't buy in to the other stuff."

"Then explain the depth of your feelings."

"I can't," she admitted, but she tilted her head and studied him. "Can you explain yours?"

He tensed, smile fading. "When Miriam died, I made a decision to spend my life alone. To be a leader to my people and forsake anything that could distract me or divide my loyalty."

"You were going to be celibate?" Knowing how skilled Fenris was in bed, Selene couldn't believe he'd be willing to live like a monk.

Laughing, Fen replied, "Sexual partners come and go, bringing earthly pleasure, which is no small thing, but it's nothing like the mate bond. It's not love."

Selene winced, ready to apologize, but Fen kept speaking.

"I never believed I would encounter a true mate. Someone I yearned for, body and soul. A thing altogether different from the partner and friend I had in Miriam." His voice was gentle. "But I would never turn from such a blessing. No matter how unexpected it is. No matter how much it complicates my life."

Selene's throat felt dry. She didn't know what to say, so she fumbled for another question. "What does it mean when you say *true mate*?"

"The connection between true wolf mates is inalterable, a union that lasts beyond death," he told her.

"In other lives?" Selene echoed Natalie's words. "And other planes of existence?"

"Yes. The bond is spiritual. But as you can attest, the physical allure of a mate is equally enticing." His irises darkened, and she had to cross her legs to assuage the sudden ache between them. It certainly felt like his body called to hers. With every breath.

"I don't know how to accept what you're saying." Her voice quaked, mirroring the tumble of desire inside her.

"But you feel it."

"Yes."

"Then trust your instincts."

His eyes held hers, and she worried she wouldn't be able to rein in her desire to lean across the table so he'd kiss her. PDA was not her thing. Except during pagan rites, apparently.

A plate clattered on the table in front of her and shocked her back to her senses.

"Steak and eggs with bacon," Tom announced.

She took a moment to look closely at their server. "Have we met before? I swear you look so familiar."

Tom ducked his head, shooting a cautious glance at Fenris before answering. "You uh . . . I also work at the gas station where you had the accident—"

"Oh my god." Selene knew who he was now. The pale face, the smashed glass and spilled coffee. The way he'd licked her blood from his hand. A vampire. Now it all made sense. She'd witnessed the real Avondale before she could grasp what she was seeing.

Fen had gone eerily still. "What accident? Explain, Tom. Now."

Tom shrank back, and Selene rushed to his rescue. "The night I arrived in Avondale, I stopped at the gas station. I dropped a bottle of iced coffee, and it shattered all over the floor. Tom cleaned it all up, and he didn't even charge me for the coffee."

She reached out to clasp Tom's hand, and, wow, his skin was cold. "Thank you again, Tom. You didn't have to do that."

"It was nothing. Really," Tom sputtered, his frightened gaze locked on Fenris.

When Selene looked at Fen, his eyes were focused on the way her hand was linked to Tom's, and she quickly pulled away, but not before she flashed Tom a smile she hoped was reassuring.

"He was very kind, Fen," Selene told the glowering werewolf. "I made so much extra work for him when I dropped that bottle."

Fen leaned back, nodding at Tom. "Generosity of spirit is admirable, Tom. I'm glad you represented Avondale in such a manner to our newest resident."

Tom nodded fervently. "Of course, Fenris."

Fen gestured to the empty space in front of him, and Tom quickly set the second plate there but frowned as if the action was troubling. "Side of bacon and side of sausage."

"Thank you," Fen said.

"You're welcome. Enjoy your meal." Tom visibly relaxed, though his expression remained confused as he scurried away.

The scent of the food wafted around her, and Selene's stomach roared to life again. Her hunger was so fierce, she almost forgot to pick up her fork and knife before she tore into the large slab of meat. She'd finished half the steak that, even dripping red liquid, still seemed overdone, when she remembered Fen was sitting across from her.

She reluctantly set down her fork. "I'm sorry . . ."

He shook his head. "You're hungry. Eat." His eyes were alight with mischief.

After offering him a grateful smile, she started in on the bacon, which wasn't as good as the steak. It tasted burned, but it didn't look charred. In fact, it was some of the floppiest bacon she'd ever seen.

When Tom came back to refill their coffee, she'd finished the steak and her own bacon. She'd taken a couple bites of her eggs but found them unappetizing.

Fen pushed the second plate of bacon and sausages in front of her, and she eagerly began cutting into the meat.

"Bring another order, Tom," Fen said and grinned as Selene chomped on a piece of sausage.

"Are you sure you don't want anything?" she asked before she took another bite. "It's really delicious."

"I'm fine." Fen began to laugh.

"What?"

He looked at the empty plates lined up in front of her.

"Oh my god." With a sense of mourning, she set down her fork.

"That was rude of me," he said but kept smiling. "Please don't stop eating."

"But this is impossible." She stared at the plates. Only her eggs and toast remained.

"You were hungry." He shrugged.

"But I never eat this much," she argued. "And all that meat. I should be sick to my stomach. But I feel like I could eat even more. I'm still hungry."

"That's why I ordered more," he said.

A cold prickling moved over her neck.

"Oh god," she murmured.

"What's wrong?"

"All the meat." She gripped the edge of the table. "I only want to eat meat. And it all tastes overcooked."

He looked unfazed as she stared at him and felt blood drain from her face.

"What did you do to me?"

"Nothing," he said, still calm.

"Then why am I eating like . . ." She had to pause when her stomach turned over. "Like I'm a wolf."

He chuckled. "Trust me, you're not eating like a wolf. Not quite."

"Then what is this?" She didn't take her eyes off his face. "Last night when we . . . Did you turn me?"

"No. Of course not." He crossed his arms over his chest. "I didn't bite you."

One corner of his mouth twitched up. "Even though you asked me to."

"I didn't know what I was saying." She blushed at the rising memory. Because amid the haze of the previous night, she did remember asking him to. More like begging him to.

"I know that," he replied. "Which is why I didn't do it."

The defensive cast of his gaze softened. "You're just feeling the aftereffects of the union. You've taken part of my essence into you. It's influencing your body right now, but it will fade. You aren't a wolf. You're human."

Selene nodded slowly, and her heartbeat grew less frantic. "Is it affecting you?"

"It is. I could eat your eggs and toast without a problem," he offered. "But like I said, I'm not hungry."

Chagrined, Selene eased back into her seat. "I'm sorry I panicked. I didn't mean to imply—"

"I would never treat you with anything but care," he interjected. "And I would not force you into anything."

She pulled in a long breath and then slowly exhaled.

"I believe that," she said. "And I do trust you, Fenris."

"To become immortal, a wolf like I am, should only happen as a choice," he said. "I would never turn you without your permission."

"I know."

He paused, the sudden sharpness of his gray eyes seeming to pierce her soul. "But I would like your permission."

20

Selene forgot how to blink. "You're serious?"

Fen nodded.

"You want me . . . to become a werewolf?"

"Yes."

She continued to stare at him because her frozen brain wouldn't permit anything else.

He offered a thin smile, as if sympathetic to her reaction. "I'd originally thought I would wait. Take more time for you to get to know my world. To know me."

Leaning forward, he placed his hand over hers. "But last night changed everything. I want you to join my pack, Selene."

Her throat was so dry, she didn't think she could speak. The touch of his hand sent her heart spinning like a top. *This is real. I'm having a conversation with my maybe-boyfriend about becoming a werewolf.*

"You belong with us. With me," he continued and stroked her fingers with his thumb. "I'm not interested in waiting."

"What if I'm not ready?" she croaked and grabbed her glass of water, taking several gulps. How could he be so calm about this when she was freaking out? And also, she was absolutely not ready. She was miles away from ready.

"I think you are ready," he said. "Your ideas are simply clouded by the past, by what you thought the world was. Let that fall away."

Selene tried to drum up a reply but found nothing. The problem was that everyone in Avondale used reasoning that relied on magic and things like past lives as if she could simply snap her fingers and let go of everything she believed about the world and its rules.

"Then you'll know that you're one of us," he continued. "The change is simply the final piece of a puzzle to be put in its proper place."

"I don't know," she said.

"You do know." He grasped her hand firmly. "You've already admitted as much."

"I said I'm falling for you." She pulled free and straightened. "I said I want *you*. I didn't say I wanted to be a werewolf."

"One leads to the other," he said quietly, his voice taut.

"Does it have to?"

This time Fen didn't have a response.

"Fenris." Selene watched him closely. "Does it have to?"

"No," he said carefully. "But I would prefer it did."

"Is it a problem that I'm human?" Selene didn't like this new development at all. "And if so, for you, your pack, or both?"

His Adam's apple rose and fell when he swallowed. Silence stretched like a gulf between them, until at last he answered, "The problem is that you'll die."

"Oh." She went still.

"I . . ." Fen cleared his throat. "I can't bear the thought of going through that again. Not when I could have you forever. Not when I know it would be even worse because of who you are to me."

When he lifted his gaze to meet hers, his eyes held a vast sorrow . . . as well as fear. "A human lifespan is terribly brief for one such as myself."

Tears suddenly burned in the corners of Selene's eyes. She was still busy catching up in this new world that had swept her and Allie up with all the gentleness of a hurricane. Knowing she cared for Fenris, a werewolf, was overwhelming on its own. She hadn't begun to consider what a relationship with him would look like, or how long it would last.

But of course Fen had. He exuded so much power and confidence that it resembled pure dominance, but for the first time, Selene understood that wanting her might be as frightening for him as it was for her. Perhaps more so.

"Fenris, I didn't . . . It didn't even occur to me that living forever was a possibility. Or what mortality means to you. I should have—"

"No." Fen dragged a hand through his hair. "I'm pushing because I want you so much. Our perspectives of what life is, how we move through the world, are very different. It's unfair of me to ask you to radically shift your beliefs without giving you time."

"Thank you." *Finally, someone is willing to accept why this is so hard for me.*

They sat quietly. The way Fen held himself, tense and impossibly still, told Selene he was struggling.

Was it the pain of his past? Her reluctance to dive into his world before she could handle how deep the water was? Her fear of her feelings for him?

He'd bared his weakness for her, and she longed to take away the hurt radiating from him. His gaze swept the diner, surveying the other guests, the employees, focusing on anything but her. The sudden distance between them clawed at her. It was awful.

But he was right. She needed time and . . .

"Time." The word slipped out before she knew what exactly she wanted to say.

"What about time?" Fen asked without looking at her, his voice thick with feeling.

"When we talked about Allie and Josh," Selene said. "You told me there are rules. They had to wait ten years before she could become his mate and join the pack."

He slowly turned his head and met her curious gaze, but his face was a blank slate. "You remember."

"Yes, I remember," she replied. "It affects Allie's future. That rule put my mind at ease about her relationship with Josh."

He nodded.

"Why doesn't that rule apply to us?" Selene bit her tongue. Ten years seemed like a good idea for her sixteen-year-old niece, but Selene was thirty-eight. In a decade she'd be staring down fifty. Yikes.

"If you want to be turned, I would ask the pack to grant a dispensation."

"I thought only popes could do that," she teased.

His bright laugh was a balm, soothing the sting of their argument.

"Would they make an exception for us?" Selene considered the question her attempt at an olive branch.

The tightness of Fen's muscles eased very slightly. "I believe so."

Selene nodded. "What about Allie? If I join the pack, does she?"

"No," he replied. "The rule still applies to her and Josh."

With a roll of her eyes, she groaned. "Allie's gonna love hearing that."

"Josh won't like it either." He smiled, and Selene's heart bloomed.

God. I'm beyond falling for him. I'm over the cliff and plummeting.

"How long do I have before you need my final decision?" she asked.

He jolted so hard he almost toppled out of the booth. It was shocking given Fen's usual grace.

Steadying himself, he said, "Selene, there's no deadline when it comes to your peace of mind. I'm sorry if I gave you any other impression."

"Okay." She wanted to touch him so badly, to nestle in his arms and reassure him of her feelings. "Fen . . . what you're offering is incredible. It means a lot."

When humans fell in love, when they promised each other forever, that promise came with an asterisk. Forever had an expiration date because no one lived forever. Fenris wanted to give Selene his life, his heart, for eternity. As much as that thought frightened her, it also wrapped her in warmth and assurance. That made the offer, and the man, very tempting.

"Come here." Fenris's words stretched toward her, carried on a soft growl. "Please."

As Selene left her side of the booth, Fen stood, gesturing for her to slide in. She scooted into the booth, making room for him. When he joined her, she had the distinct impression that he *needed* to be on the outer side of the booth, able to shield her from any unexpected threat.

Fen slipped his arm around her shoulders, and she burrowed against him the way she'd longed to. She inhaled slowly, reveling in his scent. His lips brushed the crown of her head.

"I want you at my side, as my mate," he murmured. "But I am yours whether you become a wolf or not. And I will be with you as long as you will have me."

Selene shuddered, and he tightened his hold.

"I do want you, Fenris. I've never felt the way I feel when I'm with you."

"Selene." He tipped her chin up, lowering his mouth to hers.

Their lips had barely touched when he suddenly straightened and looked toward the door. Two men hovered just inside the entrance, their eyes searching the room until they found Fen. They strode purposefully to the booth.

Selene found herself shrinking back from the approach of the two imposing figures. They were both tall and clearly muscled beneath their long leather dusters. The first man had striking gold irises and burnished brown hair with a slight wave, cut in precise layers, that brushed his jawline. He stopped alongside the table and waited with his legs slightly apart, arms clasped at his low back, as though he were standing at attention. The second man had playful sky blue eyes and a mess of dark-blond hair streaked by the sun. He leaned casually against the booth, looking very much like a surfer who'd wandered too far inland.

Selene peered at the strangers. Their faces were oddly familiar, but she couldn't place them.

"Sorry to interrupt, Fen." The beach bum grinned at her. "Looks like you've got a hot date."

Fen didn't look amused.

"Kipp and Gabriel." He gestured first to the blond man and then to the stiffer of the pair. "This is Selene Jones. You weren't properly introduced at the Beltane celebration."

Selene blinked at them when recognition finally hit her. The pair looked different in, well, clothes. The last time she'd seen them, they'd been wearing leather armor. Very little leather armor.

"Hey." Kipp kept his wide smile on her. "Heard great things about you. It's a pleasure."

Gabriel acknowledged her with a nod.

Selene eyed him with open curiosity. So this was Natalie's Gabriel? She was dying to know the story there. On first impression, the easygoing blond hottie seemed a better match for Natalie's unconventional lifestyle, where the rigid soldier appeared to be Nat's polar opposite, with the exception of the haircut, which lent him a bit of a roguish air. Maybe that cut was courtesy of Natalie and offered a clue that Gabriel's stiff-spined exterior belied his behavior when it came to sexy rituals. Or maybe it was a one-time thing? Natalie owed her a story. And this promised to be a juicy one.

Even as she watched him, Gabriel glanced irritably at his companion before turning his attention to Fen. "We need to speak to you about the violation. We can settle it tonight."

Violation? All thoughts of sexy-time tales evaporated as Selene cast an uneasy look at Fenris, but he was focused on his men.

"You finished the trace."

"We just got a call from Bannock," Gabriel said.

"They're on their way downtown," Kipp added.

Fen was already on his feet. "Very well. You can fill me in when they arrive. I'll meet you in front of the restaurant in a minute."

The two men nodded. Gabriel turned and walked away without another word. Kipp smiled at Selene once more.

"Great to meet you, Selene," he quipped. "Hope you have a fine evening."

He made a gesture as though tipping a hat to her, pivoted on his heel, and followed Gabriel out of the café.

Fen pulled out his wallet and dropped several bills on the table along with his car keys.

"Selene, I'm sorry to leave you like this. Take my car back to your house. I'll have one of my men drop me off to pick it up at another time."

"Is everything okay?" She was startled by his abrupt change in demeanor.

"I'll explain when I'm able," he said, leaning down. "Right now, I have an urgent matter to attend to."

He brushed his lips against hers. She imagined he'd meant it to be a brief, chaste kiss. But the moment his mouth met hers, her arms flew around his neck. Before she knew what was happening, she'd locked her fingers together and dragged him down into the booth. Along with a werewolf appetite, she'd gained some extra strength. She kissed him hungrily, crushing herself against him. His hands caressed the tops of her thighs, and her heart pummeled her rib cage, her body screaming for him to be closer still.

"This has to wait." His voice was hoarse as he pulled back and gently, but firmly, disengaged himself from her grasp.

She blushed and forced herself to scoot back, despite her body's protests. "Oh god. I'm sorry. I don't know what that was."

He laughed and reached out to run his fingertips along her jawline. "Yes, you do."

When he straightened, he kept his gaze on her. "May I come to you tonight?"

Her mind flashed back to her bedroom and then the shower. She knew any sound she made would be a croak, squeak, or whimper, so she nodded.

A smile broke through his otherwise serious demeanor, and Selene grabbed the edge of the table so she wouldn't lunge at him again.

"It may be late," he said with a slight furrow of his brow.

She wordlessly pulled her spare house key from her purse and put it in his hand.

"Just try not to wake Allie," she managed in a husky whisper.

"Until tonight then."

She watched as Fen left the restaurant.

"Oh." Tom appeared with another plate of breakfast meats. "Did he want to cancel this order?"

Selene looked at the heap of bacon and sausage and licked her lips. "Can I get that to go?"

◆ ◆ ◆

Gabriel was accustomed to waiting for orders, but tonight impatience set his teeth on edge. Especially when he had to watch his packmate dance on the sidewalk in the meantime.

"So what do you think?" Kipp grinned and continued to hop on and off the curb in time with some song only he could hear.

Gabriel cast a weary glance at him. "It's not our place to have an opinion."

"Drop the poker face, Gabe." Kipp jabbed at his side, forcing him to whirl away to avoid the sharp strike.

"Knock it off," Gabriel growled. "We're working. And I told you not to call me that."

Kipp's teasing was nothing new. It was always irritating, but Gabriel rarely wanted to punch him. At that moment Gabriel would have liked to flatten Kipp just to take the edge off his own foul temper.

"We can't do anything until Fen gives the order, and your man-of-stone act is creeping me out." Kipp laughed. "I've known you for five hundred years. Your blood runs as hot as any wolf's. You notice the way he is with her. We all notice. She's a good one. Fen's lucky."

"That's Fen's call." Gabriel's lips thinned. Kipp had no idea how hot Gabriel's blood was currently running. No one knew, and Gabriel intended to keep it that way. "And if he's right, luck had nothing to do with it."

Kipp rolled his eyes. "You know what I mean. Do you think she'll go for it?"

"That remains to be seen." Gabriel didn't like speculating about their pack leader's judgment. It felt too close to questioning Fen's authority—to betrayal. Then again, a new pack member affected all Avondale's wolves and was something Fenris would seek counsel about from his closest advisers. Gabriel had been so distracted by his own concerns that he hadn't given much thought to whether Selene Jones should be turned. He probably should so that when Fenris did ask his opinion, he had something reasonable to say. And that might be the right time to finally tell his pack leader . . . no. Gabriel wouldn't think about that right now. There couldn't be a less appropriate time. To distract himself, he said to Kipp, "I don't remember the last time we brought a human over."

"Sure you do," Kipp countered and did an impromptu handstand on the curb. "It was Josh."

"It was, wasn't it?" Gabriel mused, then frowned at his upside-down packmate. "Still into the breakdancing thing, huh?"

Kipp's antics were annoying, but the dancing was a definite improvement over his mime phase in the eighteenth century.

"It keeps me from getting bored while we're waiting for orders. And I get nervous if I'm too still right before a fight. I don't have your patience." Kipp flipped back onto his feet. "And yeah, the last one was Josh."

"No wonder it seems so long." Gabriel shook his head. He raised a brow as Kipp continued his frenetic dance on the sidewalk. "Forcing one's body to stillness in the face of battle is a form of meditation."

Gabriel believed his words, but he hoped there would be no fighting tonight.

"You meditate?"

Gabriel's only response was a slight shrug. Explaining the value of meditation to Kipp would be like extolling the virtues of vegetarianism to a vampire.

"Weird."

"Not as weird as dancing on the sidewalk." Normally Gabriel would have let it go, but sniping at Kipp made him feel a little better. "Especially when you have no music."

"What I'm doing is not weird, it's a distraction—and the music is in my head."

"I think you just proved my point for me."

A silver Mercedes pulled up alongside them and parked. The tinted window whirred down.

"Are you going on tour, Kipp?" Bannock leaned out and grinned before opening the passenger side door and stepping onto the sidewalk.

"Just waiting for my agent to call," Kipp returned. Ewan exited the driver's side and approached them.

The four men, Fenris Hall's guard, were like brothers, but Gabriel found it interesting that they were so markedly different from one another. Kipp, with his sun-kissed hair and golden skin, liked to play the fool, but he was as quick thinking and deadly in a fight as any of them. Bannock mirrored Kipp's playful nature to a degree, but he wielded humor like a knife, with sharp, cutting observations. He was largest of the guard, dark haired, dark eyed, and quick tempered. Bannock's opposite was Ewan, lean and lithe, with moss-green eyes that often shone with compassion. Ewan chose mercy when he could afford to. He was the kindest of them, the one who held the secrets of their hearts. But not even Ewan knew the heaviness that currently weighed on Gabriel's heart.

Gabriel was aware that his fellow guard considered him brooding and surly, often reticent. He preferred to think of himself as thoughtful, unwilling to speak without carefully considering any matter at hand. Usually that wasn't a problem. Gabriel had long been comfortable with himself and his way of living. But in an unprecedented crisis where he was caught between duty and desire, the ability to deliberate and use reason had been stolen from him. And he had no idea what to do.

"Where's Fen?" Ewan asked, pulling Gabriel back into the moment.

"Right here." Fen appeared around the corner, face drawn, gray eyes storming.

Kipp started at the pack leader's sudden arrival and barely managed to keep himself upright as he slipped off the curb. Gabriel remained perfectly still, but he threw a mocking half smile at Kipp.

"Here's the report." Ewan handed a stack of papers to Fen, who began to frown immediately as his eyes scanned the pages.

Bannock's grin vanished. "Sorry, Fen. It's much worse than we thought."

Gabriel winced inwardly. He hadn't read the full report, but Ewan had given him a summary of its contents. When Gabriel realized what would follow, it felt like barbed wire wrapped around his heart with a slow, inexorable squeeze that would ultimately kill him.

"I see that." Fen turned another page and walked to the front passenger door of the car. "Get in."

Bannock, Gabriel, and Kipp slid into the back seat. Fen was still reading when he closed the passenger door. Ewan returned to the driver's seat.

"Someone explain to me how this has been going on without our knowledge?" Fen's question barely concealed his snarl.

"She's a very clever little witch," Kipp offered, and Gabriel slugged him in the shoulder. Hard. "Fuck it, Gabriel! That hurt."

It was meant to. Gabriel bared his teeth at Kipp, who stared at Gabriel with confusion as he rubbed his shoulder. Of course Kipp was confused. It wasn't like Gabriel to hit his packmates without good reason. But Kipp had no idea what Gabriel was going through. Gabriel was having a difficult time facing the truth of it.

"Not the answer I was looking for." Fen's voice was dangerous.

Gabriel glowered at Kipp as if to say, *I told you.*

Kipp rolled his eyes. It wasn't the real reason Gabriel had punched him, but at the moment it served as explanation.

"She's covered her bases well," Bannock told Fenris as they drove through town. "Doesn't use the same suppliers for more than a few orders, doesn't move bulk. Single items only. It's a different kind of trafficking than what you usually see."

Fen nodded.

"She's been a friend to Selene, Fenris," Ewan said, meeting Fen's eyes in the rearview mirror. "And she's well liked in Avondale."

Fen didn't speak, but his jaw tensed. Gabriel's hands fisted in his lap.

"Josh seemed to think Selene and her niece will take it poorly," Bannock added and glanced at the pack leader.

Tension built in the car as they waited for Fen's orders. When silence stretched out, Gabriel dared to hope and couldn't stop himself from speaking.

"Does that change our response?" Gabriel asked, voice taut. "Perhaps—"

"No," Fen cut him off. "The response will be as the law requires. No exceptions."

There was no arguing when Fenris took that tone. Gabriel tried to pretend the words didn't slice into his gut.

Why should he make an exception? Gabriel chastised himself. *The law is the law. She knew the law. We all know it.*

A few glances were exchanged among the men, but no one objected. The five of them had been together for so long, fought and bled for each other, relied upon one another for centuries. Fenris had yet to lead them astray. Gabriel had to trust in that. In Fen.

"Right then," Kipp said. "Let's get naked."

He began to peel off his clothes.

Ewan snorted, unbuttoning his shirt. Gabriel glared at Kipp.

"Do you always have to say that?" Gabriel growled as he shrugged his leather coat off.

"What?" Kipp laughed. "Just keeping it real. I don't want to lose a shirt every time we do this. Do you?"

"Let's hope you aren't called to this task again for some time," Fen said grimly.

The car pulled up to the curb outside the storefront. It was still illuminated from within, though the sign on the door announced the shop was closed for the day.

"Stay with the car." Fen glanced at Ewan as he climbed from the passenger seat. "We should be back in a few minutes."

Ewan nodded and kept the engine idling.

Fen opened the back door, and three massive wolves emerged.

"I don't think she'll resist," Fen said as the wolves watched him with gleaming eyes. "Do not injure her unless it's absolutely necessary."

Gabriel flicked his gaze toward his pack leader, his muscles tensing at the order. He despised the fact that he'd been about to snarl at Fenris, and he could barely keep himself from whining with distress. But any inner turmoil he struggled with paled in comparison to all he owed Fen: his loyalty, his life. No matter what was asked of him tonight, he couldn't forget that.

◆ ◆ ◆

Natalie couldn't ignore the unwelcome feeling any longer. It had been there all day, like the constant scratching of a mouse in the walls or a shadow that flickers on the edge of one's vision. Natalie rolled her shoulders back, wanting to shake the uneasiness, the looming sense of danger that wouldn't leave her. She'd considered scrying a couple of times earlier in the day, but that felt like giving in to paranoia—or worse, like an invitation for trouble.

She headed into her small sanctuary, lit candles, and blended incense. Cedar for power, deer's tongue and sage for intuition. Smoke curled in the air and wove around her. She took long, slow breaths as she shuffled the cards and let the heady scents draw her to stillness and center her mind. She cut the deck and turned a card.

Ten of swords. Damn.

Natalie closed her eyes and wondered if there was still time to run. She heard shattering glass as whatever was coming for her broke through the shop's front windows. She jumped to her feet and bolted for the back door. She'd only made it a few steps when a heavy push from behind knocked her to the floor. Air rushed out from her lungs.

She managed to roll over and stared up at the snarling wolf. Its front paws came down on her chest, pinning her to the floor. Two more wolves stalked up and flanked the first. Natalie didn't scream. She knew it wasn't worth it.

Fenris Hall walked into the back room. He moved slowly, almost casually, and paused when he stood over her.

"I'm sorry, Natalie," he said as he looked down at her. The cold burn of his eyes was more terrifying than the snarling wolf that held her against the ground. "You've left me no choice."

21

Fen's car was very nice, and Selene hoped the scent of bacon and sausage wouldn't seep into the leather interior. She hadn't driven a Mercedes before and decided she could get used to it, though she'd never be able to afford the speeding tickets. The engine was so quiet, she'd been fifteen miles per hour over the limit without noticing.

She parked the car on the street in front of her house and then trotted down the walk and up the front steps. The door was unlocked.

"Allie?" Selene called and placed Fen's keys on a hook in the entryway.

Silence.

"Allie?" she called again. Nothing.

She shrugged off her coat, hung it up, then set her purse on the hall table as she walked toward the kitchen. She opened the take-out carton and began chewing on a piece of bacon. It tasted less burned now, which must mean the werewolf side effects were wearing off. She finished the first piece and started on a second.

How can I possibly still be hungry? Guess some of the effects last longer than others.

There was no denying how delicious, if overly crisp, the bacon tasted. She finished off the piece and picked up a sausage link, taking a bite as she entered the kitchen.

Someone was already there.

The chunk of sausage caught in her windpipe, and the carton tumbled from her hands to the floor, bacon and sausage spilling across the tile. She banged on her chest, managing to cough up the sausage.

"Hey, Selene." Daniel was sitting at the kitchen table. "You okay?"

He slouched in a chair, legs stretched out, his feet crossed at the ankles and resting on the tabletop.

"It's a little late for breakfast food, isn't it?" he remarked, eyeing the mess on the floor.

"How did you get in the house?" Selene caught her breath. "I didn't invite you."

"You left Allie all alone last night," he said with a mocking grin. "I thought she might need some company. She was happy enough to invite me in."

"Where is she?" she demanded, terrified at the possibilities. She'd been away for hours. "Daniel, if you hurt her, I swear—"

"Of course I didn't hurt her," he cut in as he swung his feet off the table and rose languidly from the chair. "She wasn't home when I got here tonight. I don't know where she is. I figured you'd show up eventually, so I made myself comfortable. We still have a lot to talk about."

"I have no interest in talking to you," she said. "You're not welcome in this house, and you had no right to come looking for Allie when I wasn't here."

He sauntered from the table toward the kitchen island. "I'm her father. I wanted to catch up, so I stopped by while you were . . . out. I owed her some dad time. It was a blast. She needs a man around to give her some guidance."

"You're the last person she needs guidance from."

She watched him with wary eyes. He kept moving toward her until she backed into the sink.

"Come on, babe." He smiled, and she caught a flicker of light within his irises. "Can't I get the benefit of the doubt?"

"No," she said firmly, careful to avoid meeting his gaze.

"Look at me," he purred.

"Not a chance," she snapped. "I learned my lesson the last time."

"You freaked out just when things were getting interesting." He kept his voice low and seductive, but without eye contact it had no effect other than repelling her.

"I don't know how you managed to talk Allie into inviting you in." Selene fixed her gaze on the tile floor. "But I have no doubt it wasn't completely her idea."

"Why would you say something like that?" He scoffed.

"She knows better than to trust you," she said. "And certainly better than to invite a vampire into our home."

"She's been getting some bad information." Irritation spiked his words. "I can't believe you'd let her get mixed up with werewolves."

"That's none of your business. Josh is a lovely young man." Since she'd left her purse and its crosses in the front hall, she raised her eyes to search the kitchen for her holy-water-filled bottle. It was sitting on the counter. Right behind Daniel.

"It is my business," he snapped. "I won't let one of those dogs touch my daughter. I talked to her last night, and you've clearly let things between them go much too far. What were you thinking?"

"Stay out of it," she said, running through multiple scenarios about how she might reach the bottle. "You don't have a say in Allie's life."

"I thought better of you, Selene." His voice sharpened.

"Allie cares for Josh. Deeply. You have no idea what you're talking about."

"It's not just about Allie." He hissed the words, which made her glance at his face. His eyes weren't hypnotic, but they were feverish. His lips were curled back. A skittering cold moved down her back when she saw how sharp his fangs were.

"I'm hearing rumors I don't like." Daniel leaned against the kitchen counter. The casual pose belied the fury carving hard angles into his features.

"Is that so?" She tried to keep the nervous edge out of her voice.

"Would you like to tell me what happened last night at the Beltane ritual?" His smile was like frost.

"It sounds like you already know about it." Lying seemed futile.

"I was hoping you'd have a version I'd like better than the talk around town," he said.

"What do you want me to say?" Her heart was racing. She stepped toward him so she could get closer to the bottle but was still careful not to look directly into his eyes.

"Tell me what exactly is happening with you and the wolf," he snarled, moving closer, boxing her in.

She put a trembling hand against his chest. When the moment came, she'd have to push him, and she hoped he would budge despite his vampire strength. "Nothing that concerns you."

"Are you telling me you'd let Fenris Hall take my place?" There was a madness in his eyes that matched the insanity of his question.

It took Selene a moment to grasp his meaning. Disbelief jolted through her. Was his mind that twisted that he'd convinced himself Selene could want him? If she wasn't so frightened, she might have laughed at his outrageous claim.

"What the fuck are you talking about, Daniel?" Though Selene knew it might provoke him, she couldn't hold back her anger. "You have no place with me! You never have!"

She lunged for the water bottle, but Daniel grabbed her. Her fingertips brushed the bottle, and it tipped over and rolled off the counter. He spun her around. She cried out when her lower back slammed into the edge of the counter, pain lighting up her spine.

"So you gave yourself to him in front of the whole town," he snarled in her ear. "Is that who you are now? The wolf's whore?"

Every insult Daniel spat revealed the stark difference between him and Fenris. Daniel wanted to possess her, use her, shame her into submission. Fen craved Selene in a wild, ferocious way, but treasured her as well. He struck a perfect balance between passion and respect that proved how deeply he cared for her, that he . . .

He loves me. Fenris loves me. And I . . . oh god . . . I have to survive this . . . I have to get to Fen and tell him what he means to me. He needs to know.

"Let me go." Her back throbbed, and his grip was bruising her wrists. "Daniel, please. You're hurting me."

He pulled back so his face was in front of her. His smile made her shudder, but it was his eyes that sent sickening spirals through her gut. Selene saw a promise in his gaze that he planned to inflict pain upon her, and he would enjoy it.

"I think I deserve a chance to prove myself, don't you?"

"No," she whispered. Had he always been this monster, or did becoming a vampire take his worst qualities and infuse them with pure evil?

"Too bad." He bit her lip, and she tasted blood. A throaty snarl slid from his chest. "I tried to do this the nice way. But now I want to hear you scream, Selene."

"Don't do this." She knew her pleas were hopeless, but she wouldn't give in. No matter what Daniel said or did.

When he laughed, she brought her knee up into his crotch. He grunted and dropped her wrists. She bolted for the back door but screamed when he caught a fistful of her hair and yanked her backward.

"You bitch."

Daniel twisted her hair, using it like a rope to wrench her neck and throw her to the floor. He grasped her wrists in one hand and pinned her arms to the tile above her head. His other hand ripped open the front of her blouse. She shrieked and struggled to free her arms.

"Come on, babe," he said. "Just relax. We'll have some fun, and then I'll finish it. Don't you want to be beautiful forever?"

He stroked her neck and ran his tongue over his fangs.

"Daniel." She shook her head. "I don't want this. Stop."

"Fenris Hall won't touch you again." He smiled. "Not when you're one of us. I'll turn Allie too. Take good care of her. Both of you."

"No!" She couldn't let herself think about Fen, about losing him, about facing an eternity without him. Giving in to despair would sap her strength, and she would die before she let Daniel turn her or Allie.

"Listen to your heart pounding," he purred and leaned down. His tongue flicked along the throbbing vein in her neck. "I'll bet your blood is almost boiling. Don't worry. I won't take too much. I fucked it up with Emma, but I'll be more careful this time."

It took several seconds for his words to sink in.

"You killed her." Selene was so stunned, she stopped struggling. "It wasn't a mugger. *You* killed Emma."

"I didn't mean to." Daniel had the audacity to sound annoyed. "But she fought me, and I got all riled up."

She couldn't believe what she was hearing. She thought she couldn't revile Daniel more than she already did, but he proved her wrong. Disgust and fury slammed into her with such force, she felt like she'd be sick.

He murdered my best friend, the mother of his child, and he's making it her fault.

Taking Selene's stillness as surrender, or simply wanting to hear himself talk, Daniel pushed her hair away from her face. The action was almost wistful.

"Such a pain in the ass for me," he grumbled. "I had it all set up. The perfect plan. Me, Emma, Allie, traveling the world."

His face twisted with fury. "But she didn't get it. She said no. To me. Can you believe it? She was my fucking wife!"

"You never deserved her, you bastard." Selene used all her strength to wrench her body sideways.

It was no use. Her wrists remained locked in Daniel's grip, and his other hand clamped around her throat.

"Now, now, Selene," he chided. "It's time for you to start being nicer to me."

He moved his hand from her throat to her jaw, leaving her neck exposed.

When he bent his head and his fangs pricked her skin, she screamed.

Her mind threw a desperate plea to whatever deity might hear her. *Please don't let this happen. Don't let Daniel win. He can't win.*

There was a pounding that she thought was her own panicked pulse, but then a dark shape appeared in a blur over Daniel, and in the next moment his weight lifted off her. Choking on a sob, she rolled onto her side, covering her neck with her hands.

No blood. Thank god.

Fenris crouched in front of her, in human form, snarling. Daniel tumbled along the floor but swiftly rolled to the balls of his feet, his eyes locked on his assailant.

"I thought you might turn up." He glared at Fen. "I've been looking forward to seeing you again, Fenris."

Fen didn't speak, his muscles taut as he continued to shield Selene with his body.

"I'm going to kill you." Daniel's mouth split into a wicked grin.

"You're going to try." Fen glanced at her. "Get back, Selene."

She scrambled closer to the wall, bumping against the water bottle that had rolled across the floor and stopped there.

The water bottle. Selene grabbed it as Daniel's hand slipped into his jacket and he drew out a pistol.

"I don't think I'll have to try hard." He aimed the gun at Fen.

"No!" Selene threw herself from the wall into Fen's side as she heard the gunshot. She knocked him to the floor, sprawling on top of his body to flatten him as much as she could.

The silver bullet lodged in the wall behind them. Luck was on her side. Fen hadn't expected her to push him down. Catching him by surprise was the only way she was able to leverage her strength against him. If he'd resisted even the slightest, that bullet would be buried in Fenris instead of the wall.

"Shit." Daniel took aim again. "When at first you don't succeed . . ."

With shaking hands Selene unscrewed the cap of the bottle as quickly as she could and hurled it at Daniel. She'd been aiming for his face but only managed a glancing blow to his shoulder.

It didn't matter. With the bottle open, holy water spilled out, splashing Daniel across the neck and right side of his face. As his flesh boiled, he shrieked, trying desperately to swipe away the water.

Fen shuddered, and Selene felt fur beneath her. The wolf's toenails scrabbled against the tile, and she slid off him onto a pile of shredded clothes as he surged forward.

Daniel's eye that wasn't oozing in its socket bulged as the massive animal sailed through the air. The vampire tried to aim the gun again, but he was slammed against the kitchen table before he got another shot off. The gun fell from his hand, clattering to the floor as the table groaned and cracked under the impact of their bodies. Wood splintered, and Daniel fell through the table to the floor with Fenris on top of him. Daniel shrieked curses and flailed at the wolf, but Fen locked his jaws around the man's neck. There was a scream that cut to a gurgle and a sickening crunch.

"Oh god." Selene struggled to her feet and staggered toward them. Fen's teeth were sunk deep in Daniel's neck. Daniel wasn't moving.

She parted her lips to ask, *Is he dead?* when the wolf made a single sharp jerking movement, and Daniel's head tore away from his body. Selene's knees gave out, and she collapsed to all fours.

A sound like a low hiss moved through the kitchen. Daniel's body shuddered and crumbled into a pile of dust. The wolf pinned its ears back and snorted. A moment later, Fen, naked and all sinewy muscle, crawled across the floor and grasped her shoulders.

"Are you hurt?"

She shook her head, but her limbs began to shake. Her skin felt like ice.

"You're safe now," he said.

Selene stared at the pile of dust that had been Daniel. She thought she might vomit. Fen considered her ashen face, rose to his feet, and went to the sink. He cupped his hands, filled them with water, and rinsed out his mouth a couple of times. He pulled a glass from the cupboard, filled it with tap water, and knelt by her side.

"Drink this." He put the glass into her trembling hands. "Slow sips."

She gagged on the first swallow. Her throat was parched from screaming, and the tight knots in her stomach wouldn't unravel.

"Easy." He touched her cheek. "Try to breathe."

She managed to drink a trickle of water. The sensation of liquid sliding down her throat pushed back the cold numbness creeping over her limbs. She swallowed and took another sip, the simple mechanics of her body reminding her she was alive. She'd survived.

"You tore his head off." She could barely get the words out.

Selene had never seen someone die, much less in such a violent manner. The shock of what she witnessed rattled her very bones.

"I had to kill him," he said in a neutral tone. "Beheading, a stake through the heart, or immolation offer the only true deaths for a vampire."

She shuddered. She wouldn't grieve Daniel, but his death would likely haunt her for some time. The awful tearing sound when Fenris ripped Daniel's head from his body, the sinister whisper of a vampire's flesh becoming nothing more than dust.

"Would you have preferred that I spared him?" His eyes were compassionate but his voice hard.

"I don't know," she began, then realized that was a knee-jerk reply rather than the truth. She shook her head. "No. He would have killed you."

"And he would have violated you and turned you against your will." She could see how he fought to remain calm. And she remembered what she'd realized amid Daniel's attack.

Fen loves me.

Selene closed her eyes and leaned her head back against the wall. She wanted to say something to him. To find a way to gather the torrent of emotion in her heart and offer it up in a confession, in words that could convey her desire, her need for him.

The corruption of Daniel's obsession laid bare the truth of Fen's devotion. Selene was beginning to accept what she'd been insisting to herself was impossible for a mere mortal. Her soul belonged to Fenris. But she was too shaken to find a way to say what she wished she could. Daniel's awful words and the crude hideousness of his touch still lingered, making her feel dirty and sick.

Fen brushed away the tears that slipped from beneath her eyelids.

"I am sorry, Selene," he murmured. "Sorry that you had to face such horror."

"So am I." She opened her eyes. "Thank you for stopping him. I couldn't. He was too strong."

It was so inadequate, that simple thanks, but Fen nodded. His gaze was solemn but tender, conveying that he understood how distressed she was and offered infinite patience in return.

He loves me.

"How did you know?" She pulled the remnants of her shirt together to cover her chest, though the tattered fabric was barely adequate. "I thought you wouldn't be here until late tonight."

"I didn't know." His jaw tightened with fury. "The matter that pulled me from dinner requires my further attention tonight. I came to tell you I won't be able to stay with you, and I wanted to explain what's happened."

Her breath faltered when she realized it was only by chance that Fen had come to her rescue. If he hadn't been there . . .

To stave off hyperventilation, she grabbed on to his reason for coming over. "What's happened? Is something wrong?"

"We'll discuss it in the morning. After you've rested." Fen cupped her face and laid a tender kiss on her lips. "You're in shock, and you need someone to watch over you while you recover. Is there someone I could call? I want to stay, but I can't."

Selene gritted her teeth. Everything in her being wanted to beg Fen to stay. To reassure her that the horror had passed, that she was safe. But knowing how deeply he cared for her, Selene had no doubt that whatever was calling him away couldn't be ignored. Under no other circumstance would he leave her. She knew that without question. Selene didn't want to selfishly demand his presence when someone else needed him. If they were going to be together, she needed to accept that there would be times when Avondale had to come first.

And there was someone else Selene trusted to understand what she was going through. A friend who would comfort her. "You could call Natalie. Natalie Lyon."

When Fen was silent, she looked at him and thought she saw him flinch, but she must have imagined it.

"It's getting late," he said. "What about Tim and Marley? They're right next door."

"Okay." She didn't have energy to argue. "I don't know where Allie is."

"Josh is bringing her here now," he said. "They were already on their way. I spoke with him on the phone just before I arrived. They were at the estate."

"You should get dressed before Allie gets here." Selene made an effort to smile. "I don't think I have any clothes here that would fit you."

He took her hand and kissed it. "There are clothes in my car."

She was about to ask if he could stay for even a little while and hold her, when she heard Allie's alarmed voice in the front hall.

"Auntie Sel? Aunt Selene, are you here? Why is the front door open?"

Allie came into the kitchen and shrieked at the disaster area that greeted her.

"Oh my god!"

Selene tried to stand up, but her knees buckled. Fen caught her and supported her against his body. She was all too aware that he was completely naked, but he seemed unconcerned.

Allie gasped and turned bright red when her eyes found Fen. She sought a safe place for her gaze and ended up turning around completely.

"Allie, what's going on?" Josh stormed into the kitchen. His nostrils flared, then he saw naked Fen and Selene's bruised body. "Shit."

He didn't ask what happened. Maybe he already knew. *Had he smelled the fight? Daniel's ashes?*

Nausea swam in her gut. *Daniel is ashes.*

"She was attacked, Allison, but it's over now," Fen said. "Josh, I have clothes in the trunk of my car. Could you get them?"

Josh nodded but seemed hesitant to leave.

"Attacked?" Allie half turned but reddened again and abandoned the attempt. "Attacked by who? I don't understand."

"The car keys are on a hook next to the front door," Selene told Josh.

"Get the clothes, then I'll tell you what happened," Fen said.

Josh caught Allie's hand and dragged her from the kitchen with him. "Stop it, Josh! I'm still mad at you!"

Allie is mad at Josh?

"Let me take you somewhere you'll be more at ease." Fen carefully lifted Selene in his arms and brought her out of the kitchen, through the hall, and into the living room, where he deposited her on the couch.

Finding two throw blankets, he wrapped one around his waist and settled the other over Selene's shoulders. She snuggled into the soft fabric, wishing she could get warm.

Fen sat beside her, surveying her with concern. "Marley will have something to help you through the shock. I'll get him after we talk to Allie."

"I think I should talk to Allie alone." Selene struggled to think clearly, but her instincts kicked in when it came to her niece. "It's going to be hard for her to hear about Daniel. She didn't know what he was like. Her mother sheltered her from his flaws. I guess I did too."

"It's natural to protect those we love from the dangers and disappointments of this world," Fenris said. "But I'd like to explain to her why his death was necessary."

"I can do that," Selene told him. "And she'll need time to accept it. You killed him, Fen. You had to, but he was still her father. I don't want her to lash out at you. In time, she'll understand."

He cupped the side of her face with one hand. "I can bear Allie's wrath."

"I know you can." She leaned into his touch. His warmth. "But I don't want you to."

"If that's what you wish, I'll abide by your decision," Fen said. "Josh and I will clean up the kitchen, so you don't have to worry about it."

Her stomach lurched. "What . . . what are you going to do with Daniel's . . . remains?"

"Do you want to keep them?" Fen asked with a slight frown. "For Allie?"

"No," Selene said. "But I'd rather you didn't sweep them up and throw them in the trash."

"We wouldn't have," Fen told her. "His ashes will be collected and brought to Marie. As his coven leader, he was her responsibility. She will want to know what happened here."

Selene nodded slowly. "That sounds okay."

The front door opened, and Fen called out, "The living room, Josh."

Josh came into the room carrying folded clothing and a pair of shoes. "I asked Allie to wait in the hall until you're dressed."

"Thank you, Josh." Fen took the clothes and shed the blanket around his waist. He quickly pulled on jeans, but he offered his button-down shirt to Selene.

Josh gave Fen a brief nod and left the living room while Selene discarded her ruined blouse and put on Fen's shirt. It was giant on her yet deeply comforting.

Allie rushed into the room with Josh following as Fen pulled on socks and a pair of black work boots.

"Auntie Sel!" Allie threw herself at Selene, hugging her tightly.

Selene made a small noise of discomfort as her bruised body objected to the embrace.

Fen took Allie by the shoulders and pulled her away. "Take care, Allison. Your aunt is injured."

"I'm so sorry." Allie sat as close as she could to Selene without touching her. "I didn't think."

"It's okay, Allie." Selene took Allie's hand. "I'm not hurt that badly. Just a little sore."

Allie bit her lip, and tears welled in the corner of her eyes. "Who hurt you?"

Selene glanced at Fen.

"I'll check on you in the morning." He bent to feather a kiss over her forehead. "If you need anything, don't hesitate to call."

Fen walked away, passing Josh as he left the room. "With me, Josh."

Josh nodded, but before he turned, he gave Allie a pleading look. "Allie—"

"Don't bother, Josh." The anger in Allie's voice was startling. "I have nothing to say to you right now."

Wearing a stricken expression, Josh went after Fen. From the hall, she heard the front door open and close. Fen and Josh were gone. As much as Fen's presence reassured her, it was best that she and Allie face this on their own.

Selene took a closer look at her niece and found evidence that Allie had been crying: tear tracks that hadn't dried, reddened eyes, and flushed cheeks.

"Allie, did you and Josh have a fight?"

Allie's lip trembled. "I want to know what happened to you first. I'm freaking out."

Selene hadn't looked in a mirror since Daniel attacked her, but she could imagine what Allie saw.

Placing her other hand over their already linked fingers, Selene spoke firmly but gently. "Allie, what I'm going to tell you will be very hard to hear. I wish there was a way to make it hurt less, but I don't think there is."

"Who attacked you, Aunt Sel?" Allie's voice was very small.

Selene had to swallow several times before she could speak. It felt like she might vomit, or sob, or both.

"It was Daniel."

Allie stared at Selene, then slowly shook her head. "No. That . . . that can't be right."

"I'm so sorry, sweetheart," Selene said. "But it's true. He was waiting in the kitchen when I came home."

"But I talked to him last night." Allie's voice wobbled. "He wouldn't hurt you. He likes you. He wants us to be a family."

Daniel had told Selene he'd been at the house with Allison, and that had been bad enough, but knowing now what he was capable of, what he'd done . . . The fact that he'd spent hours alone with Allie made it difficult to breathe. What Selene went through was awful, but if he'd hurt Allie, if he'd turned her, it would be so much worse. At least she could be thankful that in Daniel's insane reasoning, he decided to target Selene first.

"Daniel has always been very good at telling people what they want to hear." Selene squeezed Allie's fingers. "It doesn't matter to him if what he says is true."

Allie looked away. "He was so nice."

"I know." As much as Selene despised Daniel, both for who he was and what he'd done, she wished Allie didn't have to face this ugliness.

"Are you sure you didn't misunderstand?" Allie asked. "Did he say something mean about Fenris that made you get into an argument?"

Selene had to check the impulse to raise her voice.

Denial, shifting blame, is a normal reaction.

Rather than speak, Selene released Allie's hand. She picked up her shredded blouse and placed it in the space between her and Allie.

After taking a deep breath, then another, she said, "I was wearing that shirt tonight. Look at it."

Allie lifted the blouse gingerly, gasping when she saw the way it was torn.

"Daniel did that."

Selene opened the top buttons of Fen's shirt, parting the fabric. It was difficult. She wanted to dissociate from the violence that had been done to her. Instead, she had to relive it for Allie's sake.

Her hands shook as she gestured to her throat. "He also did this."

Allie began to cry. "I don't understand. He wouldn't . . . I liked him."

"You liked him because he wanted you to," Selene said. "And I'm sure he used his vampire charm to make sure you believed everything he said. He tried to do the same thing to me. I don't think you would have invited him into the house otherwise. Not after Josh warned you about vampires."

"Daniel said werewolves lie about vampires," Allie mumbled. The evidence was mounting up too quickly for her to counter it. "When he talked to me, he sounded so sincere. Everything he said made sense."

"I'm sure it did," Selene replied. As much as it was hard to do anything other than disparage Daniel, she knew it was vital to acknowledge Allison's feelings. Allie wouldn't be able to see the truth if she wasn't given space to work through her own experiences with her father. "Allie, I don't want you to feel bad about believing what he told you. You did nothing wrong. He manipulated you."

"Why would he do that?" Allie sniffled.

Okay, she's starting to get there. One foot in front of the other as we slog through the emotional mud.

Selene reached for a box of tissues and handed it to her. "All I can tell you is what he said to me, and I don't know how much of it was true. He told me he wanted to make you and me vampires so we would stay with him."

Allie perked up a little. "So he did want us to be a family?"

Selene swallowed a sigh. *Two steps forward, one step back. But I can't stop now.*

"Allie, he was going to turn me against my will," Selene said. "And he would have made you a vampire without asking too. That isn't a family. All he cared about was getting what he wanted." She pointed at her throat again. "That's how he hurt me. He was trying to turn me."

"He bit you?" Allie gasped.

"Fen stopped him before he could." Selene touched a bruise and winced, then she shivered, ice slipping through her veins at the visceral memory of Daniel's attack. "I was very lucky. If Fen hadn't been there, I wouldn't have been able to stop Daniel. He was too strong."

Allie swiped a tissue over her cheeks, then she began to sob. Selene drew the girl's head into her lap and stroked her hair while she cried. Selene cried, too, albeit quietly. She took a tissue and pressed it to her face to catch the tears that trailed down her cheeks.

After a few minutes, the storm of weeping subsided, and Allie lifted her head. "I'm so sorry, Aunt Selene."

"You don't have anything to be sorry for, sweetheart."

"Yes, I do." A sob welled, thickening Allie's voice. "I let him in. If I hadn't invited him into the house, he wouldn't have been able to attack you. It's all my fault."

Allie broke down again.

"No, no, honey." Ignoring the bruises, Selene wrapped Allie up in a tight hug. The last thing she wanted was for Allie to blame herself. "Nothing about this is your fault. Even if Daniel hadn't used magic, he would have used your feelings to get you to trust him. And of course you wanted to trust him."

"Can you forgive me?" Allie's muffled question came from Selene's shoulder.

"There's nothing to forgive." Selene hugged her closer, ignoring the pain of her battered flesh. "But if you need me to say it, then yes, I forgive you. I love you, Allie."

"I love you, too, Auntie Sel." Allie sat up and blew her nose. "So what happened to my dad? Did he run away when Fen showed up?"

Dread swarmed in Selene's chest. "No, Allie. Daniel had a gun. When Fen protected me, Daniel tried to kill him."

"He shot Fenris?" Allie had gone very still.

"He missed," Selene said carefully. "He and Fen fought in the kitchen. Fen killed him."

Allie swayed on the couch. "My dad's dead?"

Selene nodded and had to close her eyes. The sound of Fen's jaws crushing Daniel's neck. Daniel's scream. The tearing of flesh as his head was ripped from his body. She wanted to erase all of it from her memory and knew she would never be able to.

A choking sound escaped from Allie, and Selene gathered her close once more. Allie buried her face in Selene's shoulder and sobbed. Selene rocked her and stroked her hair as she wept, then handed her more tissues when she sat up, sniffling.

"Why did he kill him?" Allie asked softly. "Couldn't he have put him in jail or something?"

"I don't think that was an option, Allison."

"Why not? Because Fenris decided it wasn't?" There was a hard edge to Allie's questions that Selene didn't like, and again she had to temper her response. Allie hadn't been through what Selene had. She'd only seen the side of her father Daniel wanted her to. Selene couldn't lose sight of that fact because it skewed Allie's perception of everything.

Fen had saved Selene's life, and while it was fine for Allie to be unhappy with him for what he'd done, Selene couldn't let that unhappiness fester into resentment . . . or hate. But that meant she had to show Allie how ugly the world could be sometimes. What monsters could do. She wished she didn't have to rob a young girl of the innocent belief that her father had been a good person.

"Allison, don't forget that Daniel wanted to kill Fenris," Selene chided gently. "Fen only attacked your father after Daniel hurt me and tried to shoot Fen."

"But he killed my dad," Allie replied in a plaintive voice. "He could have shown mercy or found another way to stop Daniel. Isn't that what good leaders are supposed to do?"

"Allie, if you had asked me before tonight whether I thought Daniel deserved to die, I would have said no," Selene said. "But attacking me and trying to kill Fenris wasn't the worst thing he'd done."

"What do you mean?"

They'd reached the most difficult part of the conversation, the moment when Selene felt like she was about to take a hammer to Allison's heart. She hated it, but she knew offering Allie anything besides the brutal truth would be a mistake.

"He told me he found Emma in San Francisco because he wanted to make her a vampire." Selene's fingers dug in to the couch. "She said no, but he tried to turn her anyway. And when he did, he lost control."

"Lost control?" When Allie spoke, Selene could barely hear her because Allie's voice was so quiet, and Selene's rage and grief were roaring in her ears. "Are you saying . . . Did Daniel kill my mom?"

"Yes." The truth felt like twisting a knife in her gut and Allie's simultaneously.

"I think I'm gonna be sick." Allie bolted from the living room.

Selene stood on shaky legs and followed Allie to the powder room. When Allie retched into the toilet, Selene held her hair back and rubbed gentle circles along her spine until Allie stopped vomiting.

"I'm okay now," Allie said after a few minutes and sat back. Selene helped her up and gave her a towel so she could wipe her mouth.

The doorbell rang.

"Fen was going to send Tim and Marley over to be with us," Selene told her niece. "Are you all right with that?"

Allie nodded. Selene gave her another hug then went to answer the door.

Tim waited on the front step. Marley fluttered in the air a foot behind him.

"Selene." Tim opened his arms, and she stepped into them. He held her gently. "I'm so sorry. We're well rid of the bastard."

22

"Steep this for five minutes and drink it when you're ready to go to bed." Marley, who was perched on an ottoman, offered a sachet of herbs to Selene. "It will help you sleep and keep nightmares away."

Selene took the sachet. "Thank you, Marley. I appreciate it."

"If you need anything, ask." Tim was sitting beside Selene on the couch. "We'll do whatever we can."

"Would you like to stay at our house tonight?" Marley asked. "We have a guest room and a pull-out. You and Allie are welcome if it's . . . uncomfortable here."

"I'll ask Allie—" Selene began.

"I want to sleep in my room." Allie was standing at the entrance to the living room. She looked a little pale but otherwise collected.

Marley flew over to her and ruffled her hair. "Are you sure, sweetie? Tim baked chocolate croissants this morning."

"I sure did." Tim waved at Allie. "Slumber party? We can stay up late and do face masks."

Allie offered him a brief smile. "I appreciate it. I do. But I don't want to run away from this. If I don't sleep here tonight, I'm afraid I won't ever want to come back."

While Selene was proud of Allie's bravery and maturity, her heart pinched as she wished for a world where something as simple as where Allison would sleep hadn't become a painful, heavy decision.

"Whatever you want, Allie," Marley told her. "The offer stands. We always love to see you."

"Thank you." Allie's smile was stronger. "You guys are awesome."

"You're welcome, sweetie." Tim winked at her.

"Auntie Sel, I'm gonna go lie down," Allie said. "But I need to tell you about Natalie before I go upstairs."

"What about Natalie?" Selene found herself sitting up straighter as an unpleasant prickling crept over her skin.

Allie frowned and rubbed her eyes. The poor girl was exhausted. "That's what Josh and I were fighting about."

The prickling became sharp thorns of fear as she remembered Allie's anger, her tear-streaked face, and her red-tinged eyes—all before she knew anything about what happened with Daniel.

Marley shot a look at Tim, whose smile had vanished.

"Why would you and Josh fight about Natalie?" Selene had to unclench her jaw to ask the question.

"He broke his promise." Allie huffed. "About the dagger. Remember when he said he wouldn't tell Fen about it? Well, he did."

Selene already knew that, but Fen hadn't said anything about Natalie when he asked to see the dagger. What changed?

Allie began to gesture angrily as she spoke. "And because of Josh, Natalie is going to get in trouble."

"What kind of dagger, Allie?" Marley's voice was like the crack of a whip.

When Allie jumped at his sharp tone, Marley spoke again, more gently. "Can you describe it to me?"

Selene answered before Allie could. "It was silver. The hilt was inlaid with moonstones."

"Oh fuck," Tim blurted, then shot a glance at Allie. "Sorry."

"This is bad." Marley's wings flapped with such speed that they buzzed as he hovered beside Allie. "This is very, very bad."

Selene looked from Tim to Marley, frowning. "Do you . . . know about Natalie's work?"

Marley nodded. The green vines that curled over his limbs were turning brown, withering. Did that mean he was upset? Afraid?

Tim saw it and jumped up, going to Marley and clasping his hand. "Don't make yourself sick. Please."

"What are we going to do?" Marley asked in a hushed voice.

Selene stood up and went to them. "I need you to slow down. What's happening?"

It was hard to keep her voice calm when the two men were clearly panicking.

"Yeah." Allie's brow furrowed in confusion. "I'm mad at Josh for breaking his promise and making trouble for Natalie. But you guys are freaking out. I don't get it."

"We should sit down." Tim guided Marley back to the ottoman, coaxing him to land, then dragged an armchair over so he could sit close enough to hold Marley's hand.

Selene and Allie sat opposite them on the couch.

"Allie, I need you to tell me exactly, and I mean *exactly*, what Josh said to you about the dagger and Natalie," Tim prompted.

Allie bit her lip. "Um, I'll try. I was so mad. I hope I remember it right."

Though her pulse was racing, Selene put her hand on Allie's shoulder. "Take your time, Allie."

"Josh and I were in the garden," Allie told them. "And I was annoyed because I wanted to go home, and he kept stalling. Then he told me it was because—"

Allie cast a guilty look at Selene. "He said you hooked up with Fen, and we shouldn't interrupt."

Embarrassed, Selene cleared her throat. It was the sort of thing Marley and Tim would usually love to tease her about, but they were both stone faced.

"Go on, Allie," Tim urged.

Allie nodded. "Bannock and Ewan showed up and said they needed to talk to Josh. So I walked around while they were talking, then Josh came back and asked how close Aunt Selene and Natalie are."

"Oh fuck," Tim said again. He didn't bother apologizing this time.

"I told him you're really close, and then he said that Natalie was selling illegal weapons like the dagger and that she'd broken Avondale's laws by doing it and that Fen was going to have to deal with it. That's when I started yelling at him for breaking his promise, and we got into a big fight."

"Call Arachne," Marley told Tim. "Her place is across from Natalie's. She'll know if anything has happened yet. Maybe Nat got out in time."

Got out? Selene watched their exchange with increasing alarm. *What the hell did that mean?*

Tim nodded, pulled out his phone, and went into the front hall.

"Why are you so worried?" Allie's knee bounced with nerves. "I get that Natalie's in trouble, but won't she just have to pay a fine or something?"

Marley shook his head. "I wish that were the case."

"Natalie gave me the impression that her real work was a big secret," Selene said. "How do you know about it?"

"I help her," Marley replied. "There are many ways paranormals can abuse humans, but one is to foster an addiction to magical substances, in the same way a human could become dependent on heroin or opioids. Rehabilitation from a magical addiction is difficult and extremely painful, but I make medicinal compounds that assist in the process. I provide them to Natalie when she has a client who is in that situation."

"That's amazing, Marley," Selene said. She was also glad to know Natalie had allies in Avondale, despite her work falling on the wrong side of the town's laws.

He gave her a sad smile. "Thank you. I wouldn't risk doing it if I didn't believe it was important and necessary."

"That means you could be in trouble too?" Selene asked.

"I will be if Fenris finds out I'm involved," Marley replied. "But Natalie won't give up any of her associates. And Fen won't—"

He broke off, casting an uneasy look at Allie.

"Go ahead," Selene told him, ignoring the spike of dread in her gut. She needed to know everything about what kind of trouble Natalie was in, and Allie had been through too much to be shielded from the ways the world could be awful any longer.

After a brief nod, Marley continued. "He won't torture Natalie to get information."

Selene sucked in a sharp breath. She hadn't been expecting that. "Oh god."

"Fen isn't cruel," Marley tried to reassure Selene. "That kind of punishment isn't his way or in his nature."

Selene appreciated his kind tone, and she could tell he was being sincere, but she was reeling from the fact that the word *torture* had entered the conversation at all.

Tim walked back into the room, his expression drawn. "They took her. Tonight."

Marley buried his face in his hands.

"Who took her?" Selene asked Tim. She was almost certain she already knew the answer, but she didn't want to believe it.

"Fenris and his guard," Tim answered, his voice full of grief. "It's over."

"Oh, Natalie," Marley said from behind his hands.

Tim went to Marley and put his arms around him.

Images from the last several hours flashed through Selene's mind.

Gabriel and Kipp showing up at the diner.

Fen's abrupt departure.

"I wanted to explain what's happened."

That's why Fen had come to the house.

He was going to tell her about Natalie. But what was he going to say?

Whatever it was had to be upsetting enough that Fen hadn't been willing to reveal it while Selene was suffering the aftermath of Daniel's attack. Yet the ramifications of Natalie's actions were serious enough that Fenris had left Selene with Tim and Marley because he had to enforce Avondale's law.

Allie's voice broke the silence. "What's going to happen to Natalie?"

Marley lifted his face from his hands. Tears coursed down his cheeks. "They're going to execute her."

Selene didn't mean to laugh, but she did. The sound split the room like a rifle report.

"You're joking." She stared at Marley. "They . . . they can't."

Fen had kept Natalie's crime from her because the news would be upsetting. He was trying to be kind. That made sense. This, she couldn't believe. This was pure insanity.

Tim shook his head. "They can. And they will."

"But"—Selene's voice listed toward shrill—"she's *helping* people."

"She is," Tim replied. "But that's not how Fen will see it. To him, what she does is traffic in weapons that are a threat to his pack. Have you seen her storeroom? It's an arsenal."

Allie leaned into Selene, her voice shaky. "Fen won't really do that. He wouldn't hurt Natalie. She's a good person."

Selene knew what went unspoken was "not like Daniel." It was exactly what she was thinking. Killing Daniel was justified. But this . . .

"When you say 'they're going to execute her,' is there some kind of paranormal court that's going to be convened to sentence Natalie?"

Tim and Marley snuck glances at each other.

Selene let out a frustrated growl. "Oh, just tell me."

"The decision is Fen's," Marley said.

"So he could stop it." Selene was speaking more to herself than to the others, but Tim's expression became mortified.

"Selene, listen to me." He grabbed her hand. "I know what you're thinking, but you can't. This law isn't a whim or something new. Natalie was aware of the risk, and she accepted it. Fen made it absolutely clear that the sale of bounty hunter weapons in Avondale was a capital offense. She could have stopped when the law was passed, she could have moved away, but she chose to stay and continue her work."

Natalie had said as much to Selene, but Selene hadn't understood the finality of that choice.

She was on her feet before she knew she'd decided to stand. "Where did they take her?"

"No." Marley surged up, wings buzzing again. "You can't, Selene."

"The hell I can't," she snapped. "Natalie is my friend, and it is my fault she's been arrested. If I'd been more careful with the dagger she gave me—*to protect me*—she would still be safe. Still be protecting other people who need her. I won't let this happen."

Tim stood and put his hands on Selene's shoulders. "Selene. We love you. You must know that. And it's obvious Fen has fallen hard for you, but I need you to hear me. When it comes to Fenris Hall, he is the pack leader before anything else. Even before love. If you confront him, he won't choose you. You can't save Natalie."

As Tim spoke, Selene's heart turned to glass and shattered.

"He won't choose you." Didn't I have this very thought when Fen left tonight? That there would be times Avondale had to come first.

She could accept that. She couldn't accept that he would execute Natalie.

"I have to try," Selene told him. "Please tell me where they've taken her."

It was Marley who answered. "You have a beautiful soul, Selene. You really are one of us. She'll be at the estate."

"Marley," Tim voice was low. "She shouldn't."

"You're right," Marley replied, his voice snapping. "And it probably won't do any good, but if Fenris will listen to anyone, it's Selene. If she wants to try, we should let her. Natalie deserves whatever support we can offer."

Tim's mouth flattened, but he inclined his head in agreement.

"How much time do I have?" Selene asked Marley, gratitude spilling through her. "Will she be executed tonight?"

"No," Marley replied. "There's a formal process. An announcement will be issued to the paranormal community that documents the crimes and the punishments attached to those crimes. I'd say you have two days. Three at the most. But—"

Selene cut him off, moving toward the front hall. "Then I don't have any time to waste. Will you stay with Allie?"

"You're going now?" Tim gasped. "Selene, hold on—"

"I want to go with you!" Allie ran after Selene and grabbed her hand. "I want to help. If Josh hadn't said anything, Natalie wouldn't be in trouble."

Selene turned and pulled Allie into a hug. God, the poor girl had been through so much already. They both had. *And look how strong she is, how brave. Emma would be so proud.*

"Thank you, sweetheart, but I need to go alone. This is between me and Fen."

"But I feel bad," Allie protested. "It's Natalie. I love her. Mom loved her too."

"I know. It means a lot that you support me, Allie, and it will to Natalie too," Selene told her. "Thank you. But it will be easier for me to say what I need to say to Fen if we're alone. Do you understand?"

"I think so," Allie answered uneasily. "Please be careful."

Selene saw fear flash through Allie's eyes, and she paused to take Allie's hand.

"I will," Selene said in a firm voice. "And Allie, Fenris won't hurt me. Even if I make him furious, he would never do me harm."

"I know," Allie replied, blowing out a breath. "And I know that what happened with my dad was his fault, not Fen's. I just wish it hadn't happened. I wish none of this was happening. I'm sad and I'm scared. I don't know what to do."

"We're going to do everything we can to help Natalie," Selene told her. "And we'll find a way through this. Through everything. I promise."

Marley fluttered over to Allie, resting a hand on her shoulder. "We'll stay with our best girl, Allie, and take care of her. Good luck, Selene. Goddess go with you."

"Thanks."

As Selene left the room, she noticed Tim and Marley watching her as if she were the one walking to the gallows.

◆ ◆ ◆

Josh was waiting for Selene at the manor gate. She got out of the car and approached him.

"Allie texted you?"

He nodded, indecision written clearly on his face. "Don't do this, Ms. Jones. It won't end well."

She glared at him. "Maybe you should have kept your mouth shut."

"I owe Fenris everything," Josh shot back. "Keeping that secret was a betrayal."

"And if I don't try to help Natalie, I'd be betraying my best friend," she told him. "So where does that leave us?"

Josh bristled. "Natalie knew the law."

I am so tired of hearing that.

"Are you going to let me in, or do I have to climb the fence?" Selene asked.

Josh stared her down for what was probably ten seconds but felt like forever. Then, with a curse under his breath, he spun and punched a code into the gate control box. The tall iron barrier drew back.

"Thanks," Selene said, returning to her car. "I guess I'll tell Allie you're not such a bad guy after all."

At the end of the winding drive, the manor loomed, looking more than ever like an impregnable fortress from an age long since passed. On her first visit to Fen's estate, Selene hadn't known what to expect. It was strange, after all she'd shared with him since that dinner, that once again she couldn't predict what she would encounter within the foreboding stone walls.

Selene parked her car, climbed out, and marched toward the tall front doors. A movement in her peripheral vision made her slow, then pull up short as a huge wolf stalked out of the shadows. That a creature of its size could move in utter silence was uncanny. She remained still as it approached her.

When Fenris had taken his wolf form, it happened so quickly and amid the chaos of Daniel's attack that Selene's picture of what he'd looked like was muddled. Yet, she didn't think this was Fen. The size was right, but the color of the wolf that approached her didn't match what she remembered. This wolf was jet black, where she thought Fen had been a mix of gray, silver, and light brown. But she couldn't be sure.

As she tried to plot her next move, a growl at her back made her spin, only to find a second wolf, just as large, approaching from the opposite direction. This wolf was bronze tinged with black, and like the first, it moved without making a sound.

Are all wolves ninjas, or just werewolves?

The wolves stopped a few feet away from her, teeth bared, hackles raised. Had she met them in human form? Were they part of Fenris's guard?

Even if they knew who she was, it was impossible to mistake their message: *You are not welcome here.*

Selene knew Fen's wolves wouldn't harm her, but her lizard brain, with its survival instincts, screamed at her to get into the car and drive without looking back.

But she couldn't abandon Natalie. Fen might want her to stay away, but his wolves were a warning, not a threat.

"I need to speak with Fenris." Her voice came out stronger than she'd expected, and it renewed her resolve. "Please tell him Selene Jones is here."

The black wolf's ears flicked as it regarded her while the other wolf stalked closer. Selene stayed rooted in place. No doubt they could smell her fear, but she refused to balk. She'd brought nothing silver with her because she wanted to ensure Fen understood she came to reason with him, not to fight. Not that she'd win a fight. With the wolves closing in, she wondered if leaving any means of defense at home had been a poor decision.

The bronze wolf suddenly stopped, lifted its head, and let loose a long, piercing howl.

Selene yelped and jumped back. The black wolf's tongue lolled out, and she had the distinct impression it was laughing at her.

So much for maintaining my dignity.

The howl echoed in the night air and then all was quiet again. The wolves positioned themselves between Selene and the front door and sat on their haunches, staring at her but no longer growling. She knew if she took a step forward, she'd see their sharp teeth again.

How long would Fen make her wait? It didn't seem like him to turn this situation into a standoff, but considering what he planned to do to Natalie, she questioned how well she knew him.

Only a minute or two passed before the front door swung open, revealing the wood sprite, Anu. The wolves stepped to either side of Selene, and when she started toward the door, they walked beside her.

"Ms. Jones," Anu greeted her. "Fenris will see you in his study. Please follow me."

"Thank you."

Selene entered the manor. She expected the wolves to remain outside, but they continued into the house, either escorting or guarding her as she followed Anu.

Guess I'm not to be trusted, Selene thought, her heart sinking. That didn't bode well for how this meeting with Fenris would proceed.

The manor was even more labyrinthine than she recalled: long hallways, endless doorways, and myriad passages. She hadn't gotten so far as to think of launching a rescue for Natalie, but as she took in her surroundings, it was obvious that any such attempt would fail. She'd never find her way through this place, much less out of it, especially if she was being chased by wolf guards who knew the layout of the manor.

Sorry, Nat. I hope it doesn't come to that. Because we're both screwed if it does.

By the time they reached a set of wooden double doors deep within the manor, Selene had no idea how to retrace her steps to the front entrance. The sinking feeling in her stomach had become a bottomless pit.

Anu opened the door and gestured for Selene to enter. When she stepped into the room, the wolves once again followed. The wood sprite left the door ajar but walked away without a word.

Fenris Hall's study was what Selene would have described as a small library, which left her wondering what the actual library in the manor looked like, presuming there was one. Two of the room's walls featured built-in bookshelves that stretched from the floor to the high ceiling. Many of the shelves could only be accessed by a rolling ladder.

The study was spacious, furnished with a solid oak desk that looked like it had been crafted around the time Henry VIII was king. Chairs and settees that lent themselves to reading made up the other furniture along with attendant tables. A cluster of said pieces were arranged in front of a stone fireplace large enough for Selene to stand in; the hearth took up most of the wall opposite the entrance and was framed by two tall mullioned windows.

Fen stood in front of the fireplace, his back to her and his body outlined by leaping flames. His head turned slightly, revealing his strong profile.

"Thank you, Gabriel, Ewan. You may leave us." After he spoke, he stared into the fire once more.

The wolves slipped away, and the study door closed.

When Fen didn't speak, Selene slowly crossed the room toward the fireplace.

Only when she was standing beside him did he address her. Even then, he didn't look at her.

"You should be resting."

Selene had expected that when she confronted Fenris, her temper would boil over. Instead, she felt sad and exhausted.

"Do you think I can rest when I know what's happened to Natalie?"

He finally turned, his gaze searching hers, but his expression was shuttered, making it impossible to discern what he was feeling. "No. I don't suppose you can."

"I don't want to believe what I've been told, Fenris," she said quietly. "I *won't* believe it."

"And what have you been told?" His face continued to reveal nothing.

Selene took a step closer and watched his chest rise with a quick intake of breath.

So he isn't completely unaffected by my arrival. That's something. Not only could it make a difference to Natalie, but it also assuaged the sting of the distance he'd put between them.

"That Natalie's actions have led to her arrest," Selene said. "And that you plan to execute her."

"All of that is true." There was no hesitation in his reply. He'd closed himself off again.

"No!" Selene's composure shattered. "You can't be serious, Fen. You're going to kill Natalie?"

"Natalie Lyon broke a law that carried stark consequences. She knew the risk." Though he kept his voice flat as he spoke, Selene knew the unbearable weight of grief he carried was tied to the law Natalie had broken. Only such a deep, festering wound would drive him to this merciless end.

"Rather than cease her activities or move them elsewhere," Fen continued, "she chose to traffic in illegal weapons, flaunting my decree. It is a dire offense that cannot be ignored."

"I know you believe you have to take a hard line on this," she said, trying to reach the man behind the ruler, "but I'm begging you to listen to me."

She caught a flicker in his gray eyes. A spark of feeling.

"I will always listen to you, Selene," he said softly. "That doesn't mean I'm able to give you what you want."

Seizing on that tiny admission, Selene pressed on. "Yes, Natalie continued to break the law, but that in itself should prove how important she believes her work is. Fen, she only sells the weapons to people who've been abused by paranormals. She helps them escape and provides sanctuary when they have no one else to turn to."

"I don't deny what you're saying." Fen frowned. "But the presence of such weapons in Avondale presents a direct threat to my pack, whom I've sworn to protect above all else."

"Do you have any evidence that a single member of your pack or anyone else in Avondale has been harmed by Natalie's work?" Selene pressed.

"No," Fen replied. "But it's only a matter of time before one or more of those weapons falls into the hands of bounty hunters. And that is unacceptable."

"Natalie doesn't sell to bounty hunters," Selene argued. "Under any circumstances. If a bounty hunter contacts her, she takes steps to ensure their name reaches you."

He grimaced. "She's said as much. My guard are running down the names she offered against our own list of hunters we've taken out after receiving anonymous tips."

"And if she's telling the truth?"

"Then she has my gratitude," he answered. "But it changes nothing."

Selene wrapped her arms around herself as icy despair filled the space beneath her ribs. "I don't understand. How can you be so unfeeling?"

"Selene." Fen took her face in his hands, and there it was. Blazing in his eyes, hotter than the flames beside them. His love for her. His need. "I am resolved. Not heartless. Natalie is a good person, and this is a tragedy."

Her eyes stung, her vision blurred, and tears began to roll down her cheeks. "She's my friend."

"I know, and it grieves me." He bent and kissed the salt tracks on her skin. "I am loath to cause you pain."

She turned her face and caught his mouth against hers briefly. Though she longed to sink into his warmth, his taste, she pulled back.

"Then don't." She looked into his eyes, desperate. "Stop this, Fenris."

"I can't." He shut down, hands dropping to his sides, all the emotion he'd revealed gone.

"Yes, you can," she insisted. "The law isn't just. What good is it being the ruler of Avondale if you can't make an exception in a case like Natalie's? She doesn't deserve this."

His lip curled back, the first sign of anger he'd shown since she arrived. "It doesn't fall to you to decide whether our laws are just. Nor can you grasp the magnitude of what she's done."

"I know this law exists because of the horror you went through," Selene said, daring to broach the unnamed source of this conflict, hating that she was about to open a deep wound in Fen's heart. "I know it was born out of grief. But killing Natalie doesn't right the wrong of Miriam's death."

Fen spun away from her, stalking toward his desk. He braced himself against it, gripping the edge so hard, the wood creaked.

"Miriam wasn't the only wolf murdered that day," he growled. "My entire pack suffered an irreparable loss. It was and remains my responsibility to make certain that never happens again. I did not establish the ban on bounty hunter weapons without the explicit support of my people. And while it falls to me to enforce it, I did not create this law alone. You speak as if only my feelings were at stake, but I made a promise to my pack. I am nothing if I can't protect them. To set aside the law because I would prefer to would betray everything I have worked for."

And there was the key to everything: Fen's loyalty to Avondale, to his people. Selene admired that quality. Without it, he couldn't be the leader the town needed, but she believed that in this instance it would be his downfall. If he went through with Natalie's execution, even with the certainty that there was no alternative, he would ultimately regret his choice. And guilt would destroy him. Selene had come to the manor tonight not only to save her friend, but also to save Fenris from himself.

Selene approached him slowly. "What happened to your pack was unthinkable. I understand why the law exists, but—"

"Stop." He whipped around, his eyes dark with pain. "I'm sorry, Selene. I truly am."

"Fenris." She reached for him.

"The law stands." His words fell like a gavel, and she froze. "Natalie's life is forfeit. There's nothing else to say."

Selene stood there, disbelief pummeling her, but there was no mistaking the finality of Fen's voice, nor the hard set of his features. They stared at each other, Selene silently begging that he show the tiniest crack in his resolve. But Fen was immovable as a fortress.

"Actually"—she took a ragged breath, tears threatening—"there is one more thing to say."

He watched her, waiting.

"You saved my life tonight, Fenris," she said. "But Natalie saved me first."

"What are you talking about?" he asked roughly. As she'd hoped, she'd caught him off guard. She didn't like forcing his hand by revealing his vulnerabilities, but she was going to play every card she held. That meant making Fen aware of facts he wouldn't want to face.

"Tonight wasn't the first time Daniel attacked me," she told him. "He caught me alone one evening in Avondale."

Fen had gone rigid again, but his eyes were wild, roiling with fury.

"He wanted to seduce me," Selene continued, keeping her tone even. "When that failed, he used his magic to compel me. It was working, but I broke free. And I drove him off."

A deep, rumbling snarl emerged from Fen's chest. "Why didn't you tell me?"

"I didn't think I had to," she replied. "I thought it was over because I beat him that night. And the only reason I was able to do that was because of Natalie. She gave me a silver cross and told me to carry it at all times. I listened. When Daniel tried to compel me again, I used the cross to burn him and drive him away.

"That cross saved my life, Fenris." Selene didn't flinch, even when she heard Fen's claws dig in to the edge of the desk. "If Natalie hadn't given it to me, I would belong to Daniel."

"Never." Fen was breathing hard. "I would have torn his heart from his chest before I let that happen."

"I know you would have," she said. "I saw you rip his head off to save me. But that other night, you weren't there. I needed a way to save myself. Natalie gave it to me."

His eyes closed. "You should not have kept this from me."

"I'm telling you now."

Fen's shoulders tightened, then he let out a long, weary sigh. When he opened his eyes and met her gaze, ice-covered brambles twisted around her heart.

"It's too late."

23

Selene rocked back on her heels so hard, she lost her balance and toppled. Fenris lunged forward and caught her before she crumpled to the floor.

She gazed up at him, stunned and horrified. "Natalie . . . She's already dead?"

Fen's brow creased. "No."

"But you said—" She was still reeling at the thought that Natalie was gone.

"I meant I can't change her punishment." He helped Selene stand, but when he tried to draw her into his arms, she twisted out of his grasp.

She walked away, unaware of her destination until she sagged into a chair. Her limbs felt leaden. Her eyes burned. Her head was pounding.

Fen approached. "Selene—"

"I want to see her." She didn't look at him, closing her eyes and rubbing her temples. "Will you at least let me speak to her before you take her away?"

"I'm not taking her away from you," he replied sharply. "That's unfair of you to say."

She dropped her hands to her lap and glared at him. "Nothing about this is fair. If you're going to be unreasonable, then so am I, Fenris. Deal with it."

He blanched, sorrow skimming over his eyes. Her fury wavered. She hated the way they'd lashed out at each other, but she refused to show it.

"Are you going to take me to Natalie or send me home?"

Reading the determination in her expression, Fen offered his hand. "I'll take you to her."

Selene allowed him to help her up, but she let go of his hand the moment she was on her feet. He shot her a pained glance but didn't offer comment, instead leading her from the room. They walked a short distance to a wide central staircase and climbed to the second floor.

Though she hadn't expected Fen to imprison Natalie in a literal dungeon, when he stopped in front of an ordinary-looking door in an ordinary—well, ordinary for a manor decorated with priceless art—hallway, she didn't know what to think.

She was equally startled when Fen didn't retrieve a key and unlock the door but knocked.

"Yes?" Natalie's voice was muffled.

"You have a visitor." Fen spoke through the door. "May we enter?"

For a jailer, Fenris was awfully polite.

Natalie didn't reply, but a moment later the door opened.

"Selene?" Natalie's eyes widened, then she shook her head. "Oh, honey, you shouldn't be here."

"God, not you too." Selene groaned but quickly hugged her friend. "Am I the only person who hasn't lost their mind?"

Natalie stepped back to frown at her. "What do you mean?"

"Where do I start—"

Fenris cleared his throat. "Selene, a moment."

She had a sharp retort ready, but when she saw the strain around his eyes, she bit her tongue.

"Take whatever time you need," he said quietly. "But when you're ready, I'd like to speak with you again."

When Selene hesitated, he hastened to add, "If you're amenable, please come to the room at the south end of the hall on the third floor."

Still uncertain about whether she wanted to have another conversation with Fenris, Selene chose to nod rather than give a definite reply. Her heart was already in pieces. If it took any more damage, she worried she wouldn't be able to put it back together.

Fenris shifted his attention to Natalie. "Are you well?"

"Well enough," Natalie replied evenly.

"If you need anything—food, refreshment—it will be provided," he said.

"I know, Fenris," she answered. "Thank you."

"Very well." He inclined his head to her, then cast a brief glance at Selene before withdrawing and closing the door.

Natalie took Selene's hand and led her into a large bedroom, beautifully appointed, with a separate sitting area that included a fireplace.

"Have a seat." Natalie gestured to one of the chairs near the fire, which danced cheerily, giving Selene the feeling she'd been dumped in the middle of a very bad joke.

"Let me see if I've got this right." Selene sat down. "You're not locked in this room, which, rather than being a cell, is nicer than the Four Seasons and probably has better room service."

Natalie settled in the other chair. "Yep, that's pretty accurate."

Selene took a moment to inspect her friend. Nat's complexion was a little wan, her eyes tired, but she otherwise appeared in good health and spirits.

"I don't understand," Selene blurted. "They keep telling me you've committed a terrible crime, but they're treating you like—"

She gestured to the room and gave Natalie a bewildered look.

"A guest? Not shackled in a dank cell?" Natalie replied with a dry laugh. "If I was a bounty hunter, I'd be in the dungeon. But Fen likes me, other than the whole law-breaker thing, of course."

"So there *is* a dungeon?" Selene frowned.

"Oh, there's definitely a dungeon." Natalie shuddered. "Goddess forbid I ever end up there."

"Nat, I'm so sorry." Selene's face crumpled. "This is all my fault."

"Nope." Natalie waved away Selene's impending tears. "No crying. We're not crying. And we are definitely not blaming ourselves."

Selene sniffled and pulled herself together. "Ugh. Okay. I'm okay."

"I am happy to see you, Selene." Natalie smiled at her. "I was worried I wouldn't before . . . There's something important I need to tell you."

Selene leaned toward her, expecting a conspiracy or escape plan. *Thank god, finally.*

Natalie stood and went to a nearby writing table. When she returned, she handed Selene a piece of paper.

"I came up with a list of names," Natalie said. "People who can help you do a proper genealogical history, not an internet ancestry thing for humans, but a deep dive into the magical roots of your family."

"My what?" Selene sat up. This was not the jailbreak she was hoping for.

"I always had a feeling about you, Sel, from the moment we met," Natalie continued. "But you weren't part of our world, so I thought it best to leave it alone. I was planning to talk to you about it when you had time to adjust to life in Avondale, but things were happening so fast. Allie. Fen. Then Daniel. When you were chosen at the Beltane rite, I knew without question I had to tell you."

"Tell me what?" Selene asked. The room felt charged with electricity.

"You're one of us," Natalie answered.

"One of what?" Selene replied in a stilted voice. She knew what Natalie meant, but she couldn't possibly . . .

Natalie reached out and took Selene's hand. "You have power. You are part of the paranormal world."

"I can't be," Selene said plaintively. She was tired of repeating herself. And now was not the time to argue about who was or was not magically inclined. She couldn't care less about her connection to the paranormal world when Natalie's life was on the line. And she had no interest in delving into anything magical. She was done with that. It brought her nothing but grief.

"Why not?" Natalie frowned.

"Because . . . I'm me?" Selene answered, trying to keep her volatile emotions out of it. "I'm not magical, Nat. How would I, you know, miss that?"

Natalie drummed her fingers on the arm of her chair. "Your name. How was it given to you?"

"I was told I came with it." Selene's brow furrowed at the memory. "I was found on the steps of a church in Mount Shasta. Someone left me there in a basket, wrapped in blankets, with a note that said 'This is Selene Rhiannon Jones. Please care for her.'"

"Your name is a clue," Natalie told her. "It invokes not one, but two goddesses. And Jones is a Welsh name. That's something we should consider. Wales is steeped in magic."

"I don't think it means anything other than that whoever named me was a Fleetwood Mac fan," Selene replied. "The state tried to find any living relatives and failed. The name was obviously invented so they couldn't make those connections. You can't claim that Jones isn't a common last name, even if it is Welsh."

Natalie shook her head. "I doubt that very much. You need to take this seriously, Selene. It could be a matter of life and death when your past comes looking for you."

Selene rolled her shoulders back, deeply unsettled. "It already has. Did anyone tell you what happened with Daniel?"

"Fen did, and I'm sorry, Selene," Natalie said. "What Daniel tried to do is unforgivable, and I'm glad Fen killed him, but I wish you hadn't gone through that. Is Allie okay?"

"She will be," Selene replied. "She's worried about you."

"Sweet girl." Natalie smiled wistfully. "Tell her I'm fine and I love her."

Her expression grew solemn again. "But Selene, what I'm talking about is different than Daniel. He was from your human life. The fact that he ended up a paranormal was a fluke. Even if he hadn't shown up, Allie and Josh's relationship connected you to the magical world, and the Beltane ritual even more so. I'm afraid that means you're in danger if you were purposely hidden from something as a child that might now be able to find you."

"Like what?" Despite her resistance to the idea, Selene couldn't help but be curious about her past. Where she'd come from, who her ancestors were, had always been a mystery, and she thought she'd made peace with that. But Natalie offered a tantalizing possibility that Selene's family history wasn't lost to her forever.

"I wish I knew." Natalie sighed. "Even more, I wish I could be there to help you. It's good you have Fen. He'll protect you."

"How can you say that?" Selene gasped. The spark of interest in her past was instantly extinguished as the present came hurtling back into focus. "He's going to kill you."

"He has to," Natalie replied. "It's not personal, and I don't want you to hold it against him. He's a good leader, and he loves you."

Goddammit. Way to go for the jugular, Natalie. You're supposed to be on my side. On your own side.

"Natalie—"

"I'm okay, Selene," Natalie insisted. "I promise. I knew it was simply a matter of time."

Natalie may have spoken the words, but there was a flatness to her gaze. She was resigned to her fate, but she didn't want to die.

I have to stop this. I will *find a way.*

"Since we're on the topic, you can help me with an interesting, albeit morbid, task," Natalie said, resting her chin in her hands.

"What's that?" Selene asked, part of her brain still mulling Natalie's words about Fen.

"Don't hold it against him. He's a good leader. He loves you."

He was yet another conundrum. Her feelings for him were so powerful, their connection irresistible, but how could she be with him if he executed her best friend?

The answer was: she couldn't. She would always resent him for making that choice. That knowledge filled her with sickening grief, another layer over the sorrow that it seemed less and less likely she'd find a way to save her friend.

"How should I die?" Natalie's question shocked Selene out of her morose thoughts. Nat's tone was so bright and conversational, she might as well have asked, *Should I have waffles or pancakes for breakfast?*

"Wait . . . what?" Selene sputtered.

"I can choose the manner of my execution," Natalie replied. "Fenris extended that courtesy."

Selene rolled her eyes. "How generous of him."

"Selene, stop," Natalie chided, before musing, "Poison would be the most humane, but that would bring Marley into it, and I can't do that to him, so I was thinking guillotine. It would be quick . . . and the historic angle is appealing. There's also—"

"Wait," Selene interrupted. "Say that again."

An idea glimmered deep within her mind, like a firefly winking in and out of sight on the darkness of nights.

"Oh, well I've always been a fan of the French Revolution—" Natalie began.

"No, no," Selene cut her off a second time. "The first part. About poison. And Marley."

Natalie frowned and gave Selene a puzzled look. "The right poison would basically put me to sleep. Forever. I wouldn't feel any pain. But Marley would have to make it. He's the only one in Avondale who could create it without accidentally mucking it up and making my death slow and excruciating. Or fast, but also very painful. Poison is finicky and unforgiving if you aren't precise. Anyway, if I chose poison, it would be Marley who provides it for my execution."

"Choose poison," Selene blurted. Her conscious brain hadn't caught up with the strange awareness stirring below the surface of her thoughts, but her instincts were screaming at her that this needed to happen. "Choose poison, Natalie. Please."

"It would break Marley's heart, Selene," Natalie argued. "Why would you ask that of him?"

"Please, Nat." Selene didn't have the ability to explain herself. She hoped at some point she would. "Just do this for me. Promise you will."

Natalie gave Selene a long look, then nodded slowly. "All right. Poison it is. I'll tell Fen tomorrow. My execution is the day after. That should give Marley enough time."

Selene threw herself at Natalie, who grunted when Selene landed in her lap and hugged her. "Thank you."

"Um." Natalie awkwardly hugged Selene back. "You're welcome?"

Embarrassed by her nonsensical request and irrational reaction to Nat's agreement, Selene retreated to her chair. For the first time since learning about Natalie's intolerable sentence, Selene felt reinvigorated instead of hopeless. She didn't understand why, exactly. It was as though a hidden part of herself was stirring, ready to whisper secrets to her that held the solution to this crisis if she could only learn to listen.

The rational part of her brain scolded her, insisting that such thoughts were wild delusions born of desperation. But Natalie, Fenris, and, inexplicably, the crone at the Beltane ritual all believed some part of Selene was tied to the supernatural. She'd resisted that idea time and time again, but if there was somehow even a sliver of truth to those claims, and that truth could offer her the means to rescue Natalie, Selene wouldn't fight it. These tiny tugs at her consciousness that felt like instinct wanted her attention. Maybe it was time to stop resisting the paranormal and open herself to the strange and wondrous.

Even as she considered that possibility, she knew it wasn't as easy as snapping her fingers and comprehending the extraordinary. The same eerie sense that pushed her toward opening her mind told her that such a cataclysmic paradigm shift would take time and be a revelation by degrees. She could unlock the door, push it open a crack, and see what slipped inside. In the meantime, she had no choice but to be patient.

Glancing around the room again, she asked with a frown, "Nat, why don't you just leave?"

"I'm not following," Nat said, straightening her shirt after Selene's overly aggressive hug had rumpled it.

"The door isn't locked." Selene gestured to the door. "You're a witch. Can't you just, you know?"

She wiggled her fingers in a mystic-ish way . . . or tried to.

Natalie gave her an unimpressed look. "I'm going to pretend you didn't do that."

"But can't you?" Selene hunted for the right word. "I don't know. Disappear and reappear somewhere else?"

"No." Natalie smiled ruefully. "Teleportation is science fiction, not magic. The best I can do is fly short distances, which is basically a more advanced form of levitation."

Fly short distances. Selene got stuck on that for a minute.

"There must be something you can do," Selene pressed.

"No," Natalie answered, extending her arms. When she shook her wrists, Selene noticed the woven metal bracelets she wore. "These aren't for looks."

Selene peered at the simple braided design. "What are they?"

"Enchanted iron," Natalie replied. "They don't hurt, in case you're worried about that, but they dampen magic. I can't cast anything powerful. But even if I could, it wouldn't make much of a difference. I might take out a few wolves if I tried to escape, but eventually they'd catch up with me, and I'd die anyway. I don't want to kill anyone, so it's fine. This way I'm not tempted to try. So to answer your original question: There's nowhere for me to run. Fen knows that. So do the other wolves. Locking the door doesn't matter."

Selene ground her teeth. That was that. No way out.

"I appreciate what you're trying to do, Selene." Natalie smiled at her. "But it's no use. I love you, and I'm grateful you came. Truly."

Standing, Selene said, "I'm not giving up, Nat. I can't."

Natalie's smile remained in place, but her eyes told Selene that fighting for her life was futile. "You're a good friend."

◆ ◆ ◆

Selene closed the door to Natalie's room and leaned her forehead against it. She was so exhausted, and the night was far from over.

Should I go to Fenris? Will anything have changed?

No one besides Selene seemed to think Natalie's death sentence could be avoided. She couldn't understand why everyone was immovable on the subject. Were paranormals so locked in to their rules and traditions that they couldn't even imagine alternatives?

Natalie's apparent ambivalence about her imminent demise troubled Selene. She'd been hoping Nat might have some ideas about changing her fate. No luck there.

Selene was tempted to give up and go home, where she had allies. Even though Marley and Tim were doubtful that Fenris would change the punishment, they were at least upset about it. But she wasn't ready to commiserate just yet. She might not have magic, but she wasn't helpless, and she had other skills to work with.

This is what I do. I bring people onside for the right cause, and I am exceptionally good at my job.

Reframing her end goal as a work-like assignment gave her a new shot of adrenaline. She had to make at least one more attempt to sway Fen, especially since he'd asked to have another conversation. That might be a good sign?

Turning away from the door, Selene walked along the hall toward the staircase that would take her to the third floor. Not his study, and not the conservatory, which was on the second floor.

Why am I meeting him somewhere new?

As she neared the stairs, a figure slid out from a shadowed alcove, startling her so much she jumped back with a gasp.

"Ms. Jones." The man was huge, emanating raw power the way all Fen's wolves seemed to, and Selene had no doubt he was a wolf. He wore a black T-shirt, jeans, and work boots, but his demeanor was that of a sentinel.

Assuming the man was warning her away from an exploration of the manor, she said, "Fenris requested that I meet him upstairs."

He frowned. "That's his business, not mine."

When he didn't say anything else, Selene grew puzzled. "Then why did you stop me?"

His frown deepened. "You spoke with Natalie Lyon."

Oh god, is this an interrogation? Does he want me to tell him whether Nat and I hatched an escape plan?

She didn't have the patience for this. "That's *my* business, not yours."

A muscle in his jaw twitched. "Is she . . . all right?"

Selene wanted to snap at him, but the way his gaze flitted from her to the door to Natalie's room, to the hallway rug, back to Natalie's door, to Selene again, so restless, gave her pause.

She took a gamble. "Have you considered asking her yourself?"

"That wouldn't be appropriate," he answered, too quickly.

Taking a closer look at him, at the stern demeanor yet roguish haircut, Selene could identify the gruff man. This wasn't any wolf. He was one of Fen's guard.

"It's Gabriel, right? We met at the diner."

"Yes."

Gabriel, who was chosen for the Beltane ritual the same year Natalie was. And Fen said that was the last time the ritual had taken the form of the sacred union. Did that night mean something to Gabriel? Did Natalie mean something to him?

"Why wouldn't it be appropriate for you to talk to Natalie?" she asked, eager to dig for information but bracing herself for inevitable resistance. "Because you helped Fen arrest her?"

He looked away and shrugged.

No joy there. Time for a second try.

"Do you think she'll hold a grudge because you were doing your job?"

He grimaced but remained silent.

Talk about blood from a stone.

"You must know she's being treated well," Selene said. "That makes me wonder if you have a personal interest in how Natalie is feeling?"

His snarl was so sudden and ferocious, Selene took a step back.

Jackpot. But also a very touchy subject.

"I don't want to lose a hand," she told him. "So I'll make you an offer."

He scoffed. "I'm not going to bite you."

"Maybe less scary face then, Gabriel," Selene replied tartly. "Here's my offer: I'll answer your question if you answer one of mine."

Eyeing her with suspicion, Gabriel asked, "What's your question?"

"As a show of good faith, I'll answer yours first," she said. "Natalie is as well as I think she could be given the circumstances. She's calm, not sad, which surprised me."

"She's strong," he murmured as if to himself. "Brave."

Since he didn't appear to be looking for a reply, Selene moved on. "Here's my question . . ."

She waited for him to make eye contact, needing to gauge as much of a reaction from this guarded wolf as possible.

"Do you think Natalie should die for her crime?"

He almost covered it, but it was there. A flinch. Less than a second and it was gone.

"The law is the law."

An evasion. That was an answer in itself.

"Seems to be the popular opinion," Selene muttered. "I must be a renegade."

The glimmer of a smile teased his lips.

That slight break in formality prompted Selene to push further. "May I ask you another question, Gabriel?"

He took so long to reply, Selene decided he was ignoring her and it was time to leave, but then he nodded. It was the tiniest of nods, but definitely a nod.

Carefully, Selene asked, "Did Fenris ask you to stand guard here?"

Gabriel's jaw clenched, and he glared at her before he answered. "He did not."

Selene's curiosity was beyond piqued, but Gabriel's body language suggested it would be in her best interest not to investigate further. He'd obviously dedicated however many centuries he'd been alive to perfecting the whole intimidation thing. It was effective.

"Is there anything else you want to know?" Selene asked, mostly to be polite. His expression made it quite clear he did not want to continue their conversation.

But he did glance at Natalie's door before he shook his head. "Thank you for answering my question."

"You're welcome."

He stepped aside, and Selene walked to the stairs. A few steps up, she turned. Gabriel remained in the hallway. Not at Natalie's door, but nearby. Lurking? No, she didn't get any creepy vibes from him. Keeping vigil. That's what it felt like.

As she watched the solitary man at his self-appointed post, there was a sudden tightening around her heart, followed by a lightning bolt of sympathy.

"Gabriel."

He turned to look at her.

"You didn't ask for my advice, but I'm going to give it," Selene said. "If you want to talk to Natalie, you should. You may not get another chance."

That last sentence felt like sandpaper in her throat, but instinct compelled her to say it.

Gabriel didn't quite nod, but he inclined his head the slightest bit before his gaze slid back to Natalie's door.

◆ ◆ ◆

Come to the room at the south end of the hall.

Selene stood in front of the door, debating whether she should knock. Fen didn't tell her to knock, but he didn't say she should walk right in either.

The third floor had fewer doors than the second, which she assumed meant fewer rooms. The wide breaks between the doors displayed exquisite medieval tapestries. At another time, Selene would have enjoyed gazing at the intricate weaving and fascinating images for hours, but tonight she'd barely slowed her steps as she moved past them.

Considering she and Fen were at odds, Selene opted to knock. Then knock again.

When there was no answer after the third knock, Selene turned the doorknob. Unlocked. She opened the door a few inches.

"Fenris?"

She raised her voice. "Fenris, are you here?"

I should leave. If he's not here, I'm wasting my time.

Curiosity stomped on that logic, and she entered the room. While Fen was conspicuously absent, the room was welcoming, gilded by soft lamplight and flickering candles. Thick rugs cushioned her feet as she moved farther inside into what appeared to be a spacious living area. The decor was warm and comforting rather than formal. Polished wood, velvet upholstered chairs, and silk pillows. A long, deep-seated leather sofa faced a fireplace.

Did all the rooms in this house have fireplaces? Given that the manor predated central heating, the answer was likely yes.

As she explored the room, a pleasurable feeling of welcome and familiarity wrapped around her. She walked to the tall windows on the far wall. It was too dark to see whatever the view was, but Selene imagined something beautiful. Perhaps the garden Fen mentioned when he brought her tulips. She took a deep breath, remembering their spring-laden scent. That night felt like a lifetime ago. She breathed in again. The room itself smelled wonderful. It smelled like . . .

Fenris.

She whirled around, expecting him to be there, but the room was empty, save herself. Yet Fen's forest-and-rainstorm scent was everywhere.

This is his room. Not one room. Rooms.

Wary, yet even more curious, Selene surveyed the space again, noticing another door, slightly ajar, at the end of one wall. Before she could think too hard about it, she went to the door and peered through the opening. With a slight hitch of breath, she pushed the door fully open.

His bedroom.

Fen's scent was even stronger here. Beckoning. Hypnotizing.

Once again Selene thought, *I should leave.*

But her feet were already moving, and she walked into the bedroom.

Dark wood paneling clad the walls, reminiscent of Tudor England, which he seemed to favor. A massive four-poster bed of intricately carved dark-stained oak dominated the space and was framed by two windows. A smaller fireplace was set in the wall opposite the bed.

Selene saw another door on the far side of the room and assumed it was an en suite. Curious as she was to continue exploring, the bed had a magnet-like pull, and in the next moment she was standing beside it, running her hand up one of the carved posts.

Had things been different, she might have shared this room with Fen. Not his bedroom, but theirs.

He asked me to meet him here. Is this why? Did he want me to envision what life would be like if I became his mate? Or did he simply want to share this side of himself with me? An intimate glimpse into his home. A place no one else would see.

With one hand still wrapped around the bedpost, she trailed the fingers of her other hand over the deep-blue velvet that clothed the bed. Her eyelids drifted down as she allowed herself to drink in sensation and possibility. Fen's scent rolling over her as he bore her down onto that luscious fabric. His hands covering hers when he pinned her to the bed.

This is where I belong. With him.

She bit down on her lip hard, shaking away the temptation to drift further into that dream.

That future no longer exists. Not when Natalie's life is at stake.

"Selene." Fen's voice was a low rumble.

Jolted into the waking world, Selene spun around to find Fenris watching her from the bedroom doorway.

Embarrassed to be discovered standing beside his bed, *stroking his blankets*, Selene spoke quickly. "I'm sorry. You weren't here, and I got curious. I didn't mean to invade your privacy."

"I'm the one who invited you to my rooms," he said. "I intended to be here before you arrived but was called away. I apologize that you had to wait. Thank you for coming."

I need to get out of here. Her heart rate spiked.

The bed, the soft light. It was not a good idea to stay in this room with Fen. The living area would be much, much safer. Okay, not that much safer, with its velvet chairs and silk pillows, but still.

Too late. Fen was already crossing the space between them and then he was standing in front of her. So close. She could feel the heat of his body. Every fiber of her being wanted to close those last few inches. To melt against him.

"Are you all right, Selene?" he asked quietly. "Tell me what I can do."

Fenris intended the question to be kind, she knew that. It didn't stop her outrage from boiling up.

"Are you being serious right now?" she snapped. "You know what you can do. You know exactly what I need you to do."

"Please, Selene." He cupped her face with one hand. "I don't want to argue. There's no point."

No point for you, maybe, but I won't drop this.

"If you won't change your mind, there's nothing else for us to do." She grabbed his hand and pulled it away from her cheek, but when she tried to tug her fingers free of his grip, he only held them more firmly.

"Yes, there is." When she brought her other hand up to his chest to shove him, he captured it, then pinned both her hands at the small of her back. Selene gasped at the sudden thrill and surge of desire that overtook her in his show of strength, the power of his restraint on her wrists. He leaned down and nuzzled the sensitive spot where her ear met her jaw. "You're hurting. Let me take care of you."

Her body quaked, and she felt the unmistakable rush of hot, silken desire between her legs. "You're not playing fair."

"I'm not playing."

Selene moaned when his hard body molded against hers, and he kissed her, teasing her with subtle touches of his mouth before nudging her lips apart and laving his tongue over hers. Sparks erupted beneath her skin, setting fire to her veins.

He broke their kiss to scrape his teeth along her jaw before moving to her neck, licking, tasting, nipping.

"Fen, please." She writhed in his grip. "I need to touch you."

It was the truth. All thoughts of escaping him and this room had been burned away by the pure lust he stoked inside her.

When he released her hands, she buried her fingers in his hair, raking her nails along his scalp. He groaned and slid his hand to the curve of her ass, drawing her pelvis up until she ground against his thick, iron-hard erection. She gasped, and he easily lifted her, urging her to twine her legs around his waist. His other hand found her breast. His thumb circled her nipple, loosing darts of pleasure that shot straight into her core. Her hips bucked, and he growled, lowering her to the bed.

He bent over her, kissing her deeply, both of his hands palming her breasts. His fingers plucked at her nipples. She cried out, aching and desperate.

"Selene, I love you." He breathed against her lips. "I love you with all that I am. Please tell me you know that. I need you to hear it. To believe it."

Her body shuddered at his admission; his words fed a deep craving she'd only been partly aware of. She knew Fenris loved her. His actions were a testament to that. But listening to him say it . . .

"I know," Selene whispered. "I know you love me."

There was more to say. Her own feelings remained closely guarded, locked away to protect her heart. But in this moment, the truth took a siege engine to the walls she'd kept in place. If there were ever a time to be honest, to take the risk of baring her soul, it was here and now.

And yet, she couldn't. If she told Fen she was falling in love with him, that in truth she was already in love, so deeply she knew she would never resurface, that admission would forever be tied to the pain she felt knowing she was about to lose Natalie. A loss Fenris could spare her.

When his hand slid between her legs, cupping her sex, she arched into his touch and abandoned thought for sensation. Her body offered pleasure and reprieve—her mind was a trap.

Fen lifted his head and captured her gaze. "Tell me you're mine."

"I'm yours," she gasped when his fingers stroked her, hating the barriers of fabric between them. "Oh god, Fen, that feels so good."

His deft touch was a promise of blissful oblivion. His hungry mouth on her skin left her ravenous for him in turn. He made the world fall away, leading her to a place where she could be a wild creature, where she was beholden to nothing but carnal desire.

"Stay with me." He trailed kisses over her cheek, her jaw, her throat. "Let me make love to you all night. I need to feel you wrapped around me, to bury my cock deep inside you. To hear you scream when you come apart. Again. And again. And again."

He lifted his body enough to find the button at the waistband of her jeans and free it, then slowly lower the zipper. His hand slid over her stomach, lower, beneath the fabric of her panties to tease the delicate skin there.

"Will you stay, Selene?"

Through the fog of lust, Selene found his intent gaze. His dark-gray irises were alight with desire, storming with need, but fear flickered through them as well.

He doesn't mean tonight. That's not what he's asking me.

And I can't say yes. I can't.

Her voice came out in a hoarse whisper. "Stop."

Fen stilled. "Selene."

"Let me up." It hurt to say the words. Like ripping vital pieces of herself to shreds. "Please, Fenris."

If he touched her again, she was lost.

A knot of relief and disappointment tangled in her heart when he pulled his hand away and slowly stood. She pushed herself upright until she was sitting on the bed, then zipped and buttoned her jeans, unable to meet his gaze, all too aware of how closely Fen watched her every movement.

"Selene," he said again.

When she looked at him, his expression was stricken. "I wasn't . . . I need you to know I didn't plan to seduce you. I always . . . I want you so much. I couldn't stop myself."

"Neither could I," she said softly. "I'm not angry, Fen. I know you wouldn't manipulate me like that. You love me."

"I do."

She stood up. When he reached for her, she moved toward the door. "And I need you in ways I still don't understand. But I—"

She couldn't finish. There weren't words to convey the heartache ripping through her, a pain that rent her very being yet couldn't override her conviction that staying with Fenris would take her down a path she couldn't follow. Not when they were so fundamentally at odds with one another.

He followed her into the living area. "Where are you going?"

"Home." She turned to face him. "To Allie. To my life. To reality, where everything hurts right now."

"It doesn't have to be that way." Fen's voice was on the verge of breaking.

She shook her head. "I wish that were true, Fenris."

"It is," he insisted. "I will give you all that I have, Selene. All that I am. You know that."

She did know that, but it was only a partial truth. Too much remained that forced them apart.

"This is a dream." Selene gestured to the space around them. "A beautiful dream, and I want it so badly."

She hated that she began to cry. Crying felt like weakness at best, at worst like manipulation, but there was no helping it. "A dream is all it will ever be. There is no future for us if Natalie dies. That's the truth, Fenris. And no matter how much I want you, that truth won't change."

Fen's body went rigid, myriad emotions rolling through his gaze too swiftly for her to follow. "I wish you could understand why I must see this through."

He was desperate to persuade her to accept his point of view—that the law was immutable. That it was more powerful than his own wishes. His voice was edged with raw emotion: his rage and frustration, his sorrow.

"But that's what you don't seem to realize, Fen." Drawing on the scraps of will she could muster, Selene went to him and took his hands, twining her fingers with his. "I *can* see things from your perspective. I know why you're making this choice and why you believe it's justified. I understand what you're doing. I see all of that, and I still know you're wrong. You're the one who refuses to even consider a different resolution. An outcome that's justice, not retribution."

She was just as desperate for him to hear what she was saying, to know that every word came from her breaking heart. And most of all, for him to grasp that there could be no future for them if he refused to bend.

"I'm sorry that's what you think I'm doing," Fen said stiffly. "I promise you, it isn't. That's not who I am."

"I know, Fenris," she replied, choking out the words as grief strangled her. "I know who you are. That's just another reason you're breaking my heart."

Lifting onto her tiptoes, she pressed a brief kiss to his lips and turned away. Tears continued to fall. She wept for Natalie. And for Fen. And for herself. And most of all, for the promise of love torn to shreds.

Selene heard him call her name as she fled the room and down the hall. But she knew there would be no going back.

Goodbye, Fenris.

24

Sleep.

Selene needed to sleep so much her bones ached. Her eyes felt like they were going to crawl out of their sockets as she drove away from the estate.

But she couldn't rest. Not yet. Not until the other players in the scene she cobbled together over the last several hours knew their roles. Somehow, amid everything else, those tiny tugs and barely audible whispers had coalesced in her subconscious and snuck their way from hidden places into the forefront of her thoughts as she drove away from Fenris Hall's manor.

Wonders never cease, or something like that, Selene mused with chagrin. *Do I think this can work because I'm sleep deprived and delusional? Or is there an actual chance we'll succeed?*

She was depending on the others to make that decision for her.

When she pulled into her driveway, her phone chimed. A message from Tim.

Brought Allie back to our place. Come over when you can.

Selene didn't bother stopping inside her house but crossed the lawn to knock on Tim and Marley's door.

A rush of footsteps and the door was flung open, revealing Allie.

"Aunt Sel! Is Natalie okay?"

"For now." Selene rested her cheek against the crown of Allie's head when they hugged.

Allie took Selene's hand and led her inside. "We saved croissants for you. They're so good."

"Thanks, sweetie."

In the living room, Tim wore an anxious expression as he watched Marley flit from plant to plant. It looked like Marley was talking to them.

"Selene." Tim stood up and walked over to give her a bear hug that squeezed the air out of her lungs. "I'm so glad you're here."

When she'd caught her breath, Selene replied, "Did you think Fen would lock me up too?"

It was a joke, but Tim said, "I was a little worried."

"Fenris wouldn't hurt Aunt Selene," Allie said, finding her way to the sofa and another croissant.

"No." Tim sat beside Allie and patted her hand. "But he might have wanted to keep her from causing trouble with Natalie."

He had wanted to keep her, but not because of Natalie. Selene shoved memories of his bedroom aside. Hard. What she needed now was focus, not distraction.

Marley flew over and kissed Selene on the cheek. "Sorry for the change of venue. I wasn't feeling well."

He gestured to the greenery throughout the room. "My plants help when I'm stressed."

"No worries," Selene said. Marley did look much better than earlier, his skin no longer withering the way it had when they were talking about Natalie's sentence.

Oof. Her plan wasn't going to make things any easier for him.

"Sit down, Selene." Marley ushered her to a chair, and Tim brought her a croissant. "Can I get you something to drink before you tell us what happened?"

"I'm fine, thanks," Selene said, then launched into a review of her trip to Fen's estate, skipping over her visit to his bedroom.

When she'd finished, Marley sank onto the couch beside a crestfallen Tim and put his arms around the big man.

"I let myself hope, you know?" Tim's voice wobbled. "I shouldn't have. Fenris is the law. He's not going to change. Even for love."

When Selene winced, he quickly added, "It's not about you, Selene. I didn't mean his feelings for you aren't as strong as you thought."

"He said the same thing," Selene replied wearily. "Even Natalie told me not to hold a grudge."

Marley smiled sadly. "That's very in character for her. Always thinking of others."

"I know."

"Auntie Sel, did Josh let you in?" Allie asked hesitantly.

"I'm sorry, Allie," Selene told her. "I shouldn't have forgotten that part. Yes, Josh opened the gate for me. He wasn't very happy about it, but he did."

Allie's shoulders rose and fell as she sighed. "I guess that's something, but he still won't argue with Fen about Natalie. I've asked him so many times. He won't listen."

Gabriel's stern face rose to the surface of Selene's mind. "I doubt any of the wolves will. No matter how they feel about it."

"Fenris Hall has ruled Avondale for centuries," Marley said. "He's been a good leader. I don't think anyone knows how to tell him he's wrong. They've never needed to."

"Natalie isn't exactly skipping toward her execution," Selene grumbled. "But she's not fighting it at all."

Marley nodded. "That doesn't surprise me."

"It surprised the hell out of me." Selene fisted her hands. "And I am not done fighting."

"That's admirable, Selene," Tim said, his voice inching toward patronizing. "But you're tilting at windmills now."

"I'm not." She took a moment to look at each one of them. They all needed to be on board for this to work. "I have a plan."

"You do?" Allie perked up.

At the same instant, Tim and Marley frowned. "You do?"

"Poison," Selene announced, her mouth running ahead of her brain once again.

"What?" Allie's eyebrows pulled together.

"Fen is allowing Natalie to choose how she dies," Selene continued, pulse pumping hard as she got closer to revealing her scheme. "And she's going to choose poison."

"Oh no." Marley's vines began to wilt again.

"Wait." Selene waved her hands at Marley. "It's not bad. She wasn't going to choose poison, but I made her promise to."

"Why would you do that, Selene?" Marley zipped up, wings buzzing. "I have to make the poison. Fen will ask me to."

"I know!" Selene stood up to face the faerie's outrage. "That's how we're going to save her."

"How can I save her by killing her?" Marley wailed.

The vines covering the walls began to grow rapidly, wildly, sprouting long, wicked-looking thorns.

Tim rose. "Calm down, love. You're scaring the plants."

"I'm scared!" Marley glared at Selene. "I don't want to kill my friend."

"*Romeo and Juliet*!" Selene shouted.

The room froze. Even the plants seemed to be staring at Selene in utter bewilderment. Selene's heart *thump, thump, thumped* against her sternum. Saying it out loud made it too real. And too laughable when she was dead serious.

But it was all she had.

"Auntie Sel," Allie broke the silence. "Why are you talking about Shakespeare?"

"Because that's how we're going to save Natalie," Selene said, fully committing herself. "*Romeo and Juliet*."

Silence again.

"Oh. *Oh*." Marley shook his head vehemently as he flew a little closer to Selene. "No. No. No. No. Noooooooo."

Tim had gotten there as well, and his eyes bulged.

"Do you remember how that play ends?" he asked Selene, horrified. "They both die. I can't believe people still call that story a great romance. Red flags from start to finish."

"Yeah." Allie nodded. "When we read it freshman year, I had, like, zero swoon. Romeo's kind of a dick."

Tim smiled at her. "Such a dick. I'm glad you see that. It'll spare you a lot of bullshit in relationships."

Allie bounced on the sofa at the compliment. "Thanks, Tim. But I don't get how *Romeo and Juliet* is gonna help Natalie . . . oh wait. *Oh.*"

She looked at Selene with big eyes. "You want to pretend Natalie's dead and then help her escape."

Selene nodded. Now they were all on the same page of sixteenth-century literature.

"Wow," Allie murmured. "Could that work?"

"It's a creative approach, Selene. I'll give you that." Marley was flitting back and forth across the living room. "But the whole *Romeo and Juliet* scenario is a nonstarter."

"Why?" Selene frowned.

"Because Juliet doesn't actually die," Marley answered. "As ruler of Avondale, Fenris passed the sentence, and he will witness the execution. He's a werewolf, Selene, not a gullible citizen of Verona. He knows fake death from actual mortis, and it won't matter that 'no warmth, no breath shall testify Natalie liveth.'"

He hovered in front of Selene. The vines on the walls were growing again, curling around paintings and strangling mirrors. "For this to work, Natalie will have to die. Not pretend dead, 'shuffle off this mortal coil' dead . . . since we're already doing Shakespeare."

Okay, she wasn't counting on that. She also wasn't going to give up at the first of what would doubtless be many obstacles.

"But she could be dead for a minute or two without permanent damage, couldn't she?" Selene asked.

Marley scowled at her.

"If we try this," Tim said haltingly, "it's treason. Our lives are forfeit if we fail."

Ignoring Tim's warning, Selene focused on Marley. "Can she die and come back? Please, Marley."

"Possibly," Marley offered at last, the frantic beating of his wings finally beginning to slow. "But that would mean finding a way to revive her without Fen knowing about it. I don't see how that can happen."

"I'll do it," Selene said. "If you can show me how to bring her back. I'll make it happen. I have to."

Tim and Marley exchanged an even longer look. When Tim nodded, Marley sighed.

"Okay, honey, I'll roll with this, for your sake and for Natalie's," Marley said. "But you need to understand there are no guarantees. Absolutely none. We *will* be killing her. And we may not be able to revive her."

"The other thing we need to agree on is what comes next," Tim added. "If we do succeed, staying in Avondale isn't an option. We have to leave. Forever."

A little gasp escaped from Allie. They all looked at her.

"We have to leave?" She bit her lower lip. "You mean run away?"

Violence or running. Selene remembered that early exchange with Fen with a painful sense of irony. After everything, that's exactly where they'd ended up. She was running.

But she couldn't, wouldn't, leave Allie behind.

Selene went to the sofa and crouched in front of her niece. "Allie, what we're doing to help Natalie has very serious consequences. You understand that, don't you?"

Allie nodded. Her eyes shone with impending tears.

Selene swallowed. What she was about to say would rip her apart inside. "I love Fenris, Allie. I love him so much, it hurts. But I can't let him do this to Natalie. It's wrong. He doesn't understand why because he won't let go of the past. He's still in pain because of what those bounty hunters did to his mate. He's a good man, very good, but he's making a bad choice. And I have to stop it, even though I'll lose him, and . . . it hurts so much I can't breathe."

It was strange to confess her feelings to Allie when she hadn't been willing to voice them to Fenris, but Allie would be making a sacrifice of her own if she agreed to their plan. She deserved to know how much Selene was hurting too. And, honestly, it was a relief to speak the words aloud, despite knowing the person who owned her heart might not ever know it.

"You're going to leave him anyway." Allie choked on a sob. "Because you love Natalie."

"Yes." Selene's voice cracked. "I have to."

But she would reverse course if it was too much for Allie. Yes, Allison was young, and Selene knew her relationship with Josh was in its fledgling stages, but she would neither underestimate nor dismiss Allie's feelings. If she pushed Allie into a choice she didn't truly want or understand, it could have terrible costs . . . like Allie running back to Avondale, back to Josh, and hating Selene for taking her away from him. Selene would risk almost anything to save Natalie, but not her relationship with Allison.

"You're my family, Allie." Selene took the tissue Tim offered and dabbed at her eyes. "If you want to stay in Avondale, we will. You're the most important person in my life."

Allie threw her arms around Selene, weeping. "P-please let me h-help. I love N-N-Natalie too. I d-don't, don't, w-w-want to leave Josh, but I, I w-will."

"Are you sure, sweetheart?" Selene asked. "It's a lot to ask. I know how much you care about Josh, and this is all happening so fast."

Allie sat up, pulling herself together with a long sniffle. "I want to go with you. I want to save Natalie."

"Okay." Selene moved to sit beside her niece. "Thank you, Allie."

"I have to say it again," Tim blurted, still teary-eyed, looking from Allie to Selene. "Shakespearean tragedies: everyone dies. If this goes badly, there's no coming back from it."

"I know, and I'm scared, Tim, I really am. For all of us." Selene took another tissue from Tim and swiped at her eyes again. "But the other option is Natalie dies while we do nothing. I can't live with that."

Allie tucked herself against Selene's shoulder. "Neither can I."

"Neither can we." Marley groaned and took Tim's other hand. "But you already know that. You knew it before you asked us to help."

Selene wanted to shout for joy and break down sobbing. "You guys are amazing. I love you."

"Oh, honey." Tears leaked from Tim's eyes as he smiled at her. "We know."

Buds sprouted on the vines that had crept across the floor and burst into bloom.

◆ ◆ ◆

Natalie was stretched out on her bed, lying on her side and gazing into the fire, when she heard a soft rapping on her door.

She frowned. It was an odd sort of knock. As if the person on the other side of the door hadn't fully committed to the act.

It was also the middle of the night.

Who would come knocking when presumably she'd be sound asleep? Anyone with manners would let a dead witch walking rest in peace.

A grim laugh slipped from her throat. Her gallows humor was getting better the closer she danced with death.

She sat up, swung her legs over the side of the bed, and went to answer the door.

Whoever it was would be a welcome distraction. She could only practice levitation so many times, and she could barely get off the ground thanks to the iron bracelets. Maybe Fenris would lend her a tarot deck if she asked. That would pass the time. And it would be an interesting exercise to consult the cards when her fate was sealed. What could they possibly reveal?

Natalie opened the door. Nothing could have prepared her for who was waiting on the other side.

Her heart jumped with such force, her hand flew to her sternum, as if to prevent the rampant organ beneath from shattering her breastbone.

"Gabriel."

His broad silhouette took up most of the doorway.

He was here. She hadn't allowed herself to . . . hadn't dared . . .

"Natalie." He stepped into the room, closing the door behind him. "I—"

"Don't." She couldn't entertain emotions. Not now. Not when her sanity depended on perfect equanimity.

Standing before her was the one person who threatened to ruin that balance.

"Do you want me to leave?" His golden, hawklike gaze hunted hers.

And there was no hiding.

She shook her head, grabbed a handful of his shirt, and backed up, towing him toward the bed, the blood in her veins already molten. "But no talking. I can't . . . no talking. Please."

When he nodded, the air trapped in her lungs rushed out. But her next breath was stolen when Gabriel scooped her up and carried her the last few steps, gently lowering her to the bed.

He leaned over her, and she dragged his shirt up until he shrugged it over his head and cast it aside. Her palms flattened against his chest, savoring the warmth of his skin, before her fingers began to map the swells, dips, and ridges of his torso. She explored at her leisure, drinking him in, and his flesh trembled beneath her touch, but he didn't move until she caught the waistband of his jeans and pulled him down.

And then his weight, all that hard muscle, pressed her into the bed, his hips settling between her thighs. The pure sensation of it. Of him. Goddess above.

Natalie gasped, arching into him. "Gabriel, I—"

"No talking," he said gruffly and silenced her with his kiss.

25

When Selene pulled up to the gates of Fenris Hall's estate some thirty-six hours later, the tall iron barrier slid open without delay.

"Here we go," she muttered and continued up the drive.

From the passenger seat, Allie said, "I'm scared. What if Fen can, you know, sense that we're trying to trick him?"

Selene worried about the same thing. Werewolves could smell emotion, and none of her car's current occupants would be able to mask the intensity of their feelings. Except perhaps Marley. She didn't know whether a faerie's glamour could alter physical appearance alone or hide emotion as well.

"All we can do is focus on the truth, Allie," Selene advised, reminding herself of the strategy. "Natalie is going to die today. We're afraid, we're sad. Those are normal responses to what we're about to face. You can feel those things without raising Fen's suspicion."

I hope.

"She's right, Allie." Marley leaned forward, resting his arms on the backs of the front seats. He'd insisted Allie take the passenger seat because the back seat offered more room and greater, if not perfect, comfort for his wings. "Fenris will know how you're feeling, but he won't know why. We'll be okay."

Allie nodded, but her face was pale.

Marley had been the one to suggest they ride together in Selene's car. His plant delivery van was needed to serve another purpose.

"Even so," Marley continued. "He's not going to be happy you're here. Either of you. Or that we're so early."

It was late morning, and when Fenris had called Marley yesterday to request his assistance carrying out Natalie's sentence, the execution was scheduled for sunset the following day.

"The timing is symbolic," Marley had explained. "Sun going down, life coming to an end."

More signs and rituals, which Selene decided called for a little disruption.

If they forced Natalie's execution to an earlier point in the day, it was more likely they'd be alone with Fenris when it took place. That might be the case no matter when it happened, but Selene needed the best odds that there would be as few people around as possible when their plan went into action.

"He's already unhappy," Selene said to Marley as she parked the car in front of the manor. "But he won't turn us away."

With a grimace, Marley said, "I hope you're right. 'Cause there he is."

Sure enough, the front door had opened, and Fen walked to the car as they exited it. He spoke to Marley first.

"Sunset, Marley." Fenris frowned at the faerie. "It's not even noon."

"My fault." Selene moved between them. "I can't sit around all day waiting for this to happen, Fen. Acid will chew a hole through my stomach."

He shook his head. "There are reasons for the timing. Natalie understands and accepts them."

"Well, I'm sorry I'm not as peaceable about all this as the woman you're going to execute," Selene said flatly. "But it's too hard on the people who love her to stick to rules we don't understand."

She gestured to Allie, who was lingering beside the car.

Fen's expression hardened. "She shouldn't be here. Neither of you should."

"I won't let Natalie die alone." Selene crossed her arms over her chest.

"She won't be alone." Fen lowered his voice, gentling his tone. "I will be with her. So will Marley."

"Not good enough."

"I know you're going to insist on being present," Fen said. "But Allison should remain inside with Josh."

When he glanced toward the front door, Selene noticed Josh waiting there, shifting his weight from foot to foot as he watched Allie.

Damn it. It shouldn't have surprised Selene that Josh would want to see Allie, but it made the situation that much more complicated. She silently sent up a little prayer to whatever gods or goddesses might be listening that Allie could hold it together with her boyfriend present.

In the first version of their plan, Allie wouldn't have been at the manor. She was going to stay with Tim, waiting for them outside the estate in Marley's delivery van. But then Tim and Marley had started to explain the layout of the garden, where Marley was going to suggest the execution should take place, in relation to a service road that skirted the southeast edge of the manor—their best option for an extraction point. Even with a diagram Tim sketched, Selene was worried that in the stress and chaos of the moment, when every second counted, she'd lose her way.

That was when Allie piped up. "I can lead you out of the garden, Aunt Selene. I know it backward and forward. I go there with Josh all the time."

Selene initially balked at Allie's participation, but Tim and Marley agreed with her niece that having a guide was the surest way to prevent a mishap when the time came to run.

As she watched Allie walk slowly toward the manor and Josh come out to meet the girl, she hoped they'd made the right decision.

"Let her stay with Josh," Fen urged.

"She loves Natalie too," Selene replied. "If she asks to stay with Josh, then she can. But if she wants to be with Natalie, she should. She deserves to say goodbye."

After a pause, Selene added quietly, "And she needs to understand what it means to join your pack."

"That's not fair, Selene," Fen countered. His expression made it clear he was not only taken aback but offended by her assertion. "What's happening today is an exception. An unfortunate outcome that could have been avoided."

"We've already talked about what's fair, Fenris. Haven't we?" Selene said stiffly. "And it could still be avoided."

"You want this to be simple when it isn't." The defeat in his voice threatened to soften her. She longed to comfort him. To reassure him that despite everything, she still loved him. She couldn't afford that.

Selene replied with a shrug even though she felt heartless as she did it. She needed to focus on Natalie.

Josh and Allie were speaking in voices too quiet for Selene to hear, but Allie stepped into his arms after a minute. She let him hold her, then gently pulled away, shaking her head. Josh's expression fell.

Selene's heart hurt for him, for both of them, but she was proud of Allie's courage and resolve as she walked away from Josh.

"I'm ready, Aunt Selene," Allie said when she reached Selene and Fenris.

"Hello, Allison," Fen said.

Allie wouldn't meet his eyes. "Hi, Fenris."

"I'm sorry about all of this," he told her. "I hope you know that."

"Yeah, I know," Allie replied, kicking the ground with the toe of her shoe. "Can we go see Natalie now?"

Jaw clenching, Fenris looked from Allie to Selene, then he beckoned to Marley.

◆ ◆ ◆

As soon as Natalie opened her door, Allie burst into tears and hugged her. Josh hadn't followed them to Natalie's room. Instead he veered off down another hallway after they'd entered the house. Allie must have told him to stay away.

"Hi, sweetheart." Natalie petted Allie's head while the girl cried. "It's so thoughtful of you to come and see me."

After smiling sadly at Selene, Natalie caught sight of Marley and frowned. "Aren't you . . . early?"

Fenris answered, disapproval threading through his words. "It has been requested that your sentence be carried out at midday."

Natalie tilted her head. "It has?"

"Sorry, Nat." Selene didn't fight the fear and sadness welling inside her. Despite the deception at work, none of this was an act. It was all far too real. "Us humans just aren't as stoic as the paranormal crowd."

"Oh, of course." Natalie frowned slightly, but then she nodded. "I didn't think . . . You want to be with me when it happens?"

Selene's stomach lurched. It hadn't occurred to her that Natalie might refuse, which she had every right to.

"If it's okay," Selene said, voice weak.

"It's okay," Natalie said, reaching out her hand to grasp Selene's. "I would never have asked, but it means a lot to me. Thank you."

"Do you need time to prepare?" Fenris asked.

There was an odd flicker in Natalie's eyes, but after a slight hesitation, she shook her head. "No. Not really."

"Are you certain?" Fen frowned at her. It was obvious he didn't like breaking protocol one bit. What a surprise.

Marley fluttered closer. "I'd like to administer the compound in your garden, Fenris. My formula will be most effective out of doors, with the encouragement of nearby flora."

Fen inclined his head to Marley, then looked at Natalie. "Are you amenable to accepting your sentence in the garden?"

With another sad smile, Natalie replied, "The garden would be lovely. Lead the way."

◆ ◆ ◆

Natalie was right. The garden was lovely. Stunning, actually.

Sun-drenched and verdant, the garden's twisting paths and bubbling fountains exuded hope and joy. Spring flowers in hues delicate, daring, and everything in between suffused the air with their sweet, luscious perfumes.

That a place celebrating life would bear witness to the death of a person as wonderful as Natalie felt like a terrible, twisted joke. On the other hand, if Selene were the one about to die, the garden would be a better place than most to draw her last breath. A reminder of beauty and light before eternal darkness fell.

Selene groaned inwardly. All this drama was turning her maudlin.

Fenris let Natalie lead the way, making Selene wonder how familiar Natalie was with the estate grounds. Did she know where she wanted to die, or was she wandering until she found a spot that felt right?

Natalie stopped in front of a long reflection pool. Sculptures of dancing naiads decorated either side of the shining water. Natalie looked at them, smiling, before sinking onto a bench at the edge of the pool.

"Here."

Selene snuck at glance at Allie. She had no idea where they were in relation to the service road where Tim would be waiting in the van. Was it close, or had Natalie selected a location on the opposite ends of the grounds?

Allie glanced at Selene and gave the tiniest of nods. Selene breathed a little easier.

"Very well." Fen stepped beside Natalie and laid his hand on her shoulder. "Natalie Lyon, the crimes you are guilty of carry the sentence of death. Do you accept this sentence?"

Natalie looked up at him. Not even a hint of anger or resentment clouded her steady gaze. "I do, Fenris."

By contrast, Fen's eyes roiled with conflict. He gritted his teeth, then spoke again. "As ruler of Avondale, I bear witness to the fulfillment of our laws."

He paused, swallowing hard.

Hope began to beat its wings against Selene's ribs. Maybe now, at the end, Fenris would change his mind and stop this madness.

"You have requested death by poison," Fen continued, his voice steadying, and Selene's hope crashed.

"I have," Natalie replied. She turned on the bench to smile at Marley. "Thank you. I know this can't have been easy for you, my friend."

Marley nodded to her, his eyes bright with tears, as he produced a small crystal vial filled with vivid green liquid. "It will be quick . . . and quite pleasant."

"I appreciate that." Natalie took the vial and looked at Selene. "I can't say goodbye, so please don't ask me to."

Putting her arm around Allie and drawing her close, Selene said, "I understand, Nat. We love you."

"I love you too." Natalie uncorked the vial, lifting it to her lips.

Before Selene could blink, glass shattered on the ground, shards of the broken vial flashing in the sunlight.

◆ ◆ ◆

Gabriel paced in his room, fists clenched.

Not enough time. A handful of hours.

Damn it.

He should have taken her away last night. He'd gone to her again. Craving her. Needing her. It was impossible to stay away.

And he'd known, the truth singing in his blood and bones. He suspected he'd known for a long, long time, but had been too stubborn to admit who she was to him.

Even with that admission, panic held him captive, tied him tight with indecision.

How could he save her?

The only options he had were to beg Fen for mercy or run. Neither was a guarantee of success.

A scuffle in the hallway broke through his misery. Bodies slamming against the wall.

A fight? Had someone else come to free Natalie?

Fen's mate, Selene, seemed determined to help the witch, but a human would never prevail against wolves.

Gabriel lunged for his door and threw it open.

Ewan had Josh pinned against the wall opposite Gabriel's room. Bannock stood nearby, wiping blood from his lips.

"Calm down, Josh," Ewan growled at the younger wolf. "You're not helping anyone. Especially yourself."

"What's going on?" Gabriel stepped into the hall.

Bannock grimaced and shot an angry look at Josh. "Girl trouble."

"If you need to spar and blow off steam, we'll do it in the training room," Ewan told Josh, who was struggling to free himself. "You almost shredded one of Fen's favorite paintings."

"She could barely look at me." Josh heaved out a breath, miserable. "I don't know what to do."

"You wait." Bannock stalked over to him. "When it's over, you can comfort her. If you push too hard, she'll keep running away. What you don't do is sucker punch your friends."

When Josh slumped, Ewan eased off.

"I thought Allie would want me to be with her," Josh said. "I know how much she's hurting. She loves Natalie."

Cold chased up Gabriel's spine. "Be with Allie when? For what?"

"She and Selene came for Natalie's execution," Josh told Gabriel.

"What do you mean, 'came'?" Alarm surged through Gabriel with sheer terror at its heels. "The execution isn't until sunset."

Bannock grunted and shook his head. "Selene and her niece showed up this morning with Marley. I guess they're doing it now."

"Gabriel?" Ewan's brow furrowed. "What's wrong?"

But Gabriel was already running.

◆ ◆ ◆

Fen's chest heaved, his breaths coming hard and fast. His hand was still lifted, frozen in place after he'd slapped the vial away from Natalie's lips. He stared at the broken vial and the liquid seeping into the earth as if he couldn't believe what he'd done. Marley and Natalie had gone stone still, wide eyes locked on Fen. Selene stood, likewise stupefied, until Allie's fingers dug in to her arm.

"Fenris?" Selene could only croak out his name.

Silence held sway for another few heartbeats, then Fen slowly shook his head. His hand fell to his side.

"I—" He spoke in a rough voice. "I grant you a stay of execution, Natalie Lyon."

"Oh, thank god," Selene breathed. She expected Fen to look at her, but he kept his gaze on Natalie.

"I should not be the one to determine your fate," he continued. "Nor should the decision of how you should pay for your crime be made hastily. You've given much to our community. I've been made aware that the information you provided anonymously to my pack led to the capture of more than a dozen bounty hunters. That is no small thing."

Selene's heart flooded with joy. This was really happening. Fen had changed his mind. Natalie wouldn't die today.

Natalie continued to stand rigidly, barely acknowledging Fen's words with a nod.

Fen held up his hand. "You must still be held accountable for breaking Avondale's law. I will convene a council of elders to review your standing in the community alongside your crime, and I will abide by whatever decision they come to regarding your punishment. Do you agree to my terms?"

"I do." Natalie's expression was impossible to read. Then she collapsed.

Allie screamed.

"Natalie!" Selene rushed to kneel beside her friend's crumpled body. "No. Please, no."

Had Natalie somehow swallowed the poison before Fen knocked it away?

Selene's pulse hammered, her nerves screaming as she tried to make sense of the chaos. This couldn't be happening. Everything had changed. Instead of tragedy, a happily ever after. What capricious arbiter of fate would destroy such a pure scene of hope and happiness?

"Goddess have mercy." Fen's voice was stricken.

Selene looked at him, and what she saw made her sway in place until she had to plant her hands on the ground to stay upright. His features were riddled with regret and uncertainty. She'd never seen him afraid, and he was imprisoned by fear now, seemingly unable to move, staring at Natalie's prone form in disbelief.

Then Marley was there, hovering over Natalie. He leaned in close, pressing his fingers to her throat as he took a deep breath. He bowed his head.

"Marley?" Fen asked. The question came out hoarse and trembling.

Marley sat back on his heels. "She's gone."

"No! No!" Allie sobbed. She collapsed, and Selene crawled to her, drawing her into an embrace.

This can't be real. It can't be.

"It had to be powerful to be painless." Marley choked on the words. "Powerful. Even a trace ingested . . ."

Selene couldn't move. Her mind wouldn't accept that the universe would give her such a priceless gift only to snatch it away a moment later.

He'd changed his mind. She was going to live.

She looked up at Fen and found his gaze locked on her. She saw their future trampled by the stampede of cruel reality. For the briefest of moments, they had everything. Natalie was spared. Selene could throw herself into Fen's arms, into his life, without hesitation or doubt. They caught a glimpse of everything they wanted. The promise of forever.

And then it was gone.

At the sound of boots striking hard on the gravel path behind them, Fen pivoted, his eyes torn from Selene's. Their connection broken.

Gabriel stood a short distance away. His gaze locked on Natalie's prone form. And Selene watched everything she'd imagined the taciturn wolf might feel for Natalie play out on his face. Her heart broke all over again.

"Gabriel?" Fenris took a step toward his friend. Gabriel's body quaked and then a bronze-furred wolf stood in a heap of torn clothing. Lifting his muzzle, Gabriel loosed a howl that reached into Selene's bones, turning the marrow to ice. Never had she heard such keening, raw grief. Did Natalie know, she wondered, that Gabriel loved her? Because only the loss of true love could evoke that sound. Selene knew she'd never forget the way it made her shudder with awareness. She'd wrongly assumed Gabriel and Natalie's connection had been fleeting, or purely physical, but Gabriel loved Natalie deeply. Loved and lost her.

He'd appeared in the garden without warning, pulling up short from a dead run. If he'd arrived a minute sooner, what would have happened? Would he have challenged his pack leader? Fought for Natalie?

They would never know. Another tragedy, another intervention arriving too late.

In that moment Selene hated the world, hated every flicker of hope that appeared only to be snuffed out.

Gabriel the wolf bolted away. When Selene looked at Fenris, the shocked expression he wore told her that whatever connection Gabriel and Natalie shared, Fen hadn't been aware of it.

Within seconds another pile of shredded clothes lay where Fen had been standing, and in wolf form he chased after his brokenhearted packmate.

Yet another missed opportunity, she thought. If Gabriel had been honest with Fenris about his feelings for Natalie, would it have made a difference? Selene couldn't change Fen's mind, but Gabriel was a member of his guard, one of his oldest friends.

Selene shook her head. All these what-ifs were only pushing her deeper into rage and despair. It was no good.

"Aunt Selene!" Allie's face was tear streaked as she tugged on Selene's hand.

"Allie, I—" She couldn't go on. Sorrow strangled her.

Allie stared at her in disbelief. "Bring. Her. Back."

Selene drew a sharp breath. The antidote. *Oh god.* She'd been so mired in self-pity, she'd forgotten she possessed the means to change Natalie's fate. She had the antidote in her pocket. Her body trembled so violently, she fumbled with the syringe, finally getting it out of her coat and extending it to Marley.

"You should do it."

She didn't trust herself. Not only was she shaking all over, she'd been so lost in anger and grief, she'd been halfway to killing Natalie forever when they had a plan all along. Natalie was going to die, but that wasn't the end of the story. Hope hadn't abandoned them completely.

Marley took the syringe, stretched out Natalie's limp arm, and slid the needle into the prominent vein at her elbow. Without hesitating, he pushed the plunger, firmly and steadily, until the golden liquid inside had emptied into Natalie's bloodstream.

While Marley pressed his fingers over the puncture wound, Selene waited. And prayed. Without knowing why, she thought of the crone from the Beltane rite. Of the way an unnamable power had suffused her when she stood before Fenris as the Lady. The one who'd been chosen.

Everyone insisted that choice meant something. That Selene had a place in the paranormal world. That she had power. She thought of those tugs at her consciousness, of unbidden instincts she wanted to deny but ultimately followed.

If I have any power at all. Any sway in this terrible moment. Let it help Natalie.

"Aunt Selene?" Allie whimpered beside her.

"I know, honey," Selene whispered. "Just hang on."

Please, Natalie. Please don't leave us.

A sudden burst of wind rushed through the garden, lifting Selene's hair.

Natalie gasped as air flooded her lungs. Her spine bowed, life coursing through her, bringing her back.

Thank the goddess.

Where that thought came from, Selene couldn't be sure.

"Oh my god, oh my god. It worked." Allie bit her fist to muffle her squeal.

"Natalie?" Selene brushed Natalie's ebony curls back from her face. "Nat? Can you hear me?"

"Selene?" Natalie blinked at her before pushing herself up onto her elbows. "Am I back? Holy shit. I mean, *holy shit.*"

"Easy." Marley wrapped his arm around Natalie, supporting her. "You weren't gone long, but the effects will still linger."

"I get it. I'm okay, or I will be, I promise." Natalie leaned on Selene, shaking her head slowly as if waking from a deep sleep. "She said it wasn't my time yet."

Selene decided to let that go for the moment. Her thrill at Natalie's return was suddenly cut short as her chest tightened.

We brought her back. WE brought her back.

"Time to run," she whispered, more to herself than anyone else.

But Marley replied without hesitation, "I know."

He was watching her, face solemn, the syringe still in his hand.

"Run?" Allie tucked herself against Natalie, hugging her tightly. Natalie wore a blissed-out smile as she petted Allie's hair. "What do you mean? Fenris changed his mind."

"He did," Selene said slowly as cracks riddled her heart. "But he knows Natalie died, and now . . . she's not dead."

Allie's brow furrowed. "But couldn't we have, like, brought her back some other way? I mean, miraculously or something?"

"We can't risk it," Marley told Allie. "If he suspects we intervened and holds us here to investigate, he'll find the syringe. Even if I toss it now, the wolves will sniff it out. The antidote has potent and odiferous ingredients."

Oh, the irony. Shakespeare would eat this up.

"So back to the original plan?" Selene forced her voice to be steady, even as she fell to pieces inside.

Happily ever after with some caveats. I wish it could be otherwise, but life isn't fair. Is it?

Allie's face was pale, but she nodded. "If Marley says we need to go, I know he's telling the truth."

Marley smiled at her, his eyes full of regret. "I'm sorry, Allie. You, too, Selene."

"It's not your fault," Selene told him. "Now go tell Tim we're coming."

He leaned in to kiss her cheek before he rose into the air and flew away.

Allie pulled one of Natalie's arms over her shoulder, jerking her chin toward the other end of the reflecting pool. "We need to go that way."

"Aww." Natalie giggled, obviously still a little out of it. "You guys had a plan to save me. You're the best."

Wrapping Natalie's other arm around her, Selene started in the direction Allie indicated. She glanced around, searching for threats, but all appeared to be quiet. Natalie could walk . . . for the most part.

"I know you're sad, Selene." Natalie sounded like she'd had one too many glasses of wine. "But think about it. The council of elders might have decided to execute me anyway. Then you'd have to save me all over again."

"Who said?" Selene asked Natalie, desperate for a different subject.

He changed his mind. Her throat closed, and her eyes began to burn. *Oh, Fen.*

She wanted to run to him instead of abandoning him, because that's what it felt like now. Everything had changed. Before Fen tried to save Natalie, Selene believed she had no choice other than to leave him behind. That was no longer true. If Natalie hadn't succumbed to the poison, if none of the deadly concoction had passed her lips, Selene could be with Fenris now. Thanking him, finally telling him how she truly felt. But that couldn't happen because leaving now was about protecting her friends. If Selene alone had to face the consequences of her actions, she would stay. She would let Fenris be the judge of her choices. He'd be lenient toward

Allie, given her youth, of that Selene had no doubt. But Tim and Marley had risked everything to save Natalie, and Selene was the one who'd asked them to. She owed them her loyalty.

And Natalie's safety was far from guaranteed. Fen had stayed her execution, but in the next breath he said her punishment would be determined by a council of elders. Selene didn't know who those elders might be. Had she met any of them? Did he mean his guard, where someone like Gabriel would want to save Natalie? Or would they be paranormals drawn from parts unknown, who may or may not decide Natalie deserved clemency?

As Natalie just pointed out, they could hold fast to the law as it stood, and Natalie would face execution for a second time.

No, there was no option besides running. No matter how much it hurt to leave Fen behind.

"Who said what when?" Natalie replied, startling Selene out of her thoughts.

Natalie's voice was clearer, though she still snorted at her own question.

Pushing aside her inner turmoil, Selene answered, "The person who told you it wasn't your time. Who was it?"

"I'm not sure." Natalie didn't falter when Selene urged her to a faster pace. "I don't think I knew her, but she looked . . . like you."

Like me? Selene fought the urge to stop and ask Natalie more. There was no time.

"Do you think you can run, Natalie?" Allie asked. "I don't think we have a lot of time. When Fenris realizes we're gone . . ."

"Not yet," Natalie grunted. Now she sounded like someone with a nasty hangover. "But soon."

"Okay." Selene hoped she sounded reassuring. They were almost to the end of the path. "You're doing great. Let us know when you're ready."

They cleared the reflecting pool, and Allie turned them down another path, then another.

"Good job, Allie." Selene sent Allie a smile. "I never would have made it through the garden without you."

Allie grinned. "I know."

"Okay," Natalie shrugged off their arms. "Let's try running."

"Lead the way," Selene said to Allie.

Allie took off at a jog, checking to be sure Natalie and Selene were close behind. Selene hung back, keeping Natalie between her and Allie in case Natalie needed help.

When the path dead-ended at a fountain, Allie ducked around it, gesturing for the other women to follow. Behind the fountain was a small gap in the hedge, which they crawled through, earning scratches on their arms and losing strands of hair for their trouble.

On the other side of the hedge, they entered a forest that Selene knew stretched for miles across the estate grounds. Without hesitating, Allie darted through the trees. Natalie seemed to be growing stronger by the minute, staying close on the girl's heels. Selene chased after them.

As much as she trusted Allie's sense of direction, panic threatened as more and more minutes passed. She couldn't stop herself from glancing over her shoulder, expecting to see a legion of wolves plunging through the woods after them. But every time she looked, there was no one in pursuit.

"There it is!" Allie called.

A stone wall loomed above them, stretching at least twenty feet into the air.

Allie stopped beside it, a little winded but hardly struggling for breath. Natalie and Selene exchanged a rueful smile as they leaned against the wall and panted.

"All right, you two." Natalie stretched her hands to them. "Bring it in."

Allie tackled Natalie with a hug, and Selene wrapped her arms around her niece and her best friend.

They'd stopped running, but Selene's pulse continued to race. When they made this escape plan, they didn't have the luxury of timing out distances or practice runs. She didn't know when Marley would arrive or when Fen would return to the scene of their crime. With luck, Gabriel's grief would keep him racing through the forest, with Fen chasing after him. It felt cruel to hope that sorrow would afford Selene more time to flee, but every minute Fen was distracted meant the difference between getting away or facing his wrath.

"I should say I can't believe it," Natalie said, laughing, her voice and eyes clear now. "But I can. You are incredible."

"Thanks." Selene stepped back and looked at the wall. "We're not quite out of the fire yet."

Allie nodded. "We have to wait for Marley."

"Where is he?" Natalie asked. She didn't ask why. The wall spoke for itself.

"Rendezvousing with Tim," Selene answered. Once again she worried about how little time they could afford to wait.

"I'm assuming you mean in a not sexy way." Natalie laughed again.

Selene gave Natalie a puzzled look. Where Selene was gripped by tension, knowing their plans could go awry at any moment, Natalie appeared not to have a care in the world. Then again, she'd just come back from the dead. After that, maybe nothing felt stressful.

Selene shook her head, trying her best to be lighthearted. "I hope not, because if they're late, we're not escaping."

She glanced at the stone wall again, then at the forest at their backs. Caught between a rock and a green place? A rock and a bark place? Ugh. All her ideas of potential jokes were awful. They needed to get out of the estate. Now.

"Natalie, can I ask you something?" Allie spoke timidly.

"Always." Natalie gave her an encouraging smile.

"What was it like?" Allie blurted. "Dying, I mean?"

Selene turned at Allie's question, her fear about being caught temporarily allayed by the somberness of Allison's query.

Natalie didn't balk, tapping her lip with her index finger. "I don't exactly know how to answer that, Allie. Well, I can tell you that Marley made it easy. It didn't hurt at all, but it wasn't quite like falling asleep either. I felt both heavy and light, and I was . . . gone. No longer here."

"You went somewhere else?" Allie asked, eyes wide.

"Yes," Natalie replied. "But that wasn't a surprise. I've crossed the veil before."

"You have?" Selene frowned at her friend. "You died before?"

"No, no," Natalie said. "But I've visited the astral plane. Though admittedly, it's different when you're not a tourist."

Astral plane? Selene blinked in disbelief at Natalie's casual mention of alternate spaces of existence.

Just when I thought I was adjusting to magic being part of my life, she thought irritably. *This will never feel normal to me.*

A sudden buzzing had them all spinning in the direction of the sound, and Selene sagged against the wall with relief when Marley appeared from among the trees.

Marley beamed at Natalie. "Hey, you. Remember me?"

"Hey yourself," Natalie replied with a wink. "And of course I do."

"Not to be rude, but we don't have a minute to waste," Marley said. "I don't think I was seen, but it's impossible to be sure."

"Allie first," Selene told him. Natalie nodded in agreement.

Marley didn't give Allie a chance to weigh in. He scooped her up and zoomed over the wall. Less than a minute passed, and he was back.

"Now you," Selene said to Natalie. "No arguing."

"Love you," Natalie said, lifting her arms so Marley could grab her around the waist, and they were gone.

Selene closed her eyes.

Natalie was alive. They were going to make it. She'd never believed in miracles, but she did now.

The hairs on the back of her neck stood up, and her heartbeat stuttered. Her eyes flew open.

No. Please no.

She spun around, searching the forest. Because she felt it. Felt him.

Fenris was here. He'd come after them.

Even as she sent her plea to the universe that Fen hadn't pursued her, she longed for him. She craved him, no matter the consequences.

Selene waited for him to step from behind one of the ancient oaks, knowing she'd falter when his accusing gaze pierced her.

Maybe he'll understand. He changed his mind about Natalie. Maybe he'll understand why I had to save her. Even when it meant betraying him.

The buzz of Marley's wings came from behind her.

"Ready?" he asked as his arms came around her.

"Wait."

Alarm filled Marley's voice. "Selene, we can't—"

"I only need a minute," she told him. "Please, Marley. Come back in one minute. And if I'm not here, go. Promise me you'll go."

His eyes widened. "What are you doing?"

"Please, Marley."

She could see his hesitation, his fear. But he listened, rising to the top of the wall and hovering there. He wasn't leaving, but he was giving her a measure of privacy. And that was all she needed.

Maybe she should have felt foolish because there was no guarantee anyone was listening. But her heart urged her to confess.

"Fenris, if you're here, thank you," Selene told the forest. "You tried to spare Natalie. I know what that cost you, and I will be grateful for what you did with every breath, every heartbeat, for the rest of my life."

She fell silent, hoping and fearing in equal measure that Fen would emerge from the shadows. When he didn't, she spoke again.

"I need you to know I'm sorry for running. Because that's what I'm doing. Running away."

Her voice began to tremble, and she paused to take a deep breath, then said, "But I'm not running away from you. Though I know that sounds like a lie, I promise it's the truth. And I promise it's not forever."

She hesitated because what she had to say next felt like the greatest leap of faith she'd ever taken. "It can't be forever because it's impossible to feel the way I do about you. I can't—I won't live a life without the possibility that when the time is right, you'll be with me. That we'll be together. But not today. Or tomorrow. But someday. Because I love you, Fenris. I love you."

The buzz of Marley's wings sounded at her back.

"We can't wait any longer, Selene."

She didn't turn to look at him, but she nodded. Marley scooped her up. Her feet left the ground.

Neither man nor wolf burst out of the forest to chase her.

Then they were over the wall and landing beside Marley's van.

"Hurry, Aunt Sel!" Allie grabbed Selene's arms and tugged her into the back seat.

Marley zipped in behind her and slammed the door shut. "Go, Tim! Go!"

As the van sped away from the estate, from Avondale, Selene didn't look back. She couldn't. Not when she'd left her heart behind.

EPILOGUE

Fenris watched Marley lift Selene into the air and soar away.

She was running. From him. He'd listened to her pleas, her claims that she wasn't leaving him, but how could he believe those words when they felt like pity? An attempt to soften a brutal blow to his heart.

Disappointment and sorrow clawed at his chest.

Her choice shouldn't have been a surprise. She was loyal to her friends. He was impressed by her courage and the cleverness of her plan.

She hadn't expected him to change his mind, to spare Natalie. Neither had he. He was still reeling from what he'd done. He couldn't explain precisely what happened. All he knew was in that moment, as Natalie lifted the poison to her mouth, he had seen with perfect clarity the injustice of her punishment and that he would never have forgiven himself for executing her.

When he believed his attempt to save the witch had failed, that she'd died because he arrived at the truth of the situation a moment too late, he thought it might break him irreparably. Not only because Natalie's death was on his hands, but because his stubborn refusal to listen to Selene meant she would never let herself love him. And he needed her. Fenris needed Selene like he needed to breathe.

He didn't blame her for leaving. That didn't make her betrayal any less painful.

He'd been watching the conspirators for some time. After briefly pursuing Gabriel, Fen decided it would be better to let his packmate go than force him to explain himself. Gabriel would return when he was ready. When he wanted to share his grief with Fen. It was a sorrow Fenris didn't yet understand. He recognized all too well the depth of loss he'd heard echoing through Gabriel's howl, but Gabriel had closely guarded whatever feelings he'd held for the witch.

Fen had returned to the garden, ready to comfort Selene as much as he could. Guilt racked him. He'd brought this pain—and his pride, his arrogance—upon her. Upon the one he loved beyond measure. If only he'd acted sooner. If only that vial hadn't reached Natalie Lyon's lips.

But Selene was already gone. The place he'd left his mate, Allie, Marley, and Natalie was empty.

In a matter of seconds, Fenris understood what transpired. And he'd tracked Selene's scent through the garden and into the forest.

Muscles bunching, Fen prepared for the chase. He couldn't let her go. It would be no more than a handful of minutes before he caught up with them. Clearing the wall in a single leap was a simple task for a wolf of his size and strength. The service road was long and winding, and his speed would easily surpass that of their lumbering vehicle.

Fenris! The shout in his mind reached him a moment before a bronze-furred wolf stalked out of the woods.

Fen's ears pinned back at Gabriel's unexpected arrival.

Why are you here? Fen snapped his jaws at Gabriel, a warning for interrupting his hunt.

Gabriel's hackles rose. *To stop you from making a mistake.*

You know what's happened. It wasn't a question. Fen locked eyes with Gabriel, and it was clear the other wolf had witnessed the escape. *What they've done.*

Let them go. Gabriel bared his teeth.

I cannot. Fenris spun away from Gabriel and rushed toward the wall, but Gabriel surged past him, cutting off his path once more.

You must, Gabriel urged, still bristling. *If you don't, you will lose her forever. You cannot take her freedom. Her choice. You know this.*

She is my mate. Fen struggled with the instinct to attack his friend. He didn't want to hurt Gabriel.

This isn't the end, Fenris. Only the beginning. I give you my word. When the time is right, I will help you find your mate. Gabriel pawed the earth and growled.

Baring his teeth at Gabriel, Fen asked, *Why should I heed your words? What gives you the right to interfere?*

Because you are not the only wolf to lose a mate today. Gabriel took a step closer, fur bristling. *Natalie Lyon is mine.*

Fenris gazed at his packmate. The anguish in Gabriel's howl when he saw Natalie lying dead in the garden revealed Gabriel's attachment to her, but a mate? That extraordinary bond between the witch and one of his guard should have been unmissable . . . And it would have been, had it been any other wolf but Gabriel, who preferred the role of quiet observer and took great pains to reveal little about himself. Despite his reticence, over the centuries he'd provided invaluable counsel when Fenris needed it most.

Gabriel was also unflinchingly loyal, a fact he'd proven yet again by remaining silent when Fenris chose to enforce a sentence of death on Natalie Lyon. Wrenching regret seized Fen's chest. His unwillingness to bend the law had not only driven Selene away, he had also unknowingly sentenced Gabriel to an eternity of grief. It mattered little that Fenris had tried to stop the execution in its final moments; he'd been too late. It was Selene who ultimately spared Gabriel's heart and soul. Fenris was forever indebted to her for that.

And now, despite everything, Gabriel sought his pack leader out, not to accuse or berate but to ally himself with Fenris in common cause. Gabriel's ability to remain loyal, to forgo righteous outrage in favor of a higher purpose, left Fen humbled and grateful. That wisdom fought through Fen's primal instinct to hunt down his mate, reason defeating rampant passion.

So be it, Gabriel.

Will you return with me to the manor? Gabriel's voice conveyed his uncertainty. He understood how difficult it was for Fenris to back down.

Fen shook his ruff to rid himself of lingering animosity. *Yes, I will return with you.*

Gabriel trotted into the woods away from the wall that enclosed the estate. Fenris followed. It was easier to walk away knowing he would not face the days ahead alone in his longing. He and Gabriel shared a mission now, and they would see it through.

Fenris clung to the word Selene had finally uttered. The word he'd longed to hear.

Love.

She'd confessed she loved him.

He'd believed. He'd known it in his heart, his blood, his bones. But when she said the words, they'd reached into his very soul. And while the depth of her feelings filled him with satisfaction and joy, it was that much harder to let her go. Because she belonged to him, just as he belonged to her.

But Gabriel spoke the truth. And a wise leader listened to counsel. Now was not the time to hunt.

Fenris knew the day would come when he would chase her, find her, make her his own. Forever. He would wait until the time was right, but when that time came, he would pursue his mate without hesitation.

Selene's promise was a prophecy. A promise that Fen now made his own. A prophecy he would fulfill.

Not today. Not tomorrow. But someday.

Acknowledgments

Always Carry a Silver Cross wouldn't be in the world without the efforts of many talented and generous people who share a love of books and the magic stories bring into our lives. Thank you to my amazing agent, Charlie Olsen, who encouraged me to return to an idea I started playing with a decade ago and sit down and write the whole story.

Thank you also to Gideon Pine and InkWell Management. I'm so grateful that Megan Sakoi, Maria Gomez, and the Montlake team, who are a delight to work with, took a chance on Avondale and its quirky characters and ensured the novel's best self ended up in readers' hands.

Charlotte Herscher offered invaluable editorial feedback; she is incredible at her job. I'm grateful to Brenna and Tristen for their keen insights and comments in copy edits and proofreading. Beth Revis kindly read an early draft of this novel, and her input helped me immensely. Beth, you are truly a rockstar. Thank you to Jill Santopolo for being such a dear friend and always believing in my stories. (Beth and Jill both write fantastic books. Go read them!)

My husband, Eric, cheers me on through triumphs and carries me when I'm struggling. He is my hero. I will never be able to adequately express how grateful I am for my family, especially my parents for their love and support, and my brother, who has long been my best friend and insists he is my biggest fan.

About the Author

Photo © 2019 Sharon Liu Robertson

Andrea Robertson is the *New York Times* and international bestselling author of more than a dozen fantasy and romance novels. She embarked on her writing career after a horse broke her foot in 2008, but her storytelling began with imaginary worlds she dreamed up as a child in the north woods of Wisconsin and Minnesota. Before becoming a full-time writer, Robertson resided in the academic world, where she was a professor of early modern history. She now lives in Southern California with her husband and two dogs.